D1344990

Leaving Home

Lionel G. Garcia

To Marg & Chuck,
with warmest
regards,
Lionel
Garcia,
1 – 11 – 91

Arte Público Press
Houston
1985

The publication of this volume is made possible through grants from the National Endowment for the Arts, a federal agency, and the Texas Commission on the Arts.

Arte Público Press
University of Houston
University Park
Houston, Texas 77004

ISBN 0-934770-42-5
Library of Congress No. 84-072303

To my wife Noemí

Leaving Home

CHAPTER 1

It was early in the morning, no later than six. Inside the black 1939 Ford, the man held the car to the road barely seeing over the steering wheel. The car powdered the small frame houses with limestone dust as the man drove slowly toward the end of the street. At first small, now the car grew large as it came toward the house. The man slipped the car into second gear, gathered a little speed, then quickly jerked the gear into third. As he did this, the cloud of dust behind him enlarged, then grew smaller, then larger until when he stopped, the cloud overtook the car and engulfed it and the man in its powdery haze.

The man waited for the dust to pass, opened the door and got out. He had stopped at the end of the street, the last house. Next to it was a dump where children were playing with an old tire. At the far end of the dump someone had set fire to a mattress annd it was still smouldering. A dog followed the children around as they ran behind the tire.

He stepped up to the porch in front of the house and stopped at the screen door to knock. With the outside glare it was hard to see inside, but he could see a man silhouetted against the kitchen window sitting down eating breakfast. He could hear voices, noises, but not words.

He hesitated as he was about to knock, for the woman, an older lady he thought had seen him, was approaching the door. Confused, he did not know if the lady could see him or if she was merely walking into the room for some other reason. He could see her approaching the door now and he did not knock. She opened the door not speaking, expecting him to be there, like he had been there forever.

"Good morning," he said in Spanish.

"Good morning," she answered, holding the door open, almost ignoring him, looking out the door across the street.

She said something to the children playing next door, stood there for a while, then closed the door gently behind her.

"Come in, come in," the large man eating breakfast said. "Sit down here," pointing at the chair next to the wall. "You're early."

"Yes, but it's a long road and the car is not running well. The starter is out too, but it happened last night and I didn't have time to fix it."

"We'll do fine," Adolfo said, "after all, we have all the time in the world. We'll just take our time. Will you please give our friend here some coffee?"

The old woman came over with the pot of boiling coffee and a cup and served the man. "Do you want milk?"

"No, just like this. Some sugar, if you have a spoon."

She brought him the spoon and he noticed the lady was not as old as he had imagined, not the way the man had described her the night before.

"Yes, after I left you, the car stopped suddenly, then wouldn't start."

"You've got a Ford right?"

"Yes."

"Buy a Chevrolet. Fords have bad starters."

"You're right."

The small man took the coffee and tried to drink it, but he knew it was impossible. He blew on the surface for a while and then let it rest. Instinctively the lady brought him a saucer and he thanked her and poured some of the coffee in it.

The large man, Adolfo, had been eating slowly all this time. He refused to wear his false teeth. His eyes were fixed to the table, his mind somewhere else. Subconsciously he put a piece of food in his mouth and chewed it slowly. He was not aware that the small man was having trouble drinking his coffee. From a moment of awareness he had drifted back to a dream, a dream that separated him from the other two.

"Are you alright, Adolfo?" the woman asked, looking worried. She looked at the small man and shook her head. She made a circular motion with her index finger next to her temple. "Crazy," she whispered.

"Yes. I'm alright," he answered, "and don't be worried about me. I know what I'm doing."

"That I doubt. I doubt it very, very much," she answered. "A man your age looking for a future. No, looking for a fortune . . . . And at your age! Your time has come and gone. You're old like me. Behave yourself, accept what you are, an old fool." She was giving them her back as she was working at the stove, talking to the wall. "Look at you," she continued, "look at the way you look, your clothes, your mind, your senseless talk that goes on and on. And you say you know what you're doing?

"Alright woman," he answered gently.

He could not afford to get into an argument with the woman. It was her house, her food. He could, though, make a pretense at maintaining his manhood for the benefit of the small man, so he said, "Alright, alright, you win!" Then he winked at the small man when she wasn't looking.

"I win? What do you mean, I win? No one wins. Only you lose. First the beer joint and all the money you would make. Now you're leaving it. I know why too. You went broke, didn't you?"

"Alright," he said, chewing slowly, his lips moving slowly in and out.
"And you brought in the prostitutes, right?"
"Yes."
"And what did that do for you? Answer me."
"I don't know. Please, can I eat in peace?"
"They broke you, that's what they did. Buying dresses and underwear and shoes for them. And you said you didn't have money. *I. . .I* bought groceries with my pension check and you're spending money on prostitutes . . ."
"Alright, please . . ."
"And gambling. Don't think I don't know about the gambling." She hesitated for a moment then gave a short sigh. The small man could tell she was crying. She took the apron and dried her eyes. All this time she had not faced them.

He took the saucer and drank the coffee in it and refilled it.

Adolfo had a smile on his face trying to brush off the incident as a daily happenstance.

"It's just that it hurts me, Adolfo," the woman continued, now in a softer voice, "to see you like this. A man who in his prime was so admired, so handsome, so gifted. And to come to this . . . a man who pitched for the New York Yankees . . . the Cardinals . . . the Browns. Tell him Adolfo," she said, looking at him now. "Tell your friend about your career. Have you told him?"

"No, I hadn't."

"He didn't have to," the small man said, leaning back on his chair. "Everyone around here knows that Adolfo was the greatest pitcher that ever lived."

"Not the greatest," the woman said. "If he had been the greatest he wouldn't be here."

"But he drank. He drank too much."

Adolfo was pleasantly stunned. They were talking about him as if he weren't there.

"Yes, he drank and he still drinks but he wasn't the best. He was a man of talent, a talent from God, and he did nothing with it."

"I still say it was the drinking."

"What do you know?" the woman challenged.

The small man knew it was best to let matters drop. "Nothing, I know nothing," he replied.

"That's right," she said, having the last word. "Drinking? What do you know about drinking? Is it drinking when a man forsakes his family? Changes his name . . . leaves his town, state, and does not come back one single time for fifteen years? Is that the drinking you talk about?"

The small man felt uneasy, shifted his weight in the chair and crossed his legs self-consciously. "I only say what I have been told," he said, not facing the woman.

She was a rather large woman who had been beautiful at one time. Her skin was smooth, though wrinkled and very pale, for she never went out without her long sleeves and a bonnet. Her hands did not give her age. Her eyes were a gray that could turn to different shades depending on her mood. Now the eyes were light as she became remorseful. "Please, Adolfo," she said, turning to him, face to face, "be careful. Don't drink too much. Don't spend too much money. Don't go to the beerjoints, or the prostitutes or the gambling things, whatever you call them."

"I won't," he said.

There was a gentleness to the huge man, the man with long fingers and huge palms, who used to throw a ball harder than any pitcher in the majors, who used to wiggle his ears from the mound, who would make batters laugh . . . oh the stories they would tell! And she, proud that he was her cousin, would join in — stories of her own about games, baseball games played years ago in open fields, corn fields, caliche, sorghum, all fields. He was her cousin and she was proud, especially of when he had been young and virile and all the beautiful girls were her friends, just to be close to him. Those had been the beautiful days, days when it seldom rained, when to be alive was enough and was all there was to life. Now her thoughts were more of death than anything else. The games were of no importance now. Who cares who can pitch? Who cares who wins when all lose in the end? Her thoughts were of her surviving for her children. Forget about happiness. She thought, if she could just see her sons and daughters doing something, that would be good enough.

Don't leave, stay here. Work close to home. Don't study too much. They say (who is they?) that a man in the next town went crazy studying so much. He just knew so much his brain cracked, or his skull cracked, one of the two. Anyway something gave and the poor fellow is in the looney house. He must have been eternal, for his story was repeated over and over again, generation to generation. Don't do too much. It's bad for you. It will only disappoint you. Why the resentment? Because he had gone, gone to see the world and had fun playing baseball. A game, not a job. Picking cotton was a job, so was washing dishes or sweeping streets, or working from morning until nighttime crating vegetables and fruit.

"I won't do anything," he replied. Anyway, you shouldn't care. I won't be back."

"You'll be back," she said.

"No, I won't. You can slap my face if I come back. Now that I've sold the lease on the place, I have no obligations here."

"Obligations? Obligations never kept you anywhere. Obligations were something you never wanted . . . you never even got married."

"But I had a son," he said, proudly. He winked at the small man who was through eating now and was leaning back on the wooden chair.

"How can he be your son, if you never married?"

"He is still my son and he knows it."

"And what about your other sons? How many more have you got?"

"Oh," he said, laughing, "I probably have ten or fifteen scattered all over the world."

"You laugh, but look at the misery you have caused them and the women."

"Well, woman, if I am as bad as you say, then they were blessed when I didn't marry anyone of them."

"It will haunt you, Adolfo. All this misery that you have brought will haunt you."

"Let it," he said, winking at the small man.

He pushed back from the table and leaned back on the chair, patting his stomach.

"Did you send the letter?" he asked.

"Yes," she lied. "I sent it a long time ago. Well, whenever you gave it to me to mail." She was looking out the window above the stove and she could see the men and women riding on the truck beds, being hauled to work in the fields. Across the road and to the east of the house were the fields where throughout the year all her family had worked, except Adolfo. When it wasn't lettuce, it was cabbage, or okra, or tomatoes, an endless job of planting, weeding, tilling and harvesting. She had lied. She had not mailed the letter. "What good would it do?" she thought.

"Well, we better go," the small man said, clearing his throat nervously. He was not sure what would set the woman off. He had only met her this morning, but had seen her many times around town. She was always wrapped in black, no matter what the heat or cold, with a black bonnet caked with starch and lint. There were rumors about her, but one could never tell. No one came out and said, "This is the story. Sit down, please. Let me tell you about her."

He had met Adolfo the night before at the beer joint that Adolfo rented from a friend, a distant cousin. Adolfo had lived with Maria for two years. After an absence of many years, he had come to the funeral of a friend and decided to stay. The deceased friend had been a baseball catcher for different town teams around the valley and Adolfo in his youth had always liked him. The family had sent someone for Adolfo to come to the funeral. They found him in Los Angeles managing a pool hall, sleeping in the back room on a cot behind a crap table. Under the cot was a coffee can where he expectorated and urinated on and off during the night. His suit was hanging on a hanger on a nail, his yellowing white shirt draped around the hanger and covered by the coat. A tie hung from the neck of the hanger and fell stylishly across the shirt collar and, like a snake, disappeared under the vest, then reappeared below like a triangular phallus. He had a good memory. Apparently alcohol had not damaged his brain, as some have been led to believe. He could remember names, faces, places, dates, until it grated on your nerves. "Yes," he would answer to a simple question, "I knew all of those people. The one you ask me about is Carlos. His older brother is Paul and they had a sister . . . " Here he would pause for effect. Maybe he forgot? But no. He continued. "Her name was Rosa. She still lives in Los Angeles with her husband, a man named John, a large man, works for a cemetery like his father. She, Rosa, never had children, but was given a child that belonged to a woman from a small town close by. I will not tell you her name, since I wouldn't want to embarrass the lady (ever the gentleman). She is married now. If I would tell you who she is, you wouldn't believe it . . . ." Here was another pause to think since he had forgotten the original question. The question by now had lost its importance. It had been something casual, something to keep the conversation going. But that wouldn't stop him. The young man that drove him back to the funeral said later that the man talked from Los Angeles to the Valley, a period of two and one-half hours without stopping. "Paul is married to a fine woman that works at a laundry in a hotel. She had worked here for thirteen years wihout missing a day. This was told to me by Paul, her husband. He comes to play pool often. When I first saw him, I said that he had to be a Trevino from San Isidro. The nose, the teeth. You remember their father's teeth, don't you? All bunched up in front like a picket fence and little eyes like a possum. I told him that and he laughed. He remembered me as a pitcher wih Pachuca, Mexico, playing against Tijuana. Eighteen innings I pitched that day. A Sunday, August 15, the day of the Assumption of Our Lady, the Virgin Mary." Here everyone would laugh. He had not been to church in his life. "But Carlos," (He was back to the original question), "you ask me about Carlos? Oh, but he has done well. A civil servant in the Post Office in Los Angeles. Has worked there eighteen years and was given a plaque by the *Federal* (here emphasized the word) Government. Not little governments like we have here or state governments . . . *The Federal Government.* He has risen in his job to where he has five men under him. His childen are in college. He is doing well. So well, his wife doesn't work. But he wasn't like this all the time. He had taken to drinking . . . "

A young girl appeared into the kitchen from the back room. She was dressed very neatly, her hair parted down the middle and gathered in the back. This brought out her features: delicate nose, mouth, fine black eyebrows. Her eyes were almost black. She carried a suitcase.

"This is Carmen, my niece," Adolfo said to the small man. "She needs a ride. She's going with us. Do you mind?"

"No, not at all," he answered, "I'll take the suitcase."

The woman turned from the stove and looked at the girl, studied her for a long time, like this moment would be how she remembered her. Her eyes watered slightly. "Don't forget, Carmen," she said, her voice trembling, "that all that I have told you is true. Take the advice of an old woman who has seen many things in this life. As your father said many times, a dollar is a man's best friend. Don't cause any trouble at your uncle's and aunt's house. Be quiet and work. Send something home if you can." She stopped and wiped her eyes with her apron. She looked at Adolfo, but he did not respond. The small man had taken the suitcase to the car. "Remember that you have always been a good girl and that if anything happens, you should come back right away. Don't suffer if you can help it. If it doesn't work out, come back and stay with me. You can always go back to work at the theater."

"Yes, Mama," the girl replied. "I will be good. I feel bad leaving you like this."

"No, no, don't feel bad, Carmen. I'll be fine. Everything will be alright."

"But I feel guilty not being here to help."

"Go, you must go. But remember to come back if things don't work out. Now you'd better go before I cry out loud."

She sat down and wiped her eyes again with her apron. She placed her head in her hands and, looking down to the floor, she said, "You are the last to leave this house and I really feel it."

"I'll be back, Mama."

She walked over to her mother and embraced her. Adolfo left quickly and returned from the back room with his suitcase and dressed in his old suit. Carmen left the house slowly, looking back at her mother crying now at the table.

"Maria," Adolfo said, his voice firm, "it's time for me to leave also."

"You were always ungrateful," she said, "but go. It's better that you go and don't come back. But don't think that they will treat you better than I have. When you find your son, do you think he will love you?"

"Yes I do."

"Why should he? And his poor mother, who almost died from what you did to her? Will she love you?"

"That I do not know," he answered. He was standing close to the door holding the suitcase. "But at least they know I'm coming. That's why I wrote to her. Maybe if she's prepared, she will not be angry."

"Go," she said, angry now. "Go and find out for yourself that no one loves you, except your own family."

He opened the door, his huge frame filling most of it and he walked out onto the porch. He had his coat and vest and serpentine necktie on. He was back on the mound now, hiking his leg above his head, delivering the fast-ball. But he was not happy. Inside he could hear the lonely woman crying softly. "Who could she talk to now?" She had been good to him.

The girl ran back into the house and placed something in her mother's hands and kissed her. She simply nodded. Then she ran out again and got into the back seat of the car.

"Goodbye, Maria," Adolfo said, looking through the screen door, trying to force himself into the seriousness of the situation, for he had seen himself in his mind as a strange figure, even funny in his three piece suit with his yellowish shirt and tie. If he hadn't been so big a man, one would have laughed at him. Also, if he had been more self-conscious, he would have attracted more ridicule, but somehow he managed among his friends not to be made fun of, at least not to his face. To top it off he was wearing some old brown sneakers with the tips cut out to relieve the pressure on his bunnions. Half-way through the trip he would remember that he had forgotten his false teeth.

"But I thought I had them in my pocket," he would say, very worried, shaking his head. Now that he would be trying for a good impression, this would happen to him.

"They were in your room on the window sill," Carmen said.

"Why didn't you tell me?"

"I thought you had gone to get them when you went to put your coat on."

"Well I went back, but I didn't see them. I forgot them. What bad luck."

He looked at the small man wondering how he managed to see through the steering wheel.

They arrived at San Diego through Route 8, having passed through the Valley and by way of El Cajon. At the highest point of the city, they could see down toward Coronado and San Diego Bay. Beyond Coronado was the Pacific, its sequential waves forming a pattern seen from on high like strings of white erratic threads woven into a deep blue cloth. Here Adolfo had played for the Pelicans before going to the majors. Here he had been put on a ship and sent around the Panama Canal to Europe to fight in World War I. From there his thoughts turned to Germany. Who would believe him that he had fought in Germany? Had it been that long ago? He still carried a brown and white picture in his wallet showing him surrounded by two large frauleins. They (the frauleins) seemed to be giggling, each with one hand inside his army jacket. They wore printed dresses with lace tops and heavy shoes. His campaign hat was pushed back and he had a smile on his face. God only knew what he had been up to. In the background was the Cathedral at Cologne, next to the train depot. Still, some people wouldn't believe he had been there. To him it was evidence enough. "They are very ignorant." He would give a sigh and shake his head. "Can you believe that there are people here that do not know that you have to cross the ocean to get to Germany? And we consider ourselves educated?"

He remembered the ship that took him, but it was too painful to sustain the dream and it was too long ago. So he backed off.

The young girl, Carmen, had not said much throughout the trip. She thought that she would miss the Valley. She had seen the cut-off sign to Calexico and had remembered when she and her mother had gone to see some distant relatives there. Aside from that, she was relieved that the car had made it to San Diego and that she would begin a new life.

It had now surprised her how easily she had left her home. She had thought about the time when she would leave and had imagined that there would be an internal wrenching, a sort of feeling of loneliness, despair, even nostalgia. But she had left just like that. It had been without emotion, the stranger taking her suitcase and placing it in the car, saying good-bye to her mother without a sense of sadness. She had imagined herself leaving in a very different way. The night before when she thought it would be hard to sleep she had bathed and gone to bed early. She even felt like masturbating and she had done so. It was by no means her first time. She had started this practice shortly after starting her job at the theater selling tickets. The manager, a puffy faced man named Billy had started coming into the ticket booth on slow days and began fondling her. This is really when she started. She would run home and do it. Then she started going to work early. The affair was consumated one slow afternoon, a Wednesday, she remembered, in the projection room. She had lain on her back on the dirty sofa and he did his deed there. She remembered always how, on her back in the dark with her head tilted, she could see the wall and the projector light dancing on the ceiling and directly above her a window. On the ledge had been a pigeon, twitching nervously, taking small stuttering steps as the two below her made love. The pigeon had made a strange cooing sound and flown away. The man had finished. She had felt nothing but pain. Her thrill came from knowing something about herself that her mother didn't. The affair continued until she quit her job to go to San Diego. She thought she was on her way to live with her aunt, her mother's younger sister.

The small man, Jesus, had said only a few words. Adolfo had talked throughout the trip. He had covered sports (only animals play football; baseball is a game of skill and reflexes), government (everything it does is bad for you), society (whores are the only sincere individuals he had ever met), death (if it happens, it happens), life (how hard one makes it), etc. He had not taken off his coat and vest or tie during the trip. Occasionally he looked down and wiggled his toes through the holes in his sneakers.

They had descended to the southern part of the city, winding their way down from the hills and further down to the area where the small wooden houses, built forty to fifty years ago, sat side by side along the narrow streets. They had stopped to get gas and had asked for directions to the house. The small man stopped the car in front of the house and waited for Carmen and Adolfo to get out.

"Wait here," Adolfo said to him as he tied the laces on his sneakers. "Let me see who's here. Carmen?"

"Yes."

"Are you ready?"

"Yes. Let's get off."

The two of them looking oddly disproportionate, walked silently, even hesitantly, toward the house. Here was a man six and a half feet tall, no teeth, dressed in a wool suit in the middle of summer with a vest and tie and cut-out sneakers, the rear of his pants as shiny and smooth as a man having sat down on a pan of shellac and Carmen, a young girl slightly over five feet tall, very clean and beautiful, dressed neatly, having to walk twice as fast just to stay up.

He was about to knock on the door when it opened. A woman in her fifties looked at him, smiled and said, "Adolfo! Is it you?"

"Yes, it's me." He grinned slightly keeping his lips close together, showing just a little bit of gum.

"And Carmen!" she said. "How are you? I haven't seen you in a long time. You are a beautiful young lady. How is your mother?"

"Fine, thank you," she answered. "She sends her love."

"Come in. Come in." She held the door open for them and they walked into a room that was a combination living and dining room and also sleeping quarters, since one could see a folding metal cot next to an open window along the right wall. To the left was the sofa and two chairs. Opposite the entrance was a door, a piece of long cloth hanging across it, that led into the kitchen. The floor had recently been covered with linoleum. They could smell the coal tar base from which it was made.

Carmen sat at the sofa and Adolfo took one of the chairs. The lady excused herself, went into the kitchen and disappeared into another room, going by way of a side door next to the stove. They could hear her talking to someone in a low tone . . . and being answered by a coarse masculine voice. They could not hear the conversation, but it did not appear to be going well.

Adolfo and Carmen looked at each other, her dark eyes raised as if asking him to figure out what was going on. He shrugged. Again the deep voice blurted out something rapidly. Heavy foot-steps were heard and a door was slammed. Shortly, within seconds, a car door slammed and an engine started. A car pulled out by the side of the house next to where they were sitting. As they both looked out the window and down into the narrow driveway, they saw a man, the woman's husband, angrily backing the car out into the street. From here he gave the car a good jolt and took off down the street, barely missing the old Ford and the small man in it. The woman returned. "He's angry today," she explained. "We have had so much company. You know how he is. He gets it in his head that he is supporting everyone in this house and he doesn't like it. He's been drinking a lot, too. He's been gone for three days at a time. I don't know what to do with him. I'm in the middle. I can't refuse his family if they are in need, and I can't my family either. What do I do?" She sat at one of the chairs and looked out the window in disgust. "How does he think I feel? Does he think I enjoy all of this?" She spread her arms out and took in the whole room. "Does he think I like cooking all day long. Working all day long . . . washing, all the other things."

It was obvious to Carmen and to Adolfo too that the woman had not received the letter or, if she had, she was doing a good job of hiding the fact. Of course she hadn't received the letter. It had never been mailed. Carmen had trusted her mother to mail it for her and she had burned it, just like she had burned Adolfo's letter to his old flame and mother of his son. Or maybe it got lost in the mail? Don't kid yourself. She, the old woman, Maria, had burned it, had burned both letters.

"Look," the woman was saying to Adolfo, "this is where he hit me the other day." She was bending toward him and showing him a spot behind her ear. "It still rings inside my head all the time and I can't hear well. Why does he do it?" She sat down again, this time next to Carmen and, woman to woman, she asked, "Why does he do it, Carmen? He was so gentle as a young man. He never used to hit me. It seems he hates me more than ever." She sighed, smiled and touched Carmen's hand. Adolfo? In these situations, serious, he did not say much. These were the few times that he would not hog the conversation. As a matter or fact, he was embarrassed with the scene and he wished it were not happening. He wished the husband had not been there in the first place. It did something to him to have the husband leave in anger, just because he and Carmen had arrived. It embarrassed him to know that the husband hated him so much, and that the woman knew it. And now Carmen knew. He could not stand not being liked, for being liked was what he had based his life on.

"I'm sorry, Adolfo," the woman said.

"Oh, don't apologize. You know better than me how some husbands are. He's probably drunk."

"No, not really. He hasn't been drinking this week. All I said was that you were here and he flew into a rage." She was still holding Carmen's hand and she looked down and sighed. "And you, Carmen?" she asked gently.

"Did you receive my letter?"

"No." She looked puzzled. Had she received it and forgotten? Had the blow to the head made her forget? "What did it say?"

"Well," she said, "it was about my staying with you until I could find a job." She had the feeling one gets when you know you are going to get rejected even before you ask.

"I didn't receive it, Carmen. When did you mail it? Maybe it's still in the mail."

"No, it couldn't be. It was mailed almost a month ago."

"Then it's lost."

"They lose more mail now than ever before," Adolfo said.

"What can I say now," Carmen said, hesitating. "I had said it in the letter. I wanted to see if I could stay here for a short while, of course, until I had enough money or found a friend to share an apartment or something."

The woman squeezed her hand and looking at Adolfo said, "I wish I could, Carmen." Then softly she repeated the words, "I wish I could . . . Do you see the situation I am in here? Even If I wanted to, you couldn't stay. The man is an animal. The only one who can control him is our son and then only part of the time. I just said that Adolfo was here to see if he would come out and shake hands, say hello and he goes crazy. Have you seen the side of the house where he hits it when he backs out? Did you see how fast he went . . . and in reverse! He's carrying a pistol in the car now. I don't have any pots and pans because he shoots at them. The neighbors complain, but it doesn't do any good. Also, they are afraid of him, too. He almost killed a sailor in a bar downtown. He beat him up so badly that they felt he wouldn't live. Thank

God he survived and didn't press charges." Then she looked at Carmen and said, "I'm sorry, but you can't stay. I would have written back to tell you, but I never received your letter. I'll swear to that. Maybe when things settle down. Maybe then you can come. You know I've always liked you."

"I should have known," Carmen said. "That's why I never got an answer and Mama kept telling me that you were busy and wouldn't write. She said it would be alright if I came."

"Don't blame her," the woman said. "She is old and doesn't know my situation."

"I won't stay if you don't want me," Carmen said. "I don't think there's much need to stay any longer."

The woman released Carmen's hand and reached into the apron pocket and took out two crumpled bills. She smoothed them out on her thigh and put them in Carmen's hand. "Here is something for you. It's not much, but it will help." It was ten dollars, two fives.

"Thank you," Carmen said, not proudly, but realistically. She had learned not to turn money down when offered. Although it might make her appear cheap, the feeling afterwards of having more money made up for this slight, fleeting embarrassment.

"It's not that I don't want you to stay, Carmen. Remember that. I have never turned anyone down before, but unfortunately the situation is bad here and I wouldn't put you in it for anything in this world."

Adolfo by now was fidgeting in the chair, uncomfortable to be sitting in a conversation and not contributing to it. He was very awkward in a situation involving anything serious, especially between women. Laughter, bantering, joking, drinking, that he could take and enjoy. This serious stuff was not for him. Besides, he needed to urinate.

Just then came the screeching sound of a car turning into the drive-way. They saw the top of the car fly past the window and a very large man sitting in it, driving wildly trying to avoid hitting the house. They heard the brakes lock the wheels in place and the car skidding to a stop. The car door slammed shut.

"You must go quickly," the woman said, jumping to her feet. "Quickly, quickly! He's back!"

They both got to their feet, tried to act casual as their hearts pounded in their chests. They couldn't run. It would surely incite him. So they moved as fast as possible without trying to show fear. Carmen ran for the car as soon as she got to the door. Adolfo, for his part was now more angry than afraid. That it should come to this: that a man who was idolized in Pachuca and Saltillo, Mexico; and in San Antonio, Amarillo, and Corsicana, Texas; and in Albuquerque, New Mexico; and in Phoenix, Arizona; and yes, in San Diego, California, would have to leave a house like an unwanted dog. But those had been other times when baseball players, even the minor leaguers were idolized. Yes, those were other times; now no one knew him except once in a while when he met an old timer in a bar in a strange place and the stranger would come up and ask if it was really he. "Yes, it's me, one and the same and the only one," he would reply. And even though he was short on cash, he would buy the gentleman a beer just to have an audience. In reminiscing, he would live again the days of his youth and he would feel the old surge inside him, but that was all he had now. "An old athlete," he would say, "one that does not provide for his older years, may as well be dead." He had not provided for himself, but still he had saved enough money to open a beer joint in his old home town after his friend's funeral. He had not given up the lease, as he had told the old lady. That was a lie. He had gotten his cousin to run it for him while he came to San Diego to arrange for his later years. Those years were fast approaching.

Carmen was already in the car wetting her lips nervously when Adolfo got in and angrily slammed the door.

"What happened?" the small man asked. "Why was she running and you walking so fast?"

"Don't ask questions," Adolfo said, looking straight ahead, his lips, without teeth for support, fluttering as he breathed. "Just drive away slowly."

As he said this, the huge dark man came out of the house and pointed a revolver at them. He took aim and held the gun steady, as if ready to shoot. The small man had the car started and slowly, as they watched in horror at the man with the revolver, the car moved away. The man did not fire. Adolfo could hear him cursing them.

"That it should come to this," Adolfo said. "That I should be run out of a house like an unwanted dog. Those people, especially him, never had the education, never had the training to treat a person in a civilized way. They come from bad people. Very ignorant. There you have his mother, whom I knew as a young girl, always picking cotton because she couldn't find anything better to do. Her brothers were the same, a bunch of ignorant people who could never see that a man should try to rise above all this shit! His parents were bastards. All of them from his great grandfather to the present were a bunch of bastards and ignorants. And to have Carmen subjected to this also. Don't be afraid Carmen," he said. He looked back at her. "Everything will be fine. But now you know what type of people your aunt married into."

"He was never like that before." she said.

"Well he's that way now."

"I wonder what has happened to him? He used to come and visit and be so polite. He laughed so much at our home."

"I don't care what happened; he should not have treated us like that. Especially you, Carmen. Me, I'm an old man. I can take it."

"I've got to go to the bathroom," Adolfo said.

"Me too," Carmen said.

"Where do we go from here?"

"We'll ask at the service station," Adolfo replied. "I have the address."

The car pulled up slowly to the house, a small white frame house trimmed

in blue with a cedar shingle roof that had molded over with the humidity and
the shade from several large trees. The house sat well into the lot and had a
small porch with a portico. On either side of the house was a wooden fence.
The three in the car strained to read the numbers on the pillar that supported
one side of the portico.

"Two, two, eight, four," Carmen said.

"That's it then," Adolfo said.

The car came to a stop.

"Let me get off first and talk to her. If everything is alright I will come for
you, Carmen. Don't worry. I'll see about you also."

"Fine," she replied, "but don't worry about me. I can always go back."

"I don't want you to go back, Carmen," he said. "You have got to get away.
That town is no place for you."

"I don't mind it, Adolfo. I really don't."

"That's what you say now. Wait until you get older. Anyway, you have got
to get away from your mother. It's not good for you to be there with her. She'll
drive you insane. I'm getting off."

He opened the door and slowly got out, pushing his pants down trying to
hide his high top sneakers with the holes cut out, but it was no use. As he
walked away, they could see that he had sat on something white that had
stained his seat.

He stepped up to the porch and knocked on the screen door. A dog that had
been sleeping under the porch growled. He knocked again and the dog came
to life, running from under the porch and going up to the top stair. There he
barked and growled and would not let Adolfo move. From inside the house he
heard a young girl shout at the dog and immediately the dog backed off and
returned to his post under the porch. The screen door opened and he asked for
the lady of the house. She was in back washing clothes.

He went around the side between the fence and house and the dog growled
again but Adolfo paid him no mind, although he glanced at him out of the
corner of his eye. He noticed that the dog had a cloudiness over one eye. The
ground here was muddy from a leak that seemed to be coming from under the
house. Someone had placed boards to step on. He followed the long boards
along the house and to the back yard. Here he saw her for the first time in
many years. How many? He couldn't answer, although he knew. Not right
away he couldn't, although he knew. He could figure it out, but he was too
excited. Thirty? Forty? More like forty, he thought, since he had been playing
for San Diego at that time. Her back was small and she wore a dark blue
cotton sweater that had rolled up little balls of lint all over it. Her hair was
combed back into a bun like Carmen's hair. She was standing over a tub rhythmically kneading a piece of cloth over a wash board.

The back of her neck had wrinkled and he remembered briefly how beautiful that neck had been in her youth. Forty years ago was right. Where had they
met? That, he would never forget. He saw her at the ball game between neigh-

borhood teams. He was there as a star attraction to autograph baseballs and throw the first pitch. After all, he was the star pitcher for the Pelicans. She was there with two friends to see the game. He had been impressed with her, had asked her name from a friend, and had introduced himself after the game. She had always been a very neat woman and being slovenly himself, he had been attracted to her and her neatness. When she had taken her clothes off for the first time in front of him, she had folded them neatly and placed them on a chair. Even her shoes were tucked neatly under the chair. Oh, how he remembered now. He had not loved anyone before or since. What had happened to the skin on that beautiful neck? He had kissed it many times, those times when he had all his teeth, before he lost them to the Tijuana dentist. Why had he pulled them all? Wasn't it the trend in those days that whatever ailed you was caused by bad teeth? He had said it many times, but he would say it again that the dentists of that time had done more harm to the human race than Adolf Hitler, his namesake. Now his teeth were gone, his lips curved inwardly like the end of an apple and he would lisp as he talked.

They made love many times and he left one day on a road trip to northern Mexico; by the time he returned, she had already left. He knew why, too. She hadn't told him, but he knew just the same. As luck would have it, he was sold and shipped to the Yankees before he could make up his mind what to do about her. He didn't know if he loved her enough to marry her. Now he knew he had. Now he was hoping it was not too late.

He was standing close behind her. She sensed his presence and turned around startled.

"Isabel?"

"Yes," she answered, placing a soapy hand over her eyes to shield them from the sun.

"It is me, Adolfo."

"Who?" She was still confused.

"Adolfo," he repeated.

"Adolfo?"

"Yes, me."

"What are you doing here?"

"I was in San Diego for the day and I thought I would drop by to see how you were doing."

"How did you know where to find me?"

"I ran into a friend of ours in Los Angeles. He knew where you lived." He realized that she had not received his letter. In the letter had been an apology for all the years that he had neglected her and lastly a plea to take him in now that he was old and had no close relatives. Maria, he explained, was a first cousin who was nice enough to put up with him for a while, two years to be exact, and could not be counted to help him much more. (This last statement was a lie, of course. Maria had complained about him and about spending money on prostitutes and beer and gambling, but she had never threatened to kick him out. Why else would she, Maria, lie about mailing the letters? She didn't want anyone to leave, not Carmen, not Adolfo. She had connived to keep the rest of her family from leaving home. She had wanted Carmen to stay at the theater and she wanted all her sons and other daughter to stay there, to stay in the fields or do menial work, but the important thing had been to stay.)

"I guess you didn't receive my letter?" He was dejected. He had thought the letter would break the ice and she would have made up her mind by now. He hated to have to explain all over again. Serious words never came easy to him.

"No, I didn't. But the mail service is bad and, even then, the mailman refuses to deliver because of the dog. But what can I do? Without the dog they would steal everything I own."

The young girl came out from the house with a pair of wet sweaters wrapped in towels and she unwrapped them and hanged them on the clothesline that ran from the house to a small washing shed. When she was through, she walked back into the house.

"How have you been?"

"Well, Adolfo, after all these years. Do you really care?" She was not angry. She had gotten over that a long time ago.

"Yes, I do."

He really hated himself now for forgetting his teeth. How nice he could have looked. He thought about placing his long fingers over his mouth as he spoke, but he felt it was too late. She had already noticed. And even if he had done it, he couldn't keep it up throughout the conversation.

"I do want to know how you are. That's why I stopped in to see you."

"Where were you when I needed you?"

"I was gone. You didn't leave word."

Her father had come in drunk one night and pulled her out of bed by her hair and had beaten her. He had been insulted at a beer joint. The word around there was that his daughter and Adolfo had been seen naked on a country road. A man and a friend of Adolfo's had surprised them. They had laughed at the sight of her running naked into the brush, Adolfo following her, his gangly figure trying to shield her naked bottom from the men. The father had run home and taken her by the hair and dragged her on the floor around the small house, hitting her on the head. At last when he was exhausted, he began kicking her until she could scream no more. She crawled behind a wood burning stove, but he took a piece of fire wood and hit her over the head with it. She crawled as fast as she could, the pain becoming unbearable with each breath. He came from behind and kicked her between her legs. Her mother watched in silence. Then, the beating had been enough. "Poor girl, maybe it's a mistake," the mother said, holding a kerosene lamp in her hand. "No one takes her out. Men are not attracted to her yet. Let her explain." She managed to get to her feet, but her father caught her from behind and slammed her head against the floor. That's all she remembered to this day. Her mother had intervened finally, before she was killed (while Isabel's father looked for a knife), and had taken her to a neighbor's house for the night. She had been shipped like a mare in foal to Tijuana the next day. There she had stayed with her mother's friends and relatives until she had the boy. She had named him Adolfo and everyone thought she was crazy.

The following year she had received a telegram saying that her father had died. It didn't say how he died, but later she was told by her mother that he was killed in a brawl with the same man that had seen her naked running into the brush that night. The man had been carrying a knife in his sleeve and, in an instant after words were exchanged, he had taken the knife out and shoved it into her father's chest to the left of the breast-bone. Everyone had laughed. Everyone thought it was a clean punch, but when the father fell over a table and turned around, they saw the rhythmic spurting of bright red blood coming from the hole in the chest. Everyone ran.

She came home after that to live with her mother. Her mother loved her and the child and never mentioned her pregnancy or the child or the child's father to her. She had made a mistake and both knew it. That was enough for both of them. Her anger had been that she had been violated by her father and Adolfo, a feeling she would never forget. She had hoped that her father would forgive her, but he couldn't and didn't. It was as if he had been beaten down by life so much that he could not accept the desecration of his daughter. That had been the last straw, as they say. Maybe if he had had money or power or even a decent job, he would have taken it as one of those things in life, a mistake of the flesh, a mistake of the young, a mistake, period. But he was a poor and ignorant man with a terrible temper. It did him in. She had also found out on her return that she was not the first, that Adolfo had impregnated many women. Along with her anger she now added bitterness.

"I have come to talk to you," he said. "If you will only listen."

"Let's go in then," she said, drying her hands on her apron.

She led him into the house by the back door and into the small kitchen, through there and into a fair-sized dining and living room. He sat at the sofa, an old maroon velveteen piece with worn out arms. In front of the sofa was a chair which she took. He looked around and saw the picture of a girl on the wall, her head resting on her arm, the head tilted sideways. The picture had faded, the colors of the face being a squalid blue and the teeth extremely white. Next to it was a picture of a man dressed in an enlisted-man's navy uniform.

The young man was grinning broadly and below him in the same frame was a picture of a navy battleship. At the corner of the frame was glued a small picture taken at an arcade showing the man droopy-eyed, holding a beer in one hand and his other arm around a snaggled-toothed Japanese girl. In the background were some painted palms.

"Do you want some coffee?"

"No, thank you," he answered.

In the soft light of the room it was more noticeable that his teeth were missing. There was a darkened shadow around his mouth. He started to cross his legs, but remembered his sneakers. She had noticed them while outside.

"Well Adolfo, tell me what you're here for."

"Isabel, I know that you have suffered because of me. And I have suffered too. Not as much as you, but I have suffered."

"And?"

Everything had been explained in the letter. If only she had received it. It was so much easier to write it down or rather, have someone write it down for you. He had paid two dollars to have the letter written. But he gave the letter to Maria to mail. How could he have trusted her? The letters, both his and Carmen's, had been burned the same day.

"I'm living with Maria now."

"How is she?"

"Fine. She never changes. Still the same."

"She came out of her troubles a stronger woman."

"Yes, I guess you could say that. She's very possessive."

"With you?"

"Oh no. Not with me. That's the reason I'm here."

"She doesn't want you around?"

"Well, Isabel, let me just say that I feel like a stranger there. I've never felt like I belonged. She is only a first cousin and it makes it hard for me."

"Are you moving then?"

"I would like to."

"And you still don't have a steady job?"

"I have a beer joint that I lease from my cousin and I make a little money. Not much, but I buy groceries for Maria and have something to spend for myself. I also have saved a little from my veteran's pension."

Outside, the small man was lighting a cigarette. He got out of the car and opened the hood. The dog came out to the sidewalk and barked at him. He checked the starter and the battery, wiped his hands with a rag and took a drag from the cigarette. Carmen was sitting quietly. He leaned against the door. "I wonder what he's doing and why it's taking him so long?" He knew Carmen. He knew about her and the manager at the theater.

"He's talking to the woman. But you're right, it is taking a long time."

"I don't have all day. I wish he'd come out so we could go."

"I'm getting nervous."

The small man had known Adolfo for several years, but last night was the first time that they had been drinking together. Adolfo had somehow talked him into driving him to San Diego. The dog came over to him, smelled his cuffs and went back under the house. The small man wondered what this was all about.

"And what did the letter say?" She was rolling the edge of her apron.

"In it I explained everything. It's so much easier to write about it than to say it. But what I said was that I wanted to tell you how sorry I was."

Isabel was about to say something, when the young girl appeared from a door next to the kitchen and crossed the room. She was well dressed and looked like she was ready to go downtown. She waved at the woman, smiled and left.

"Is she your daughter?" he asked.

"No. I never married. She lives with me. She works at the naval base, but she's on the night shift this month. That's why she's leaving so late. I always rent a room or two. It helps me so that I don't have to work anymore. She's leaving in a week. Getting married. You know how these young girls are nowadays. They all want to get married." She looked at her apron and folded it neatly at the hem. "I'm retired, you know. I retired from the base last year."

"You worked there many years, didn't you?"

"Yes, almost thirty-five."

"And now you don't have anyone."

"Well, my son is gone, if that's what you mean. He's in the Navy."

"I noticed the picture on the wall."

"Yes, he's a fine man, but he's never married."

"He will some day."

She thought about what he said and he did too, but she did not take the opportunity to embarrass him. Her son was like his father.

He would never settle down.

"Well, you were saying something about the letter."

"Oh, yes. I explained everything Isabel. But the most important thing to me is that I apologize for everything that I did to you and to my son. It has taken me a long time to come to my senses. Do you realize that I have lived sixty-seven years and I don't have anything?"

"Do you blame me?"

"No, I don't. I blame myself. I have no one left. You probably hate me. All my friends are gone, dead. All I do is live from day to day. There are days I don't eat, because I don't want to impose on Maria. There are nights I sleep at the beer joint, so I won't bother anyone. In Los Angeles I ran a pool hall. Do you know that's where they found me when they came looking for me to attend my friend's funeral? Imagine the embarrassment at having to face someone that knows you under those circumstances."

"And what do you want from me, friendship?"

"More than that. I want for both of us to be together."

She lowered her head and played with the apron. He was leaning forward.

"I couldn't do it," she replied.

"Why not?"

"Because my life is simple now. I have a routine. You would disturb that and, besides, I've never forgiven you and I could never forget. You weren't around when my father ran me out of town. You weren't around through the difficult years when I was raising our child."

The thought of her running naked through the brush came to her and she could hear the men laughing as they saw her naked rear.

"Think of your son."

"I am. He hates you, Adolfo. I never said anything bad about you, but he still hates you. As a child he would say that I had suffered because of you and that someday he would kill you."

"It hurts me to hear that."

"He doesn't mean it, Adolfo, but sometimes even now, when he gets drunk, he curses you."

"I'm sorry for everything I did to you and to him. What's sad is that I can't do anything to change it. Maybe someday I'll write him a letter."

"I'm sure he would read it," she said softly.

"What's the use," he said shrugging. He leaned back.

"That's the way it has to be. We are happy now and we wouldn't want the change. I'm sure Maria will take care of you."

"She's getting old. No one can take her anymore. Her daughter came with me to get away from her. Maria fights with her all day long. The poor girl can't take it anymore. We had hoped that she could stay at her aunt's house here in San Diego, but she couldn't."

"What happened?"

"She came here to stay with Maria's sister, but they ran us off. They didn't have room for her. The husband took a gun to us. It was all very bad."

"You mean he shot at you?"

"No, but he pointed the gun at us as we drove away."

"Is he crazy or what?"

"Well, Maria's sister married into a bunch of ignorant people and now she's stuck with a madman. I don't know if he's crazy, but someone is going to kill him one of these days."

"Do you mean to tell me the girl has been sitting in the car all this time? Why didn't you have her come in?"

"We just didn't want to impose. But I was thinking that, since you take in boarders, maybe you could find a place for her here. She's a good girl. It would help her a lot to get away from her mother."

"What can she do here?"

"She's got a job at home, but she wants to learn to do something else."

"Is she willing to work?"

"Yes. She's a hard worker."

"I don't know. Can she get along with people? I have the other girl to consider and myself also."

"She can get along. I've lived with her a long time now. If she can get along with Maria, she can get along with anyone else."

"Does she have any money?"

"No, that's the bad part. But I'm sure that she can find a job, maybe at the base like the other girl. And I'll give you what I have with me now and, if she has a hard time finding a job, I'll send you the money for her room and board every week. That I can promise. Can you do it?"

"Well, it's hard to say. I hadn't planned on it. I'm fixing up a small room in the back and putting in a new bathroom . . . "

"I promise to you on my mother's grave that I'll send you the money." He reached into his pocket and took out a ten dollar bill. He gave it to her. "Will that be enough to start out? I can send you some more tomorrow."

She thought for a while, the memories came back to her. She saw herself running naked; she saw herself degraded, but it didn't matter any more. All in all, her life had not been so bad after all. Her mother had been wonderful. She had not realized it at the time, but it had been so.

She took the money. "Is she in trouble?"

"No," he answered. "She's a good girl. She has made some mistakes, but who hasn't."

"I suppose I owe you something, Adolfo. I'll do it as a favor to you. We'll see about getting her a job."

"Thank you, Isabel. You are a good woman, as always. Now that I think about it, it is more than I should expect from you."

She smiled at him. "Adolfo," she said, "I knew that this day would come. I knew you would want to come back and I knew that you would wait until I didn't need you. That's the way you are. I knew what I would say. Don't get me wrong. I don't hate you. There was a time when I hated you and I loved you at the same time. Both of those feelings have died. I knew I would refuse you. That's the way things have to be. I feel sorry for you. You have come to the age when it is not easy to be loved. You are just like me. Who wants someone like me? Who wants someone like you? You made your move too late. For you and me love has to become a habit. That I found out a long time ago. You just don't belong anywhere."

"You are right, Isabel." he said. He stood up, "I'll talk to Carmen and see. I'm sure she wants to stay."

"Are you sure? What will Maria say?"

"Nothing. What can she say?"

"She never liked me, you know. She blamed me for everything. You know the things she said about me."

"She's old now, Isabel. She doesn't remember anything anymore."

"Well, we'll see." She stood up beside him and led him to the front door.

The dog was sticking his head out from under the porch and the woman scolded him. He retracted his head like a turtle back under the house.

When he reached the car, Adolfo was in full stride, but favoring one leg that had gotten stiff sitting down. He put his head through the window, looked at the small man and asked him how he was doing. Then he turned to Carmen.

"Carmen, do you want to stay here? This is Isabel's home. Isabel is my old girl friend."

"What does she do?"

"What do you mean, what does she do? She's retired. Retired from the naval base. She rents rooms, furnishes meals, everything."

"And what does she say about me?"

"She wants to meet you. Haven't I always told you that I would get you out of that house? Now I'm doing just that."

"Does she really want me to stay?"

"Sure she does. That's how she makes money and, besides, she knows you're my relative."

"But what about money?"

"I gave her some already, enough until you find a job."

"But what if I don't find a job?"

"You will. She'll help you. Don't you think that someone who worked for the government for thirty-five years has some connections? She'll talk to someone and you'll have a job in no time. A good job too. Not selling tickets. No, that's not a job for you. You'll be working for the Federal Government, Carmen. Think of that. The Federal Government."

"And you, Adolfo? What about you?"

"I have to go back. I need to take care of my interests."

"It didn't work out, then?"

"No. But it's for the best. I was never born to be tied down."

"You're going back to the prostitutes, aren't you?"

"Yes. That's where I belong. With friends."

"What do you think? Do you think I ought to stay?"

The small man turned the key and checked the gas gauge. "It's getting late," he said.

"Come on Carmen, let's get down. Do you want to fight with Maria every single day for the rest of your life?"

"No."

"Well, then, let's get your suitcase and let's go in. I need to introduce you properly. This is a good woman you're going to meet, not like your aunt's family. You're going to see what a good woman is like. I never associated with anything but good women."

"And the prostitutes?" the small man asked.

"I never associated with prostitutes until I became an old man. I never needed to either." He winked at the small man and the small man laughed and hit the steering wheel.

"Adolfo, you're an old has-been."

"Never mind that, Carmen, you need to get down."

"If you think that it's okay, I'll go."

"I know it's okay. Don't be afraid."

"Alright, but if I don't like it, I'm not staying. After what happened this afternoon at my aunt's home, I don't know what to think."

"Oh, don't bother yourself about that. Those are low class people. This is a higher class you're about to meet."

She got off the car finally and followed Adolfo to the door. Adolfo opened it with not as much as a sound from the dog. He was bored and had fallen asleep.

Adolfo led her to the sofa across from where Isabel was sitting. He introduced them and Carmen slowly sat down next to Adolfo.

"What did I tell you, Carmen? Didn't I tell you that Isabel was a lady, a lady in the proper sense of the word? A lady of good morals."

Isabel blushed. She had never been referred to like this and she knew Adolfo was bragging on her to impress Carmen. She wished her father had been alive to hear this. Adolfo was in his element. He was joking. He was happy. Teeth or no teeth, he was happy. Slowly he shifted the conversation to Carmen and Isabel until he had them both talking. He knew that they would get along. In Carmen Isabel saw herself at that age. How lucky, though, that Carmen had the choice of leaving home. She had not been that fortunate. She wondered if Carmen was pregnant, but that didn't matter. She realized the kindness that had been extended to her by her mother's family when she had been pregnant. Carmen's pregnancy didn't bother her at all. Although she wasn't sure, she could tell something about the young girl that only another woman would notice.

It was dark now and at the top of the hill they could see San Diego stretched out to the Pacific. He thought of Carmen and what she would be doing at that moment. He made the small man stop at a store and he hurried in and out. He carried a small paper sack in one hand and two six-packs in the other.

"Something for the prostitutes, eh? Panties?"

Adolfo winked at him. "Don't go tell Maria."

"I won't. I don't want to talk to her about anything."

"Oh, she's alright. Don't take her seriously. She's a good woman."

"I guess she's good if she's put up with you all this time."

He ignored that remark and opened a beer for each of them.

On the road at the outskirts of town he could see stadium lights. It looked like a baseball game. San Diego was a major league city now. He thought about asking the small man to stop. Maybe someone would recognize him. But it would be too much of an imposition.

When they reached the Valley, they could see the large head-lights from the tractors working the fields. With the lights they could see the workers like two dimensional puppets following the tractors, picking vegetables and placing them in large wooden boxes. Others were throwing the full boxes into flatbeds towed by trucks.

They were on their last beer.

"Have I told you about the time I pitched eighteen innings without allowing a hit?"

"No," Jesus said, "but I'm sure you will."

"It was a Sunday, August the fifteenth, the feast of the Assumption of our Holy Mother, the Blessed Virgin Mary . . . "

CHAPTER 2

They arrived at 3 o'clock in the morning. Adolfo had been sitting in one position for so long that he felt numb. His legs were asleep. He placed his fingers under his knees and picked up one leg and then the other. He could see his feet by the dashboard light, but he couldn't move his toes. The small man, Jesus, shifted the car into second and the engine whined through the small downtown. They passed the theatre where Carmen once worked and Adolfo thought about her. She would still be asleep at this time, he thought. Next to the theatre the small cafe was open and through the large glass pane, he could see some men drinking coffee at this early hour. Across the street was the only large building in town, a two story bank made of brown cut-stone with barred windows. A solitary light was on inside the bank and Adolfo thought he saw someone moving around inside. But wasn't that always the case? No one had ever robbed the bank and no one would. Next to the bank was the grocery store, its glass panes smeared with lime paint announcing to the people the cost of everything on sale. Two men, drunk, were on the side-walk weaving their way home. One had stopped to try to light a cigarette. His pants were about to fall off.

Past downtown, what little there was of it, Jesus went straight for about a mile, then turned left unto the limestone road. This was Mexican town. At the corner was a beer-joint silhouetted against a darkened sky by the head lights of Jesus's car. This was not Adolfo's place or Adolfo's Place as the tavern was known.

The car went up a slight rise to the top of a small hill and below was the section of town where the Mexican workers and their families lived and died. There was only a scattering of lights. The small area of the town had gone to sleep. Once more another day had come and gone and all the routine of the day-to-day work was about to begin. Adolfo and Jesus had seen them as they came into town, the workers, each with their hoes or rakes or whatever they owned, walking to the fields. This area was such a fertile one and the growing season was so extended that almost all the workers lived here permanently. Occasionally one heard of a family that had gone to Michigan or the Dakota's as migrants. There was enough work to be done where they lived. They were not allowed to participate in any of the "town" activities. Once, when a Mexican tried to get a haircut downtown, he was bodily thrown out of the barbershop. They were not involved in politics. They had been told to keep to themselves and that all would be taken care of for them. And they were satisfied.

Midway from the intersection to Maria's house was Adolfo's Place and, as they passed it, he looked over, tried to move his feet, and saw it still standing there, as if being away one day would have destroyed it or visibly altered it. It was still the same. He gave a sigh and Jesus yawned. His lips puckered in and out as he moistened his tongue. He had that vague feeling of having had only a few beers to drink and had slept them off and his body did not know how to respond. The body was used to much more punishment than that. So he wet his tongue. It was dry and it felt odd.

Behind Adolfo's Place was a row of small rooms, like the motels of the forties, except that these rooms were not for sleeping. The whores lived there for sure, but they only went to sleep late, late at night. They were all asleep now, perfect soldiers in their little barracks after having put in a heavy day. He didn't own the whores. They belonged to several men. Those were the guys, Adolfo had said, that made all the money. And of the men who pimped at Adolfo's Place, the most feared was a dark man they called "El Tigre," the "Tiger".

Further down the road was the Catholic church, in the middle of this separate town. Adolfo and Jesus crossed themselves as they passed the church. The priest was from Spain, and he hated the people. The Spaniard, with his gentle ways, refined ways, had been thrust into the society of ignorance and violence. The priest could not understand these people. He had seen brother kill brother, brother kill father, father kill son, mother kill father, father kill daughter. He had seen strangers kill each other over nickels, quarters, dimes, card games, anything he could think of. It had been his fate to be sent down to these miserable people. It was, he thought, an act of God and he didn't appreciate being put to the test. For his part, he would just as soon let this cup pass. He took care of his resentment by drinking all day long as soon as daily mass was over. He could have been drunk during mass and no one would have noticed anyway. So few people came to church. Always the same ones, old women who did not understand the significance of the liturgy. He would turn from the altar to the people, the old ladies, and he would see them praying the rosary. At a time like this, he thought, when I'm in the middle of the mass and these ignorant old hags are praying the rosary. He would say a "goddammit" under his breath and then reluctantly ask forgiveness. It made him angry. He was mostly in a bad mood all the time. He drank so much that the old women never mentioned it. They would think it was a sin to accuse the priest of anything. He treated them with much the same contempt that the Spaniards before him had had for the Mexican indians. They would bring him rosaries to bless and he would wave his smallish hand over them and pronounce it done. They would give him fifty cents; two beers, he thought.

He particularly did not like Adolfo. He would see Adolfo walk past the rectory by the side of the church every day. "That man is up to no good," he would tell his housekeeper, another old woman who had visions of sainthood. He knew that Adolfo was the one and only big-league pitcher turned bar-keeper and the man who ran Adolfo's Place. He knew everything. Between confessions and the housekeeper, he was well up-to-date on what went on in Mexican town.

The old women loved him. His contempt brought out in them the feeling of worthlessness, which he had taught them was a virtue in God's eyes. The more worthless they were, the more God loved them. They loved this. They could feel the spirit move inside them. Some would cry at his door after some abuse, not from the abuse itself, but from the movement of the spirit within them.

The men didn't care. The few who attended church were the sick or the dying old men. The younger men never felt much for religion until the chips were down. They ignored the priest except to insinuate that he was screwing the housekeeper or some middle-aged widow that might be attending church too often. The ones who didn't think the priest was screwing, thought that he was a homosexual. To these men, Sunday was for drinking and, since early afternoon, the old cars would fill the parking lot, a dusty place, in front of Adolfo's or one of the other beer joints.

It was not the best thing for your health to go to the beer joints. Almost every family in Mexican town had had a male member injured or killed in a fight. And it wouldn't stop there. The injured family had to have revenge and these feuds lasted forever. No one was pardoned. Not even the priest could control the fighting nor did he much want to try.

He tried to sneak in the house, but the noise from the car and the barking dogs in the neighborhood woke up Maria. She was a light sleeper anyway and she had been worried all day. She had felt badly about burning the letters. Whatever happend to Adolfo and Carmen would be her fault.

She got up and turned on the light in the kitchen as Adolfo walked in. She looked behind him, looking for Carmen. It really hurt her that Carmen had stayed behind. Or maybe she was still outside.

"Where is Carmen?"

"She stayed with Isabel", he said.

He kept on walking and went into his room. There on the window ledge where he had left them were his teeth. He quickly put them in his mouth and went back to the kitchen. He did not want Maria to know that he had forgotten them. She would have enough to lecture about as it was. Maria was warming some coffee in an aluminum pan.

"What happend to Irene? She couldn't stay with Irene?"

"No, Alfredo's gone crazy. He won't let anyone stay there anymore. He tried to kill us. He ran us off. Imagine a man like that, with no education, a common laborer running us off. If he hadn't had the pistol, I would have beaten him up." He took a drink from his coffee. Maria had sat down across the table from him. There was a slight tremble to her hands. She hadn't thought at the time she burned the letters that she would place Carmen in such a situation. Now she wondered what effect burning Adolfo's letter had had. "A pistol?" she asked, as if she had not caught what Adolfo had said. "What was he doing with a pistol?"

"He pointed the gun at us, but we drove away as fast as we could and I don't know whether he pulled the trigger or not. But he did point the gun. We left him there. God only knows what he did to Irene. He's gone crazy. Irene says that he has beaten her and her son is the only one who can control him and then not all the time."

"And Carmen, what happend to her?"

"She stayed with Isabel. That's the best I could do. No one knew we were coming. Irene had not received the letter Carmen had sent her. Isabel had not received the letter I wrote."

Maria was not about to confess. It was not the right time. To do so would only aggravate the situation. She had plenty of time to confess, she thought. There would be a more opportune time. "And tell me about Carmen. Is she safe there? Was the house clean?"

"She'll be alright. Isabel will take care of her. She rents rooms and I gave her some money for Carmen until Carmen finds a job. The neighborhood is safe." He had begun to take off his sneakers. "I'm tired," he said.

"Well, at least she can be by herself now. Poor Carmen. I hope she's happy now. She always said that I kept her from being happy. I missed her so much today. It's hard when the youngest one leaves home."

She felt better. Carmen had not been injured, scared yes, but that would pass. They would laugh about it later on. And yet she still had that vague uneasy feeling about what she had done. Why had she done it? She couldn't say. And if she could, she wouldn't. It seemed an act of selfishness and yet her feeling was, although unknown to her, one of self preservation. She had not wanted the last bird to learn how to fly and she had tried to keep the oldest bird (Adolfo) in her nest.

This is not so unusual for a woman that had lived under her circumstances. Given to her aunt as a child, as was the custom in those days, she had learned the value of a strong family bond. Her parents had too many children. Some had to go. Her aunt was married and childless, so Maria at the age of five had been given to her. The giving away of a child was not unusual and did not seem to bother the parents. Whether it bothered the child, no one asked or seemed to care. The aunt was happy to have Maria, but she had to give up her prior relationship with her husband. She had to lower her standing in the marriage in order to get Maria. She became more subservient, more docile. The husband, who resented the child, assumed a more powerful role. He began to stay away from home, was drunk every night, would keep other women, would beat her up. He never hurt Maria. He could hurt her by hurting her aunt and he knew it. He also knew just how far to go. He knew his wife would kill him if he hurt the child. The aunt was content to suffer through the marriage, as long as she had the child. Without knowing it, he welcomed the child, for the child had made married life more bearable to him. At least it had given him the excuse to seek the freedom that he had not had before.

Her parents gone to New Jersey, Maria gradually became used to being alone with her aunt. One thing she never did was to call her "Mother." It was always "Aunt" this and "Aunt" that.

They had lived many years by the railroad tracks close to where she now lived in a one room small house. At night she and her aunt would sit in front of the house and watch the train as it moved the produce slowly from the giant warehouses to the eastern states. It was the same train that would kill one of her brothers later in her life.

She went to school for a few months and then she was taken out. Her uncle said she was needed around the house to help her aunt. Educationally, that was it. She knew the alphabet and how to count. Later she could read in Spanish, but not in English. The teacher had said that the child was smart but the uncle had said no.

Her real father had not been a mean man, but he had been hard to handle when he drank, and that was mostly every night. On Saturday nights, she and her brothers and sisters could count on their father coming in drunk and abusing their mother. Whether this abuse was physical or not depended on the mood of their father. If he had had a hard time at the beer joint, he would surely beat her. They could count on it. So they lay awake in their little room waiting for their father to hear what he would say. If he started cursing and complaining, they knew it meant a beating and all they could do was be still and bear it and imagine it. That was the hardest part, imagining the beatings. They could hear the thumps and the crashing of tables and chairs, the breaking of dishes, the muffled cries of the mother, muffled so that the children would not hear. Little did she know that the children knew what was happening. And that, if they had been big enough or powerful enough, they would have killed him. "Some day when I grow up and I'm big and strong I'll beat him up so bad that he'll cry like a little pig. I'm going to make him squeal like a pig. I swear to God," her brother had said. He was the one killed by the train.

If he arrived happy and talking freely about his friends and gossip, then they would rest easy in their little room. He still abused her though, but it was a verbal beating, a harangue about other women he had had or drank beer with.

In the mornings she remembered what her mother was like before and never showed a mark on her. The mother worked around the house as usual. Then, since it was Sunday, she would get herself and the children ready for mass. The father never attended. He was hung-over until noon, then he would walk to the beer joints and would start drinking again. There were no beatings on Sunday, for he came late in the afternoon drunk again and would go to bed. He would be up by five o'clock in the morning to start the week at the canning plant or in the fields.

They had had six children. Maria was the fifth child. Her younger brother, the sixth child, also was given away and Maria would see him every day, since the family he belonged to now lived just two houses down the street. But mostly she stayed with her aunt.

The fact that she had been given away shaped her personality. She was at once humurous to the point of making everyone around her laugh and yet she used this humor to hide a deep resentment for the happiness of others. She would out-grow the second part of her nature as she developed a stoicism toward life. As a child she would play at being someone else, preferably an adult she knew, pantomime that person, to the delight of her stepmother. Her stepmother did not realize that there was a viciousness to the charade. Instead, she laughed at little Maria, as the young girl limped around the yard mimicking the old man with the wooden leg that lived in the neighborhood. She imitated her stepfather coming home drunk, stumbling over a small weed and rolling on the ground. Among the other children she was the leader. She would take them to the railroad tracks and there they would place little nails on the track and wait for the train to run over them. Afterwards they would run to the track and pick up the flattened nails. They would use them as scissors, although they would not open or close, or instruments for cleaning their fingernails or for prying loose little rocks on the ground. Or they used them to groove the dirt in the yard to make drawings and boundaries for games. She had a collection of these nails in her room.

One day as they gathered to go to the railroad track, her younger brother also went along. This was the day the train would kill him. They were doing the same thing, taking nails and crossing them and placing the cross on the track. They ran as they saw the train coming. As the train came up to them her brother ran to it to see the iron wheels flatten the nails. The children watched, mesmerized. The young boy stuck his hand between the iron wheels to get the nails now flattened into a cross. His sleeve got caught by a bolt sticking down from the floor of the boxcar. He was dragged under the wheels and all they could see was the tossing about of his body under the boxcars. It was an incessant moment to see the full body being thrown up and down and side to side as each train car passed over him. Finally after the caboose went over him they ran away. She would never forget that day.

So Carmen had stayed with Isabel and not Irene, her sister. Maybe she had been right after all. She was beginning to feel better. If what Adolfo said was true, everything had worked out for the best. And the best thing she had done was not send the letter. She knew that Irene's husband was going crazy the last time they had visited. Now she knew why she burned the letter. She was protecting Carmen and that was what mattered most.

"And she stayed with Isabel?" she asked, more to herself than to Adolfo.

"Yes, I told you she had. She'll do well there."

"Poor, poor Carmen. She's never been away from home. She must be homesick already."

"Maria," he said, "you have got to leave her alone."

He drank the last of his coffee and excused himself and went to bed.

In the morning he could hear Maria in the kitchen working and crying. He got up, bathed and dressed and left without eating breakfast. His only words were "Good Morning" and "Good-bye." From the house he walked the dusty road to the tavern. Maria wiped the tears from her eyes, dressed quickly, and went to see the priest.

The priest was very fond of her for she made him laugh. She was the only one of his parishoners that was reverent and had a sense of humor. There were times when he caught her in practices outside the Catholic faith, when he could be stern with her. This included going to faith healers, promises made to God in return for His goodwill, the use of cards to tell the future and voodoo. When he saw her open the gate in front of the house, he was sitting at his small office. He greeted her at the door.

"Good morning, and God bless you," he said.

"Good morning to you, Father, and I hope I get all the blessings that are due me. God knows I need them more than you."

The priest laughed at Maria and showed her into his office.

"I have a problem," she began. The priest sat down slowly and asked her to sit down.

"Tell me about it."

"Someone gave me a letter to mail and I read it and burned it and afterward it caused some problems, but no one was hurt. It was, to think about it, a blessing since everything came out for the better."

"Well, you see, Maria, that was one blessing you got. You ought to be grateful to our Lord for that . . . " Then he looked at her sternly in the eye and brought his clasped hands to his chin. "But in the matter of the letter and the way you acted, it is a sin. I would classify it as a theft and a lie. These are two commandments that you have broken. Now, who was the person that you wronged?"

She gave him a glance and looked out the window to the church next door. She wished she had not come, but it was the only way she knew.

"It was my daughter . . . Carmen."

"And what did she say to you when she found out?"

"She doesn't know."

"And where is she?"

"She went to San Diego to look for a job."

"And she never found out? And she was not hurt by what you did?"

"No," she answered limply. This had gone far enough. She wanted penance, not an inquisition. And she hoped she didn't have to explain the whole story.

"Then the sin is more venial than mortal," he said. "Go to the church and pray the stations of the cross and I'm sure God will forgive you."

He sat back in his reclining chair and placed his hands on the arm rests. "And I hope," he continued, "that you do not repeat this sin again. No one likes people who read other people's mail. And no one, especially God, likes someone who does not do what is expected of him."

"Yes, Father," she replied. She truly felt bad and, of course, that's why she had come. No one could make her feel as undeserving as a priest. "But I have another problem," she continued. The priest came forward slowly toward the desk and again placed his hands to his chin. "I want to make a promise, a covenant, with God, if Carmen does well."

"You know that I don't approve of those things. It's sacriligeous to say to God that, if Carmen does well, you will do something for your God. You cannot barter with the Lord. You and the other people around here that do all kinds of crazy things are really insulting the Lord. I see you people at night carrying candles, walking backwards, on your hands and knees. I don't approve of that. We should look at religion in a more civilized way. Those days are gone forever!" He pounded the desk.

"But why?" Maria asked. "Those days were so beautiful."

He smiled. He thought of the day his own mother in Spain had crawled into church, a lit candle in each hand, and had gone all the way to the altar to fulfill a promise she had made to the Lord. It had been a beautiful experience for him, an experience that, on the one hand, embarrassed him and yet, on the other hand, made him proud that his mother had the faith to do it. Afterwards he had expected his friends to make fun of him, but they didn't.

"We don't do things like that anymore. If you want to barter with God, go ahead, but leave me out of it." He felt sorry for her.

"Well then, I'll do it on my own," she said. "When Padre Antonio was here, he never said anything about our promises. One time, a woman walked backwards on her knees from the stairs of the church to the foot of the altar during mass and he acted like nothing was going on. He never said a word. He also told us to eat meat on Fridays. 'If you have it, eat it,' he would say. 'You're too poor to let it go to waste. God will forgive you. He understands,' he would say."

"Maria," the priest said, adding emphasis to every word, "Padre Antonio had no right to change the laws of the Church. It is a sin to eat meat on Fridays. That is the law."

"And promises? Covenants?"

"There is no law against them, but if you want something from the Lord, ask him. Pray to Him. Don't tell him you will perform some idiotic thing if he grants you your wish." He paused to see if he had gotten through to the old lady. "Now, I have things to do and you must leave."

He opened the desk drawer and took out a book mark that had the picture of the Virgin of Guadalupe and on its reverse side a small prayer, blessed it and gave it to Maria. Maria took a quarter from her pocket and gave it to him as an honorarium.

On the way back she made her promise to God: If Carmen did well — here she stopped to think of what "well" meant. What did doing "well" involve? Getting a job, being happy, getting married, having children, a good husband, a home? — she would go on her knees from her front porch to the altar, a distance of about a mile. It would be something, she thought. All her neighbors would see her. They would wonder what great windfall had come to her in order for her to do this painful thing. She would even have to pass several beer joints on the way. She could make each of them a station of the cross. It would be on a Sunday early in the morning. It would take several hours, and on the way she would pray the rosary over and over again. She could see herself, her eyes pointed upward to the heavens, a tear barely oozing over her lower lids like the statue of the Virgin Mary looking up to the crucified Christ. No one would forget that. But, she thought with a little anger, God would have to produce. Carmen had to do well. God had to meet her definiton of the term as she, Maria, defined it.

She had walked so fast talking all the way home that she arrived before she realized it. She had forgotten to tie her black bonnet or, if she had tied it, she had undone the string during her revery.

Adolfo was sitting at the kitchen table. No one ever sat in the small living room, except when there was company. The people of the house would never dream of sitting there. It was a place to be looked at, dusted, cleaned and mopped, but hardly ever used. If you wanted to sit and relax, you went into the kitchen or took a chair outside.

"Why are you back so early?" she asked him. She sat down, tired, across the small table from him.

"They won't let me have my place back."

"Your cousins, Adolfo?"

"Yes. We had an argument. They say that when I left yesterday that I told them I wouldn't be back for a long time . . . that they have already made plans to paint the place and fix it up."

"And your contract with Oscar?"

"I never had a written contract with Oscar. It was a monthly thing. I never promised to stay a long time and I didn't intend to. How could I sign a contract? You know me. I could have left any time. They say that, if I didn't have a contract, I don't have any rights to the place. I talked to Oscar and he says that it's up to them. If they want me to have the place, it's alright with him. He says I have to fight it out with them. Oscar just wants his money."

"And what are you to do?"

"I don't know. I could go back north. I would find a job there. Or I could go to San Diego. Maybe Isabel can help me find a job. But I really don't know what to do."

She stood up slowly and placed the coffee pot in the fire and sat back down. She unbuttoned her thin sweater, the one with the rolled balls of wool on it, and took it off. She got up again and went into her room. When she came back, she straightened her hair and went to the stove, turned it off and served two cups of coffee. She asked him if he was hungry and he said no.

They sat there quietly looking out the window at the children playing in the garbage dump. One child had found a small tire from a tricycle and was rolling it along and running behind it. Two others were sitting on a can, playing with the dirt. Their dog was with them and it would run around sticking its nose into the debris, then rear back and bark excitedly.

"This may be just what you needed, Adolfo," she said.

"What do you mean?"

"Maybe now you can get out of that situation and lead a better life. It may even be God's way of telling you something. Remember the old saying, 'There is nothing bad that does not have some good behind it.' "

"I never did understand that," he said.

He was more dejected than she had ever seen him. He had not touched his coffee. She, on the contrary, had finished hers. "What it means, Adolfo, is that some good always comes out of bad situations. Look at it this way. You won't have to associate with those men at the beer halls anymore. You won't have to gamble. You won't have to get men for the prostitutes. The pimps will leave you alone."

He thought about the prostitutes. He had taken the panties to them this morning, waking each of them in their small rooms one at a time. They had made fun of him. "A man of your age," they had said. "You ought to be ashamed." He had laughed, but that was before he found out that he no longer had a place to call his own. Now they worked in someone else's place. He didn't mind giving them gifts. He still would have given them the panties.

"I'll help you find a job," Maria said. "Tomorrow I'll take you with a friend and we'll see."

"I don't want to pick or can vegetables," he said, angrily. "I don't want to work as a slave."

"Everbody else has," she replied. "Why all this pride?"

"It's not pride. I just don't want to do it. Besides, I'm too old for that sort of work."

"It's another job. Don't get angry. Let me help you."

That night, he stayed home for the first time since he had lived at Maria's. They talked about the past, about Carmen, about baseball and how it had been many years ago. They spoke of Isabel and the many other women he had known. They spoke of Irene, her sister, and her crazy husband, Alfredo, the one with the gun who almost killed them and the sailor in San Diego. They sat outside in back of the house under a beautiful clear sky. Beyond the dump and the hill they could see the glow of the football stadium lights and they could hear the echo of the crowd as it roared during the game. They spoke of

Maria's husband, dead now many years, and how he had died of a heart attack at the cannery and how she had been told of his death and how she had panicked and run to the cannery through the fields, how she had arrived exhausted and found her husband on the loading pier, fallen, like a sack of produce, with all the men around him. No one had bothered to cover him up. She wiped the tears from her eyes with her apron. Adolfo had not been there. No one knew where he was.

Someone had said that he had heard that Adolfo was pitching in Pachuca, Mexico, at that time. You see now how long ago it had been? He cried some too, but in the darkness no one knew. He cried because, since his baseball days were over, nothing had ever gone well for him. He had lost everything except for the few clothes he had. He had never before taken inventory of himself. He did not know why, but this night it seemed that in the darkness he could no longer hide what he felt. He realized what a waste of time his life had been.

And as the night went on, he spoke to her about the war, how it had been in Germany and the battles, the horror of it, the blowing away of people, the poisonous gas that had been used, the life afterwards in small German towns where they had marched through. It had been fun at the end.

At the end, they were laughing about something that had happened when they were young. They laughed at the silliness of youth that had not prepared them for this night. They felt closer now than they ever had before. Though they always argued, they realized how much love was between them.

She did not tell him of her promise to God. There were some things that were sacred.

In the morning she had cooked breakfast before he was up. When he did show up she had everything on the table and they both ate. The air was strained. Maybe they had relived or revived too many memories last night. He had gone into his shell and did not talk. The hopelessness of the situation had been reinforced during the restless night.

"Do you still want to go back to selling beer?" She asked this, not as a sarcasm, but out of real concern for his happiness.

"No," he answered. "I don't want to see those people again. I don't beg anybody for anything."

"I'm glad to hear it, Adolfo. Have some pride. Be a man."

She took him with her, he, dressed in his suit and sneakers, and, when they walked by the church rectory, she stopped. She opened the iron gate and they walked to the door. Maria twisted the knob for the bell and the maid opened the door. The priest was shaving and they said they did not mind waiting. They stood in the dark hall-way and soon the priest started down the stairs putting his coat on as he came. When he saw Maria he remebered yesterday's conversation and wondered what she was up to now. Was this part of her promise to God, to bring the wretched Adolfo to be baptized? He did not know their relationship. Was she here to marry him?

"Maria," he said, "may God be with you."

"And with your spirit," she replied.

"What can I do for you?"

He had reached the bottom of the stairs and had his coat on. He showed them into his office. Maria went in, but she motioned for Adolfo to stay out in the hall. The priest had his back to them and, when he sat down, he noticed that Maria had closed the door and had left Adolfo behind.

"Where is Adolfo, that wretched man?" he asked.

"He prefers to stay in the hall while we talk."

"That's fine with me," he said. "That man as I understand it, has never set foot in any church and I would prefer not to talk to him."

"You don't understand him, Father. He has suffered much. His life has been different from yours and mine. You might say that he was cursed from birth."

"Cursed? And in what way?" Then he remembered the promise. "And let me tell you that if this has something to do with your illiterate promise to God, I won't have anything to do with it!" On that point he was emphatic. The veins on his forehead stood out.

"It has nothing to do with the promise I made."

"And you've already made your covenant with God? Is that it?"

"I have made my promise, but this has nothing to do with it."

"And what did you promise to do?"

"That's between me and God. But I do need your help in another matter and it concerns Adolfo."

"And why should I be concerned about him?"

"Well, Father, he's very depressed."

"Can't the prostitutes and his friends cheer him up?" he said with a touch of sarcasm.

"No, not anymore. That's the problem. He left town just for one day. It's true that he thought that he wouldn't return, but in the meantime someone else had taken over his place of business."

"The beer joint?"

"Yes."

"He lost it?"

"Yes."

"And what business is that of mine? He will infinitely be better off. Don't you realize that?"

"Yes. I do. And you do. But he doesn't. He needs something else to do."

"And why did you bring him here?"

"I thought that maybe he could work here, outside the church. Gardening, mowing, that sort of thing. He could fix the house. Be of some use to someone."

Adolfo could hear the priest raise his voice. He wondered what it could be that Maria wanted that had infuriated the priest so much.

He banged his fist on the desk. His face was red and a prominent vein had engorged itself with blood right down the middle of his forehead. "And you say he is cursed? And, you say you want him here with me? In this house?"

"He wouldn't need to come inside. He can stay outside. Never come in. He would promise you that."

"And what is this curse?" he asked. He was slightly calmer now, but his hands were still locked to each other.

"Well," she said, "he was cursed to be born with talent. You may think it has done him good, but it has made his life complicated. He was never like the rest of us. That's what I meant."

"For a while I thought that you had gone into witchcraft. No telling. If you believe in promises, you could believe in witchcraft. But it's out of the question. I cannot have a man of his character, of his morals, around the church yard. And that, my dear lady, is final."

He stood up and without even giving her a glance walked out of the office, turned past Adolfo and went back upstairs. As he passed Adolfo, he couldn't help but notice the three-piece woolen suit, the tie, the sneakers. Once upstairs, he wondered why, why the suit, the sneakers? He was an orderly man trained as a priest for many years and he couldn't imagine, no, he couldn't understand someone like Adolfo.

He went to the small icebox that he kept in his room, opened a beer and sat down to read by the window. From there he could see down as Maria and Adolfo walked past the rectory.

"You must be crazy, woman," Adolfo said, "to try and get me a job with the priest. He doesn't like me. You know that."

"It's more than that. He hates you," she said. Her bonnet was on her head tied neatly to where the string was hidden in a wrinkle in her chin. Only the bow fell softly from the wrinkle.

From atop the priest could see them walking slowly, talking all the time. He took a long drink from the beer and began reading his book.

"This is a sad time for me," Adolfo said. "It reminds me of the time in Puebla. Fernando Soto and myself had been stranded there. The team had not been paid in months. The players left in droves. Menchaca, the catcher, who also sometimes played first base, was the first to leave. He left for Monterrey. He just caught a ride. He happened to be sitting at a bar drinking a beer and this man approached him and asked him if he was the same ballplayer from Monterrey. And Menchaca said yes he was and he found out during the conversation that the man was going back and he left with him. Then the others left. Soto and I were the only Americans. We had no place to go. The manager left the hotel without saying a word. His name was Esquivel. He had played in the majors like me. Soto and I had no place to go. We were desperate. We found a ride to Mexico City and from there we got money from a friend, a loan you understand, to get us to Laredo. And you know who loaned us the money?"

"Who?" Maria asked. She had followed the dialogue. She was one of the few who enjoyed his stories.

"A priest friend of mine in Mexico City. He loved baseball. I had met him several times at the games. He was nice enough to give us food and lend us money. I'll never forget him, Father Emilio Carranza."

"Well, this priest is different. He doesn't like you," she said.

"That's alright. He doesn't know who I was in my youth."

He clicked his teeth and they walked slowly and silently back.

"What we need," Maria said after a long silence, "is a promise."

After much objection, he agreed to the promise: That if he found work, that he would, under Maria's watchful eye, go on his knees from Maria's house to the church. For Maria it was a triumph, because she felt that if Adolfo could do it, she could too. What better way was there to help Carmen? The only stipulation was that Adolfo insisted on doing it at night. "Of course," Maria agreed. "I would never think of doing it at any other time but at night. I don't want anyone seeing us doing it. I'm no fool."

When they arrived home, they were happier than they had been in a long time, although Adolfo still had his doubts.

Several nights later, as they sat outside, they saw the lights of a car from a far distance come slowly toward the house. They expected the car to turn, but it never did. And after each intersection, when it did not turn their expectations grew. The car stopped in front and the priest got out. By this time, Maria and Adolfo had walked to the front of the house. They exchanged greetings in the dark and Maria showed the priest into the house. They sat in the small living room. Even by the light of the small exposed bulb, they could tell he had been drinking. Adolfo excused himself, went to his room and inserted his teeth and came back. Maria had stayed with the priest alone, but he had not said a word. When Adolfo sat down, the priest began.

"I came to apologize for that day," he said. He wore the traditional black suit, white collar and black shirt. His hair was rumpled. He gave the impression of a troubled man. "I was born in Galicia, in Spain, and things were a lot different there. The customs, the traditions, the people, are very different. Do you know that in Galicia, when I was a boy, I was not allowed to do heavy work? I would spend my spare time away from studies playing the guitar, reading books. I never knew people like you existed."

They both nodded their head at the insult. They were embarrassed for the man. Maria especially didn't care for all this. She felt her esteem for the man slowly fading from her. She preferred him to be tough and arrogant. Adolfo was confused by it all, but he tried to act normal.

Maria got up and asked him if he cared for some coffee. He said no. He would be leaving soon.

"I'm sure you don't care about all this," he said. "But it's important that you understand why I do some things. And I wanted to apologize to you, Maria, for the way I acted. However, this thing about promises that are made by the ignorant people of my church is distressing to me," he said. "It is a sacrilege, and I'm sure it offends God more than it pleases him. But enough of this. I know that I cannot change you or your ways. If some ignorant ass wants to stand on his head during mass, I won't object to it. I'll ignore it. But enough of that. I came to tell you that a priest who is a distant uncle of mine from Mexico is coming to visit me and, in the letter I had from him this morning, it turns out that he knows Adolfo and heard that Adolfo was here. His name is Father Emilio Carranza and he will be here Friday. Today is Wednesday, so in two days he will be here. He wants to see you Adolfo. We will send for you when we want you to come."

They both silently marveled at the coincidence. Hadn't they just been talking about him? Surely, Maria thought, there was divine intercession in this matter. Adolfo wondered also. Surely this must mean something.

"I didn't know you had an uncle that was a priest?" Maria asked him. Of course, she thought to herself, there are many other things I don't know about him.

"Well," the priest replied, looking about the house for something to criticize later on, "he's not really an uncle but a friend, when you stop to think about it. He is an uncle three or four times removed, but you know how mothers are. She had me look him up. He has been in Mexico many years. He says he loves it, although I can't see how."

"The Mexicans are fine people," Adolfo said to him and then immediately realized he had spoken out of turn.

"How would you know?" the priest said, cutting him down to size. "Unfortunately," he continued, "Father Carranza is sick. And that is why he is coming to San Diego. He feels that this is his last pilgrimage to the United States. Apparently he likes Adolfo very much, although I can't figure why. My mother always said that he was the oddest of the family."

The name brought memories back to Adolfo. But being in the presence of the priest and having been put down before, he refrained from starting his dialogue, he looked at the priest and lowered his eyes to avoid direct contact with the man who he considered his intellectual, but not physical, superior. Maria looked at the priest and sighed. She had expected much worse, maybe an ex-communication or something of that order. In other words, she felt that she had not been that out of place and that Adolfo at least had a friend in the clergy that would do him some good.

The priest excused himself, looked around the room with disrespect and left. The screen door was slow to open and he ran into it, but without saying a word, he kicked the bottom and forced it open.

They, Maria and Adolfo, agreed that the priest had been drinking. They did not realize that the priest was always drinking. Only tonight they had seen him drunk.

The car had a hard time starting but eventually he got it running and was gone.

Once home, the priest went to his room, opened another bottle of whiskey and sat by the window looking down at that small section of town separated from the rest by the fields and railroad tracks. Across from the fields and the warehouses, he could see the lights from the main part of town, a part to which he and these people did not belong. He had been discriminated against for the first time in his life when he arrived at the San Diego Diocesan Center when he arrived from Spain. The Bishop had been courteous to him, but later he found out that the politics was such that a Spanish priest never was assigned to a good parish. He had been fed and sent off to this wretched place the same day. It was one of the poorest parishes in the Diocese. He had arrived in this country with a lot of Spanish pride, but now he wasn't so sure. That pride would get the best of him. This was in fact the reason he behaved so badly among the people. He was blaming them for his bad luck. He considered himself superior to everyone around him, but what galled him was that the Bishop considered him inferior to the American-educated priests. And there was nothing he could do about it.

He had been born in Galicia, an area of Spain devoid of trees on the upper northeast coast, in the small city of El Moro. At the age of thirteen, he had been taken to the largest city on the province and had been enrolled in the seminary there. He had done well, although his heart was never really in it. He knew that to be there was an honor to his family and that seemd to be enough. His mother would send him small packages of food or clothing, mostly underwear, often. She never forgot him on special occasions and the packages would be larger then. Once or twice a year they would come visit. They stayed in town at an inn and they spent as much time as they could with him. As his education continued and his knowledge of theology grew, they began to respect him more and love him less. After all, they considered him to have a special relationship with God. Their respect grew and, by the time he had finished seminary at the age of twenty-six, they treated him with reverence. When he went home the last time before sailing for the States, they held a small banquet in his honor. His mother had tried to kiss his ring, but he had asked her not to. His father had been proud of him. Of all his sons, he was the only one to receive a formal education. All of his other brothers, three in all, were married and fishing for a living. One sister was married and living in Portugal. The other sister had died at an early age.

So here he was now in California in a small farming town in the valley between San Diego and God knows where.

The town had been a shock to him. He had never seen such a clear cut division into two societies: the Anglos and the Mexican-Americans. Sure he had seen poverty in Spain, but the people had not been physically isolated as in this town. In the first place, he noticed that all that was new and clean and orderly was in one section of town. The Mexican side, beyond the fields and the railroad, was dusty and dirty. The streets were not paved. The houses were usually not painted. It galled him always that these people, the descendents of the Spaniards, had not learned the values of the motherland. They were, he was convinced, more Indian than anything else. What Spaniard would allow his home to go unpainted? Even the poorest in Spain would take pride in their homes. Why were the yards always littered? Why was there no pride in ownership? In Spain they had, along with everyone else, painted their homes every year or so. They had cleaned their mess daily. He could not believe that an old abandoned car could sit in front of a house for years.

At first he appealed to them to clean up, but when that didn't work, he kept quiet. But he still seethed everytime he walked or drove around the neighborhood. He tried setting an example by having the rectory and the church painted and cleaned at regular intervals. He had a man plant grass and shrubs in the yard, but he was the only one to do so. He tried to get men that were out of work to clean the small park in front of the church, but no one came. They had too much Indian blood in them he thought.

It was as if living in squalor for so long had made them immune to the sight of it. And yet, he could see it. Why couldn't they? Especially if someone pointed it out to them. Paint your homes, he would say. Get rid of the old cars in your yard. He had a sermon one day on abandoned cars and no one got the point.

And yet he found them a paradox. They were good people. He couldn't fault them there. But placed in certain situations, they would do things to each other that he couldn't believe. It was the damndest thing he had ever seen. Nothing in Spain had prepared him for these people. Not even the Basques.

He still couldn't get over his first involvement with a family feud. He had only been there one week when he was called to administer the last rites to the only surviving male member of a family, an old man in his sixties, who had been knifed to death in full view of all the neighbors in his own front yard. There had been six killings in that feud. It had started over a chicken that had crossed over into someone's yard. What kind of people were these? What part of the world am I in? And yet he stayed. Drinking, he found out, was the only way out.

He had acquired this drinking habit gradually, like a good education. He started with one or two beers a day, then he started with more and then he added the whiskey. It had crept up on him so easily that he did not realize the problem. He would use the handy man as the errand boy to get his liquor. He would pay the man off in order to keep him quiet. On the days that the old man was ill and he was out of beer or whiskey, he was like a caged animal. He tried reading, praying, anything to keep his mind off his need for alcohol, but eventually he would succumb and would send for something with the maid. The maid didn't think it out of place; since her husband drank heavily also, she assumed all men did.

This, in a round about way, was the reason Adolfo went to work for the priest. The handy man died one afternoon while mowing the grass between the rectory and the church. The priest had by coincidence looked out of his study and had seen the man's legs wobble and then he saw him stagger behind the lawnmower until he fell clutching his chest. He was dead before the priest got to him.

Adolfo had dressed himself neatly in his suit and Maria had washed and ironed his shirt. His corn was better and now he could wear his black pointed shoes. He sat at the kitchen table and Maria served him coffee. This was the Friday that his priest-friend would be in town. He waited until early afternoon, talking gibberish with Maria about life in the earlier years. Then a small boy came running up to the house and said that the priests, two of them, wanted to see Adolfo. He got up quickly from the table and said his good-byes to Maria. She wiped her hands on her apron and patted him on his back and wished him well.

Maria was born in the valley and had never gotten away, except for short trips to San Diego and Tijuana to see her relatives. She had married at the age of eighteen to a man older than she. He was in his middle thirties. He had seemed like a nice man and the younger men did not attract her. It seemed at the time that the crop of males her age were not men enough for her. Or so she thought. That was the excuse she gave. The truth was that the men her age shunned her because she had had an illegitimate child. But to hear Maria talk about her youth, she never even mentioned that as the reason men were not attracted to her. Sure she was beautiful, but among this race, a woman with a child and not married was a used woman and no one, especially the young men, would want her for a wife. The identity of the father of the illegitimate child was somewhat of a mystery. Several men had been talked about as being responsible, but no one, especially not Maria, said a word.

There was a rumor that the father was the owner of a small grocery store in town and that he had refused to marry Maria because she had another boyfriend at the time she became pregnant. Another rumor had it that Maria had become pregnant from the town barber and he too refused to marry her. The blacksmith — there was one at the time in town — also was believed to be involved. In all, four or five men were accused of being the father, but no one came forward. Maria never revealed the name of the man. Or maybe she couldn't. Had there been more than one? No one knew. It became a town joke then that even the accused men played. Eventually, as everyone got older, the joke died and became town lore. Her husband was spared any loss of pride, for when he walked into any place no one spoke of Maria's problem. He was more or less respected in the community. He was a big man with a ready laugh who was foreman at a cannery. He spoke English well, although he was not formally educated. He did not work with his hands, but was considered one of the boys. He always had a car and wore clean clothes. Maria saw to that. He brought to the marriage three children: two boys and one girl.

Her marriage had been the talk of the town. They had been seen together several times and the women had made comments to each other about them, but the marriage had caught everyone by surprise. He was a widower and no one expected him to get married again. As for Maria, no one expected her to ever get married, not after what had happened.

He moved her from her parents' house to the small house at the end of the road where she now lived. Maria took the three children and her own daughter and started her married life at the age of eighteen. She raised them all and had a relatively happy marriage until her husband died thirty-five years later. She was a widow at fifty-three. From that day on she wore a black dress with long sleeves and a black cotton bonnet whenever she went out. Carmen had been born sixteen years after their marriage. She adored Carmen from the moment of her birth. The two neighbor women in attendance for the birth had told her almost immediately how beautiful Carmen was. And that she was, and she was also a gifted child. She did well in school and her teachers were always telling Maria that Carmen should go to college. Maria never had thoughts of Carmen going off to school. She would remain there and marry someone in the community. There was no need for further education. No one had ever finished high school, except the Young Maria, the illegitimate child. Carmen would be the second. But college was out of the question.

Her husband had treated Maria well, except that she found out later in marriage that he enjoyed seeing other women. This did not hurt her as much as it irritated her. He spent considerable money on the prostitutes that he could have spent on the family. Several times when he disappeared for two and three days, she had gone to the shacks behind the beer joints and had physically dragged him out and away from the whores. It didn't seem to bother him and the other men did not make too much of it. Sure they laughed about it, but he joined in and it never led to violence.

The truth about little Maria was never known. Not even Adolfo had been able to get it out of her. She had kept the secret and kept it well. The truth was that none of the rumors were true. None of those men had done it, although as they grew older they enjoyed being talked about. Her pregnancy had come about from a secret affair.

As was the custom in those days among Mexican-Americans, the courting of the female was usually done behind the family's back. It was normal for the boy and girl to have to meet secretly and only at night; there was no open courtship. In the first place, the father would not allow it and, in the second place, her brothers would seek revenge on the suitor. These meetings at night in hiding places led to many pregnancies. They also led to elopements. The true marriage ceremony in white bridal gown and pin-stripes was not common. The marriage usually took place after the father and brother found the couple, brought them into town and forced them to marry. For the most part they did want to marry. It was just that deflowering the girl was the surest way to get her. Refusing to marry meant severe violence to the suitor, even death. How they reconciled after the wedding was funny in a way. The priest never could understand it. A few moments before the wedding, the family would threaten to kill the young man and immediately after the wedding the whole relationship would change. Now, the new groom was one of them. It was the damndest thing he had ever seen. It reminded him of the Sicilians. "Now," the priest would tell the housekeeper, "if someone touches a hair on that boy's head, his new family will die for him." After the wedding and forevermore nothing was ever said between the groom and the family about the pre-nuptial threats to his life. This bond existed and held firm through many circumstances, except one. The boy could be unfaithful, violent, lazy, a bad husband in general, but he could not leave the girl. If he left, it was an insult; he would no longer belong to the family and became fair game. Usually this type of man had to leave the county or even leave the state. The woman was never consulted in these matters. She may have been relieved at being abandoned, but that didn't seem important. Now, if she left with another man, it was a different matter. Not only would his family turn against her, so would her own family. It was a double standard, to be sure, but the priest had known several families that had killed their own unfaithful sisters and daughters, not to even mention the husband killing the wife. The priest often wondered how these people had ever survived all these killings. If they can't fight someone else, he thought, then they'll fight among themselves.

In Maria's case, things worked out differently. On the night she was supposed to elope, her lover never showed up. They had planned to elope during a community dance, but when she arrived with her friends, she did not find him there. She danced with other men, the barber, the blacksmith, the grocer, but her lover never arrived. He had been prevented from going to the dance. It seems his father suspected something was about to happen. It had been a heart-breaking blow to her. He never tried to see her again. She cried and would not eat for several days and everyone became alarmed. She would not say what her problem was. Exasperated, they called a healer, an old woman, who was the town expert on herbs and witchcraft. Her diagnosis was that Maria had been a victim of the evil eye. The probability was that some man at the dance had done it to her. Several men were brought in to touch her forehead, but it didn't seem to help. An egg was placed overnight under her bed and the next day the old woman cracked the egg and confirmed her diagnosis. The egg had an eye (a white spot) visible in the yolk. It was the evil eye. She swept her body with a broom, and gave her herbal teas. Eventually she came around and confessed. It was the most terrifying time in her life. Nothing equaled it before and nothing came close to it after. She still panicked when she thought about it. This episode she had in common with Isabel and she knew what Isabel had gone through when Adolfo left. Adolfo had been lucky to be alive. He was lucky that baseball kept him away for so many years, until Isabel was an older lady.

What was considered the evil eye lasted for several months. In fact she had had a nervous break-down. But in the community of the poor and ignorant, no one knew any better. She drifted in and out of reality and no one could understand why. Sometimes she would be well enough to take her meals with the family, her step parents. Usually, though, she wouldn't eat. It got so severe that one time, while her mother was washing clothes outside, Maria left the house and walked down the railroad tracks undressing herself. As she bent over the caldron of hot water, her stepmother had noticed her out of the corner of her eye. She ran to her and quickly covered her up and led her back home. She did not let Maria out of her sight from then on. Maria recovered slowly, but she was never the same again. Sure, she was quick to laugh and cry and talk, but she was more serious in between those times. Her stepmother thought that Maria was thinking too much. What was happening was that Maria was continually having small relapses of fantasy. She would lose touch with reality. Her strength came back to her, though, and eventually she was able to accept what had happened.

Maria ignored the gossip. Her stepfather was not particularly angry. After all, Maria was not his child. He had nothing to prove, so revenge was not his affair. He was able to talk about her just as easily as any other man or woman. He even took part in trying to figure out who the father was. Her mother suffered in silence. It was the mother's role in these situations to also be the penitent. They stuck it out together. Maria was left with few friends, however. The ones that did come to visit were the same ones that she considered friends now.

Later on, the gossip began to take on a different aspect. Many believed that Maria's lunacy was the work of the devil. So it followed, they said, that the child was the child of the devil. A boy would be born the likes of which had never been seen in those parts. That would also explain why no man had stepped forward to marry her. But luckily for Maria, the baby was a girl and that rumor died quickly. With nothing left for them to talk about, the guessing game about the identity of the father began again.

Maria's troubles were never completely over. She found that, once you have been thought insane, you can never be respected again. There was a primordial instinct among the people to regard her as defective, one who could not withstand the vagaries of life. They kept wondering when she would fall back again. It was only after many years, when most of her contemporaries had died or moved on, that she was able to mix among the people with some confidence. For instance, the priest didn't know her background and she felt at ease with him.

After some time, no one spoke about Maria and the gossip died away. The people turned to other things to occupy their minds.

For all the years later, when she saw the father of her child, he would give no sign that he recognized her. In her heart she still loved him, but she could never forgive what he had done to her and the child.

As to what kind of life the young man led, no one can say. To what extent he had suffered, no one knew. Only he and his father knew that he was the one. A few years later he married a woman more beautiful and with a little more money than Maria.

Adolfo rung the bell at the rectory and waited for the old woman to open the door. She led him directly to the office. She knocked very lightly with the knuckles of the middle finger and asked to come in. She opened the door and stuck her head in. "Adolfo is here," she said. From inside he heard the priest tell the lady to let him in.

Once inside, he recognized his old friend, the Reverend Carranza from Mexico City. They embraced and sat down. The priest watched them and smiled as he saw the two large men hug and pat each other.

Father Carranza had aged more than Adolfo thought possible. He had become an old man. How long had it been? They both figured it was the early twenties, just before World War I. It had to be, since no one was at war when Adolfo played for the Mexico City Aztecs. The conversation seemed to swell into dates, games, innings pitched, until both were not conscious that the priest was there. Finally the priest excused himself and left. Adolfo and the Reverend Carranza did not mind. Even the episode where he had lent Adolfo the money to come home was retold. But in all, this Adolfo could not get over how the priest had aged. He looked at his face to find an old familiar wrinkle. Now and then he found one, but it was larger now or if not, it was deeper. But taken as a whole, the face was recognizable. It was hard for him to explain this change. He was the same person, but still not the same face.

There they stayed together and spoke to each other for several hours. The priest had gone to his room to study. To them, Adolfo and the Reverand Carranza, there was no end. They remembered when Babe Ruth had come to Mexico City with the New York Yankees for an exhibition. Ruth had remembered Adolfo from his short playing career with the Yankees. Adolfo had fed him a fat pitch during the exhibition and the ball cleared the center field wall. The crowd went wild. As Ruth rounded third, he tipped his hat to Adolfo. The Reverend had never seen anything like it before. They remembered and laughed about the time when a friend of theirs, a nut, had stolen first base, to the astonishment of the crowd, not to mention the manager. They agreed that those were wonderful times. Now things had gotten hard. Mexico, the Reverend said, was not friendly toward the church nor the priests. He was tired, tired of the whole thing: religion, people, politics, even life. He was in reality in San Diego for medical tests. He believed he was dying of cancer of the prostate. That was what he had been told in Mexico City, but he had come to San Diego for a second opinion. He tired easily now. Before he had been able to do the work of several men. Now he could hardly walk from the rectory to the church. It had been a good life but he felt it was time to go. As to why he was there, he explained that he had known the priest's parents in Spain and had recently seen them during his vacation. He was here to deliver their blessings and some things which they had sent their son. In actuality, he didn't know the priest at all. He had called San Diego from Mexico City to tell them that he would be in the city as an out-patient. Then he had called the priest. He took the opportunity to bring the priest the gifts from his parents in Spain.

The visit with Adolfo was a coincidence for which he thanked the good Lord. After two hours, Adolfo noted that the Reverend was tired. He was not the same man he had known in Mexico City. Adolfo, for that matter, was not the same man either. He realized that the Reverend had looked at him and found him older, more lined in the face, the same as he had found the Reverend.

He kept on though. He told Adolfo of his troubles with cancer, the pain emanating from the pelvis and around the urinary bladder and shooting down the back of his legs. Some mornings he could hardly rise from bed. Urinating was frequent and so painful it could make him cry. He hoped the Lord would take him soon, for he did not know if he could endure the pain much longer. He had prayed that Adolfo would become a major league star, but that wish had not come true. He understood the disappointments in life and he realized that Adolfo felt worse for it than he. After all, he had just been a poor parish priest most of his life and he could never be anything else. What made him admire Adolfo was that the man had gambled his life on being able to make it. The Reverend felt that he himself had taken the easy way out.

It was getting dark and through the window the old women could be seen arriving at church for the nightly rosary. The younger priest came down from his room, his eyes red from drinking and crying. He had opened the packages he had been sent from Spain and he longed to be there. His parents, now very old, had sent him some clothes and a pocket watch that belonged to his father. He was wearing the watch in his small pocket by the belt loop, the small gold-filled fob, gold filled dangling limply on the outside. The inscription read "To Our Son" and had the date at the center. He promised himself that he would go to Spain this year.

As he passed by the door of the study, Adolfo came out and paid his respects. The priest stopped him and asked him to come by the next day in the morning. He needed to talk to him. He hurried out of the rectory and went inside the church through the back door.

The Reverend Carranza saw Adolfo open the door quietly and leave. He stood and walked to the door and watched him walk away slowly, his shoulders stooped.

He left early the next morning by bus. Adolfo never saw him again. He died within the year. It was a Saturday, he recalled, when he was working in the flower beds of the rectory that the priest came to him and told him he had just received a letter from Mexico City announcing the death of the Reverend Carranza. In the obituary enclosed in the letter, it mentioned that he had played semipro ball as a young parish priest. It also mentioned his undying love for baseball and the children's league he had founded in Mexico City.

"They were all dying around him," he thought.

The priest had slowly folded the letter and the long obituary column, replaced them in the envelope and walked away.

Adolfo's job with the priest involved keeping the lawn mowed, the flower beds weeded and planted, cleaning the church floors and pews, mostly handy-man jobs. He fixed some things that were simple to do. The things which he didn't know how to do, and they were many, the priest would call someone in to do them. Having never worked in his life in a normal sense of the word, Adolfo was at a loss more often than not. He did not like the job and he had mixed feelings toward Maria for having helped him. He appreciated her concern, but still he was not cut out to do this sort of thing. He did know, however, where to get beer and everyday he made his pilgrimage to the taverns to get the priest his quart of beer. He also took the opportunity to have some himself while he was at it. He would leave early afternoon on his errand and would return a couple of hours later. The priest did not seem to care how long it took and he didn't seem to mind the beer breath on Adolfo when he returned. He was in a situation where he could not complain. Once in a while, when the mood struck him, he would complain to Adolfo that he had drank too much. But as a rule, he let it slide.

Adolfo's problem was one of pride. He had, it seemed to him, lost a lot of respect with his fellow drinkers and the prostitutes. Where once he had ruled a tavern, he now came in, he thought, with his hat in his hand. They kidded him about this and he accepted it. What else could he do? But inside he seethed at the turn of fortune that had made him a gardener.

He developed some skill at growing things. He enjoyed seeing things grow, and it baffled him to think that during his lifetime and his travels, he had not noticed the things that grew around him. What irritated him was that he was now doing it as a common laborer and not strictly for his own enjoyment.

The priest was nice enough to him, although he still considered Adolfo someone who had squandered his life. Adolfo came to work early, cleaned up, and left when he was supposed to. That was more than the former gardener had done. And Adolfo was good at keeping his mouth shut. Never did he talk about the priest to his fellow drinkers. Never did he say the beer was for the priest. They knew who it was for but Adolfo didn't add to the priest's misery by publicly branding him an alcoholic. And that the priest appreciated.

Adolfo's home life at Maria's had deteriorated somewhat. They still talked about many things when he arrived from work, but he began to resent the fact that she had thought of him as no better qualified than a gardener. She should have, he thought, helped him get the tavern back. The tavern began to occupy his mind more and more. He did not realize that to Maria a job was a job and nothing else and was not necessarily the index to the worth of a man.

And now this thing about the promise was bothering him. Maria was planning the deed and he didn't want to go through with it. He was worried about getting back to his own tavern and she was worried about how he was to walk on his knees from the house to the church.

Finally, to keep her quiet, he relented. He would do it alone, but Maria would not agree. So one night, shortly after midnight, he walked on his knees from the house to the church. Maria walked slowly in front of him holding a kerosene lantern for him to see. She talked all the way through, telling him where the rocks were, to slow down, to speed up, pointing to the ruts on the ground, until finally they arrived at the steps only to find the priest standing there waiting for them!

Adolfo slowly came to his feet and sat at the stairs, exhausted. He unraveled the pieces of cloth he had tied around his knees for padding. Maria stood with the lantern held high.

"Put out that lantern!" the priest said. "What in God's name are you two doing here?"

Maria quickly blew the lantern out.

But the priest was impatient. "Put the lamp out immediately!" he demanded. "Do you want the whole town to see you? What are you doing?"

He had seen the lantern light from his bedroom window and had followed the erratic path it took until it approached the rectory. He had quickly put on his black coat and had gone to the church steps. From a distance he had not been able to make out the two figures. As they approached he could see a woman with a lantern walking in front of a man walking on his knees. He had cursed. "So we're back to this again," he said. "And after the sermon last Sunday when I told them I didn't want to see this type of worshipping."

It didn't surprise him when he saw Maria with the lantern. What really upset him was that behind her on his knees was Adolfo, his gardener.

"And what is the meaning of all this?" he asked. He placed his hand to his chin and shook his head slowly.

Maria was hesitant. Adolfo groaned in pain as he stretched out his legs, massaging his knees.

"Adolfo made a promise to walk on his knees," she said. "It was a promise made, if he found a job."

The priest did not know what to believe. It may have been the truth but he wasn't sure. So he resigned himself to the fact that they had done it, and felt it was better to let matters be.

"Go on home now. Go to bed, it's late," he said. "Adolfo, I expect you here tomorrow or today, whatever hour this is. And I expect you to be on time."

With this he slowly walked away to the rectory. The two, Adolfo and Maria, sat down on the step and Maria felt proud that Adolfo had accomplished the feat which she herself had promised to do. She also decided that from now on, if she couldn't fulfill a promise, Adolfo could do it for her.

They argued for a while before leaving. Adolfo was angry because Maria had given the priest the impression that the whole thing had been his idea. Maria, knowing full well that he spoke the truth, apologized.

"But what could I do?" she asked him. "I was so nervous. He almost scared me to death. I couldn't tell who it was. Could you?"

"No," he said. He was still rubbing his long fingers over his knees. "He scared the shit out of me. I thought he was the devil!"

"Me too. I thought it was the devil or someone's spirit haunting the church steps. I kept thinking, who's spirit would need to enter the church for redemption? He really scared me."

"I was looking down and when you gasped and I looked up and saw him with the flashlight . . . Well, I thought we were done for."

"He shouldn't scare people like that," she said. She had already started to change the situation around in order to blame the priest. "He ought to know better. He should make a little noise, clear his throat, anything to tell people he's there. What a fright!"

"And you, woman, had to tell him it was my fault. I'll never forgive you for that." He was able to stand now and he was trying to exercise his legs.

"I didn't say that. I just said it was a promise that you were fulfilling."

"But he thinks it was my idea."

"Well, it was both your idea and mine. After all, you're the one who got the job."

"The job? Do you call that a job? Cutting grass? Weeding flower beds? Sweeping the church? Is that your idea of a job?"

"It's something, Adolfo. It keeps you active. It keeps you out of the beer joints all day long."

"But don't you understand that I want to be at the beer joints all the time. I like it. I enjoy it. There's nothing I would rather do."

"Well," she said, lighting the lantern and getting up from the stairs, "you have no one to blame but yourself. I told you not to go away. But you wouldn't listen. Come on, let's go. Anyway, what you really want is to hang around the whores."

He could barely get up, but he did with much effort. At first, with much pain, he appeared as if on a string, his legs almost giving out on him, but, as he warmed up, he was able to walk normally.

The following day he was in agony. He couldn't kneel down to tend the flower beds. He was erect all day acting busy, but doing nothing. When he went in the church to clean, he sat in the pew and looked around, killing time. When it was time to go for beer he stayed longer than usual. Every beer he drank made his pain a little less severe. By the time he left, he was staggering. The combination of the aches from the night before and the beer was too much. Two of the men there took him in a car back to the rectory. He held the beers for the priest in a paper sack in the crook of his arm.

The priest had become impatient and, when Adolfo arrived propped up by the two men at the front door, he was enraged. He grabbed the beer from Adolfo and gave him a severe tongue-lashing. The two men slowly released him and, as he swayed back and forth, the priest kept up the harangue. No one can scold like a Spanish priest. The two men made their get-away quickly and left Adolfo to his fate.

After the priest was through with him, he slammed the door. Adolfo staggered back to Maria's. He fell several times on the way. Once he didn't feel like he had the strength left to get up. He lay there quietly for awhile and gazed at the stars as they careened through the dark space in his intoxicated mind. This is what he enjoyed. He was a man again!

In the morning, the priest wouldn't talk to him. Instead he spoke to him through the housekeeper.

"Tell him to clean out the garage," he told the old lady.

The old lady dutifully went out and he could see her talking to Adolfo. Adolfo looked toward the rectory and saw him standing beside the screened porch at the back of the house. He took up his hoe and rake and walked to the garage.

The priest was intent on teaching him a lesson. He was angry because he felt Adolfo was using him. He was reaching the point where he didn't care whether the people knew about his drinking. After all, whatever he did, he was still so much better than they.

That afternoon Adolfo decided he would quit. He couldn't take the job, demeaning as it was to him, anymore. He had taken it reluctantly for Maria's sake. The priest had been fair to him at first and it made conditions tolerable. But now with the priest against him, he felt that he had reached the end.

He cleaned out the garage, took the house money to buy beer and returned quickly. He handed the beer to the old lady and told her to tell the priest that he would not be coming to work anymore.

"Don't go, Adolfo," she said. "You have been a good worker. Father Angel needs you. He's just a little angry over what happened yesterday. He feels you took advantage of him."

She was an old lady of small stature, hardly over five feet and on the heavy side. The sides of her face moved as she spoke. Her hands were wrapped in her apron, a habit she had as she spoke. Adolfo, with his height, looked down at the woman. She kept her eyes down as she spoke. "He doesn't mean what he says when he's angry. If I paid any attention to him, I would have left years ago. And he's not bad considering the other priests that have been here before him."

"I know he's not bad," he said. "It's just that it won't work out for either of us. I'm not made to do this kind of thing. I know I was wrong."

"Don't go yet," she said. She was nervous and fidgety with the apron. She looked up to Adolfo and it seemed to him that she had gained weight since he started working there. "Let me talk to him."

"It won't do any good. I've made up my mind."

With this, he turned and walked away. They had been standing inside the screened porch and he opened the door, walked down the step, and left.

From his room the priest saw Adolfo leaving early, another cause for dismissal. He opened a beer. Before he could bring it to his lips, the old lady knocked on the door.

"What is it?" he asked.

"It's Adolfo," she said, excited.

"What about him? Why is he leaving early?"

"He's left," she said.

"Left? Left for where?"

"He's left for good," she said.

"Good riddance," he said, muttering slowly.

"What?" She could not hear from behind the door.

"Nothing!" he shouted.

"Praise be to God," she said, nervously walking away from the door and down the stairs. She was rolling her apron around her hands as she fled.

CHAPTER 3

Maria started to cry softly as Adolfo told her what had happened. Had it been because of the episode two nights before? Had it been because of last night's drinking? Had it been a combination of the two? Adolfo quietly sat at the small table and told her it had been his idea. The priest was angry, that he couldn't deny. But all things considered, he felt he was out of place there. It just wasn't what he wanted to do.

"But what do you want at your age? You want to work in an office?" Maria asked him. She was losing her patience with him.

"No. Besides I couldn't get a job like that. I'm just not a yard man, that's all." He wondered what it would take to convince her.

"And what, in truth, are you?" She knew that the question was a brutal one.

"I don't know." He sat down, dejected.

She had quit crying and was sitting across from him. She didn't know if she felt anger or pity for the man. In fact, she felt more disgust than anything else.

"I don't know about you, Adolfo." She was shaking her head slowly. "How could you do this?"

"Something else will come up, I'm sure."

"And we know what that something else is, don't we?" She had sat down with him at the table and was eyeing him with disgust.

"What do you mean?"

"You know what I mean. I don't have to say it."

She wished she had not burned the letter. She could have gotten rid of him. Or maybe not. There weren't that many fools around like her to keep a man like Adolfo.

"I'm going to tell you something, Adolfo, that's been on my conscience. Now that you've done this, that you've shown how ungrateful you are, I'm going to tell you. You remember the letter to Isabel that I was supposed to mail?"

His face changed expression. He knew what she was about to say.

"I burned it!" she yelled. She hit the small table with an open hand and the salt shaker tumbled over. "I burned it! Do you understand? I burned it because I felt you would be better off with me. Now I realize how foolish it was. I should have let you go. Let someone else take care of you."

He got up slowly. He was still feeling quite a bit of pain in his knees. He walked toward his room and, as he reached the entrance, covered by a long narrow cloth, he turned and said, "What bothers me is that you burned Carmen's letter also. And I'll see about moving out of here."

In the morning, a small boy ran up to the house and brought Adolfo his pay. The priest had added five dollars to it. He took the money and got dressed in his old suit. He wore his black leather shoes. He strode proudly to the tavern that had been his. He felt empty since Maria had not been around to cook breakfast. And even if she had been there, he doubted that she would have fed him. His days were numbered there. He wished that Carmen would have been there yesterday to hear about the letters. But then he thought about it and decided it was best that she hadn't. He didn't know how to feel about the whole situation. His life had been one of so many compromises and accomodations that he was slow to form an opinion and even slower to anger. He could see her side of it too. Losing Carmen had been a blow to her. And although they wrote to each other, it was not the same as living together. For his part, he rationalized that he was better off not living with Isabel. She would have been tougher than the priest to live with. He really wasn't as old as he thought. He could still take care of himself. He had gone through desperate times before. He knew how to do it. He was a survivor.

When he arrived at the beer joint, it was almost empty, except for the die-hard drinkers who didn't work. These men showed up as soon as the doors opened and didn't leave until they closed. They spoke to him and snickered about the suit, but it didn't bother him. It never had before. Why start now? Instead, he kept on walking to the rear and opened the door by the bar that led into the back room. Two men were sitting there drinking beer. He sat with them as they greeted him. One of them was his cousin, the one who had taken over and wouldn't give back the business. The other was "The Tiger," a heavy set very dark-skinned pimp. He owned three of the best prostitutes in town and he had the scars to prove it.

After the light conversation was over, the cousin broke the ice. "And what brings you here? I thought you were working for the drunkard?" He was referring to the priest.

"I quit yesterday."

He hated to be placed in a position of weakness. He knew his cousin had his friend at his side. He should have asked for a private conversation. "The Tiger" was grinning. His gums were purple. His teeth were short.

"And what are you doing here? You want a beer? Get a beer on the house."

"I've got money," Adolfo said.

"He's got money," "The Tiger" said, smiling. "Lot's of money. He's on a pension. He's got Veteran's Pension. Maria's money. The priest's money. He's rich. You don't need to work."

"I came for what is rightfully mine. You know this place is mine. I didn't leave except for one day. You had no right to take it."

"Tell the owner. He's my cousin too. He said I could have it. Your argument is with him."

"I talked to him. He says it's up to you. If you want me to have it, I can have it. And I think you ought to give it back."

"Look, Adolfo, we had an understanding. You were leaving. I was taking over. It's not my fault you came back the same day. I cleaned up the place. We painted it. We've done a lot since I took over. This place was a mess when I got hold of it. I won't let you have it."

"Do you understand what your cousin is saying," "The Tiger" said. He was not smiling. The scar on his face had healed a darker color than the rest of him and it ran from the top of the hairline to the corner of his purplish mouth on the right side.

"Does he have to be here?" Adolfo asked pointing to the dark man. "I'm used to talking to people with some intelligence, not an animal."

"The Tiger" stood up quickly. The cousin intervened. Adolfo is an old man, he reasoned. Leave him alone. He's always talking. He was able to pacify the man.

"You don't scare me," Adolfo said, calmly. "In my younger days I could take on two of you. In Pachuca I broke one man's neck and another man's arm and they were bigger and meaner than you, and I fought them at the same time."

The cousin intervened again and led the furious "Tiger" out of the room.

"What are you trying to do, get yourself killed?" he asked Adolfo.

"He doesn't scare me. He might scare you, but not me.'

"If it hadn't been for me, he would have killed you. Have you ever seen him fight with a knife?"

"Have you ever seen me with a baseball bat?"

"Don't you see you can't do things like that anymore? Don't you realize that you are old. Old! Adolfo, you're old! You're an old man. You can't fight anymore. How long do you think you could last here now? People here have lost a lot of respect for you. You're not a hero anymore. You're a has-been who never shuts up. You bore people. You talk too much."

"You're just saying that because you're jealous. You never amounted to much. I told your father before he died that you were not much."

"At least I don't go around making a fool of myself. The people here don't like you anymore. You've stayed too long in one place."

"I'll talk to my *good* cousin about the contract. As for you, I don't consider you a cousin anymore."

He stood up slowly to leave.

"It won't do you any good," he said, getting up and finishing his beer in one swallow. "This place is mine now. My cousin and me, we have an understanding."

As he left he noticed that "The Tiger" was sitting at a table by the bar. He tried to stare Adolfo down, but Adolfo kept walking. As he reached the steps, he held on to the door jam to help lower himself. He slowly took the steps one at a time.

He straightened out his dirty tie and pulled down his old vest and walked back to Maria's.

"Carmen wrote," Maria said. "She hasn't found a job yet, but she has applied at a theater where Isabel's next door neighbor works. She says she has a good chance to get the job. The first thing she's going to do is buy some clothes when she gets her first pay check. She can't believe she's living in San Diego. She likes it a lot more than being here, she says. Isabel has been very good to her. She makes her work, keeping the house clean. You know Carmen never did anything like that around here. I guess I had her spoiled. Anyway, she's all excited about her new life."

Adolfo sat in his customary chair at the table. He was glad Carmen had written and was doing well. "She'll find a job, just you wait and see."

He appeared weary to her and it bothered her to think that he was so worried over his misfortunes. But what else could he do? Anyway, it was not up to her now.

"Are you angry over last night?" she asked. She placed a cup of coffee in front of him. She was feeling better. The letter from Carmen had cheered her up and she was not one to stay angry. If Adolfo didn't want to work, that was it. She would have to find him something more suitable.

"Why should I be angry," he said. "You're the one who was angry."

"And the letter?" she asked, hoping that he had forgotten. "I think you did right in burning my letter," he replied to her. He was very tired and he didn't feel like talking about it. Besides he didn't feel it would have made any difference. "I don't think you did right in burning Carmen's letter. I think you did wrong, very wrong, there. But with me, I don't care. It was probably the best thing to do. It couldn't work out. Isabel was too set in her ways after all these years. My son would not have allowed me there either. It gives me a strange feeling to know that he wants to kill me. A son wants to kill his father. What kind of world is this?"

He took out his teeth and placed them at the edge of the table by the window. He rubbed the itch in his bare gums with the tip of his finger. The coffee numbed the soreness in his mouth. Maria set a plate of beans and rice and he ate slowly.

"Enough of this, Adolfo," she said. "Let's not feel sorry for ourselves. This afternoon we'll go to the store. We'll buy some groceries. We'll pay the grocer. I'll even buy you some beer. Let's be happy together. What are we worried for? We're at the evening of our lives. We've worked hard. Now is the time to enjoy ourselves. My children are grown and gone. Carmen was the only one I hated to see go."

He stood up, took his teeth and put them in his pocket and went to his room.

"Don't change clothes," she said, hurriedly cleaning the table, "we're leaving in a little while."

"No, I won't," he answered from inside the room. "I just want to lay down for a second."

The next day, he was given breakfast. Maria had been in a good mood. She had completely forgiven him and decided that everything would work out for the best. He had washed his face, shaved over and over again with an old razor blade and felt somewhat better. He had gone back to the tavern and had argued his case again. And again he was turned down. Next, he had gone to see the owner of the building, the one he called his *good* cousin, to see what results that would produce. He was been turned down.

Now in the solitude of his room, he was contemplating his next move. He knew he had to leave town. How would he break the news to Maria? He could hear her outside drawing water from the faucet and watering the geraniums by the side of the house. He could also hear the children playing in the dump. He had to have at least one friend left that would help him. He thought of Jesus, but he hadn't seen him since the day they went to San Diego. But Jesus was not a friend in his sense of the word. They had only been together once, twice, if you counted the night before going to San Diego. Most of the people he had known, and known well, were dead. He thought that maybe he could go back to Los Angeles to the bar where the young man found him and told him about the death of his friend. Could he go back? He felt the road closing in on him. He had traveled it and had made so much use of it that he was now, he felt, at the end. There were not many choices. He could stay with Maria. That was one. He didn't want to, so that eliminated that. Not that he didn't like her. It was just as his cousin had said: he had stayed too long. The trouble with being well known, he always knew, was that you had to keep people from finding out who you really were. The job as a gardener had done him in. And yet, if he hadn't left for that one day to see Isabel in San Diego, he would still be in good standing. He cursed his fate. He had only wanted something better. If only he had settled for what he had. No, he had to make a mess of things. What Maria did with the letter was not important anymore. It wouldn't have helped. But what to do? He had to leave. But would that turn out for the worse also?

So he set out to look for Jesus. He looked for days, walking to every tavern and store in town. He found him one day sitting in his car in front of the barber shop. He was with another man and they were trying to empty a fifth of tequila. Adolfo spoke cautiously. He didn't know how he would take it if Jesus turned him down. He was relieved to find out during the conversation that Jesus did not know about his handy-man experience.

"Where have you been?" Jesus asked him.

"Here and there," he said, trying to give the impression that he had been doing something interesting.

"And the girl we took to San Diego, is she still there?"

"Yes, she's there and working now. Making good money too. She's working at a theater." After all, Carmen had said that the job was as good as hers.

"What about the crazy man?"

Here Jesus told the story to his companion about Alfredo and how he had pulled a gun and threatened to shoot them.

"It scared the hell out of us," he said, shaking his head at the thought.

"It would scare the hell out of anybody," the companion said. "I don't know what I would have done."

"He didn't mean any harm," Adolfo said. "I've known him since he was a little boy. All talk. All bluff and no action. Just like some pimps around here." He adjusted his pants and tucked his shirt in.

"Well, I didn't think the girl would stay. She was so scared."

The conversation stopped and the bottle was passed around. Adolfo took a small bit. He didn't like hard liquor anymore, not today anyway.

"By the way," Jesus said, "the car is fixed. I got a starter from the junk yard and my friend here and I put it in."

"You know," Adolfo said, "I've been thinking about going to Los Angeles. I've got some friends I need to see. Haven't seen them in years now. Maybe we ought to go. The car's fixed. I'll pay for the gas. We can stay at my friend's place."

"Not me," the companion said and he appeared serious about it. "I'll start work again tomorrow. Besides, I don't think the wife would let me go."

"And you, Jesus," Adolfo asked. "Are you working?"

"Not right now. But I've got a lot of things to do around here. Why don't you take the bus? There's two buses leaving every day for Los Angeles. I'll take you to the bus station. How's that? You tell me when and I'll pick you up. But I can't take you to Los Angeles."

He had not wanted to go by bus. He knew the bus schedule. The point was that it was more personal to go by car. It seemed to him that everytime he had been on a bus he had regretted it.

"Listen, Jesus, I'll pay for everything if you take me. I've got a little money saved. We can have a good time. I know some of the prostitutes in Los Angeles. I know some of the bars, good beer joints. We'll have a great time. We'll get up late, sleep all day, if you want, and party all night. I'll fix you up like you've never been fixed."

"You didn't fix me up in San Diego," he replied, "why should you be able to set me up in Los Angeles?" He knew Adolfo was lying.

"That was different," Adolfo reasoned to him. "That was a trip to help out Carmen. We couldn't do anything with her around."

"Why not?" he asked. "There were rumors about her. Like mother, like daughter."

The two men laughed. Adolfo just smiled and winked an eye. He had no loyalty when he was around the men. They passed the bottle again. This time Jesus' friend took a long swallow and passed the bottle to Adolfo. Adolfo refused. "I've had enough," he said, making a face as if the thought of having one more drink would make him sick. The friend took another long drink. Each time he swallowed he shook his head and blew hot breath through his clenched teeth. "Man, that's good," he said after regaining his composure. Jesus was more of a steady drinker, slow but sure.

"There's this young woman I wish you'd meet." Adolfo was persistent. "She's the most beautiful girl you've ever seen. The whores around here are awful. They're either fat or skinny and they're hard and ugly. But this one in Los Angeles, she's like an angel. I could introduce you to her. You've never met anyone like her. You can take her out. Do whatever with her, if you know what I mean." He winked at the companion. He laughed and slapped his thigh. He appeared more interested than Jesus.

"No, I better not," Jesus said. "I appreciate it, but I can't. I've got too much to do. But like I say, I'll be glad to take you to the bus station. It's more comfortable anyway. This old jalopy probably wouldn't make it there and back." He played with the steering wheel and looked at his friend. The friend just stared straight ahead. They knew, and especially Jesus, what they would be getting into if they took Adolfo.

Adolfo was slowly eased out of the conversation and in time was just standing there by the car door. He straightened out and rubbed his back and then said his good-byes. The men stopped what they were talking about and acknowledged his departure. Adolfo slowly walked away.

Although she had been happily married, Maria could not help but think once in a while of the love that had eluded her. The night of the dance, when she was to elope, she had had no idea that the young man would not show. She had talked to him the night before and he had the whole thing planned. They would, he told her, leave the dance during the last intermission, get in his wagon and go to the next town. They would spend the night there at the little hotel and then come back the next day. They would be forced to marry that same day. By the end of the day they would be husband and wife and she would go live in his house. From there things would work out. They could, if she wanted, move out and live by themselves or, if she wanted to, they could stay there. Whatever she wanted. He knew that she was pregnant and there was no question in his mind that it was his child.

Why, she would ask herself later, did he do it? Why was she denied his love? How many other women did she know that had married under similar circumstances? There were many. Why had he cast her aside without a word? Was she the only one of the two brave enough? Was he a coward?

By the end of the dance she was acting abnormally. She couldn't sit. She was walking around and around the dance hall looking for him. At the end she didn't wait for her friends. She ran back home crying.

For all these years she felt that the young man had thought her not good enough to marry. He never spoke to her again nor tried to see her again. To her he acted as if the whole thing had never happened. She saw him afterwards and he acted as if nothing had ever happened. Her pregnancy reminded her that it had, though.

She gave birth to a girl that she named Maria. This child was a thorn at her side. She nagged constantly and was hard to raise. She was bright, though, and she was the first one in all of the family to graduate from high school. She left shortly after graduation to work in San Francisco. And since neither of them got along, she seldom came home. This is not to say that they didn't love each other. Maria could count on her to come through anytime she needed her. At Christmas she always sent gifts for everyone, the largest and most expensive for Maria. And the fact they never got along did not diminish the respect one had for the other. It was a respect born of mutual adversity. Things had not been easy for both of them. Little Maria, as she was affectionately called, was always at her mother's side. Her stepfather, Maria's husband, liked her, but he didn't have much to do with her. She was a bastard and a small imposition on his life. She kept away from him. For the most part, he was a good man, and he had been married before. He was a widower with three children, two boys and a girl slightly older than Little Maria. Maria brought Little Maria with her into the marriage and he brought his three.

The marriage was fairly successfull by community standards. That is, they seldom fought and he seldom got drunk. He did enjoy going out with the prostitutes. And many were the times that Maria and the children would have to go and get him out of the little houses in back of the beer joints. He was jovial and enjoyed telling a good story.

Maria tried to be fair with all the children, but with Little Maria's personality it was impossible. It was as if she demanded more of her mother, just to prove to the others that she was the preferred child. The other three children moved out as soon as they could. They saw the hopelessness in the situation. They knew their father would never take up for them. None graduated from school. The boys set off to work in the fields and the girl went to work in New Mexico. They saw each other occassionally — funerals, weddings, and the like — but they were never close as a family. Their father, Maria's husband, was just not much for children.

Adolfo arrived drunk. He startled her. She was sitting at the table reminiscing when she saw his head pass through the kitchen window. He opened the back door and swayed backwards holding on to the door frame and he fell as if someone had shot him in the chest. Down he went from the top step, reeling, trying to get his long legs under him and he fell on his back, his legs open. She could see by the wet crotch that he had urinated on himself. She glanced quickly away from the dark spot on the pants. His shirt tail was out and his vest was twisted to one side where she couldn't see the buttons. His tie was twisted and the knot was hidden under the dirty collar. He had lost his coat. She noticed that the soles of his shoes each had a large hole through which she could see his feet. She ran to him.

"In the name of God and my mother who is in heaven," he cried, "someone help me. Maria!" he yelled. "Where are you?"

"Right here," she answered.

She picked up his head, but that was all. He was a big heavy man.

"Help me, will you?"

"Yes, be quiet," she said. "Don't make too much noise. Everyone will see you."

The children playing in the dump had run over and gathered around and they stared blankly at the great figure of a man so powerless to get up. One of the smaller ones started to cry. He wanted to know if Adolfo was going to die. He was comforted by one of his playmates. "He just looks drunk to me," he said. "He's not going to die. But I'll tell you, if he's like my father, he'll wish he was dead in the morning."

When they saw that Maria could not help Adolfo, the older boys helped her. First they got him to sit and then they held Adolfo's arms as he tried to get his feet under him. Finally they had him on his feet and held him up as he ascended the stairs. From there they all took him to his room and he collapsed on the bed. Vaguely, in his stupor, Adolfo remembered the time that he had been carried on the shoulders of a delirious crowd after a well pitched game.

It is sad when a man reaches a point where all he has is memories. For Maria the sadness was doubly hard, for she had known him most of his life. She regretted what he had done with his life. What a mistake it had been. No matter what he had been, life had not forgiven him for his unstableness. She only knew that if she felt miserable for him, that he must feel worse. And she couldn't imagine how he could survive under those circumstances.

The next morning she was glad when Adolfo told her that he was leaving. He had found it hard to say, but when Maria encouraged him to talk he came out with it. He wasn't happy there, although he loved Maria and considered her his favorite cousin. Things just had not worked out for him. No, not even if she had sent the letter, it wouldn't have made any difference. It was good that even Carmen's letter had not been sent. "Look at that crazy man in San Diego," he said, holding his head between both hands. "He would have killed Carmen."

"I knew it," Maria said. "I knew something or someone made me do it. God works in very mysterious ways. I shall pray a rosary for that."

"Don't forget," he said, "that you still have a promise to fulfill."

"I'll do it," she said. "It's just that I haven't had time. And," she added, "I want the priest to get over the last one."

They laughed and immediately Adolfo started to talk about his plans. He would leave and go to Los Angeles where he was respected among his friends. He would go by bus. Jesus was not to be trusted, he said. He didn't like Jesus now and never did. Jesus was from a lower class of Mexicans, a man who would never amount to anything.

"Watch out for him, Maria," he said. "He doesn't talk well of you and Carmen."

"I don't care about that," she said. "I've been talked about for many years. It's not important to me."

He would take the bus to Los Angeles. There he would look up his old friends, visit with them, enjoy the talk of the old days. He would, if he were in luck, get a tavern of his own. He wouldn't work for anyone else. No women, he promised Maria. Just his friends sitting around having a good time. He would stay with friends for a while, then get a place of his own. He knew several people that let out rooms. He would eat his meals at work. Everything would work out, just wait and see.

A small boy knocked at the door and Maria went out to see who it was. Adolfo could hear her talking and thanking the young visitor. She came back with Adolfo's coat.

"Someone sent you your coat. It's a mess."

The boy had rolled up the coat or had been given the coat rolled into a ball and, when Maria unfurled it, she could see that he had fallen with it on. There were some grass burrs and mud spread over the front and back. The elbows were caked with mud and debris. He looked at it and wondered where he had fallen and how he had taken it off. She took the coat outside and spread it across a clothes line. She swept it with a broom.

"Look at what you did," she said. She looked at him as a mother would an errant child. "And you urinated in your pants."

"No, I didn't," he said defensively. "I would never do a thing like that."

She went into his room and brought out the pants.

"Look at that," she said. "Now tell me you didn't urinate on yourself."

She held the crotch out to him and he looked at it very carefully.

"I spilled some beer on myself, that's all. Woman, you're always dreaming up bad things about me. It's beer."

"Then smell it and see if I'm dreaming."

She put the crotch of the pants to his nose and he sniffed gently.

"Is that beer?" she demanded.

He sniffed some more.

"No," he admitted. He was serious. "It's urine."

"I told you."

"How did it happen?"

"What do you mean, how did it happen? Don't you know how you urinate?"

"Yes, I know. But I still don't understand."

"You were drunk. You fell somewhere and you fell asleep and urinated on yourself. You woke up. Got up somehow, or someone helped you up. Then you got here. How you got here only God knows."

"I swear to you on my mother's grave, I don't remember," he said, baffled.

He took the pants and went outside and washed them by the faucet and hung them to dry alongside the coat. He looked at the coat and took it off the clothes line and washed it also.

Maria came out running.

"Don't you know wool will shrink if you wash it in water?"

"I don't care what it does," he said. "I'm not going to Los Angeles smelling like that!"

By the end of the week he had prepared himself to leave. Maria had made a half-hearted try at changing his mind, but he ignored her and she didn't press him. She felt realistically that it was better for him to leave. She didn't want him to, go but then again she did. It was hard for her to explain her feelings. One part of her would miss him dearly. The other part felt it was for the best. She knew that if he stayed, he would get hurt and she didn't want that.

He came out of his room wearing his suit for the first time after being washed. His pants were shortened and his white socks made a contrast between the end of the trousers and his shoes. The coat was short, but he felt that it would stretch out as the day went along. Maria told him it wouldn't and this irritated him. He had packed an old suitcase, the same one he took to San Diego and they said farewell. Maria was crying as usual and she kept up the advice and admonitions she often repeated to him. Be sure to eat, she told him; and be sure to bathe and get enough sleep and don't fool around with the whores; don't bet your money; go to bed early; be sure to keep track of your teeth; don't drink too much.

After this bombardment, he hugged Maria tightly and said that he would see her again. Jesus was waiting outside and he released her, grabbed the suitcase, and walked briskly to the car. He felt like a new man. Jesus could not help but notice the condition of the suit. He wondered what could have happened. Knowing Adolfo, he wasn't about to ask.

From here, Jesus took him directly to the bus station and saw him off to Los Angeles. He later told his friends how Adolfo looked that day. The trousers were about six inches short and the coat looked like he had stolen it. The men laughed. They wondered if he would ever return. "The Tiger" was glad that he was gone. He felt, he said, like someday he would have to kill him, if he had stayed. No one said a word. They looked at each other, for they knew he meant it.

Adolfo purchased his ticket and counted the change slowly. He knew now he had to be careful with his money. There weren't any Marias around to feed him and house him. He sat down at the waiting area and re-counted his money. It was not much, but as always, it was less than he expected. Maria was to keep the Veteran's Pension checks for him until he wrote her his new address. He could make it, though, if he were careful. He really didn't like to eat breakfast, he thought.

Across from him sat a middle aged lady with two children, a little boy and a girl about six or seven years old. She kept trying to keep them still, but she was having little success. No sooner did she plant one of them down on the chair next to her, when the other one would get up and start running around. By the time she gathered that one, the other one would be gone. He thought about his life and figured how lucky he had been not to have had the experience of raising a child.

At the end of the row of chairs where he sat was an older lady somewhat in her early fifties, he calculated, and dressed rather smartly. She wore a tight black dress and black patent shoes and her hair was combed up in a bun. Her face was heavily made-up. She looked to neither side and was oblivious of the woman running after her children.

Shortly before departure, the waiting room was getting crowded and he stood up and walked to the door that led to the loading area. He had not noticed, but the lone woman had walked over to the door also. She looked at him suddenly and smiled. Then, just as abruptly, she looked away from him. He was overtaken by the smile. Surely, he thought, she meant something by it. His immense ego at work, he began to think of her as a conquest.

Once in the bus, he sat by her. As that was his forte, conversation flowed. He had his teeth on and he looked handsome enough, except for his clothes. He kept pulling his pants down at the knees as he sat. He took off his coat after excusing himself. He had much difficulty doing this since the sleeves had narrowed and were very tight around his arms. She helped him out of the coat and he thanked her for it.

It developed during the conversation, when he gave her the opportunity to speak, that she was a widow, this being the reason for the black dress and shoes. Her husband had died in Los Angeles three years ago. He had been a surveyor for the city and had worked at that job for some thirty years. He had died of a heart attack one afternoon while surveying a sewage line around one of the hills in Los Angeles. Death, she said, was more or less instantaneous. The co-workers had told her that he was dead before he hit the ground. It was funny, she said, that he had never complained about anything before this happened. It had been a great shock and to this Adolfo agreed. He himself, he said, had had a friend die under similar circumstances in Torreon, Mexico, when he was pitching for the Falcons. And from here he took off on one of his one-sided conversations and took her with him through Torreon, Pachuca, Mexico City, and a few other places he had pitched. She was impressed. He was too, especially since she had relinquished her conversation and was genuinely engrossed in his. After all, her husband's death must have been very important to her. He took a liking to her immediately.

When he was through, she began anew. Most of her children were grown now and only two of them, a teenage girl and boy, remained with her. Her oldest daughter lived in Los Angeles in the south side of town with her husband, a brick-layer. Her oldest son was married and was a concrete finisher. He had three children. Another son was in Albuquerque and he worked as a house painter. This is why she was on the bus. She was returning from New Mexico after a month's visit. That son had three children also. Here she began searching through her purse and produced a big bill-fold. She opened it and unfurled a series of photographs inserted into a long folded celluloid sheet. When she was through, the pictures reached almost to the floor of the bus. One by one she named off the faces — men, women, children — and she even had a picture of her dog sitting on the porch. Her late husband was a handsome man, although very short, shorter than her, and he had a very thin mustache and small mouth. His nose looked large in proportion. He had eyes that appeared to be smiling all the time.

Adolfo took out his wallet and showed her a picture of Carmen. Then, from the inside where he had his folding money, he took out an old photograph showing him in his Yankee uniform. Oh yes, he informed her, he had played for them. And also the Cardinals.

He had found a friend. She lived in Los Angeles in what she described as a humble home.

The fact that she was still interested in his rambling conversation after several hours made him feel good, better than he had in a long time. Let's face it, he had lost respect in the old community. He had stayed too long, as they said. He felt that this would be his lucky day. After all, how long had it been since he had had a good conversation with someone that he could impress. She had not heard any of this before and she still had a long way to go.

Periodically she would lift her skirt and fan her thighs ever so demurely. It was hot. He tried not to notice, but such a warm feeling came over him. "The heat is insufferable," she said. He only agreed. "You must be warm in that shirt and tie and, besides, you have a vest on," she said. He agreed and removed his vest. And since she hadn't ever seen him before, she couldn't tell whether the shirt was old and white or fairly new and yellowish.

By late afternoon, they were in Los Angeles and he hardly wanted to arrive, such had been the pleasure of the trip. Her genuine conversation and her occasional flapping of her skirt had made the trip seem so much shorter. Even when they had stopped to eat lunch, they had sat together eating like two old friends. They had left the bus crowd and had gone to one side to a small table and he had graciously paid for the meal.

It was obvious to him at least that she was lonely. Her conversation sounded as if she were starved for attention. She had gotten excited just talking about the sites on the trip. This to him had made him feel both comfortable and excited also, as if he were the cause of her change in character. After all, he had imagined her to be a very silent type who only spoke when spoken to.

The two children had been on the bus and she had talked to them patiently as they ran up and down the aisle. This was also a good sign. In fact, he had also spoken to the children and it had been many years since he had done so. Children, to his way of upbringing, were not only to be seen and not heard, but were to be slapped around.

As the bus came into southern Los Angeles, she pulled the cord. She gathered the small package from under her seat to await the bus stop. He realized he had come to an important moment in his life. Should he get off with her or stay? He looked at her for some clue. What would she say? What did she want him to do?

She was very frank. "Would you like to come and visit for a while?" she asked, her heavily made-up face fixed in an innocent smile. "I would like to hear some more of your interesting life stories. My children would enjoy meeting you. After coffee, maybe we can drop you off wherever it is you're going."

He felt like a man who had won when all was lost. No game ever gave him such a thrill. He agreed and hurriedly put on his vest and coat. And like this, stooped from the tightness of his coat and the shortness of his pants, he walked behind her down the aisle and they both disembarked. The bus driver was out already and had opened the luggage hatch. He took out four large suitcases and his one, locked the hatch and thanked them. The bus roared off spewing exhaust and dust on them.

They walked for what to him were ten miles. He was carrying the four large suitcases while she carried his thin one and the package. Each suitcase must have weighed thirty or forty pounds and he had to stop in ever shorter intervals to catch his breath. Once he felt his pulse to make sure everything was alright. He grew dizzy after a while and they had to stop to rest. She was always the lady, one time picking up a small piece of cardboard from the ground and fanning his face. He could hardly talk. His mouth was dry. He craved a beer. No, two beers or more. And still they walked. She was doing all the talking now, pointing out little places of interest along the way: where she shopped, her friends homes, the different trees. It was all for nothing, because the perspiration had gotten into his eyes and had clouded his vision. As he walked in this stooped crouch, he appeared like the large apes in the circus, ill-fitted, and carrying two suitcases in each arm.

When they reached the house, he could go no farther. He dropped the suitcases on the sidewalk and staggered to the stairs. Here he sat for a while, his hands dangling limply between his knees. She had gone before him and unlocked the door. She went in and came back shortly with a large glass of water. The indispensable dog had come from behind the house and was looking at him curiously, first one way, then tilting his head another way. He was the same dog in the photograph. He caught Adolfo's eye and instantly Adolfo saw he had made another friend. This was an intelligent dog. He was almost entirely black except for his paws and a small ring of white around his muzzle. His eyes were dark and shiny. His ears perked as if ready for action, each ear moving independently like periscopes attached to his head. He was a medium-sized dog, maybe forty pounds. He loved people, especially strangers.

He drank the water slowly taking deep breaths between swallows. She was standing behind him. "Are you alright?" she asked, knowing full well what torture he had been through.

"I'll be alright in a few moments," he replied. This reminded him of the time in Puebla when the bus had broken down ten miles from the ballpark and they all had to carry their luggage and equipment into the heart of town. In those days he had pitched that night. Now he would be lucky if he could walk by nightfall. He couldn't help but smile at the passage of time.

The dog went in with them and she had him sit in the living room, the room reserved for visitors. The woman had collected all sorts of bric-a-bracs from all over Mexico and California: little dolls, ash-trays from various cities and places, Indian pottery, silk pillow cases, a small Mexican hat, and most conspicuously, a large serape hung on a wall. The furniture was high caliber poverty, all cheap vinyl with burnt wood. This escaped him, since he wasn't used to anything better. She was doing something in the kitchen, then she came in and sat by him. The dog had kept on going and had gone out the back door. He had come around the house and was sitting tightly against the front screen.

"Are you hungry?" she asked, fanning her thighs. "I hope you are," she kept on without waiting, "because I'm going to fix something for us. The children will be coming home from school any minute now. What time is it?"

He didn't have a watch. She got up and went to the kitchen. "They should have been here by now," she said. "I think I'll go change."

She walked past him to the bedroom and he could hear her unzip her dress. She changed, coming out in a housecoat and slippers, and sat by him. He was feeling better. She sat close to him, closer than he had anticipated. Her weight made him lean toward her. "Here, take off that coat and vest. Remove your tie and be comfortable." While he was struggling to remove his coat and vest, she got up and stirred something in the frying-pan. He could hear the sizzle and smelled the meat cooking.

When she came back, she had a different look about her. He couldn't quite figure out what it was. She sat by him and placed her hand on his shoulder. She undid his tie. She looked at him and it embarrassed him. He quickly looked away. And when he caught her eye again, she was staring at him. She offered to massage his neck and, as she sat side-ways to get to him, her housecoat opened ever so slightly and he saw her thighs. He really didn't know what to do. She kneeled beside him to get more comfortable and she started to massage his neck. He thought he could feel something, a warmth inside, but he thought it was something else. The old fire was apparently gone. She kept up her girlish stare, but he couldn't take it. He looked the other way. "Are you bashful?" she asked. "You seem bashful around women." He had yet to speak. Her housecoat was opening and closing, showing a small portion of her breasts.

The fire was coming back.

She reached gently and pulled his face toward hers and kissed him lightly. She unexplainedly jumped up and started dancing in the middle of the room. She did the waltz. Then she had a fair try at a belly dance, exposing some of herself as she danced.

Someone was stoking the fire.

She jumped on his lap and almost made him fall. He had quit being embarrassed and was on the verge of feeling passion for her. He held her tightly to him and opened her housecoat and buried his head between her breasts. He couldn't breathe down there and she wouldn't let go of him. He had not realized how strong she was. She should have carried the damn suitcases, he thought, submerged among the soft flesh of her breasts. Finally he wiggled his head to where his nose pointed downward between the breasts and he could breathe. The curious thought came to him then that he had to write Maria and give her his new address. The checks would come in handy.

His trouble was that he couldn't keep the fire going. Just when he thought he had it, it flickered. Embers wouldn't do with her. He needed a roaring fireplace. He was breathing down her belly. If Maria could see me now. No, not Carmen, that would be too embarrassing. Jesus? Yes! And all the other bastards that had run him out of town.

She was up as suddenly as she had jumped on him. "Maybe some other time," she said, messing up his hair, and hurrying into the kitchen.

He was left with a sobering feeling. Was it possible that this was happening to him? Or was it a dream? He surveyed the room and felt of himself to make sure it was him and that it was happening. When the reality of the matter came to him and his mind settled down, he was able to produce a grin. It wasn't the most unusual thing that had happened to him, but it came close. In Germany, he remembered, a girl had walked up to him and grabbed him by the crotch. This was in broad daylight too. At that time, he had been able to do something about it. Now, today, he doubted very seriously about his manhood. After all, he hadn't used himself in a long time. But as the saying went, a good rooster crows in any henhouse. At least he had felt something, something apart from the near suffocation he had endured. Her breasts were enormous. He had no idea from seeing her in a dress that she was that big. He felt like going back just to tell the men about his good fortune. Then he would hurry back. He would be sure that the priest found out about it also. He could just see the smallish priest with the dark eyebrows and close-set eyes enraged at the story . . . or enraged that it had been Adolfo and not him.

The two children arrived as she was setting the table. Adolfo had all his clothes on and sat ready to eat. The son was a young teenage boy. He reminded Adolfo of the type of child who works and sits straight without making an effort. He seemed only to be able to bend from the neck. He was taller than his father had been, or so he was told, and had fine long hands. The daughter trailed behind him and, from what he had seen of her, she was no Carmen. She was pretty enough, but she did not have the classical Mexican beauty. She appeared more Anglicized, more gangly, as if she would fall apart when she walked.

"This is your uncle Adolfo," the mother said, slowly and with the effect of some finality. In other words, there wouldn't be an argument over the matter.

To Adolfo, this was another of a series of small jolts he had had during the day. Uncle Adolfo stunned him, but it sounded nice to him.

"He comes from the Imperial Valley of California. I had not seen your uncle in many years. As a matter of fact, I had forgotten about him. That's how long it has been. We were very close as children, but we were separated when our parents went their different ways. Imagine my surprise, my delight, when I met him on the bus today."

Adolfo marvelled at the lady. She sounded so genuine that he was inclined to believe her himself. The children sat in silence as she continued her story.

"Just imagine the coincidence," she said, continuing the farce. She stirred the food in the skillet slowly and smiled to herself, a self-assured smile showing she was in complete control. To Adolfo she appeared more radiant than he had seen her all day. Her face was flushed. Excitedly she told the children of how she had sensed something about Adolfo that had made her recognize him. Indeed, it had been him.

The children were happy for her. They asked about their brother in Albuquerque. She placed the food on the table and they ate as she told them all about her trip. She even told them about a filthy old man she had had trouble with on the bus on the way over. He had insulted her, tried to grab her by the "you know what." Now her face was twisted in anger. Who did he think he was? More important, who did he think *she* was? The children agreed. The bus driver had made the man move. She looked at Adolfo and smiled. She grabbed his hand and rubbed her cheek with it. He had never seen a person change emotions quite as rapidly as this woman, and it frightened him. Also of some concern was that he didn't even know her name.

"What's the matter with your coat, Uncle?" The boy was being sarcastic.

"I got caught in the rain last night," Adolfo replied, looking at his clothes. These were the first words spoken by him and, oddly enough, they had been to answer a question. His bashfulness around strangers made the conversation awkward.

"I thought it didn't rain in the Valley?" The young girl added to the insult.

They were not thrilled to have Adolfo there and, although their mother told them about his life as a ballplayer, they were not impressed. The girl in particular had a whining way about her. She was abrasive, or so Adolfo thought. The mother absorbed this filial punishment as a maternal obligation. Adolfo wouldn't say anything. It was not his responsiblity, and also, he was sure that in any event the mother would side with the daughter.

"Did you enjoy the supper?" the woman asked the daughter.

"What supper?" she answered.

"The one you just had."

"The one I just had? Or the one we *all* had?"

"The one all of you had."

"Why ask me?" she answered bitterly.

It was this particular habit of answering a question with a question that was beginning to irk him so much. The mother, to his amazement, didn't notice it. Or if she did, she ignored it.

The son was more subdued and, being in the presence of his sister most of the time, Adolfo knew why. Even Adolfo could not talk. The son was quiet and grinned only on occasions when his sister's habits had irritated someone. He appeared to be completely dominated by the two women. He was subjected to a doting love from his mother and an abrasive tenderness from his sister. Yes, his sister turned on him too. Both loves did nothing but bring out the helpless child in him.

"It's time for both of you to go to bed," the mother said. She had already cleared the table. She looked at Adolfo and smiled.

"Why is it time to go to bed?" the daughter asked.

"Because, it's been a long day."

"How do you know it's been a long day? You haven't been around us all day long. We didn't have a long day. Did we?" She looked at her brother and he grinned.

"No, we had a short day," he said. "We've had longer days before."

"We sure have," the girl responded. "Longer, longer days."

"Yes, I know," the woman said patiently, "but it's been a long day for your Uncle Adolfo and me."

Adolfo agreed. He told them how their mother had made him carry the suitcases. How exhausted he had been.

"I thought you said you were a ballplayer?" she said. "I thought athletes were in good shape."

"That was a long time ago," Adolfo pleaded, sure that he had made his point.

"It really looks it," she said, tersely.

"Now, now, now," the mother said. "That's no way to talk to a guest. You should have more respect for your uncle."

The son was grinning at Adolfo. He had a perfect row of teeth. The daughter rose and went to her room. Her brother followed her.

"You've got to understand them," she said to Adolfo, "they have been this way since their father died. They loved him so much. They just don't like company, especially another man. They're still jealous for their father, since he isn't here. But what am I to do?" she kept on. "I'm alive and I have my needs. They would never understand."

"I can see that they wouldn't," he said.

"But let's not have them spoil it for us. What do you say?"

"That's alright with me," he replied, hoping for a repeat of the afternoon.

"Do you want to stay?" She looked at him seriously. She meant it. He had seen that determined look in a woman before.

"Yes," he replied. What did he have to lose? How quickly he had forgotten about his friends in Los Angeles. But weighing the two alternatives quickly, he had come to the conclusion that this was the place to be.

The children kept interrupting them as they sat drinking their coffee in the living room. Not that they spoke to them, they just kept walking in and out of the kitchen and out the door and would come back in. Obviously they were doing something, since they didn't seem to acknowledge the mother's or Adolfo's presence. Finally they settled down and the house was quiet. The only faint sound they heard was periodically when the dog scratched himself and rattled the front door.

"How are you feeling?" she asked.

He wished she hadn't asked. Now that he was cold, his arms and legs ached. So did his torso. The pain radiated from the neck on both sides and through the shoulders to the arms. His insides hurt from the abdominal pressure he had had to exert. The ligament from the urinary bladder to the umbilicus had stretched and then contracted in a spasm, making it hard for him to stand up straight.

"I feel alright," he said. "A little sore, but alright."

She sneaked over to him and, holding the coffee in one hand, she opened up the housecoat with the other. Her breasts were the biggest he had ever seen. There was no doubt about that. She quickly covered up as she heard footsteps.

"Mother." The daughter was standing at the door. She seemed to have appeared from nowhere. "Where is Uncle Adolfo going to sleep?"

The woman's face had turned pale, but in the darkened room, the daughter couldn't tell. "I'll fix him a bed here on the sofa, Eloise. Don't be worrying about it."

"Oh, I wasn't worrying," she said emphatically. "I just wanted to know. I just wanted to make sure he didn't sleep in the same room with you, like Uncle Joe did."

Adolfo couldn't figure out what the daughter was saying.

"No, of course not," she answered. She stood up, but didn't know where to move. She had a look of desperation about her. She cleared her throat and looked quickly at Adolfo, then at Eloise. "Your Uncle Joe was different. He needed constant attention at night. Cancer, you know." She said this to Adolfo as if *he would* know. Adolfo nodded in agreement, although he felt as if he had missed the point. After all, he said to himself later, he had seen people dying of cancer who required constant watching during the night. The pain, you know.

Eloise was gone before the woman could say anything else. She had disappeared as quickly as she had come. They both looked at each other wondering what effect that scene had had on their relationship. Adolfo had not registered any emotion. He was there and he was happy. Nothing much could affect him. He had been through so many embarrassments that one more meant nothing to him. The woman was embarrassed. She tried to explain and really concocted a good story in which she had been the good Samaritan for Uncle Joe. She had been the only one to volunteer to help the poor man. Miraculuosly, he had survived his ordeal and recovered enough of his strength to leave. It was he who had given her all the bric-a-bracs he saw in the living room in appreciation for the return of his health.

"He was a true gentleman," she concluded, and in a way signaling the end of the conversation, she left the room in exaggerated anger.

"I thought Uncle Joe was your husband," Adolfo asked her as she left the room.

Either she didn't hear Adolfo or she chose to ignore him. Regardless, she didn't answer.

He could take any abuse without showing emotion. The only thing that had upset him recently had been losing the beer joint. But aside from that he was used to defeat. He had learned many years ago that, if you live as a dependent, you don't accumulate privileges. He was used to people talking about him in front of him, being served last, served smaller portions, to sleeping wherever anyone told him to, to wearing hand-me-downs, to drinking warm beer, and hitching rides. He had not had the genuine love of a woman in many years, more years than he cared to remember.

Antonia was good to him. She had shown him not only her enormous breasts, but treated him with some respect, had paid some attention to him. He felt a little piqued at himself at not being able to be himself around the children. He could have impressed them, he thought. But that was not his nature.

He slept on the sofa that night. She had given him a quilt and a pillow. She was still feigning anger. She knew Adolfo didn't believe her Uncle Joe story. She was more angry at herself, though, for not having had a good lie prepared beforehand. She should have anticipated that Eloise would bring it up, bitch that she was.

In the morning he could hear the subdued voices in the kitchen. He could see the three moving around in the kitchen, though the drape hung across the door sill. He could hear the children eating breakfast and Antonia walking back and forth from the stove to the table. It was an awkward situation for him. He knew he was better off staying in bed and, yet, he didn't know whether he was expected at the table. He decided to stay under the covers. He had taken his trousers off under the covers with a lot of difficulty, considering how tight they were and how sore he was. He knew it would be hard to put them back on without making much noise. The coat and tie and shirt and vest he had placed on the table beside the sofa. He had placed the bric-a-brac under the table neatly. He had slept with his teeth in place. He would have thought it embarrassing if anyone, especially the children, had seen them on the table. So he stayed in bed clicking his teeth gently and allowing his mind to float in a neutral state. Subconsciously, though, he knew they were whispering about him.

When he was sure the children had left for school, he began the heavy task of putting his pants on while still under the covers. When he was through he flipped the quilt off and sat by the side of the bed, his long thin thighs almost pointing upwards. Antonia came in and greeted him. She was in a better mood. She had coffee ready for him.

"About last night," she began. She sounded apologetic.

"What happened?" he asked, surprised. He felt that she did not owe him an explanation. That went with being an *arrimado*. No one owes you an explanation about anything.

"Uncle Joe was not an uncle. He was a man that lived in the neighborhood. When his wife died, he was left with no one to take care of him. His children were all gone. After his wife's funeral, the children said good-bye and left him. He had expected for someone to take him in, but no one said anything. The children felt, Uncle Joe told me, that he had more than they and that he would be more comfortable staying at his house. He did have a little pension, but that was all. I could tell by looking at him when he walked by the house that he was losing weight. It bothered me. So one day, I went by to visit him." She sat down by him with a cup of coffee of her own. "I went into the kitchen and I found out why he was losing weight. The dishes had not been washed. The stove was filthy. He was eating salt crackers and water. The house was filthy. I went back the next day and started cleaning up. He was grateful for me. I started taking care of him. Naturally he gave me his pension check for me to cash. He gave me money." She stopped here to see what reaction Adolfo had. "He didn't give me much. But soon I figured I was spending too much time at his house, working, cleaning. You should have seen the floors. So I moved him over here with me."

"You did the right thing. You were very kind," Adolfo said. He wished that he could get up and go to the bathroom to urinate. He needed a shave and a bath. He wondered where his suitcase was. He hoped Maria had packed his underwear.

"Do you honestly think so?" She was surprised Adolfo agreed with her.

"Yes."

"I'm glad you agree, because the children didn't. That's why Eloise was asking all those silly questions last night. They resent anyone being here. They love me so much that they're jealous of anyone I meet."

"I could tell that they were not in a good mood."

"You could tell? I knew you could."

"And where is Uncle Joe?"

"I put him in a state hospital for old people. But I still see him once in a while, whenever I need to. I still handle his affairs. His check comes to me. I buy him whatever he needs. He doesn't need much, but the check isn't much, either. I keep the house rented. He really appreciates me."

"I've got to go," Adolfo said, a look of pain crossing his face. He had not heard much of the conversation.

"Where?" He had caught her by surprise.

"To the bathroom."

"Oh," she said, relieved.

"If you'll tell me where my suitcase is."

"It's behind the sofa."

While he was taking a bath, she opened the door to the bathroom quietly and stood there watching him. Adolfo sensed someone in the the room and turned to see her. She opened up her top and walked toward him. He had a terrified grin on his face. He wasn't sure what she would do. She grabbed his wet head and massaged her giant breasts round and round with his face. He quickly lowered his nose between the breasts. He had learned quickly from yesterday's experience.

"You want your momma?" she asked. She was trying to be coy, but she was much too rough for that.

From between her breasts and from what sounded to be the inside of a tin can came his reply: "Yes."

Nothing happened, of course. He was too old and his preoccupation with his age and his sexual performance made it even more difficult. "It'll take time," she said, "but I'll fix you up."

He hoped she could.

He stood dripping wet on the tub for an instant. Then he decided he might fall, as his equilibrium was not what it used to be. So he held on to the sides of the tub and crawled out. His paunch was greatly exaggerated by his thinness. His long skinny legs came up like two rubber tubular appendages interrupted by the bulges at the knees and ended somewhere inside the fold of his belly. From behind, his buttocks were very small, so that side-ways his back seemed to descend down to his feet. The once taut and lithe muscles were like a mixture of flour and water. Age, inactivity, and gravity had taken its toll. He seemed like he would have to stand on his head to get everything back in place.

She brought him some clothes that belonged to Uncle Joe. She had no more use for them. As she had walked in, he quickly covered himself with the towel. "Take these and try them on," she said and without even looking, turned back and left. He wondered if she were disgusted with him. After all, he knew, a woman like her that has been around and not satisfied usually becomes very hard to live with. It may be the one thing that would make him unwelcome. Not that the children didn't feel that way already. At least he could deal with the children.

He tried the clothes and they were a decent fit. Apparently Uncle Joe had been a tall man, but he had been stouter. He had left behind for some reason or another a fairly good pair of trousers, but again they were heavy wool that itched when he sat. She had brought several shirts. These were all cotton and at least he felt better around the chest than around the legs. There was no coat and it bothered him. Maria had packed his underwear and socks and one old shirt, plus his shaver. A shaved man was a decent man, he had always heard.

That day after breakfast, they had gone walking around the neighborhood to be introduced to Antonia's friends. He met the neighbors on either side. One was a widow lady that was, in his estimation, less than four feet in height. He had only seen someone smaller in size in a circus in Mexico. The circus had called her a freak of nature and she could be seen lying on an old lounge behind a glass pane. Antonia's neighbor was comparable in size. Her face was large for her body and her eyes were extremely wide-set and her nose was a short glob of flesh rounded at the tip. Her mouth was very wide. She appeared in good spirits, though, as if she had managed to live with her physical appearance and done quite well. She was so small that her every motion seemed exaggerated and very quickly done. Her small, short arms moved very fast when she spoke and she had the habit of trying to cross them when she was through speaking. This was impossible, because she didn't have arms long enough to cross and they fell limply to her side. Her breasts were huge for her size but not as big as Antonia's. She was very happy to meet him and she was properly impressed that he had played for the Yankees and the Cardinals, although she didn't seem to recognize the names. She had changed the conversation quickly and was more interested as to what he was doing there. He felt awkward and itchy as he heard Antonia tell the story of her cousin Adolfo and the chance encounter on the bus. She changed the story just enough to make him think that she had given the story more thought. *He* had recognized her, she said. The dog came up to them and sniffed around their crotches and Antonia shoved him away. The dog only came up to the neighbor's waist and, to Adolfo, he wasn't a large dog. The small lady had unconsciously placed one hand in front of her and one behind as she spoke and the dog sniffed at her. She did have a beautiful back yard. She had bordered the yard with neatly trimmed ligustrums and in front of them she had planted red creeping geraniums.

The other neighbor was married but separated from her husband and she spoke of him as if he still lived there. She was happy to meet Adolfo and she knew a little more about baseball than the other lady. She had had a brother who umpired in the city leagues for many years until he developed tuberculosis and had lost one lung. Two other younger sisters and the tuberculoid brother lived with her. The brother was not contagious, she volunteered, just in case Adolfo might want to befriend him. She was as tall as Antonia, but very heavy. From inside the house he could hear an argument and the dog who had followed them over lowered his tail and went back home. The neighbor and Antonia apparently didn't hear the commotion inside the house or, if they did, they were ignoring it. Antonia had the lady engrossed in her story about their encounter on the bus. He couldn't help but be distracted by the argument going on inside. And when the noise grew louder, he could tell that the obese woman was beginning to concentrate more on the argument than on Antonia's story. The neighbor started looking back toward the house and he noticed that she was becoming irritated at the noise. Before anyone could run out of the way, the kitchen door blew open with great force and banged against the house. Next to come out flying was a thin frail man who Adolfo instantly surmised to be the tuberculoid brother. He flew through the air in a crucified posture and landed on his face. Behind him, a large woman, larger than the newly acquainted neighbor, came running with a cast-iron skillet in her hand. "You ate my breakfast," she screamed. "You son-of-a-bitch, you ate my breakfast!" She was on top of him before he could get to his feet. She raised the skillet and was about to hit him when he cried out, "I didn't know. I didn't know. I thought you had eaten already. Please," he implored, "please let me go."

The woman who had been talking to them ran swiftly to the scene and started cursing the both of them. "You two dumb son-of-a-bitches. What's your problem now?"

"He ate my breakfast," she shouted, still holding the skillet ready to strike. "I ought to kill him. The no good bastard. Son-of-a-bitch," she added as an after thought. Then, "mother fucker."

"That's enough," the new acquaintance screamed. "You can't kill him. Did you eat her breakfast?" she asked the downed man.

"Yes, but it was a mistake." He was begging for his life.

"A mistake?"

"Yes," he pleaded.

"And the other day when you ate Cristina's food . . . you said that was a mistake too."

"Yes. And it's the truth! Get her off me, please. I can't breathe!"

Cristina came out running. She was bigger than the other two sisters. "He did it again?" she shouted. She was running to her brother. "Did he do it again, the son-of-a-bitch? Did the goddamn son of a bitch do it again?"

"Yes, again," the woman on top of him said.

"Well, hit the son-of-a-bitch! Kill the bastard."

The older sister grabbed the skillet and took it away from her sister. "You always took up for him," the woman said as she rose to her feet. Cristina was jumping in circles around the brother. "Kill the son-of-a-bitch!" she yelled.

"I'll protect you this time," she said, angrily pointing a crooked finger at the man. "But if you ever do it again, I'll let them kill you."

He stood up and dusted himself off. By this time, the three women had gone inside. Then a hat came flying out the door and landed by his feet. "Take your goddamn hat and don't come back until tonight," someone said from inside. He strode along briskly, dusted his hat, not showing any signs of the defeat just handed him. And he walked with the peculiar side-ways caved-in angularity of his upper body, the result of the cavity left behind when his lung was removed. Adolfo and Antonia, who had not moved during the entire time, looked at each other and she shrugged, "They're like this all the time. When it's not the three sisters against their brother, then it's the sisters against each other."

Adolfo looked over to Antonia's house and the only movement he could see was the dog's tail as he moved it rapidly from side to side. He was a smart dog, Adolfo thought.

Later that night, after a supper he had had to endure with the children, when he and Antonia sat on the porch, they saw the three sisters dressed in black wearing shawls over their heads walking by the house on their way to Rosary and the Stations of the Cross.

It was odd to him that Antonia didn't try to explain her strange neighbors. "That's the way they are," she said. "They've been fighting among themselves, since I can remember. It's a blessing too, because when they quit fighting among themselves, they start on someone else. They beat up Uncle Joe one day, just because he cut across their yard on the way home. Even Blackie, the dog, got caught up in that fight. He's never liked them since. Poor Uncle Joe never knew what hit him. But they're okay, if you side with them. They've never bothered me, yet. The children hate them. They've wanted me to move out of here because of them, but I don't mind."

The other odd thing to him was how quiet he had become. He had not been given the chance to say much. This was obvious when the children were around. They took over the conversation and, whenever he tried to join in, they quit talking or attacked him with a vengeance. Even when he was alone with Antonia he wouldn't say much. It seemed like his mind was drying up. She, in turn, seemed to open up more while he was alone with her. In her children's presence she was content to stand back and let them have their say. Eloise was becoming a more dominant force in the household. She could manipulate her brother easily and, once she had him on her side, the mother surely followed.

One evening after supper, Adolfo had tried to tell them about the correct way to round the bases. "You should step on first with your left foot. This allows you to turn toward second base by swinging your right leg across first base. That way your turn is tighter and you don't lose time."

"Who cares?" Eloise asked. "No one here will ever run around the stupid baseball field. Will you?" She looked at her brother, giving him a wink.

"No," he replied, "I like basketball."

"Yes, *we* like basketball," Eloise said. "Don't we mother?"

She was sitting next to Adolfo. "Yes," she replied, a hint of resignation to her voice, "we like basketball. But don't you think your Uncle Adolfo is interesting?"

"He's more interesting without his teeth," she responded, viciously. Adolfo could see the hatred in her eyes.

"How do you know?" Antonia was a mixture of curiosity and feigned anger.

"I've seen him asleep without his teeth and his mouth looks like an asshole."

The brother jumped up laughing and banging the table. The daughter rocked back in her chair, throwing her head back in uncontrollable laughter. Antonia at first raged, then slowly changed her mood and started giggling. "What a bad girl you are, Eloise. You should apologize to your uncle."

"I'll apologize when he apologizes," she said. She was still on the verge of laughing again. Her brother had gone into the living room and was still laughing, rolling on Adolfo's bed.

"Adolfo, apologize for what?" Antonia asked her.

"For being here," she replied. And as she said the words her whole countenance changed and fury came to her eyes. "And for sleeping with you. You two old farts."

From the big room the boy started the hysterical laughter again, stomping his feet and hitting the sofa with his hands.

In the morning he was awakened by Antonia throwing plates across the table, a sure sign that she was still irritated by the children's behavior. He felt good to think that she was siding with him, or at least respected him enough to feel that the children should treat him with some courtesy. He could hear her saying something in a loud whisper, but he couldn't hear the children answering. He was staying in bed again for fear of facing them early in the morning. He checked his toothless mouth to feel what it felt like. Surely not an asshole, he thought, even though he had a small mustache.

After the children left, he could hear voices coming from the neighbors. He thought that they must be at it again. Then he heard Antonia scream and run out the kitchen door. He immdiately got up and dressed quickly. He went to the door and saw that the three sisters had their brother down on the ground again. This time he saw blood. He could see it coming down the brother's forehead, over the bridge of his nose, and dripping to the ground. One of the sisters had hit him with something. He couldn't see very well at that distance, but it looked like a big board. They were standing over him and yelling obscenities. Antonia was trying to help him to his feet, but they kept pushing her out of the way. As the brother tried to get up this time in his lop-sided way, he was hit on the head again. Antonia screamed.

"You son-of-a-bitch," one of them screamed, "you used my comb! I saw you, you no good bastard." She was the one with the board. It was Cristina again. He could tell by her size.

A new bleeding place had begun, or else he had smeared blood to that part of his face while protecting himself.

From the periphery came the short woman, the other neighbor. She was running in a comical way, her short legs moving very rapidly under her skirt. Her forward motion was slow. Her short arms pumped in time with her legs and it seemed like her whole body was about to fall apart, limbs flying in all directions. She quickly threw her arms around Cristina, but they were so short that she couldn't hold on when Cristina shrugged her off with a twitch of her body. She landed beyond the scuffle. But quickly she was on her feet and jumped on Cristina's back. This time she had hold of her neck and Cristina couldn't get her off. She had the tenacity of a small dog. The more Cristina swung her around, the tighter she held on until Cristina, dazed by her revolutions, staggered and fell to the ground with the short lady stuck to her neck. Antonia in the meantime had verbally subdued the large neighbor. The in-between sister was still trying to hit the brother as he lay with his arms crossed in front of his face. Antonia said something to her that Adolfo could not hear, but she apparently said it with enough conviction that she stopped the fusilade of blows. Cristina was still struggling with the short neighbor. "Alright, you win. Turn me lose," she said to her short opponent. "You're killing me. I can't breathe with you around me. You're like a snake around my throat!"

The short one let her go and, surprising enough, to Adolfo at least, who was still watching the melee from the door, the brother got up, wiped the blood from his face and dusted himself off much the same as before. Adolfo had seen many men play possum before, but this man was a master at it. For all purposes, it always seemed as if he were being killed. But after the fight, he was the calmest one of the family. This time he left without his hat, or so Adolfo believed, but Cristina ran to the house and came out with the gray fedora and ran after him and threw the hat at him hitting him on the back of the head. He, in the instant of surprise, gave a little jump and covered his head with both arms. He turned around slowly expecting a rain of blows and wondered what had hit him. When he saw Cristina running back home, he picked up his hat and dusted it off, combed his hair back between his fingers and set the hat at a rakish angle on his head. Off he went in that peculiar stride, his upper body tilted to one side.

The whole thing ended as quickly as it had begun. By the time Antonia was at the door and saw Adolfo, the sisters had picked up their board and had gone inside.

He was to see many more of these incidents. If they didn't occur daily, at least they left the impression that they did. So frequent were the squabbles, in fact, that he had the temptation to set the date by a particular fight. "Last Wednesday," he would say to Antonia, "when they fought over the comb." Or "Saturday, when they fought over the egg." It did afford him a place of reference and it also imbued him with a sense that he was alive on a daily basis and that his life was not a maze of days grown together.

After a while, when the nature of the violence had rubbed off, he was able to enjoy seeing the four or the three or the two fight it out. Somtimes he could not see them, since they fought inside, but he could imagine what was going on when he'd hear the cursing, the dishes crashing about, and the furniture being tossed around. He wondered why the brother stayed, but then again, they wondered the same thing about Adolfo.

Antonia had written to Maria and told her that Adolfo was living under her care, a situation that she explained was to Adolfo's benefit. She also told Maria that they thought they were in love and that the only thing that could prevent their marriage would be that the children might object. She had Adolfo sign the letter also and he dictated a few words to Maria as a postscript. In the letter Adolfo asked for his veteran's check to be mailed to Antonia's address.

The fact that it had been two weeks and they hadn't heard from Maria or received a check didn't seem to bother Antonia. Adolfo, in turn, was relieved that she hadn't brought it up. He had been there now two weeks and he had not contributed very much for the household expenses. Sometimes, though, he would make a great show in front of the children and extract a worn bill from his pocket and give it to Antonia. "This is for groceries for the children," he would say. "Buy them some bananas."

"What do you think we are, monkeys?" the girl replied. The boy laughed. Then he flapped his arms like a chimp and made noises to make his sister laugh. The mother naturally laughed a little.

But that small amount of money he gave her was by no means covering his expenses. He was eating three good meals a day. Just how long the honeymoon would last, he couldn't say. He did know that she had big breasts and she loved to smother his face with them. There were days when he felt he couldn't survive, days when he felt he couldn't catch his breath among the mass of flesh and fat that were her breasts. He wondered sometimes, while trapped from both sides, if she thought he was enjoying this. No wonder Uncle Joe is in the hospital, he thought. If he hadn't been, he'd be dead by now. For the first time in his life, he was glad he hadn't smoked. A touch of emphysema would have done him in.

It became a ritual, this smothering. It occurred every day, or if it didn't, like the neighbors' fights, it sure felt like it. She grabbed him whenever the urge over-took her. She would throw her top open and grab his head with both hands and place him forcefully against her breasts. And for this she wants the check? he thought.

After three weeks he could now hold his breath for a long period of time. He also somehow felt better, more rejuvenated, youthful. Even the children noticed it and would say things to that effect, always snickering, of course. He took it as a compliment, for he knew that that was as close as one would come his way. The ruddiness to his face was actually due to the chafing the large breasts produced. The youngish look he attributed to the sebum, a skin oil being transferred almost daily into his face from the breasts, an oil he sometimes described to himself when down-under as smelling like curdled milk.

Not that she was a bad woman; in fact, he thought of her as someone who could handle herself in any situation and seemed to care about him, to boot. This led him to feel secure around her, except when the children were around. But he had grown accustomed to this feeling of inadequacy and knew it would wear off as soon as the children were out of sight. He thought about her more and more as a guardian, something he had never had. And if she had proposed to him, he probably would have accepted.

One day on their regular walk in the morning, when they had managed to get by their neighbors without experiencing any violence, she took him to meet the Professor, a run-down old man who urinated in a can and lived in Uncle Joe's old house.

"Adolfo was a baseball player. One of the best," she explained to the Professor after she had introduced them. "He played in the major leagues. Who for, Adolfo?"

Adolfo stretched himself out fully. "I played for the Yankees and the Cardinals," he said.

The Professor was impressed. He began talking of his career and he seemed never to run down.

Again Adolfo had met somebody who wouldn't let him talk. He cursed his fate for throwing him in these surroundings.

"I have come for the rent," Antonia said, finally interrupting his long conversation.

He was a small man and frail, enough so that most men would have feared hitting him for fear of breaking him in half. He had a long aquiline nose and thin lips and, from what Adolfo could see, he still had most of his teeth. He had been spared going to the dentist, he thought.

"I can see that you are still not using the outdoor toilet, like I told you to use. You'll use the toilet from now on, or I'll kick you out of here." Antonia was angry and apparently she and the Professor had argued about it before. This was all new to Adolfo. He felt odd in their presence. He hoped the Professor would agree, so that all would be forgiven.

"All right," the Professor responded. "It's not that important to me." He reached into his pant's pocket, counted his money and gave her the money. "Here," he said, holding the money out to her without looking at her.

So this was the Professor he had heard the children talk about. The man did not appear to be the ogre the children had painted him to be. Apparently he had lived with Antonia much like Adolfo had been doing. He was a strange man, according to Antonia, but to Adolfo he seemed more like a lot of friends he had had.

It had been a month before the first check arrived. Maria had scratched out her address and had, in very crude writing in pencil, printed Adolfo's new address. Adolfo noticed that the envelope had been tampered with and that Maria had partially torn the flap in order to see inside the envelope. She had always wanted to see the amount of the check and Adolfo wondered why, since it never had changed.

"This is for me," Antonia said, holding the check against her breasts.

"I'm sorry it took so long," he said. He knew the money rightfully belonged to her. "But Maria is probably angry."

"Why should she be angry?" Antonia asked him. "She sure sounds like a busy-body to me. What's the matter? Doesn't she think you can take care of yourself?"

They walked to a bank nearby and cashed the check. He had felt embarrassed at not writing his name clearly, but she didn't seem to notice. The bank was one of those small two-story buildings that didn't seem to have much security. Upstairs were the lawyers and notary offices and, as Adolfo noticed, the ever present dentist. The dentist had had someone draw on the window-pane a large mouth with huge white teeth. Antonia knew the woman teller and she introduced Adolfo as her friend, no cousin this time. "We need to cash his check every month here, so you'll be seeing us more often now.

In this section of the neighborhood were the small business places of every *barrio*. There were a few grocery stores, ice houses, professional offices and a mortuary, several restaurants, their fronts thick with old paint and greasey screen doors that opened at the sidewalk and that had the aroma of plate-lunch. These were the busy places, usually at noon, when workers in the area came and ate their *carne guizada* and rice and beans, or their *picadillo* and and *fideo* with rice and beans, or their *caldo de res* with beef and potatoes and cabbage and rice and, if you were a steady customer, a big spoonful of beans in with it. These were stick to the ribs, working-man's lunches, something you could burp all day afterwards.

As they walked past one of these restaurants, *El Imperial*, a man came out blowing his nose and wiping tears from his eyes. Adolfo had seen people like these that ate the raw *jalapeños* in their soup. Antonia had also.

"He looks like he just lost his morther," Adolfo said.

Antonia laughed. "You are funny sometimes," she said, stopping to look through the restaurant door. Then she thought a while and looked into her purse, a large black bag that hung from her shoulder. She moved the contents around and came up with Adolfo's money. "Let's eat out," she said, waving the money around. He followed her into the dark restaurant. It took a while to get used to the small amount of light. Then he followed her to a table. A waiter came and set a glass of water before each of them. She ordered the *picadillo* with *fideo*, or the ground beef with spices and vermicelli. He ordered the plate-lunch. He ordered a beer and she ordered tea.

That was the first beer he had had since living with her and it amazed him how good it tasted and how long he had been without one. He had noticed that she never drank or kept any liquor in the house. "It's bad for you," she said. So he had to make do without it. There were days when he could hardly stand it. Her first husband (first husband?) had been an alcoholic and had suffocated in his sleep. It probably had something to do with her breasts, he thought; surely it couldn't have been the liquor only. He would be more careful next time. As a matter of fact, she had only recently taken to smothering him again. She had quit as a punishment for his behavior around the children. But, about a week later, she had started again. She had jumped him as he lay on his sofa after the children were gone. It seemed to him that she had returned with greater determination and he wondered down there whether she actually was arriving at some satisfaction from the process. It had become for him more work than play. The chafing which had healed over during the absence of one week of mauling had returned almost immediately. The sallow hue that had returned to his face in that period had been lost in five or ten minutes of vigorous massage. One time he wondered what would happen if someone would make a movie of the both of them. He wouldn't have to worry about money anymore. That morning, she had caught him wihout his teeth and it had made it almost impossible to breathe. She was pushing his nose almost into his mouth. She never explained why she did this. He wondered if he had given her a subconscious suggestion that this was what he liked. Anyway, he thought, as he ate his meal and drank his beer, he was tired of it and yet he felt he was satisfying the woman to some degree.

The whole direction his life had taken seemed odd to him. In all his dreams he could have never imagined the set of circumstances that had brought him there. Surely if he had his pick, he would have been with his friends on the other side of town, drinking and playing cards or shooting pool or just hanging around the whores, poking fun at them. He wasn't unhappy and yet he wasn't satisfied. He felt he was wasting his time. But wasting his time on what? He had done plenty of that all his life. He was better off here than as a gardener or a bartender, which is really all he ever had been after quiting baseball. He had an itch to leave, but he didn't know to where. Maria would take him in, but it was too soon to return. His friends would be glad to see him, but would he wear out his welcome as he did in the Valley? He would stay, he decided, but only as long as he felt like it. He had another beer after the meal and Antonia frowned at him. He wasn't allowed to talk and now he couldn't drink.

"Don't you ever drink two beers in front of me again," she said as they walked hurriedly back home. She was strutting a half-step in front of him, her rear and huge breasts bobbing under her black dress.

She gave him no choice. If he agreed with her, he would never drink again and that was unthinkable. If he disagreed, he was out and with no place to go.

"I'm not giving you any money to waste on liquor." She was definite and she patted the bag strapped over her shoulder. She was a step in front now.

As they passed the Professor's house, they saw an arm poke out the window and pour a can of urine into the ground.

He was beginning to feel vague about his existence. He felt he was being treated like a child and an unwanted one at that. Not that Antonia didn't show her love for him in her peculiar way. He often thought of what he had done or said that made her so sure that she was satisfying him in some way. His face was a mass of debrided, flakey skin which fell on his suit and on his shirt like termites. It hurt just to touch his face. Shaving was becoming unbearable and there were times he thought he could smell fresh blood on his face. His eyebrows had dandruff, like millions of immovable lice clinging to the hairs. He decided to grow a beard, but the children made fun of him. He had not had a beer since the lunch at the restaurant. It was truly unbearable.

That he had placed himself in such circumstances still kept bothering him. He had thought about leaving, but it seemed everytime he did, she sensed it and smothered him in her giant breasts once more. He had to behave, he felt, or if not, suffer the consequences.

The children took him for granted now. Eloise, it seemed, had realized that he was ineffectual, or harmless to her mother and she more or less accepted him. Bobby did what Eloise said, so he was not much of a problem. They came from school late and ate and it seemed they went to their room and never returned. Once in a while Adolfo would ask Antonia for some of his money to give them so that they could go to the movies or walk to the drug store for an ice-cream cone. They took the money and, of course, this made him proud. It was the custom in those days for a visiting male to give the children money as they were introduced to him, just a nickel usually, sometimes a dime. The families were large and the man usually couldn't afford much more. It was a show of wealth of sorts and it ingratiated the hosts and made the visitor more at ease. He never felt he could give them enough, such was his desire to be accepted. He felt that if he could turn them over to his side and with Antonia's help he could live a good life, if only he could drink once in a while. Finally, in desperation, he told Antonia about an imaginary war wound that painfully flared up once in a while and that it required a shot of alcohol to relieve the pain. She took him to the doctor and he couldn't find a scar and Adolfo insisted it was internal. He told her about the insanity that ran in his family, of the need to drink to stay normal and she wouldn't buy that. She couldn't afford a psychiatrist, nor did she know of one, so she made her own diagnosis. She said he seemed sane to her. She was immovable when she felt in the right. She prescribed herbal teas for him. They would go to the grocery store and she would pick out the remedy from the tea rack. She concocted a special tea, *toronjil*, for his nerves; *flor de canela* for his complexion, which was getting worse; *anise* for the urinary tract; and *yerbabuena* for the mind and wound. She had him up at all hours of the night urinating. His urinary flow was such that he could be heard throughout the house even with the bathroom door closed. The children complained.

In the end he succumbed to the power of alcohol. He began by stealing his own money a little at a time from the great black womb that was her purse. She didn't miss it. He would walk by himself and buy hard liquor, *barreteada*, at the liquor store, and hide it inside his shirt. He started drinking at night alone as he lay on the sofa. When she complained about an odor in his room, he quickly went to the store and bought a bottle of liniment which he used to cover his entire body before retiring. He was careful to rub it around his mouth in the morning to protect his breath. The children, of course, objected. They imagined they carried the smell to school with them. "What's the matter with him anyway," they asked their mother as he slept on in the early morning. It was the war wound acting up she explained. She would talk to him about it.

His attitude changed for the better, now that he was drinking. He didn't feel as sore throughout his body. He could walk better, think more clearly, laugh and even talk more. If the liniment wasn't enough, his new outwardness helped the children dislike him more. They had been growing apathetic to him, but now they were openly contemptuous and he didn't seem to mind. The change somehow startled them, as if they realized that he had just been regrouping all this time for an assault on them and their mother. The words started to come to him as freely as before. He talked incessantly at the table before, during, and after the meal. He retold stories he hadn't told in years. His mind was back in gear and he even felt a twinge between his legs. He hadn't urinated so well in years.

In the morning when he awoke, he could hear the neighbors fighting again. He dressed quickly. He didn't like to miss the fights. By the time he was out of the house and standing at the property line trimmed with dwarf scraggled euonymous, the fight had come outside. All four of them were on the ground, but this time the brother was on the giving end. He and the two smaller sisters had Cristina down. Her huge bulk rolled under them whipping them up as she moved. They were hard pressed to keep her down. They kept yelling about an egg. An egg was missing! She had apparently taken it. He stood with his arms folded, a smile on his face. Just as suddenly as the fracas had started, it stopped. Antonia had joined him. From underneath the stack of people, he could see Cristina's angry face casting him a stare that would chill a man's heart. When she quit struggling, they instinctively let go of her and, noticing what she was doing, they looked up and saw Adolfo and Antonia.

"What are you looking at?" Cristina bellowed from underneath. "Don't you have anything better to do?"

"Has he been watching us all this time?" the older sister growled in anger. "Doesn't the son-of-a-bitch have anything better to do?"

"The goddamn bastard is just standing there looking at us."

Antonia grabbed Adolfo's arm and quickly turned him around and eased him toward the house. "Don't say anything," she murmured, "they'll jump on you."

He left the smell of liniment behind as he quickly entered the house. Antonia came behind him and closed the door.

"Who the shit does he think he is?" the brother said, holding his side. Cristina had rolled over his caved-in chest. "Who the shit does he think he is?"

"Sonofabitch," Cristina said, growling under her breath.

Just that small incident was enough to set them off against him. From now on, he couldn't step outside the house without one of them making some off-handed comment. "Look at him walking around the yard like he owns the place," he could hear them say. "He doesn't own shit. He's just a leech, a little worm sucking on her big tits, thinking he's a man."

It was distressing to him. He was used to being liked, or if not liked, at least ridiculed in a good-humored way. They made him nervous and Antonia was beginning to resent them.

The fight between them, Antonia and the neighbors, occurred when he wasn't even there. He had gone to get his *barreteada* and liniment and, as he walked by the house, one of them had called him an obscene name. Adolfo, in his customary gait, walked on by without saying a word, but Antonia heard them. She had come out running, seemingly fed up with their abuse and they met her in their yard. The short neighbor had gone in on Antonia's side and the fight was finally broken up by the police. By the time he returned, she and the short neighbor were sitting in a police car and giving their side of the story to the police. One large policeman, he noticed, was holding the neighbors at arms length away from the car. He had never heard Antonia curse until now. The short one was sitting crying and holding a wet handkerchief to the top of her head. Even the Professor was there peering into the car and making all knowing comments to himself and to anyone else who would hear him out. The police quickly shoved him out of the way and escorted him down the sidewalk. He kept moving, shaking his head. The smell of urine faintly flowing around him. The dog went to him, sniffed, sneezed and shook his head and ran back to his house. Adolfo was of no help. He tried to explain what had been going on, but the police wouldn't listen. The four neighbors looked at him and he could almost hear a growl, a primordial noise that indicated he would be next. The policeman stretched his arms toward them and waved them back. For the first time he noticed that Cristina had a hammer clutched to her paw like a gorilla holding a lollipop. He could have used a beer then. It seemed that all the neighborhood had gathered in the commotion. Everyone was talking simultaneously. The police car departed with Antonia and her faithful neighbor and he was left alone in the crowd of people he did not know. Disconsolate and afraid, he walked briskly into the house, peering back now and then to be sure he was safe. Once inside, he watched from the door as the crowd finally thinned out. Cristina and her family went in, grumbling. He could hear them laughing and calling Antonia a whore.

He had seen many fights at beer joints and in homes and countless other places, but this one disturbed him more than any one. How could someone live as they did? Usually, a fight was between two men over some form of injured pride. These people were geared for fighting from the moment they got out of bed. This he couldn't understand.

The affair with Antonia came to an end shortly afterwards. The children had been embarrassed and Antonia was rather cool toward him from then on. She had received a citation, and on top of that, had been placed under a peace bond. Her name had appeared in the papers along with the short neighbor's in the small print in the daily court records filed under the caption, "For Disturbing the Peace."

But that was not all. She had suspected something ever since he began using liniment and one night she caught him drinking in the sofa as he anointed himself. She had packed him and sent him on his way that night. She had never intended to marry him.

CHAPTER 4

The Professor's sparse furnishings had not afforded him a peaceful night's sleep. He had curled up on the floor on top of an old mattress that the Professor had gotten from a back room where it had stood behind an old unused refrigerator. The faint stench of urine still permeated the room. He had gone to the house as an exile from Antonia's well kept home and had entered into a world more to his liking. Had it not been for the burning light in the house, he would have never stopped. "Who is it?" the Professor had asked as Adolfo knocked on the door. The smell of kerosene had come through the door as he opened it. "What happened, dear friend," he had asked as he surveyed the tall gangly man at the steps, a suitcase in his hand. "They've run you off. And in the middle of the night. You must have done something terribly wrong. Maybe mashed one of those big tits." He grinned with the thought in his mind and held open the door.

"I appreciate this," Adolfo said, laying the suit-case down and nervously brushing his coat with his hands.

"Think nothing of it," the Professor responded. He was dressed in long cotton pajamas that reached to the ground.

He started to the back room and Adolfo followed him. "Take off your coat and tie and your vest. Let's have some coffee."

"I've got something to drink," Adolfo informed him. He went to the suit-case and returned with his bottle of *barreteada*.

And so began a friendship that would last throughout their lifetime.

The house was divided into two rooms. The larger room in front served as sleeping and living quarters. The small back room was the kitchen and the toilet. In the toilet was a commode as dirty as any one he had ever seen. There was a small shower crammed into one corner that had been stuccoed but never painted. The customary leak from the shower pipe was there and it had turned the floor of the shower white with its incessant dribble and had bored a small depression into the concrete.

The ammoniacal smell infiltrated the first room, blended in with the kerosene odor from a lamp the Professor used to read by. Amazingly enough, the smell did not float as a miasma into the back room. It just stayed in the front of the house. Thank God for that, he thought, for it would be hard to eat under those conditions. The refrigerator was disconnected and the Professor kept some books in it and other items that he felt the rats had a notion to eat. The sink in the kitchen had lost its glaze at the bottom. There was a yellow streak at its side that broadened at its base and continued into a fine line as it worked its way upward toward the faucet. It leaked also. A small table with two chairs served the two men for eating their meals. The front room had the Professor's bed, a rickety affair made of iron and Adolfo slept across the room on his mattress. He had found an abandoned nail on which to hang his clothes. Otherwise, he lived out of his suitcase. He found through desperation that a small amount of liniment dropped into the urine can did away with the odor. The Professor didn't object when he noticed the new smell and to Adolfo this made things more tolerable. And after all, he had use for the liniment now.

The next day they had gone to Antonia's and returned the clothes that she had given him, the clothes that had originally belonged to Uncle Joe. "Always return everything someone has lent you. Neither a borrower nor a lender be," the Professor had said, seriously, squinting his long thin nose, knowing that Adolfo would never figure out where the quotation came from. Antonia had dispatched them without a word, her huge breasts heaving in what they felt was an indication of her anger. She refused the clothes at first, but the Professor took them from Adolfo and threw them on the stairs.

As they walked past Antonia's neighbors, Cristina came out with a broom in her hand and made a sweeping motion toward them. "I'll sweep that sona-fabitch out of the way and his little friend too!" she said. They lowered their heads and quickened their pace.

The Professor, Manuel Garcia, was a native of Mexico. He had explained to Adolfo during their drinking bouts that he had taught primary school in rural Mexico for a short while and then decided to leave when a woman he was courting turned out to be married. "How was I to know?" he implored, as if Adolfo could help him, his small eyes intent on Adolfo. "The husband was never home. No one had the decency to tell me." So he left hurriedly, the husband in pursuit, taking only his clothes and the little money he had saved. He taught mathematics, Spanish — "the true Castillian," he explained — and spelling. He had not graduated from a university, that was for the sons of the rich. His basic secondary education had qualified him to teach the indigent, though, and he had done the best he could. In that period, because of loneliness, he had taken to reading and found that there was more to be learned from books than from classrooms and professors. He had left behind the small library he had accumulated. Once in the United States, he had taken all sorts of work from field-hand stoop-labor to shipping clerk, but he realized he could never advance beyond that so he made life so miserable for his employers that he was promptly fired from many jobs. Now retired, he subsisted on the social security that his naturalized citizenship entitled him to.

He thanked Roosevelt for that. He paid no allegiance, he said, curling up his eye-brows in a habit of his, to any country. No country he had ever lived in treated him with dignity. Here he would mention Mexico, the United States, Guatemala, Honduras, British Honduras and several more. Adolfo never knew which ones he would include in the list. He would lean back, his hands inside his waist band, waiting patiently to see if he had offended anyone.

In a few days Adolfo came to admire this small, hawkish man who wrinkled his nose and curled his eye-brows as he spoke. He had never been around an intelligent man before. His own ramblings took on less meaning and importance to him and for once he realized there was more to talk about than baseball and beer and liquor and whores. Not that the Professor didn't enjoy his stories. He was particularly fond of listening to Adolfo and the things that he had gone through in his career, for truly Adolfo had traveled much more than he and that interested him. In particular, he enjoyed the stories about Germany and the war. He wanted to know about how the war was fought and he would pour some more liquor in the glass and Adolfo would lean back on his chair in the small kitchen and regale him with the details of hand to hand combat. "The Germans were the finest and bravest soldiers the world has ever produced. And if it had not been for the Kaiser who in his ignorance tried to advance too fast, they would have won the war. If it had not been for us also, the French would not be free today. Now they were a sorry bunch, the French. Everytime they've had to fight, they lower their pants and point their ass to the enemy." The Professor would laugh and, starting this, he couldn't stop until he began a coughing fit. Adolfo would feel good. After all, a man of letters appreciated him. This was no beer-joint fool and he appreciated the audience, even though the Professor still urinated in a can.

"Why should I have to walk all over this house with all the stuff on the floor at night just to urinate in a receptacle, when I can do it right here from the bed?" It was a rhetorical question. It had no answer.

"I don't know," Adolfo responded. He knew that he was being set up. With the Professor, he knew that usually no response was best. Such was the respect he had for the man.

Adolfo had been without money for some time and one day the Professor convinced him to go see Antonia about his check. So, accompanied by the Professor, Adolfo went to see Antonia. At first they had thought she was not at home. They knocked on the door several times and only the dog came to greet them. They were careful not to walk to the side of the house next to the mean neighbors, so they couldn't get to the kitchen door. As they were leaving, they heard the faint sounds of a conversation at the other side of the house. Antonia was talking to the little short neighbor, her little flipper-like hands folded above her breasts. The short neighbor was saying something and was emphasizing by pointing her short square finger upward toward Antonia's face. Antonia appeared stern, and not in a very good mood. As Antonia saw them coming toward her, she dismissed the neighbor hurriedly and walked toward them. As she left, the neighbor said, "Good morning" to Adolfo. He returned the greeting.

"What brings you back?" asked Antonia. He was sure she wasn't going to take any foolishness from him today. It scared him, but he got up enough courage to ask for his money.

"It hasn't come in. But when it does, you can have it. But I'm going to have to take out something for the lawyer."

"What lawyer?" He looked at the Professor, but received no encouragement. The Professor was looking down at his feet and shifted his weight between them. His eye-brows were wiggling nervously.

"The lawyer, my good friend," she said fuming, "that had to go to court with us. The lawyer, my friend, that got us out of all the trouble you got us in."

"I'm sorry," he said, "and I understand. I think it's only fair for me to help pay for that."

"You're not only going to help," she replied, "you're going to pay it all."

"I understand." That's all he would say. He didn't realize it had gone that far, that he had caused so much damage. "How much is it going to be? I'd just like to know, just to plan what I can spend. I need to give the Professor here some money. I'm broke, you know."

"It's going to cost one hundred and fifty dollars." She said it so emphatically that he didn't question the amount. Mentally he had already been prepared to pay more. Afterwards, the sum did appear to him to be steep. Even the Professor, who had no regards for money, thought it was excessive. "From now on," she continued, "you will go with me to the bank and you will cash your check and give me fifteen dollars a month for ten months. Since your check is for twenty-nine dollars, you will have fourteen dollars to live on a month. Maybe that way you can control yourself and that drinking habit of yours. I also ought to charge you for the sofa. It smells so bad I'm having to air out the room all day long. The children didn't want to use it anymore and, to think, it was their favorite studying place before you came." He felt guilty about this, of course, and shuffled his feet as an act of atonement.

As she tried to walk between them, the Professor quickly reached out and touched her breasts. She swung around as quickly as a spring and hit the Professor a shot on the ear that made it ring for days. At first he complained about the numbness to the side of the face and Adolfo had prepared some hot olive oil patches. The following day the ache started and he was barely able to chew. "Always duck after you touch," he remonstrated to Adolfo.

The first check after the fracas arrived and Antonia came by one late morning and took him to the bank. The Professor walked behind them. Antonia refused to walk next to him. He spoke to them from this rear position and Adolfo was the only one to answer. Antonia had been furious when the Professor insisted on going with her and Adolfo. She felt, and rightly so, that his interference would only lead to some kind of trouble. The Professor had said he was going anyway. He needed to cash his check also, and didn't Antonia want to be paid the rent he owed?

"This is a free country, my dear woman," the Professor said. "If I want to go to the bank, I can go to the bank and no one can stop me." His long thin nose had moved slowly up and down, causing that characteristic movement of his eyebrows.

"You can go wherever you please," she answered, acting like she would give him the back of her hand, "but not alongside of me."

"Let's all go together as friends," Adolfo said, stepping between them.

"We'll go together, but not alongside each other," she reiterated. "I won't have him next to me. He'll never touch me again, or try to. I'll slap you harder next time. I'll hit you so good I'll cross your eyes!"

"Forget the eyes," the Professor said remembering the pain, "just don't hit me on the ear. I still have trouble hearing out of it."

"You deserved it. Just keep your hands to yourself. I won't put up with you anymore."

"He's harmless," Adolfo said. "You don't have to hit him anymore. I think he's learned his lesson."

"That's how well you know him," said she. "I've never known anything to stop him. I'm just warning him right now that, if he tries anything, I'll hurt him." Her breasts were moving rhythmically as she breathed the fire that was in her.

He wondered what had attracted him to her, what he had seen in her. She was a well proportioned lady and her appearance of reticence at the bus station had been, he surmised, just a momentary slice of boredom. She had been peaceful on the bus. And she had fooled him then, appearing at once innocent and lady-like. How she had changed, especially since he had moved out. He saw in her more fire and determination than he had ever seen in a woman, and for someone of her physical stature, since she wasn't a small woman by any means, she presented an awesome figure. Her face in particular was very handsome, her features chiseled as they were, without a wrinkle, but in her anger she acquired a demoniacal intensity that frightened him. He was, after all, a man of peace, of live-and-let-live, of *status quo*.

The Professor, on the other hand, enjoyed bringing out those qualities in her that made her bile rise. Adolfo had cautioned him after she gave the Professor the blow to the ear and the Professor had agreed to let her be, but here he was at it again.

Once inside the bank, Adolfo noticed that Antonia not only had his check but several others. One, he presumed, belonged to Uncle Joe. The other checks he could see were for a man named Gutierrez and another one to an Hernandez, plus she had her own and her first husband's check. Then there was his check and the Professor's rent money that the Professor had counted out to her before she made her deposit.

She came from the teller's and counted out fourteen dollars and gave them to Adolfo. At the far end of the bank a woman was complaining that the Professor was standing too close behind her in the line.

"The trouble with these women, Antonia especially, is that they like me but won't admit it," he told Adolfo, later, as they sat in a tavern.

"The trouble with you," Adolfo corrected him, pulling on his beer bottle, "is that you smell like urine and you won't take a bath."

"The trouble with you, Adolfo, is that you smell like linimint, like a dying horse."

Adolfo laughed. It was true. It had not been like this always. He had dressed well and smelled well during his prime. "Our trouble," he said, philosophically, "is that we have no one to clean up for."

The Professor thought for a while. He stripped the wet label off the beer bottle with a long thin finger. "I'll tell you what, my friend," he said, finally, "tomorrow we will clean up and dress up and we'll enjoy the small amount of money we have."

Together they had eighty-nine dollars. Adolfo had thirty-seven and the Professor, fifty-two. They counted their money out on top of the Professor's bed and divided it up in half. The Professor kept the extra dollar.

"This is for a tip," he said, about the extra dollar, rubbing his hands in anticipation.

Adolfo had showered under the water pipe in the small vestibule and had put on his old suit and vest and shirt. The tie was left dangling loose from both sides of his open frayed collar. He almost looked debonair. He was wearing leather shoes, the same ones that had given him trouble walking and the ones he felt were responsible for his bunions. He had combed his thin hair over to the side and had cut it square against his head with a sharp pair of scissors.

The Professor had showered also and had dressed in a black suit that had been hanging on an iron hanger behind a bedspread next to the shower. Adolfo had not seen it before, so well had it been hidden. He wore a short-sleeved print shirt buttoned at the neck. He also sported a pair of old cowboy boots that he had hidden under the bed.

"Where did you get the boots," asked Adolfo. He couldn't remember seeing them.

"They're from my younger days, comrade," he said. "They're old, but good. I don't like to wear them often," he said, turning the boots from side to side admiringly. "They hurt my feet. God never intended for Mexicans to make boots, but they look good. Whoever invented the boot, and I'm sure it was the Spaniard, never had to walk far in them. The Indian was smart, he invented the *huarache*. Those things you can walk on forever."

He stood up from the bed and admired himself. Although he wished he were taller, he still felt that he was a handsome man. At least his head was well proportioned in relation to his body, he thought. He had seen some short men with huge heads and they looked grotesque. He was, he thought, well proportioned, except he was short. Adolfo, on the other hand, was tall, maybe six-three, six-four. There was about a foot of difference between them. Naturally the men in the neighborhood had taken to calling them *los cuates*, the twins, as a form of derision.

By the time they arrived at the bar, the regular drinkers were in their places, mean looking men, some of them, with black mustaches in undershirts with cigarette packs rolled up their sleeves, sweaty men who wouldn't look clean no matter how often they washed, their hair pasted down with Four Roses Brilliantine with the sweet sickening smell of a funeral wreath. You could almost tell what they did for a living by looking at their hands, and smelling their bodies, the carpenters with the blood blisters under their finger-nails, and a phalanx missing from the fingers smelling of pine. The mechanic (the one who washes and never looks clean) with the greasy hands and neck who smells like cup grease and varsol, the meat-packer with reddened hands that are missing the whole finger and smells like old, spoiled hamburger meat, the body- and paint-man with colored nails and knuckles who smells like thinner and tac-rag, the barber with delicate hands and a pendulous belly that smells of talcum powder with little short hairs stuck to the fabric of his shirt, the painter with his colored hands and shoes that smell of turpentine, the plumber with burned hands and crooked fingers that smell like standing water, molten lead and burning okum.

The smells had permeated the large room like a sheet of vapor that one could almost see. And although there was a breeze with the doors and windows opened, these odors, intermingled with the smell of stale beer, stayed as if locked into the atmosphere.

They found a place to sit next to the window after exchanging greetings with several of the men. Adolfo and the Professor knew almost everyone by name and they got along well with the men. Adolfo was very popular; after all, he had lived in Los Angeles before and had acquired a reputation as a bon vivant and beer drinker without equal. Someone made a remark about being careful with two men living together and they had a good nervous laugh. (What if they were homosexuals?)

They hadn't finished their first beer when an argument started. They were too far to one side to see who was involved. The crowd had gathered around the bar and obstructed their view. It didn't amount to much and the crowd dispersed. Not that the crowd wanted a fight; on the contrary, they were there to keep things from getting out of hand. No one really wanted a fight, for that would ruin the whole evening. And on top of that, there was a rule, unwritten as it were, that a bad fight would sour the place for a long time. The bartender was in charge and everyone, or almost everyone, respected him. When he said no more, that was it. He also had the power to injure anyone who wouldn't mind him. He was, in effect, the referee, and almost everyone went by his rules. Once in a while someone, a renegade, like *La Bruja*, would cause serious trouble, but he wasn't allowed back. Adolfo had seen plenty of those types of troublemakers. So the argument, as small as it was, was put down by the bartender. "Please, don't start anything in here," he said. "I have a business to run and it's no good for me or for you to get into any argument. Let's shake and forget it." He was amiable. And the two parties stood and they shook hands and had a beer together.

Much bad had been said about Mexican beer joints, but that was usually the way things ended. More times than not, the men arguing would wind up being friendlier than ever before, as if that act of aggression opened the way for their communication. It amazed Adolfo sometimes how often this phenomenon happened and it seemed that now he understood the psychology of the matter, although he couldn't put it into words. This is not to say that there weren't any fights, but they were rare. After a while everyone knew who was an untouchable, a fighter, and he was left alone. Even if this type insisted on fighting, usually no one would take him on and the bartender ended up running him off at gun-point. The law intervened rarely, usually represented by Anglos who didn't care what happend to the Mexicans. They would show up after the fight or after someone was dead. By that time there was no one at the scene, save the bartender. He usually knew nothing and he was closing up.

The idea was to have a good time away from home, not to fight. The conversation was nothing startling, but consisted of daily happenings, gossip and such, and it passed the time: work-a-day stuff, death, births, visits, neighbors, whatever came to mind. The weather was prominent among the old timers. They spoke of how hot it was, or how cold it was, how dry it was, or how wet it was. Things were just never right with the weather.

"This year is the wettest year since I moved here," one old man would say. "It's wetter than last year," his neighbor would reply. "There's no doubt about it. I've said it before, but this is the wettest year yet."

One old-timer asked Adolfo it it had rained in the Valley and, not having been there in several months, he replied he didn't know. "But it doesn't rain there much anyway, does it?" he was asked. "No, it doesn't. It didn't rain there for six months one time."

"I knew it," the old man said, looking at his neighbors. "What did I tell you. Whenever it's wet here, it's always dry in the Valley."

The Professor eyed the two old men sitting next to them. When their conversation on the weather was exhausted and they both looked away from each other, he intervened. "Do any of you two know who this man is?" he asked, pointing to Adolfo.

"No, sir," they said, eyeing Adolfo for some faint hint of recognition.

"This is Adolfo Arguelles, the famous baseball pitcher from the Mexican leagues."

Adolfo felt uncomfortable. At least, the thought went through his mind, he could have mentioned the Yankees and the Cardinals. Why start out so low? He was sure he had emphasized to the Professor that these were his major league teams. The Professor didn't seem to care. One team was as good as another.

"No, we never heard of him," one of the old men said. "Have you?" he asked his companion.

"No," he replied. "But I've never been to a baseball game. Never had the money."

"You should have gone," the Professor said. "Especially if Adolfo Arguelles, the great, was pitching. It is said," he lied, "by many who know, that he was the greatest fast-ball pitcher who ever played. Who else did you pitch for, Adolfo?"

He was truly uncomfortable now at hearing his own words, spoken strictly in confidence to the Professor, from the Professor's mouth. "I played some for the Yankees and Cardinals," he replied. He combed his thinning hair back with his hand in a nervous gesture. He hadn't been prepared for the Professor's out-burst.

"The Yankees are from where?" the old man asked, adding to Adolfo's discomfort.

"They're from New York!" the Professor shouted.

"Oh," he answered and turned away. After a while he said to his companion, "It'll probably be dry next year *and* very hot."

"Yes, hot and dry. I'll bet it'll be hot and dry."

"That usually happens after a wet year here. I've never seen it be wet two years in a row."

The Professor looked at Adolfo and shrugged. Then suddenly he looked up above Adolfo's head and Adolfo turned around in his chair. There behind him was a large fat man silhouetted against the sun-light and he couldn't make out who he was.

"Adolfo?" the large man asked.

"Yes," he replied, shielding his eyes from the light.

The man came around to the other side of the table and Adolfo recognized him instantly. It was Francisco Garcia, Pancho, as he was called. He had gained a lot of weight so that his small nose barely fit in his face and protruded like a small ball. His once thin lips had become fleshy and tumescent. His eyes were still dark and flashy and jerked around inside the lids like nervous mice.

"Pancno Garcia!" Adolfo cried out. "What are you doing here?"

"Had to bring the wife over to see her aunt and I thought I'd drop in here to see what's going on."

Adolfo quickly introduced him to the Professor. "Manuel Garcia," he said, "my friend."

He sat down with them and ordered a beer. Adolfo and the Professor ordered another one also.

"What are you doing here, Adolfo?" He was surprised to find him in this neighborhood.

"I live close by now. Manuel and I share a little house. You're welcome there anytime."

"And when did you leave the Valley?"

"About three months ago. I decided to leave. There was no future there for me. Things are slow there right now."

"And how is Maria?"

"She's fine."

"Is she still as mean as ever?"

"No. Maria is not mean. She can be hell sometimes, but never mean. Not intentionally," he corrected himself.

"She could be awfully mean sometimes with me when we were young. Remember?" He winked at Adolfo. "Adolfo and I grew up together," he told the Professor. "We were pretty wild in those days, weren't we?"

"Yes, we were. Those were the good days."

"And why hadn't you come to see me?"

"I haven't had time. I lived in another house for a short while and the moving around . . . I just didn't have time. And your family?" he asked, trying to get the conversation away from that vein.

"They're doing alright. We could be doing better, but you know how it is. We're in good shape for the shape we're in. I've been doing fine, as you can see. Eating a lot of tortillas and beans. I've gained about fifty pounds since you used to live on the other side of town . . . . When you left for the Valley."

"You say your aunt lives here?" the Professor asked. He couldn't think of anything else to say. He was sorry he asked. It seemed the conversation was better left to the other two men.

"It's not my aunt," Pancho explained, "it's my wife's aunt. She was operated on her eyes last week and the wife wanted to see how she was doing."

"She's doing okay?" Adolfo asked him. They were all sorry that the conversation had turned to something serious.

"Yes, she's alright. She's going to need thick glasses, but she'll be able to get around." He said this rather quickly, so that maybe this would end the conversation.

"She'll do alright," Adolfo said, as if his saying it would make it so.

"She can already see some things."

Pancho looked at Adolfo and grinned, his globular head shaking slowly. "They still talk about you, Adolfo. I mean the men at the bar. Why did you leave? You seemed so happy there with us."

"Well, you know me. I went for a funeral and I just stayed. Maria was very good to me. I've never known a finer woman, even though I'm her first cousin. I think it means something when I say it. She has gone through a lot in her life. She treated me well and I stayed. You know how it is. One day went by and then another and, before I knew it, I had a bar in town and I was doing well."

"So why did you leave there?" He still couldn't understand the logic.

They had finished their beers and ordered another round. The bartender, a large man with huge hands and a bear-like frame, came over and silently placed the beers at the center of the table. He collected his money from a small stack of bills on the table and gave them their change. *"El Oso,"* the Bear, they called him and with good cause. He was law and order within those four walls.

"I left because there was nothing else for me to do," he said after the bartender had left.

"What happened?" He knew Adolfo well enough to know that there was more to the story than what he was being told.

"I lost the bar," he finally admitted. "My cousin, if you could call him that, forced me out. It was a shady deal."

"You got screwed," he said, emphatically, "you got screwed again."

"Yes, you could call it that. But part of it was my fault. I told them I was leaving, but then I didn't. In the meantime, this other cousin rents the place to my other cousin and I came back after being gone one day, just one day, and he had taken over."

"They screwed you good."

The Professor had heard the story, so he was listening patiently, curious to see if Adolfo had told him the truth. The story remained unchanged, so he figured it must have been so. The Professor was a man who didn't like to be fooled and on any new friendship he examined a man and questioned him, sometimes nonchalantly trying to set a trap, to see if he could detect a lie. So far, Adolfo had not lied to him, as far as he could tell. Who knows? For all he knew Adolfo could have been lying about his baseball days, about Maria, Isabel, Carmen, Jesus, the priest. The fact that the two old men that were sitting next to them didn't know who Adolfo was had made him a little suspicious, but now he attributed their ignorance to their economic station. There were people who never had been to a baseball game or anywhere for that matter. These were the type of people he complained about, as the priest did, who never knew anything about anyone. He had frequently said that the United States coud be at war and they wouldn't know who our enemy was. Their lives revolved around work and drinking and to hell with anything else. They would fight, though. Just give them a rifle and point them in the right direction. After all, he said, the most war-decorated race of people was the Mexican-American. It was hard to figure them out, he admitted. If they would only learn to read the newspaper. His thoughts were interrupted by a slap on the shoulder from Pancho. "Don't fall asleep old man," he said, "let's have another beer."

At closing time, the table was jammed with empty beer bottles. The bartender hadn't had time to pick up after everyone. Only a few people remained and Pancho was still going strong. Adolfo was wavering in his seat or so he appeared to the Professor. Adolfo thought he felt good. Pancho said something about some musicians he knew or he said something about some music he knew. Both could not hear well anymore. They saw him get up and felt a sort of uneasiness, as if the whole room had simply dropped and Pancho was left standing. Adolfo knew he was in trouble when he looked out the window and the window narrowed into a thin rectangle and then enlarged right before his eyes. He had been this drunk before. He didn't remember the last time he had urinated, but he was feeling a hurt around the neck of the bladder. He stood up to go and weaved his way around the chairs and table. He was self-conscious and he knew it and it embarrassed him to think that the other men were seeing him. The Professor followed him and staggered behind him.

They came back and sat down feeling the dull ache in their bottoms from having sat for six hours on wooden chairs. Pancho was drinking his beer and it nauseated Adolfo and the Professor slightly. The smell of his beer, their breath, the smell of beer spilled on the table, all the smells were starting to nauseate them. Someone started a car outside of the window and the exhaust from the engine wafted past them. The Professor lowered his head and tried to shut his eyes but the room started to spin. Adolfo stared blankly and kept his hands on the table to keep the chair from moving slowly up and down. He was conscious that his feet were on the floor, but he couldn't keep from feeling the sensation that his body was swaying. Pancho took a large swallow from his beer and they looked away. Adolfo tried counting the bottles on the table but they melted into each other and slowly separated in a nauseous illusion. His brain had had enough. He dreaded the night before him and the morning after.

While they had gone to the urinal, Pancho had gottten his friends, the musicians, together. "Let's go seranade someone," he said, as fresh as they had seen him during their first beer.

"Wha, wha, what about your wife?" Adolfo asked him. He tried to keep his slurs to a minimum, but he knew he was making an ass of himself. Better, he thought, than to go off serenading. He didn't think he could make it.

"He's, he's, he's right," the Professor agreed. "Your wife."

"She's used to this," Pancho said. "She'll sleep with her aunt. Let's go." He acted so gingerly and with so much enthusiasm that Adolfo and the Professor swayed back away from him, fearing he would slap them on the shoulder. That's all it would take.

They stood up and off they went. They piled into an old car with a leaky exhaust pipe: Pancho, Adolfo, the Professor, one man with a guitar, and one man with an accordion. Adolfo and the Professor would never recognize the musicians again. They appeared to Adolfo and the Professor like illusions, men with double heads and faces: four eyes, two noses, two mouths. One had a pencil mustache that looked like two worms lying side by side, moving up and down copulating. He spoke with a gentle lisp that brought visions of saliva drooling from his lip. The accordion player sat to the right of the Professor in the back seat and the Professor would look at him out of focus as he talked and then quickly he would close his eyes to keep fom vomiting. Then he would smell the exhaust inside the car and would open his eyes and look ahead at Adolfo. Now there were two Adolfos, his mind would tell him, and Pancho driving wih four arms and two steering wheels. The guitar player on his left held the guitar between his legs and he swore he had never smelled a guitar before, but he did that night, as if the damn thing had just been stained and varnshed, thinned with gasoline.

They serenaded Pancho's wife and aunt. They started off with "*Mujer Ideal*," then followed it with, "*Noche de Ronda*," then "*La Barca de Oro*" and finally "*Sin Ti*," while the Professor and Adolfo vomited behind the car.

Pancho's wife came out to the porch, insulted them, and told Pancho to come in and ordered the rest to leave. "I can't," he responded, ignoring the insult, "these are my friends and I have to take them home."

"Well, take them right now," she demanded, "and then come straight here. We've got to go. My aunt is not supposed to be disturbed."

"Maybe we can play a song about eyes," the accordion player said, "in honor of her surgery." He seemed satisfied with himself for having thought of the idea.

Adolfo and the Professor, feeling better, started to laugh from behind the car.

"There is no honor in surgery, you fool," the wife said.

"I was just thinking," the accordion player said. "It's nothing to get angry over."

"Play something about eyes," Pancho requested. "Can you think of anything?"

"*Green Eyes*?" the guitar player volunteered.

"No, her eyes aren't green.

"*Dark Eyes*?" he said.

"That's it!" Pancho cried out. "Play *Dark Eyes*."

"In what key?

"I don't give a shit about the key. Just play it."

"Listen, Pancho," the accordion player said, solemnly, "you don't have to talk to my friend like that. We're not here to be abused. We're here to entertain, to serenade."

"I'm sorry," Pancho said, "but what do I know abouь keys?"

The two musicians faced each other and the guitar player strummed a few chords and the accordion player played a few bars, repeating this over and over again. Finally they turned away from each other and got into the song and it was beautiful. Even the wife was crying. They heard a noise from inside and the wife rushed in and brought the Aunt out, although she couldn't see and they played the song again for her.

"I'll be right back," Pancho said and they hurriedly got into the car. Adolfo and the Professor had by now joined the crowd. As soon as the exhaust started soaking the car, the nausea began again. Pancho took a bottle of tequila from under the seat and passed it around. The Professor feigned a drink, but he was caught in the act by the accordion player. "Drink it man," he said. "It'll do you good. It'll keep you from getting a hang-over."

"Yes, because you'll never sober up," the guitar player said.

It was Adolfo's fault that they wound up at Antonia's house. Pancho had asked him if there were someone Adolfo wanted to serenade. The force and conviction with which he turned down the request made Pancho and the musicians sure he was hiding something from them. They refused to take them home until they were told who this woman was. Finally Adolfo relented, after turning backward and giving the Professor the eye. The Professor didn't say anything. He had the look of a drugged hostage seated firmly between the two musicians. The tequila was passed around again. Adolfo couldn't take anymore.

The house was dark and only the dog came out to greet them, at first barking loudly and then recognizing them, lowering his voice to a disapproving growl. They took their place by the bedroom window at the side of the house and began their repertoire.

After the serenade, the lights were not turned on. No one seemed to move inside. "Maybe she's a heavy sleeper," the accordion player whispered.

"Not her," Adolfo replied.

"Tell me something about her so we can play a special song."

"She has big tits," the Professor said, laughing, and they all started laughing gently.

"I don't think we know any song about big tits," the guitarist said as the laughter broke out.

Pancho was impatient. "Who the shit does she think she is? After all the trouble we've gone to." He turned to Adolfo and the Professor. "Are you sure we're at the right house?"

"Yes. I ought to know," Adolfo said, "I lived here a while with her." He thought for a moment that in his state he might indeed be at the wrong house. He remembered the dog. He had to be right. All eyes were on him. "Let's go to the other side of the house and see."

They went to the other side of the house, the one with the kitchen door, and before Adolfo could stop them the musicians started to play. "Don't start," he whispered.

"Why not?" the guitarist asked, confused. "Is this a serenade or not?"

"Let's make sure first," the Professor said, walking over to the door and knocking gently.

No one answered.

The musicians started up again. Their original repertoire spent, they started with a polka, *La Playita*, a piece requiring considerable dexterity with lots of runs and arpeggios. It was impossible to play. They were too drunk. The guitarist started to laugh. Then the accordion player started to laugh also and quit in the middle of the piece.

"What's going on?" Adolfo whispered to them. They were doubled up in laughter.

"We can't play it," the accordionist said and continued to laugh.

Suddenly the lights next door came on. It was Cristina, the meanest one of the three sisters. "Who's out there?" she demanded.

"No one," the accordion player answered. "At least no one who would be serenading you."

"Just you wait and see," Cristina yelled. "You stay where you're at and we'll see what kind of man you are!"

"Let's get out of here," Adolfo pleaded, trying to hurry them away. "That woman will kill us all."

"He's telling the truth," the Professor said. "We'd better leave in a hurry." The accordionist didn't move. "No woman can scare me," he said.

"Me neither," the guitarist agreed.

"This one will," Adolfo said. "Let's get out of here." He didn't feel drunk anymore.

The Professor was already hurrying to the car. Adolfo was pleading with the three men to leave when Cristina, Inez and Margarita came out running in their night clothes. Cristina had a shovel, Inez had a club like a baseball bat and Margarita had a large cast-iron skillet. Seeing this, the men took off. The Professor was already safe inside the car. Luckily they didn't follow Adolfo and Pancho. They took off after the musicians, shouting obscenities. The accordion must have come undone, because with each running stride, they could hear a discordant squeal from the instrument. They could see by the street light the two of them running, the guitarist holding his instrument in one hand like a huge relay baton. They quickly started the car and went around the neighborhood looking for the musicians.

They found them a good thirty minutes later, sitting at the curb, gasping for breath. The guitarist had vomited between his legs.

"Who the hell was that?" the accordion player asked.

"Those are the 'Mean Sisters,' " Adolfo said. "How do you like them?"

"They ruined my accordion, the whores."

The guitarist still couldn't talk. He held his hand to his chest and rested on his guitar.

"I thought you said a woman couldn't scare you," said Pancho. "What do you say now?"

"They almost caught us," the guitarist said, shaking his head. "They almost, almost caught us. Sonofabitch!"

"She didn't scare me," the accordionist said. "She surprised me. I thought it was a bear coming at me with a shovel. Goddam, she is big. And tough. But what gets me is I tore my accordion."

"That can be fixed," the Professor said, "but not your head if she had caught you."

Pancho went to the car and brought out the tequila. They drank from it and for once it tasted good to Adolfo and the Professor. Pancho went behind the parked car and urinated. "Where do we go from here?" he asked.

"Nowhere," the accordion player replied. "I'm going home. You've got to take us all home. I've had enough."

"He's right," Adolfo said. "It's late and we need to get to bed."

"Adolfo's right," the Professor agreed. "Let's go home. We're all tired."

Adolfo was tired. He was not sober yet by any means and the tequila that had just been passed around had seemed to go directly to his brain. The Professor was beat. Adolfo had never seen him drunk before. It wasn't funny now, but they would laugh about it later on.

"But first," Pancho said, "we've got to finish this bottle." He passed the bottle around once more. "I can't keep it in the car. If my wife finds it, she may suspect that I've been drinking."

They all began to laugh. "Shit," Pancho continued, "the truth is, if I didn't drink, *then* she'd start to worry."

"That's what I was thinking. That sounds more like it," the accordionist said, laughing.

Adolfo and the Professor sat on the curb next to the guitar player. They had resigned themselves to drink the whole bottle.

A police car came by, but they waved at the officers and indicated all was well. "Just talking and catching up on the news and world events," the accordion player said to the police. Then they all began to laugh again. Adolfo had to clutch at his belly to keep it from hurting.

A string popped from the guitar and they started laughing again. It had made a funny twangy sound like a poorly played note and they had all stared at the instrument as if it had come alive. "I think she's trying to tell us something," the guitar player said.

"That's the way my pecker does after it's been strung out for a while," the accordion player said, and then again they started to laugh.

For the first time, the Professor realized what an enjoyable evening this had been. He was feeling a lot better, although his ribs ached from laughing.

Pancho farted several times and he made it into a staccato musical piece that lasted several seconds, lifting up his leg as the gas was passed. The accordion player had fallen backwards in laughter. Adolfo and the Professor were slapping their thighs. The guitar player was beating on the back of the guitar. Pancho kept up his little jig and danced around the car, first on one foot and then on the other.

"I can do that all the time," Pancho said to his laughing friends. "That's why they call me 'The Skunk' at work."

They couldn't control their laughter. The accordion player, on his back, was rolling from side to side, a painful expression of laughter on his face. The guitar player had gotten up and was walking stooped over, holding his stomach and dragging the guitar. Adolfo was bent over his long legs, his head between his knees, his arms crossed over his belly. The Professor had stood up and was leaning forward against the car, trying to keep from vomiting.

After a moment of silence, the accordion player began to make a sobbing noise, as if he were crying.

"Are you crying?" Pancho asked.

"Yes," he answered.

"But why?" they asked.
"Because I didn't know a song about big tits," he replied.
They started laughing again.

CHAPTER 5

To Carmen, life with Isabel had been a drastic change. She was used to not having to do anything for herself. Maria was possessive enough to insist that only she could do things right around the house. With Isabel, she learned quickly that she was responsible for her own room and would help clean the rest of the house. She had to do her own laundry and help in the preparation of meals. The two were alone now since the other boarder had left to get married. She had not been much company to either Carmen or Isabel. She had apparently come to San Diego to find a man and, having done so, she acted like her life had been fulfilled, as if she didn't need any more friends. She had stayed mostly to herself in her room while Carmen and Isabel talked.

All in all, Isabel was good to her. Carmen and Isabel realized that Carmen's ineptness was Maria's fault. She would give Carmen a stern look if she didn't clean up after herself and Carmen soon learned what it was she was expected to do.

She was not pregnant after all.

She found a job at a movie-house downtown with the help of one of Isabel's friends, Carolina, who also worked there. This friend, younger than Isabel, cleaned the theater and it was convenient for Carmen to ride to work with her. At least that was one worry out of Isabel's mind. She had feared that Carmen could not function in a large city, that she would have difficulty getting around. Carolina was friendly and loud. She spoke non-stop on their daily ride to and from work. She would make sure Carmen learned her way around town. Carmen had visited San Diego various times but now as an inhabitant, actually living in the city was exhiliarating to her. She couldn't understand it, but she felt like she belonged. There was an electricity to the air that made her feel more alive. She marvelled at the traffic, the constant noise in the streets that the old city dwellers took for granted. These were exciting times for her.

Her job was similar to her previous one. She sold tickets, made sure she had enough change, made sure she gave out the right change and, in general, all the things she had done before, except on a larger scale. In the Valley, she considered it a good day to have twenty people in the theatre. Here she was dealing with hundreds, sometimes a thousand people a day. She wondered where they came from, these people that could go to a movie in the morning, in the middle of the day. They were people like she had never seen before, mostly red-eyed men and women with liquor on their breath who either had not been to bed or had no place to sleep. Some were workers coming out of their late shift who couldn't go to sleep.

The theater itself was an old building that had been grandly decorated to simulate the fine movie houses of that day. The street entrance was framed on either side by two large red and gold barber pole columns. In the vestibule were the glass-case displays of still photographs taken from the movie being shown. Around the display cases someone had ordered pink tile glued to the stucco walls. The floor here was made of small blue tile with a type of white runway leading to the ticket booth.

One of the strangest and yet most humorous things that had happened to her was when a young man came to the booth, bought his ticket, looked over the photographs and then left. He never realized the movie was going on inside.

The lobby behind the entrance door reeked of mildew. The carpet was worn to the mat, especially at the two side entrances where people stopped to adjust their pupils before entering the dark cavern that was the movie house itself.

She had noticed a faint smell inside when the theatre was empty and had recognized it immediately as coming from a dead rat stuck somewhere in the walls. They had had the same problem in the Valley. Later, of course, with the theatre full, the smell intermingled with the people, the popcorn and the candy, and no one could tell.

One morning Carolina found a rat bloated with pop-corn stuck to the concrete floor in a corner. There was no way to tell if that one was the only one causing the odor. There would be others though and the lady stoically scraped it up with a dust pan and threw it behind the building.

The manager was a man in his late fifties or early sixties who nervously counted the house every spare moment he had. He was the type that trembled until they balanced at the end of the long day. Then he would thank her profusely, as if his job depended on her efficiency. He had had many bad experiences with ticket sellers, he would say. One had even taken off with all the day's receipts. She had spent three months in jail, he would remind Carmen in an off-handed threat. But she was different, he would say, wringing his hands nervously. Apparently he had had tuberculosis, for he walked slightly askew with his upper body angled to one side, as did the mean sister's brother.

The man could hardly fit in the booth with Carmen, but he insisted on helping her out when the lines grew long. He'd hold folded dollar bills between his fingers and make change for her, counting out the bills in the air and popping them to make sure they weren't stuck to each other.

She liked the man and, instead of making her nervous, he had a calming effect on her. She would consciously try to remain calm around the storm that was his nervous energy. He was married to a lovely and gracious lady who seldom interfered with his work. Carmen had met her the first week and saw her only on occasion when she came by the theatre on her shopping days. She spoke to Carmen and all the employees in a kind manner, as if secretly telling them that she understood, that she knew full well what her husband was like.

Even she, though, did not go into the projection room where the hated Marcos ruled. Not many people spoke to Marcos. He was abusive to the manager and no doubt the manager's wife knew about it. He had not said much to Carmen. He arrived on time and set up his projector and stayed in his room until quitting time. No one, not even the manager, could get in to see him.

Whenever a film would break or a splice would jump the sprockets, all that could be heard through the door were muffled sounds and the clanking of tools being picked up, used and replaced quickly. But no one was allowed in, not while he was there. The few times he would open the door would be to accept food or drink that he had ordered from Carmen, using an old pipe intercom that ran from the projection room to the ticket booth.

The manager had a key and after Marcos would leave, he would sneak into the room, turn on the lights and look around suspiciously, his nervous eyes darting about, but he could never see or find anything out of order.

No one realized it until later, when the county health authorities came by and arrested him. Marcos was an infectious tuberculoid and had been a carrier for several years.

The manager didn't contract the disease. He had built-in immunity, the authorities said. The older woman escaped the disease also. No one else got the disease, except Carmen.

Her letter to Maria was short and simple. She knew that if she left any doubt about her condition that Maria would seize it as an excuse to delay her treatment.

She had been taken along with the other employees to a county health laboratory and had been given a patch test, a chest radiograph and a sputum test. All had been positive, except for the radiograph. It was too early to detect pulmonary lesions, the doctors said, but all the other tests showed she had an active case. To confirm it, they brought her back in two weeks and her skin test showed a more severe reaction: a higher titer. This titer business was explained to her, but she didn't understand. She tried to explain it to Maria, but that's when she gave up and shortened her letter.

Isabel had been tested also, but was found negative. Doctors found that she had had problems at an earlier age. There was some scarring of the lungs. Either that or she had suffered from attacks of pleurisy, they said. And since she could not recall any chest pains during her life, it was assumed that the scarring was from the disease. In fact, the doctors were pretty sure that had been the problem. She had walked out of the lab with Carmen, wondering how many people she had contaminated during the active phase of her disease. Not Adolfo, she thought, he was much too strong for that. She felt sorry for Carmen, so young and only starting to live. What would become of her? The frail-looking Carmen walked alongside her and they both cried and embraced as they felt like the only two people in the world that cared for each other.

Isabel made sure that during the two weeks between tests, Carmen did not exert herself. "Maybe it's a mistake," she said, trying to comfort her. "They've been wrong before. They could be wrong again. I don't think you worked there long enough to get TB."

Isabel brought meals to Carmen in bed, brought her magazines to read, a deck of cards, anything to keep her preoccupied. She was closer to Carmen than she had been before.

The house was quarantined. Soon, after she left, Carmen realized that her mattress and pillow would be burned in the backyard along with any belongings she left behind. Her entire room would be scrubbed with lye.

She could not go to her mother. She, her person, her body, was quarantined. The only one she could rely on now was Isabel. "I don't mind," Isabel would say, carrying trays and mopping the floor around the bed with coal tar soap. "I can't get TB. I've had it before and I don't think I can get it again."

After the second test she was allowed to go to Isabel's and pack her few things. Then she was taken in a small bus along with other diseased people to a sanatorium fifty miles north of San Diego, by the sea.

Her trip had been uneventful, except that she noticed that she tired more easily with each succeeding day and this trip had left her exhausted.

The old man sitting by her made the trip worse. He kept coughing up something that she dared not look at as he spit it on a handkerchief. He kept up a steady complaint about his health that only depressed her even more. "And look at you," he said to Carmen, "you're so young and you've got it too." It was too much. She got up and went to sit by a middle-aged lady across the aisle.

The small bus moved slowly as it took to the hills on the coast. The engine labored on in first gear, the noise causing the ears to hurt as it climbed steadily, slowly up the hill. Finally, when he had enough momentum, the driver, his face wrapped in a surgical mask, shifted to second and the noise decreased ten-fold. An inadvertant sigh came from the passengers. But still the steady drone in second gear would set the nerves on edge and, when the noise became unbearable, when one wanted to scream, the driver shifted into third and a more relaxed pitch. By this time he was at the top and he would begin his descent and once at the bottom, he would start his shifting all over again. Peace came finally at the top of the highest hill. Overlooking the sea was a large central building four stories high in Spanish architecture with stuccoed walls and arches and covered walk-ways. In front was a large sign with the state emblem, a bear, burned into its boards and the words, *California Department of Health* and, around the top of the emblem and underneath in a

straight line the words, *State Tuberculosis Sanitaruim*. Below, as an afterthought, on a sign dangling from two "hook and eyes" were the words "No
visitors beyond this point."

They were taken from the bus and sat in a lobby at the entrance of the main
building. The routine seemed so pat for the employees that the process took a
surprisingly short while. It seemed to Carmen that something else needed to
be done, that an experience so critical to her required so little time and effort
bothered her. She did not realize that this was but a small part of her admit-
tance procedure.

Her room-mate was to be the middle-aged lady she had sat by on the trip
over. There were two to a room, she gathered, because when they were taken
on the grounds behind the main building, only she and the lady accompanied
the orderly, a large Mexican lady.

"The main building you just came from is called the Administration
Building," she said to them, taking in the whole building with a sweep of her
hand. She pointed to the ground floor. "On the first floor where you were are
offices for doctors and nurses. The office for admitting patients is also there.
That's where you were right now. The second floor is a clinic for out-
patients." She realized Carmen didn't understand the term. "Out-patients
are sick people that don't need to be in a hospital. They walk in, we treat them
and they go back to their room or back to work. The third floor is surgery and
part hospital. The fourth floor you don't want to know about. That's where
they take you to die. It's always full."

She turned back to them after having faced the building she was describing
and she shook her head. "You don't want to go to the fourth floor." She
walked past them and they followed on the pathways lined neatly with flower
beds. The salt air breezed through them and gave Carmen a chill. She
clutched her thin arms. "The air is cool, but it's good for you to breathe," the
orderly said when she noticed Carmen's discomfort.

They walked slowly behind her. The older woman had not said a word.
Her eyes were fixed to the ground as she walked. Who knows, Carmen
thought, stealing a glimpse at her, what problems the poor woman had. What
had she left behind? How much — children, perhaps grandchildren, a husband, a home, a place to belong — had she left? And now thrown into this
world, not even two hours away from home, a stranger in her own territory,
she had arrived. Carmen's breathing was labored and she stopped to rest. She
placed the suitcase beside her and sat on it. The older woman touched her
elbow and helped ease her down. All she would remmeber of that day was
looking as if into a fog toward the sea and then lowering her sights as the large
lady waddled on without them, talking, the heels of her shoes worn unevenly
to the outside. The orderly faded into the fog as she spoke. Little by little she
disappeared.

She had fainted and had been brought to the cabin with the help of the
orderly and a handsome tubercular young man. He had noticed her as she

walked slowly behind the orderly and was in fact following them. His name was David and he was a thin male of average height with thick black straight hair and heavy eyebrows. His eyes were large and brown and expressively fixed in a state of sadness, no matter the occasion. He had picked Carmen up with the orderly's help and they had taken her to her room. There they laid her on her small iron bed and, with the older woman's help, they placed cold towels to her forehead. She awoke slightly disoriented and her first words were about Maria. "Where were you?" she asked confusing her room-mate for Maria. "I've been waiting for a long time."

They dismissed the talk as the incoherent rambling of a person coming out of unconsciousness and did not try to make meaning out of the words. "Here, here," the orderly said, gently rubbing her hand, "you will feel well in a minute. You have been over-exerted today. This has been a long day for you."

The older woman had found her bed across the small room and had sat down on the edge of the bed to rest and watch the other two, the orderly and the young man, help Carmen come to her senses.

By dinner time they were left alone and Carmen had the strength to walk to the cafeteria. She ate a little. "You've got to eat more than that," her friend said. "You've got to fight this thing. You're so young." Carmen looked at her and smiled. "I'll try," she said. She wished she had Maria by her side. Maria would be strong at a time like this. She wondered what Maria was doing at that moment, where she was.

At night she and Luz would talk themselves to sleep. Luz, being much older, used that time to moralize. She tried to pick the specific misdeed that had brought on the retribution, this illness, from God. Surely these things were not left up to fate. Had it been, she asked Carmen, an abortion she tried after her first child? Was it that she didn't love her children as much as she ought to? Was it her husband? The list was endless. What was it? Why her? She had an uncle, she said, still living at ninety-two that had never been ill, and here she was in a sanatorium. Then finally she asked, "Why you, Carmen?" and the silence that followed lasted a painful length of time. Carmen didn't answer. There were no answers as far as she was concerned. She had never done anything to deserve an illness of this magnitude. Luz's attempt to find the causative relationship between the deed and the punishment led her nowhere. God was not to be dealt with logically. Until, finally, with the passage of time, she grew to accept her condition. She prayed. They both prayed — the Rosary usually — after their talk. Toward the end, by the last mystery, Luz's voice would waiver, drop to a whisper and soon they were both asleep.

Luz had married young and had five children, all grown and married. It appeared to Carmen that she didn't look that old. In fact, she was in her late forties, she said. She had ten grandchildren and her husband was alive and well working at the Naval Station. No, he didn't know Isabel or, if he did, he had never mentioned her. It was a big base. She had worked at the Naval

Station when they met, but she quit to have her children and went from job to job with each pregnancy. Her favorite job had been at a hospital as an orderly, much the same as the fat woman they knew. She had seen many things there and her eyes had been opened to medicine's limitations. Carmen felt uneasy. But, she continued, this was not true of tuberculosis. She was referring to grave illnesses. Tuberculosis wasn't like a stamp of death, she said. She enjoyed the work because, more often than not, people would get well and, although she had no part in the healing process, she felt good for the patient. She wished she had been a nurse. Carmen was usually quiet and very tired by this time of the day and she lay in bed and rested. Luz's voice would soothe her and she would be as in a trance. She could hear the muffled crashing of the Pacific waves beyond and below Luz's voice and their rhythm added to her hypnotic state.

Every night Luz would divulge a little more of her past, until some months later her story was exhausted. That night Luz ended where she began, a circle had been completed and she realized it. Carmen knew all about her, except for her secret thoughts and only God and Luz knew about those. She faded at the end of her story and, when she stopped, it startled Carmen. She could only hear the sea now. Luz said, "Well, that's it. Now you know all about me. From now on you will be with me and you will know everything that happens to me."

The day's routine was such that she and Luz spent most of the day together in adjacent beds. They awoke early at the sound of a buzzer that had been screwed on to the wall between the two beds. They showered and dressed and walked to breakfast. They returned to clean their room and police the grounds around the cabin. There were four rooms per cabin, each one housed two people. Each was responsible for the yard directly in front of the room. They could grow flowers, if they so wished, in the small box containers in front of the small patio by the front door. Luz and Carmen had gotten geranium cuttings from David and they had propogated the red flowered plants in their box.

Afterwards, they would report at a specified time to the second floor for a daily physical evaluation, a sort of short physical examination consisting of auscultation of the lungs and a sputum smear. This was followed by chemotherapy. The drug of choice was isoniazid, a new discovery, and indeed Carmen was lucky that it was available. Before now, the treatment of choice was the chest surgery that caved a person in side-ways for life. It was also believed beneficial to give the patient as much bed rest as possible, so that after the morning treatment, the patient would return to bed and spend the rest of the morning there.

At the sound of the buzzer they would return to the cafeteria for their noon meal, then back to bed if they were tired. By late afternoon, they would receive their second treatment and would go directly from there to the cafeteria in the basement of the Administration Building. After dinner, they returned to bed or they were allowed to walk the grounds or visit among the less ill. The more seriously ill were kept in beds in the hospital and were not allowed to walk the grounds. The terminally ill, those who had no chance of recovery, were sent to the fourth floor. Very few ever survived that ordeal.

At night, Carmen strained to hear the sounds of the fourth floor, the moanings she had been told about by the other patients, but she never heard anything. And if she sometimes felt she did, she could not be sure, because the surf interfered with her concentration.

One morning as she and Luz walked to breakfast, they saw a group of people standing around a fallen patient. The patient's head had been covered up by the orderlies before they could reach the scene and they were ordered to move along. They were told by the others that had seen the whole thing that a woman had jumped from a fourth floor window. There were pustules all over her body. Where she hit the concrete sidewalk she had oozed a reddish creamy discharge from her skin.

She learned quite a bit about the disease while she was there, enough to know that after six months she was not feeling any better. The doctor was evasive about her recuperation. Her healing powers were slower than normal, he said, but that was no cause for concern. She still had difficulty sleeping. The fever seemed to start as soon as the sun set and the constant surge of the waves from the sea below her seemed to nauseate her. She could not breathe well. One thing she knew for certain, she was not worse, but she wondered if she would ever feel well again.

Maria was writing often. At least once a week she received a letter from her in her scribbled hand. She realized how easy it was to detect ignorance by the way a person wrote. After all these years, she had not realized how ignorant her mother was. She enjoyed the letters, though, and any criticism she had of her mother was purely a detached observation. She loved her mother. Maria now had two promises to fulfill, she wrote. The first one was for her finding a job and the second was for her recovery. She prayed every night, the rosary, in bed. She went to mass every morning and she went to rosary every night. Father Segura was also praying for her, as were all of her friends. She had not heard from Adolfo in a long time, but believed he was doing alright. Adolfo was living with an old degenerate man like himself and she could imagine the filth in which they lived. He no longer lived with that hateful woman. But she had gone into that before and she wouldn't bother Carmen wth Adolfo's problems.

It was amazing, she wrote in one of her letters, how many people she talked to that had had tuberculosis. It seemed like half the people had it and they were doing fine now. She had been trying to visit her, but could not find anyone to take her. Jesus was in Kansas working some harvest and, as soon as he came back, she would get a ride.

Carmen and Luz both noticed that David was paying more and more attention to Carmen. "I think he likes you," Luz told Carmen when David stayed on longer than usual. He was beginning to be a frequent visitor. He spoke to Carmen about his dreams, what he wanted to do as soon as he was released. He said this with anticipation, waiting to see how Carmen reacted. Did she like him in return? He brought flowers from his garden, a little piece of soil he had tilled on his own at the edge of the manicured lawns, to the northwest of the property. He loved flowers. He loved to grow things, he said. He would be an agronomist or a horticulturist, he told her. He had read books about things like that.

"Be careful with young men like him," Luz advised her as they talked alone. "He has a lot of dreams, but he doesn't have an education. He didn't even finish high school. How can he do what he says he wants to do? Don't you have to go to college to be what he wants to be?"

"I don't know," Carmen replied, defending him. "He seems intent on doing it. I feel he can be whatever he wants to be."

"Oh, how innocent young people can be," Luz said in exasperation. "You just don't say this is what I want to be and then be it. You have to study, go to school." Then she thought for a while, her head down, and she told Carmen, "Look at me. I married someone like that. And we never amounted to much. Sure, we raised our children and had something to eat and had a modest home. But, is that what you want?" She didn't wait for Carmen to reply. "You should be thinking big. Try to do more in your life than anyone expects you to. Don't settle for the ordinary life. You're young now. Look at me, dying fom tuberculosis and do you know what bothers me the most? I could have been somebody. I spent my life on my husband and my children. I never lived life for myself. It was always for someone else. Someone always came first, always. Don't get me wrong. I love my husband and my family, but God I wish now I could have done something besides raise a family. Isn't it horrible that the most anyone ever expected of me was to be married and raise a family?" Carmen was stunned. She had never heard her talk this way. She was expressing her true feelings, now that she knew that she probably woud not survive this illness. Why hadn't she done something about her life?

"Because," she explained, "I was afraid. Here I was an orderly, and a good one too, and I gave it all up for the family. It seemed that whatever job I had, it was not of any importance," she said. "Be somebody. If you ever decide you want to help the sick, go into nursing; if that pleases you, be the best nurse in the whole world."

She was exhausted from talking. "Anyway," she said rolling over on her side on the bed, "don't be fooled by the innocence of youth. It's a guaranteed way of getting hurt. Remember, nothing turns out the way you plan it."

The next morning, David was sitting on the porch steps. He had brought flowers. It was still too early for breakfast.

Carmen came out and they both sat close to each other.

"I've been thinking," David said, "that I've been coming over here two or three times every day. I guess I better not be bothering you so much, especially since I don't think Luz is very fond of me."

"Oh, I wouldn't say that," Carmen lied, trying to ease his concern. "Luz speaks highly of you. She thinks you are a fine young man."

"I don't believe that, Carmen," he answered. "I feel that she doesn't think I'm good enough for you. She acts like you belong to her."

"I know," Carmen said, "but she means well. All women that age mean well. She's like my mother."

"Well, do you mind if I come over to see you as often as I do?"

"No, not at all," she replied. She liked him.

Carmen was feeling a lot better, good enough to stay out on the porch with David or walk gently with him on the wooded grounds until the ten o'clock curfew.

He had kissed her one night and she quickly backed off realizing that she was still infective. He didn't care. He grabbed her in an untypically forceful manner and kissed her again, this time lingering until she relented and held him close to her. She felt total relief, as if she had been needing to be kissed and held for a long time. How long had it been since she had had an innocent type of relationship with a man? Maria would not allow her to date anyone around her. They were never good enough.

They held on to each other for a long time. He had forgotten how beautiful it felt to have the body of a young girl pressed against him. He felt he could never let her go. "I love you," he whispered to her. "I love you very much."

She did not answer. She did not know whether she loved him or not. Luz had partially ruined him for her.

He insisted that he loved her and his persistence almost paid off.

They were inside her room talking while Luz was in the infirmary. He kissed her gently and again told her he loved her very much. "Why don't you ever say you love me?" he asked her.

"Because I don't know," she answered. "I'm not sure. You wouldn't want me to lie, would you?"

"No, it's because of Luz, isn't it?" he asked.

"No, it's not Luz," she replied. She was feeling awkward, as if she needed to apologize for herself.

"It's Luz, I can tell. You can't fool me."

"It's not Luz," she said, "It's not Luz," and she started to cry.

"Then why? Why? Carmen?"

She didn't know why, but she put her arms around him and kissed him. She wanted to prove something to him, that she was in fact capable of love.

They were undressed when Luz came in.

She allowed him only enough time to put his clothes on and then she banned him from ever coming into the room again. "I can't control what happens on the grounds," she said, "but there will be no sex in this room." And to Carmen she said, "Carmen, I thought you knew better."

Later, when they were by themselves and after Carmen had tried to explain what had happened, she gave Carmen this advice: "Take it from someone who has traveled the road, Carmen. I was just like you, so I don't blame you one bit. Don't give it away. Make them pay dearly for it. Men may think they want it for free, but they really don't."

Better advice was never given a female. Carmen was smart enough to take it.

She began feeling even better one night when she noticed that the fever was not as severe. In fact, it was gone. She kept touching her forehead, her cheeks, her arms, and she could feel cooler than before. Or was it her imagination? It was not. That night she slept well, better than before, and the surge of the tide below the escarpment was a rhythmic beat that kept pace with her breathing and deepened her sleep.

She awoke refreshed and could hardly wait to tell Luz. Luz was happy for her, but deep inside she felt an envy for Carmen. If only she could do as well. The truth was that Luz was doing worse. Carmen sensed that Luz had not been as happy for her as she had imagined Luz would be. The last weeks she had to be helped out of bed. "It's not that I'm not happy for you," she told Carmen one night, in a voice as faint as a whisper, "it's that in here it's everyone for himself. I want to get well. I want to get well and so, if you get well, that's fine, but it's me I'm worried about." She coughed and held her chest from the pain. She had lost much weight. What had been a rather distinguished looking lady when she first arrived had shriveled into a long-nosed creature with sunken eyes and a pallid, almost death-like color to her skin. She would cry herself to sleep in pain. She would shake the bed in her fevered tremors. She coughed the cough of the fourth floor and that's where they took her. She said not a word to Carmen. Stooped as she walked, she was helped to gather her belongings and the last Carmen saw of her alive was as she stood by the fourth floor window one early afternoon as Carmen strolled the grounds with the young David. She waved at her and she hardly raised her arm in return, but Carmen knew that Luz had seen her.

The day after she died, Carmen met Luz's husband, her two daughters and three sons. Her husband was a well-dressed, well-mannered, good-looking short man with a thin face and a thin mustache who spoke very gently and thanked Carmen for all she had done. Luz had written to them about her and how much she admired Carmen's courage and her will to live. "She was old," the husband said. "She just couldn't fight it. She was a good wife and mother. But that is life." He took out a handkerchief and wiped his eyes. He took out a business card and handed it to Carmen. Carmen had held back the tears, although she had cried through the night. She missed Luz now that she was gone. "If you are ever in San Diego, please come to see us," he said.

Luz's children stood behind the father as he spoke to Carmen. They were all married, but had not brought their families. They each thanked Carmen for her help and for her generosity toward their mother. They were sure that Carmen had made her stay more bearable. They would remember her at the funeral.

Luz's husband left briefly and spoke to an administrator in the hallway. They went into an office and came out shortly. The husband placed an envelope in his coat pocket and walked back to them. "All the papers are in order," he said. "I guess it's time to go."

Carmen accompanied them to the drive-way as the hearse came slowly around from behind the main building. The family stepped into the car and they departed. She cried for her friend. She would never forget her.

After many attempts to visit Carmen, Maria was coming! It would be the first Sunday in August. Jesus had arrived back in town and had promised her he would bring her over as soon as he replaced the radiator in the car. She was giving him five dollars to help with the radiator and ten dollars for the trip. She had heard from Adolfo. He was still living with the filthy old man, but not in the same house. They had been forcibly removed from their house by the sheriff, based on a complaint citing unsanitary conditions filed against them by the hateful woman. This was all a pretext, Maria wrote, according to Adolfo, so that she, the hateful woman, could rent the house to a couple from Mexico. She had other news. Father Segura had been found drunk, sprawled out in the yard, by the gardener. Everyone knew he drank, but no one said much about it, at least not the women. Who knows what the men said at the taverns.

The situation in town was one full of rumors. She knew that the United States had declared war on the Germans. Most of the young men were being drafted. She didn't understand beyond that. She knew war was horrible. She had lived through World War I, *la Primera Guerra*, they called it.

Carmen was over-joyed with the letter. It had been close to a year since she last saw her mother. She was feeling well now and her strength was gaining daily. She took longer walks each day and she could climb the long tortuous stairs up and down the escarpment to the rocky shores below. Still, the constant pounding noise of the waves bothered her somewhat at night. She could get used to it. David had become her dear and close friend. They had both agreed to forget their short love affair. They were just not meant for each other. He realized Carmen was looking for something in life that he could not give her. He was completely recovered now and would be released soon, within two weeks, he had been told. They celebrated by walking on the shore not saying much, grateful that both had survived the ordeal.

When they did speak, it was to tell each other what they would do once they were out. He wanted to go to a university, he said. Somewhere where he could improve himself. In a way what Luz had said about him had made him realize that he needed to do something with his life. He felt he had been spared for some divine reason. He felt he had gained strength as Carmen had from the experience they both shared. He was ready now to get down to the serious part of his life. He did not want to follow in his brothers' footsteps. He would not go to CC Camp, a federal government work project, as his brothers had done.

He would strike out on his own.

Carmen, inspired by him the last few months, believed that she could do better. She was thinking seriously of nursing as a career. She had watched the nurses there and felt she would find gratification in helping the sick.

"It's a hard life," David said, "if what we see here is an example."

"I know it is," she replied. "But it's more important than what I was doing before. Do you know what it takes to sell tickets?"

"Not much."

"Yes, not much."

David was gone in a tearful farewell, but Maria was coming for her birthday. She would be twenty-one. She felt a sadness in seeing him leave. She had lost a companion and the only person she could confide in. Her new roommate was an old lady who cursed and chewed tobacco at night when no one was watching over them. For her size, she ate more than anyone Carmen had ever known. She passed gas in large bellowing sounds throughout the night. Carmen wondered, with her being so small, where did all this flatulence come from? She was delirious sometimes or acted so and she would scare Carmen out of her sleep. After all, Carmen thought, you never knew from one day to the next who would die or who would survive.

It amazed her how fast a person with tuberculosis deteriorated. One day she would see someone looking normal and the next time the same person would look different. Then that same individual who looked unhealthy would later be withered and sallow, the body drained of all energy, and confined to a wheel chair.

Marcos had been one of those that she particularly remembered. He had appeared on the grounds one day, robust and with a genuine laughter that could be heard not once but twice as it echoed off the wall of the Main Building. She had talked to him and he had made her laugh. Everything said to him he could take and with his wit make it humorous. He had been diagnosed late, but it seemed like almost everyone assumed he would get well. He didn't. In two weeks time or so, he had shriveled into a small, frail, bitter man who hardly spoke. His mind was preoccupied with death, not with laughter. All his energy, it seemed, was directed at the cruel turn that had sentenced him to a short time on earth. It was bad enough to know you were dying, worse still was to know you were dying soon. His laughter never reverberated again. The last time she saw him he was being wheeled toward the Main Building by a large Mexican woman. He died two days later.

But the other side of the coin brought happiness and, more importantly, hope. Some of the patients who no one believed would make it, got well, thrived in the sea salt air and daily doses of isoniazid, and walked out discharged and clear-eyed to fight another day.

She often wished that Luz had been as lucky, but it was not to be.

Carmen developed a strength from this ordeal, an inner fiber that was to serve her well in her life. She would no longer be the timid little girl that

Maria had raised. She came to feel good about herself.

She would marry well, she hoped.

Maria came. She made her typical loud entry. When she saw Carmen, she fell to her knees by the car door and lifted her arms to the sky and looked at God and began crying loudly. The people in the Main Building and those strolling on the grounds quickly rushed to her, thinking that she might have fallen and injured herself. Some, thinking that she was a new patient coming to be admitted for treatment, tried to pick her up and place her in a wheel chair that had been rushed from inside the building. Jesus, who was familiar with both Maria and Adolfo, stood by the car on the opposite side and lit a cigarette. A young doctor tried to calm Maria down while two orderlies tried to force her on a chair.

"Take your hands off me," she yelled. "Take your dirty hands off me. Can't you see I'm well?"

If her mother hadn't looked so old, and so large, Carmen would have laughed. Indeed, later she would. But in her preoccupation with her mother, she could think of nothing amusing in the situation.

"Carmen," Maria yelled, "Carmen. Please let me embrace my daughter. Carmen. Come help me."

She flung the rosary as one would a ball and chain at the two orderlies. The crowd around them was stunned. The doctor couldn't think of what to do. Finally he spoke to Carmen. "Is this your mother?" he yelled above the commotion.

"Yes," Carmen replied.

"Is she sick?"

"No, she's come to visit me."

He ordered the men to release Maria and Carmen rushed to her. They embraced for a long time as Maria rocked her gently back and forth.

The crowd finally understood what had happened and they stood and watched as the large woman held her daughter pinned against her, her expansive back racking with sobs. Those around them cried also. Most knew Carmen and loved her. The orderlies apologized. The doctor walked back to his office and soon the crowd dispersed and they were alone.

Carmen went to Jesus and shook his hand. He removed a straw hat from his head and took her hand. He asked her how she was. He had not heard from Adolfo, he said, as a nervous afterthought, not knowing what else to say.

They sat at one of the concrete benches facing the sea close to the edge of the cliff. Maria caught her breath, holding both hands to her chest. The rosary fell like a heavy chain from her hands and reached her lap.

"I made a promise," she said, "that when I first saw you I would fall to my knees and praise God in a loud voice." She thought for a while. "But I wish God would make it easier for me. He didn't have to cause all that commotion. He *would* embarrass me. Don't you agree?"

"Yes mother," Carmen said and she looked at Maria and a grin came to her face and then they started to laugh.

"Did you see those men trying to carry me?" she laughed. "They couldn't do it. Who did they think they were picking up? A young pretty girl like you? They were mistaken. They were trying to pick up a heavy old woman, someone with lots of years in her. After all, I'll be fifty-nine this year."

"You'll be fifty-nine?" asked Carmen, seriously eyeing her mother for signs of age. She was getting old. In those days, 1941, life expectancy was late fifties, early sixties.

"Yes," she replied with an air of resignation.

"And Adolfo?"

"He'll be fifty-eight. He was born in eighty-four. I was born in eighty-three. He was thirty-three when he went to fight in nineteen-seventeen."

"That was old wasn't it?"

"Not really. They took any Mexican they could."

As painful as it was and as easy as it was to ignore it, they finally began to talk about Carmen's illness.

"It was those people in the theatre that gave you this horrible thing. You couldn't have picked it up in the Valley."

"I think I know who it was. We had a man who ran the projector who never associated with anyone. The doctors say he was spreading the disease everywhere he went. He must be dead by now."

"I knew it, Carmen," Maria said. "I knew it had to be one of them."

"But I'm doing well now. I feel very good. I can walk and exercise and not feel tired anymore."

"I knew you would get well. I felt it and I knew God would help you. Not to mention the promises I made."

"Well, I hope the other promises turn out better than the one you just did."

By this time Maria had begun to ignore what had happened to her. Such was her nature that the whole episode would fade quickly from her mind. There was no room there for any unpleasantness, especially self-ridicule. All of that would be locked out. She ignored Carmen's remark. "And you're feeling better?" she asked.

Carmen realizing that she had hurt Maria's feelings by bringing up the subject again, Carmen answered sweetly. "Yes. Thanks to you and your prayers and your promises."

"And don't forget the ladies of the Altar Society and Father Segura. They had a lot to do with it. No, it wasn't only me. They prayed many rosaries for you Carmen. They lit a lot of candles for your recovery. You must thank them when you return."

"Speaking of Father Segura, how is he?"

"Oh the things I could tell you Carmen. You knew he drank a lot. We all knew it, but we didn't say anything. What difference does it make? He's a priest and he knows right from wrong. Let him have his few beers now and then, I say. What harm does it do? The poor man sits alone all day long, except for that ignorant housekeeper. His juices flow, Carmen." She looked at Carmen a sort of side-ways glance to make sure Carmen understood what she had said. "His juices flow too," she repeated just in 'case. "He's a man. Don't think for a moment that he isn't. And no one but the ugly housekeeper to look at. My God, his juices must have exploded a long time ago." She gave Carmen the side glance again. Carmen stared out to the sea. "There's a rumor he wants to go out with the widow Fernandez. It's only a rumor, mind you, but that's what they say." Now Carmen became interested and it spurred·Maria on. "They say some people have seen him climbing the fence and jumping into her backyard. Some say they've seen him looking through the windows. They also say Adolfo made him an alcoholic. That anyone Adolfo is with becomes an alcoholic sooner or later. They say Adolfo was the one that bought him beer and hard liquor, *trago fuerte*, but he had been drinking for a long time before Adolfo worked for him."

"And what does Adolfo say?"

"Adolfo?" She made a gesture of disgust curling her lips. "Adolfo only cares for Adolfo. He only writes for his money. Do you see that rock sticking out of the water?"

"Yes."

She had pointed at a large rock standing alone at the shore-line.

"What that rock has done for you, that is what Adolfo has done for me since he left. Not a word. Not a penny. He knows I'm a poor woman. If it wasn't for your sister Maria, I wouldn't eat. But you know what he does? He takes up with this horrible woman and gives her his checks . . . a woman who has never helped him in anyway. All I do is send the check every month to her. God only knows what she does with it. And I hear he's living with a dirty old man like himself, a Professor he calls himself. Jesus told me all about it. I know I wrote to you about it, but I've found out more since then from Jesus. Adolfo hasn't worked since he arrived in Los Angeles. He's living on the southern side of town. Why? All his old friends were on the west-side. Why?" She didn't wait for an answer. She already had one. "Because the woman has him in a spell."

Carmen laughed.

"Don't laugh, Carmen, these things are true. You're too young to know about these things. She has Adolfo in a spell. She uses herbs, teas, that kind of thing. Don't you think the widow Fernandez could cast a spell on the priest and have him jumping fences and looking through windows? That's what some say. Maybe the priest is under a spell too. That I don't know. I do know that if a man gives all his money to an unknown woman whom he doesn't live with, that he is in a spell, *enhierbado*. She has him by the balls, *los huevos*, and he doesn't know it." She gave Carmen that little side-ways glance again to see what Carmen thought about that.

"Maybe he loves her," she said.

"Love? What does Adolfo know of love. He never loved anyone. That's why he's in the fix he's in. He has no home, no friends, real friends I'm talking about, no money. He could be out in the street for all we know and nobody would care except me. He always got what he wanted, if you know what I mean."

"Well, he must care for her. If not, he wouldn't put up with her."

"Carmen, Carmen," Maria sighed. "You are young. Don't you know about the herbs that a woman can give a man and render him helpless? Do you remember Virginia and Roberto? Do you remember how she used to run around on him while he stayed at home and cared for the children? And he worked too! He would come from work all tired and dirty and find his children abandoned most of the time. Would he go out and raise hell, get drunk, like the rest of the men? No! Of course not. He came home and cooked supper and took care of the children while his wife whored around town with anyone that would have her. She did it in cars, behind sheds, under trees, behind bushes, in the dirt, on the gravel, in the field, in the streets, on the floor, on the top of cars, railroad tanks. The woman was a whore and everyone had seen her do it. Why Carmen? Why didn't her husband kill her? She had a hex on him. She gave him a concoction of teas for that special purpose. He was under a spell. What normal man with normal senses would have permitted that? Who killed her finally? Her husband? No! Her son. She couldn't put the hex on him. He was too smart. Shot her like a dog in heat under the stairs of the old lumber yard, like she should have been put away many years earlier. These things happen. And it's happening to Adolfo right now. She's giving him cow female organs, or something like that. He's drinking her tea. His balls are dangling like dried prunes by now."

Carmen let out a laugh. "You can really carry on, can't you? You could keep on like this for hours, if someone didn't stop you."

"Why not. It's the truth."

"And you always tell the truth?"

"Mostly," she answered. She looked forlorn, her gaze took on a preoccupation with something else, a new thought that had come to her.

"Like you told the truth about the letters."

Maria had known it was coming. That had been the vague thought that had previously escaped her conscious. The letters. The truth. "No," she said, not wanting to lie anymore.

"You could have gotten us killed," Carmen said.

"I never thought of that. I did what I thought was right. I didn't want to be left alone. You have no idea what it is to be there alone. Young Maria doesn't come to visit and even if she did, she couldn't stay for long. I'm lonely. You may not know it, but I'm old now." She wiped a tear with a handkerchief she had balled up in her hand that she had taken out of her flat imitation patent-leather purse. "Anyway, Father Segura understood perfectly. He said I was completely forgiven. He said it was you and Adolfo who should be in the confessional. It was not a sin, he said, but a small infraction, and I only had to go through the stations of the cross twice."

"I'm glad for you," Carmen said. She had not intended to hurt Maria's feelings. It was just that sometimes she had to put her in her place. If not, Maria could overwhelm her. "I'm really glad he forgave you. I forgave you a long time ago. It probably was for the best."

"I know it was," Maria said emphatically, positively. "Look at that crazy Alfredo, with his gun trying to kill Adolfo. Look at poor Irene, my sister, how much she has suffered with him. He's still the same. Or maybe worse. People like that never get better. If he ever finds out that the middle boy is not his, he'll kill Irene. I'll swear to that!"

That came as a complete shock to Carmen. She realized that her mother kept a lot of secrets from her. She knew that when she walked into the room and Maria and Adolfo quit talking and would change the conversation, that there was something being discussed that she should not know about. Now this secret had come out.

Maria continued as if she had expected Carmen to know about Irene's indiscretion. The trouble was that Maria had so many secrets in her that she never remembered who knew what about who.

Carmen started to laugh. Maria stopped and looked at her. "What's the matter Carmen?" she asked.

"I didn't know about Irene. I didn't know." She tried not to laugh at the irony of the situation for fear she would start coughing. "And we all thought Irene was so afraid of him." She laughed silently, her head bowed. She looked at Maria. Maria had a look of discomfort.

"You didn't know?"

"No." Carmen said. She was still trying to laugh as easily as possible. Her sides were beginning to hurt.

Maria started to laugh, but with her it was different. She laughed as hard as she could, the sound echoing through the buildings. They were both laughing and each time they looked at each other, they would begin to laugh again.

"That's why . . . " Maria couldn't continue. She had to compose herself first. "That's why . . . " she said, and started laughing again. Carmen couldn't help herself. She knew there was a tremendous ending coming on. She knew Maria. She was laughing uncontrollably.

"That's why," Maria said, determined to say the words, "the priest allowed him to marry his first cousin on his father's side! They weren't related!"

It was too much laughter. Carmen began to cough and Maria doubled forward in glee at the thought she had evoked and they both rocked back and forth and laughed until they cried.

When the laughter had ended, when their sides were hurting where they couldn't laugh anymore, Maria began to talk of her eldest daughter.

She had loved but yet resented her illegitimate daughter, although she had never said it. The daughter had been a constant reminder of her stupidity.

"How could I have done it?" she wondered many times. From the beginning, the child represented to Maria a barrier which had kept her from leading a normal life. Should she have aborted the child? Why hadn't someone come to her aid? It would have been a small thing for someone, an older woman wise to the world, to take her by the hand, sit her down and explain the facts to her. She never imagined that child would be such a burden. And even in raising, the child had been difficult. Not that she was ever in any trouble, it was just that she always imagined herself better than her mother. She wouldn't wear just any clothes. Maria had to sew for her and fit her just right. She ate only the foods that pleased her. She slept in the best bed. In short, she was spoiled and there wasn't anything Maria could do about it. If she thought about disciplining her, she immediately felt sorry for the child. After all, she didn't have a father. She didn't have the home-life that others had. What harm was there in letting her have her way?

She grew up a complicated mixture of selflessness and the uncontrollable need to dominate. She could be terribly irritating and yet the family put up with it because they knew that they would be rewarded for their patience.

She had worked at many jobs and had given her mother all her pay-checks, as was the custom in those days. She never asked for anything for herself, knowing full well that Maria would give her more than she herself would have taken. Many were the times when she was the only one working. She really ruled the household then. And yet, such was her personality, that under these conditions she was most loving toward her family. But pity the individual that questioned her authority.

By the time she left (and no one knew why she did), she had completely dominated the household. That included men as well as women. Maybe she left because she needed others to conquer. She never said.

She created a void on leaving that was never filled. The rest of the family, like dependent children, were lost. Maria knew it, not in so many w ords, but she knew that things were not right when she was gone. They missed her. It was the eternal case, when personalities like that existed, when you couldn't stand to be with them and yet their absence created a void that was unbearable.

Even when she was gone she sent money home. She also sent admonishments to whomever she suspected of not pulling their weight. She knew, of course, through Maria, who that person was. So Maria used her to help keep the family in line, except for Carmen. Maria never told her what Carmen was doing.

She married an Anglo, a trashy but nice man who was thin and tall, and who looked like he would topple over at the slightest wind. He was a welder and a part-time mortician. (In those days you didn't need licenses to embalm anybody. The big funeral homes did have the trained embalmists, but in the small towns, anyone who had seen it done once could do it.)

She had brought him to the Valley shortly after their honeymoon. No one but his side of the family had attended the wedding in Sacramento. He was the first Anglo brought into the family. This created a stir. To some in town it was a triumph for the young bride. Others thought of it as a disgrace, especially since he had no money or education, and Young Maria was so beautiful. He took to the Mexican customs right away. He ate menudo, although the men had anticipated that he would turn it down. After he was through, he asked what it was and when they laughed and told him it was beef tripe stew, he said he enjoyed it. They did not know at the time that he had been raised in Missouri. They found out later that the Missourians ate a lot worse things than the Mexicans. The spiceyness of the food didn't phase him. In fact, he ate more than any other person they had ever seen.

Once, at a beer joint, they made him eat a part of the vulva of a cow that somehow had been thrown into the stew and had floated to the surface and he ate it without comment. He smiled afterwards.

His brothers-in-law loved him. Young Maria hated him when he was around them and often cut short their stay and took him home. She returned every two or three years thereafter, but she couldn't stand his behavior when he was among her half-brothers.

Eventually she settled him down and made him appear even more frail. And after she had completely dominated him, she would complain that he was always underfoot and not much of a man.

"She's coming to visit," Maria said. Carmen knew who "she" was. "I hate to see her come, really, I do. It's so much work with her around. It's so much fighting. They eat so much. I have to cook all day. Now that Adolfo is gone I barely light the stove. Now that they're coming, I'll have to cook and work. I've never seen anyone eat like he does. In the letter she said that Eddie wants some menudo. I haven't made menudo in years. Who wants to cook that stinky stuff." She held her nose and looked at Carmen, expecting Carmen to start laughing once more.

The time passed quickly and soon as they sat on the bench in front of the main building to where they had moved. They could see the old Ford coming up the long red drive-way and Jesus barely looking out through the steering wheel, building up his cloud of dust once more.

"It's Jesus," Maria said. "And I must be getting ready to leave, although I hate to." She took a handkerchief and wiped her eyes. Carmen cried softly. "Of all my children," Maria said, "you are my favorite. And I don't mind the other ones knowing it. Your sister and your two brothers I can do without. It's just that I had you so late in life that I feel closer to you."

Jesus had stopped the car. He jumped out and tried to act normal, as if his reflexes were intact, but the two women could tell he had been drinking. They had seen enough drunks in their lives. "How much did you drink, Jesus?" Maria asked.

"Oh, just one beer, that's all," he lied.

"If you are drunk, God help you," Maria said. "I'm not giving you any money for the trip then. I may even be taking my life in my hands riding with you."

"Never fear," he replied, leaning against the fender, "I will get you home."

Maria's departure was less eventful than her arrival. Although her getting there had caused quite a commotion, her leaving was quiet, subdued, tearful. She did almost fall as she stepped off the curb and she did let out a small scream and a supplication to God (ever expecting the worse) and she and Carmen laughed afterwards. She had covered her mouth immediately so as to squelch the cry. She feared she would get the orderlies out again. She blamed that misfortune on Jesus, the driver, not the Diety. "*Mondado*," she said, which was the equivalent of calling someone a dumb ass, as she boarded the car.

As she left, Carmen wished that time would come back, reverse itself, so that she would be waiting once more for her mother. Wouldn't it be fine if I could do that, she thought, bring back time, bring back Luz, her mother, her father, all the people that had been so good to me. Yes, Isabel also.

CHAPTER 6

Adolfo and Manuel, the Professor, had moved, or maybe I should say they were evicted by the Public Health authorities. Antonia had complained to the Sheriff and he had suggested that the way to do it was to call on Public Health, have someone go to the house, and he was sure that the house would be condemned. *Dicho y hecho*. Said and done. Just as the Sheriff had predicted, the two were evicted and their possessions piled neatly in City Health boxes outside the house. Later a team of city empolyees appeared and enveloped the house in canvasses and began fumigating. Manuel later said that the newspaper had carried the story, but had exaggerated the part about how filthy the house had been.

Adolfo had made a phone call and reached Francisco (Pancho) Garcia, the Skunk, and Francisco had driven over and picked them up and took them to a boarding house that he was familiar with.

"This is Adolfo Arguelles," Pancho had told the boarding-house lady. "He is a fine and honorable man. He was at one time a famous baseball player, but you probably don't remember."

"I sure do remember," the lady replied. "My late husband loved baseball. That was his favorite sport. Of all sports, he loved baseball the most. He often spoke of Adolfo and the San Diego Pelicans."

For the first time since arriving in Los Angeles he felt appreciated. Oh, he knew the Professor appreciated him, but he was talking about being recognized as a ball player. He winked at Manuel. He was going to be in his element. Oh, the stories he would tell.

"Well," Pancho said, "he was a hero to many of us. Not too many from our race amount to anything. You know what I mean."

"Yes, I understand," the lady replied. Then after a brief hesitation she said, "Come in, come in." They had been standing outside the front door.

Once they were in, she turned to Pancho and asked, "And who is this other man?" She was referring to Manuel.

Manuel was a handsome man and by no means did he appear to be crude or uneducated and the woman sensed this. His fine linear features made him appear distinguished. After all he had graduated from high school and then attended a university. She seemed impressed.

Pancho had forgotten Manuel's last name and he fumbled the introduction deliberately. "Excuse him," Manuel said, "my name is Manuel Garcia, the Professor, I'm called."

"How nice to meet you," she said. "I'm sure we will have a good relationship."

Adolfo laughed. He was ready to have a good time.

"Why didn't you tell us about this place before?" he asked Pancho after they had been given a room. "It beats living in that rat-filled hole we were in all this time."

"How was I to know? I thought you guys were happy where you were. Didn't you both tell me about resting your head on Antonia's tits? You sounded happy there, didn't she let you play with her part?"

"Well," Adolfo said, winking at Manuel, "we did have a good time while it lasted."

"Yes," Manuel replied, "but the trouble was it didn't last long enough. You got more than me Adolfo and I bet I paid more for it."

"What do you mean?" Adolfo said, "I still can't get my pension check away from her."

"That's stupid, Adolfo," Manuel said. "I did it and you can too. All you have to do is go to the office and file your claim. I keep telling you and you don't do it."

"I'm expecting a little more tit, that's why," Adolfo replied and they both laughed.

The room was sparse but clean. Again, the ever present linoleum was on the floor and it had been worn in the most used paths by many footsteps belonging to many people that had lived there. There was a faint acrid smell to the room. There were two twin beds and between them a night stand with its lamp. On the far wall was a dresser with mirror and on the near wall was the chest of drawers.

They unpacked the boxes after Francisco had left. Adolfo took the two top drawers because he said he was the taller of the two. Manuel, not to be outdone, chose the right-hand drawers on the dresser because he was right handed. They both agreed.

Francisco had brought a bottle of cheap bourbon along and had left it there for them. Adolfo took a large swallow and handed it to Manuel. He, more delicate and well-mannered, only took a small swig. Then they hid the bottle in the small closet.

Before they would finish closing the closet door, the woman opened the door to their room. "I will not allow drinking in this house," she said. "I may have forgotten to tell you."

"That's understandable," said Adolfo, being very serious. They both had thought the woman had seen them drinking.

"Do I smell liquor in the room?" she asked, sniffing out the different odors in the air.

"No," Manuel said, "it is the liniment that Adolfo uses for his old pitching arm. Right?"

"Yes," Adolfo replied, adding to the lie, "If I don't use it once in a while, my whole arm begins to turn to stone and hurts to where it becomes unbearable. It just now started hurting, what with all the boxes we had to carry."

"It sure smells like whiskey to me," she said.

"It's the same base," Manuel said. "It's all alcohol. All that stuff athletes use has alcohol in it. It is used to refresh the body."

"It sure does," Adolfo said. "In Mexico we used a liniment from the cactus that had been fermented and allowed to spoil. We skimmed the top off, then we added chewing tobacco to it and then applied it to the body. Now *there* was a smell. Thank God we don't use that in this country.

"Well," the lady said, "I just don't like anyone drinking or getting drunk in the house. It disturbs the other tennants. No one here drinks. Not inside the home, anyway," she corrected herself.

"Will we be allowed to drink outside the house?" Adolfo asked. He was hoping for an affirmative reply. If not, he and the Professor were in trouble.

"Sure," the lady said, much to their relief. Now they could sneak the bottle out. "I will, also," she continued, "try to keep your room clean. I can't do them all and I can't be thorough. All you can hope for is that I come and straighten out the little things once or twice a week. The rest of the time you are going to have to clean up yourselves."

She had them sitting on the edge of their beds, as if she had been lecturing two small children. They appeared remorseful, looking down at their shoes, but yet happy that they would be allowed to come home drunk.

It amazed them that in Los Angeles all one had to do was change neighborhoods and one became an unknown all over again. The city seemed to be divided into small sections ten or so blocks square and all activities within that neighborhood belonged there and nowhere else. Adolfo had not known the area where Antonia lived or the area where the boarding house was when he had lived in the west part of town — the time when he lived in the pool hall. They had in reality moved east from where they were evicted, a distance he calculated to be about one mile. This area too had its own beer joints, grocery stores, ice-houses and small retail stores. They were in business again.

That night after they had heard a lecture about table manners from Anna, they decided to get even with Antonia for having them evicted.

"Oh yes," the lady replied to the question. "We have an apothecary about four blocks from here. You can find anything medicinal that you might need."

"It is just that my arm is still hurting," Adolfo told the lady. He was lying. What he really wanted to buy was some withcraft potion that would place a hex on Antonia. Manuel believed very strongly in such hexes and so did he. It was just a matter of deciding what harm they wanted to befall Antonia.

The apothecary was full of potions. There were herbs and powders and roots and twigs and leaves for most afflictions, physical or spiritual, that in one way or another affect man during his life. They displayed a bearded man, a so called healer, on the outside of the box.

"Here's one," said Manuel, "for the affairs of the heart. For all those," he read, "that have lost their true love. How to make him or her come back."

"Here's the one we need," Adolfo said, showing Manuel the box. It showed a woman being rejected by all around her. Everyone was turning their back to her and making a face as if she smelled bad. Since he couldn't read very well, he passed the box to Manuel. "Hatred Potion," Manuel read aloud. "Secret recipe of herbs guaranteed to make the object of such a hex the object of hatred by all who know him or her. Guaranteed also to make such a person lose all monies and possessions and render him or her destitute. Your money-back guarantee is included in the contents of this box." He whistled silently at the enormity of the curse, at the power that was in his hands. "Can you believe this," he said, "that in this box lies the power to destroy a person?" After some reflection and looking at Adolfo, he said, "We'd better be sure we use this properly. I wouldn't want to injure Antonia's children also."

"We won't," Adolfo said, "it doesn't say anything about children, does it? I've never known children to be affected by these potions."

At the counter, the pudgy-faced clerk with pock-marked face and bulbous lips looked at the potion and read its heading. "Is this all it will take?" he asked.

"What do you mean?" Manuel asked him. "Are we missing something?"

"If you want the job done properly," he lisped, "then I suggest you buy a candle to go with it."

"Where are the candles?"

"In back of you against the wall," the man said.

They turned around and walked behind a middle counter that ran almost the length of the store. This counter was filled with all kinds of potions and liniments and candles that had apparently lost their strength or their style, either one. They were on sale. Against the wall were the large yellow candles imprinted with their respective cures or hexes. For every hex their was a counter-hex. They ranged alphabetically from *amor* to *voyages*. Each one was guaranteed to unleash its power through its light and give solace or revenge or aid to its intended victim.

Amor, one candle said boldly, *to be used when a person is trying to find love when the chances appear very dim. Use only as a last resort. Caution! Be very careful that the entire candle is burned at one time. Do not save portions of the candle and re-use, to do so may result in a reversal of the desired effects. If a loved one is merely angry and one denies their return, use in conjunction with either the relocator or lost and found candle.*

They could not find a "hatred candle." "There is more," the clerk explained. "If you are using a hatred potion, then I would recommend a revenge candle. Look under the R's."

They found the perfect candle. *Revenge!* it said in large red letters followed by a large exclamation point. *To be used very sparingly and under extreme circumstances where nothing worked*, Manuel read aloud. Adolfo scratched his head. "Do you believe we need to go that far, Manuel?"

"I sure do," he answered. "We must use everything at our disposal. After all, the woman deserves it. Remember your pension check, why don't you?"

"You are right," Adolfo answered, "but it's just that I hate to over-revenge anyone. I don't mind getting even, but this sounds like we're over-doing it."

"Too much sometimes is not enough," the Professor said. He picked up the candle and took it to the counter and paid for both the potion and the candle. Lately he was the only one that had any money.

"Don't forget," the clerk said, as they walked out, that if you really want all this to work, you must turn a picture of the victim upside-down for twenty-four hours."

They hurriedly returned to the boarding house and, since they did not have Antonia's picture, they decided to turn a wallet photograph (Rita Hayworth) upside-down on the mirror on the dresser. "Upside down she looks somewhat like her," Manuel explained.

"Yes," Adolfo said, his hands on his chin looking at the photograph upside down. "They both have faces!"

It was ten o'clock at night by the time they arrived in front of Antonia's house. They were exhausted, especially Manuel, who had to walk twice as fast as Adolfo just to keep up. They traveled through part of their new neighborhood and into the old one and it took them about two hours.

"I don't know if this is worth it," Adolfo said, panting. "We may just be over-doing this revenge thing and we're not going to accomplish much."

"That's where you're wrong," Manuel said. He kept falling behind. "I have seen this witchcraft work all my life. In my native Villa de Santiago, Doña Teresita our local witchcraft lady, could put a hex on a person and make it work. Just to give you an example, there was a man," he said this while tiring out. "Can we walk slower? You're killing me, Adolfo. Remember that your legs are a lot longer than mine . . . . As I was saying, the man had a wife who would make a fool of him with other men."

"Haven't you told me that story before?" Adolfo asked. He had slowed down and was allowing the Professor to take his time with the story. It was Maria who had told him the story, the same one she had told Carmen.

"I may have," Manuel replied, "but it bears repeating. Such are the powers of women who practice witchcraft. And you would imagine that I, an educated man so to speak, would not believe in such things. Anyway," he continued, "the man was cuckolded repeatedly. The woman had no shame. She did it in the house, his own house, Adolfo, with other men while her husband washed the supper dishes. Can you believe that? She did it behind trees, bushes, in the grass, under houses, the woman had a tremendous apetite for *it*. You understand what I mean?"

"Yes, I do," Adolfo said. "It reminds me of the same woman Maria always talks about. Surely it's not the same one."

"I doubt it," he replied. "But in your life have you heard of anything like that? A man as docile as a contented dog? And yet his testicles were there."

"How do you know?" Adolfo asked. He was starting to laugh.

"I was told, that's why I know. But that's another story."

"If you don't finish this one, I'm going to start walking faster."

"Well, you could say I'm finished. But do you get the idea of the power of witchcraft? The man obviously had been hexed by some form of witchcraft. He sees things and doesn't believe what he sees."

The house was dark, except for the kitchen. They walked slowly and softly up to the house already knowing what to do. Manuel went under the house. He crawled to the center of the house, as well as he could measure in the dark. The dog was there asleep and he recognized Manuel after emitting a soft growl. Manuel took the potion out of the box and unwrapped its contents. It was a substance that he determined in the darkness to be pieces of leaves and twigs. He rubbed some between his fingers and smelled it, but could not discern any recognizable odor. Adolfo had stayed behind, for he was too large to fit under the house. He would be the sentry. If he whistled, he had said, it would be a signal to Manuel that someone was approaching.

The directions had been very explicit. In order for the potion to work, the contents had to be about equally distributed toward the four corners of the house. The candle had no directions on it, so they had decided to light it under the house and allow it to burn itself down during the night.

Adolfo could see inside the house through the open door. Antonia was talking to someone seated at the table, but he could not see who it was. Her daughter, Eloise, walked up to her and both talked and laughed as Antonia washed the dishes in the sink. He could see her robust body through the dress and cursed himself for not having taken advantage when he had the opportunity. Bobby, Antonia's son, came into the kitchen also and walked to the door. There he stood for a moment, not being able to see outside in the dark. Adolfo waited nervously. If Bobby walked out, they would be caught. Manuel would have no time to get out. Bobby said something to Antonia and he walked away from the door. Adolfo heard the strike of the match and the glow under the house. The glow grew larger as the candle took over. Now it flickered gently under the house.

Bobby came out through the door. Adolfo stepped behind the house and at the same time he noticed the light from the candle extinguish. Manuel had heard the door open and slam shut. Bobby walked around for what seemed like an eternity to Adolfo and then abruptly he walked back in. "Come finish your homework," Antonia had told him.

The light from under the house came on again. Manuel had re-lit the candle. "I swear that woman will pay for everything she's done to us, Adolfo," he said afterwards. "That is one hex that she cannot remove, for in the first place, she doesn't know the hex has been placed on her and then she doesn't know who did it. She will just assume she has hit upon a rash of bad luck. You just wait and see." He smiled a wicked, crooked smile that Adolfo had never seen from him before.

As he was coming out from under the house, he was spotted by one of the mean sisters that lived across the yard. "Who's there?" Cristina demanded. She already had a hoe in her hands. "Answer me, you bastard. Whoever is out there. What are you burning, you sonofabitches."

Adolfo saw her coming toward the house. He tried to whistle, but his lips wouldn't pucker. His damn teeth were at the boarding house. He tried again and again, but no sound came from his mouth. Finally in desperation as the woman drew nearer, he yelled for Manuel. In the meantime, Manuel had heard the woman and had started crawling from under the house as fast as he could. He came out running on all fours much like a dog, as Adolfo would describe it later. As he gathered momentum, he finally straightened out in full stride. Adolfo had already started running before the Professor came out from under the house and he looked back down the street and he could see the Professor running and gaining on him. Behind the Professor was Cristina running after him, followed by her other two mean sisters, Inez and Margarita.

"They were trying to burn the house down, the bastards," Cristina yelled.

"Whose house?" Inez asked her as she ran to her.

"Antonia's," Cristina said, exhausted.

"Well fuck Antonia," Margarita said. "I thought they were doing something to our house."

"Oh no, they wouldn't dare," Cristina said as she stopped running. "Let the sonsofbitches go."

"Yes," Inez replied, "I don't see what you're so excited about. It's no skin off our you-know-what. Fuck Antonia and her house. What has she ever done for us."

"You're right, Inez," Margarita agreed. It was a perfect place for the put-down. "Cristina is always getting excited about any goddamn thing that doesn't concern her."

"Yes," Cristina said. "Like I'm getting excited about taking this goddamn hoe and hitting you over the head with it."

"You try it, you sonofabitch," Margarita said, "and I'll kick your thing in to where you can't find it with your favorite banana."

The reference to the banana was guaranteed to set off Cristina. Somehow, through the years, it had become a sore subject with her and the other two, knowing the nature of her personality, used it to start her off on an anger binge that lasted sometimes for days.

"What happened?" Antonia asked as she stood by the house. The wind had blown the candle flame out by the time she stepped outside. What was all the commotion about?"

"What do you care, you goddamn whore," Cristina answered. She was really angry now. "Who the shit do you think you are, asking us what's going on? What have you ever done for us?

"Someone was trying to burn your goddam house down," Inez answered her. "If it wasn't for us, you'd be in a lot of trouble right now. My sisters and I are getting tired of all this crap," Margarita said. "What with your whoring around all the time, fucking all kinds of men, there's bound to be someone who's after your goddamn ass, big as it is. We don't mind telling you that we're tired of all this and all the stuff that goes on in your house." With that, and without allowing Antonia a spoken word, they went inside.

The hex was on! It didn't matter that the candle flame had been blown out almost immediately. The important thing, according to the Professor, who had somewhat of a legal mind, was that it had been lit and that no unused portion had been reused. Nowhere could he find where the candle said that it had to burn for a specified time. Granted, he said later, that the curse would be better, more everlasting and profound, if it burned for a long time. After all, he rationalized to Adolfo, they really didn't want to injure the lady, just scare her, put her in her place, so to speak.

That night, in bed on his back, Manuel spoke to Adolfo as he gently scratched a wound on his arm and stared at the ceiling. The small lamp light was on. "What is going to happen?" he asked. "I wonder what will happen? Isn't witchcraft interesting?"

"Not as interesting as running down the street with three crazy women chasing us. And to think that this has happened twice," Adolfo said. "I'm getting too old for this. I don't care about revenge anymore. I just want to be left alone. He had taken the bottle and placed it under the bed. From here it was easy enough to reach under and bring the bottle out, take a swallow, then place the bottle back in one continuous, swift, motion. Manuel refused a drink. He had had enough troubles for the night.

Manuel thought a while on what Adolfo had said. "I don't blame you," he answered. "Wouldn't it be nice if they left us alone?"

Adolfo started to snore and the Professor turned off the light.

In the morning, they met each one of the tennants at breakfast. The lady introduced them around. There were four besides themselves. From the youngest to the oldest, this included a young lady in her twenties named Raquel or Rachel, a slightly older lady named Sylvia, a fortyish man named Domingo and the oldest, a man that appeared to be in his fifties whose name was Isaac. The young lady, they found out during their conversation, was a seamstress. The older lady was a personal correspondent and notary public for a bookkeeper. The younger of the men, Domingo, was a salesman in a hardware store. Isaac was a helper at the farmer's produce market.

They were all pleasant, but this was not enough for Adolfo. "Can you imagine these people," he told the Professor. "All their lives doing nothing but getting up and going to work, then coming home to go to bed, just to rest up to go to work again. Is this life?"

"I don't know if this is life or not," Manuel said thinking over such a profound question, "but that's what most people live for."

They all ate at a long table. The food had been prepared by Marta, the cook. She did not live at the house. She was married, had children of her own and came to work on foot. She served the meal in large bowls and it was everyone for himself. The men did allow the women to serve themselves first, though.

At the end of the meal, the lady of the house, Anna, would help Marta pick up the dishes and she would collect the money from each of the diners. At night she would be informed as to who would be eating breakfast the next morning. She charged twenty cents for breakfast, thirty for lunch and thirty-five for supper. This suited Adolfo and Manuel fine. They hardly ever ate breakfast and lunch there, but they really went after the supper. That made up for the rest of the meals they had missed.

The two women boarders lived downstairs in a bedroom adjacent to Anna's. The two men lived upstairs across the hall from Adolfo and Manuel. They shared a bathroom upstairs and the women shared one downstairs.

Anna had taken special care to decorate the house in her "style." She had seen a photograph of the interior of a house and she had in her own way tried to duplicate it. What she really had done was tried to cover most of the furniture with doilies. In the entries where there were no doors she had placed heavy curtains that were hard to move as one passed through them and which were very hard to keep clean.

At night the three women stayed in the living room and talked. The men never came in. Adolfo and Manuel took off after supper and no one saw them until the following day. Domingo and Isaac were usually in bed early in the evening. "They go to bed with the chickens and rise with the roosters," Adolfo said of them. Anyway, they never went anywhere together.

Anna had lost her husband in a train accident. He had been employed for several years at the rail-yards as a laborer who hitched and unhitched rail cars. One rainy afternoon he stumbled over the track and fell perfectly between two moving rail cars. It was as if divine providence had taken special care that this would be the manner of his death. "He was almost cut in half," she sighed as she recounted her misfortune to Adolfo and Manuel one rainy afternoon when they had failed to go out. "He was so strong and virile," she added, and then she raised an eyebrow to them and said, "you know what I mean, don't you?"

"Yes," Adolfo had replied, meekly. Here he was again in the uncomfortable situation where the only one to talk was a woman. He couldn't think of anything to say. Sure he knew what she meant. In those days "virile" meant sexual prowess.

"But he was cut in half," she sighed again, this time a longer sigh and she gave a look of wonderment, as if she could not believe she had survived it all. "They opened the casket, although it was against my wishes. But his family wanted it that way and in those days I was naive. I believed everyone was right except myself. I guess you can say that I did not have courage. Not like I do now, anyway. So they pushed me into it. And when I saw him in the casket, he did not look at all like my husband. I thought for an instant that maybe this was all a dream and I would awaken from it, relieved, my husband at my side. Virile as he always was. But it was him. I couldn't help but look at his waist. God knows I tried not to. And I could see that there was an emptiness to him there. How cruel they were." She wiped tears from her eyes.

Adolfo did not know what to do. He had no handkerchiefs. Manuel didn't either. After she blew her nose gently with her own handkerchief, she continued.

"You both realize," she said, "that a woman who had been initiated by a virile man suffers greatly afterwards. Not only are you placed in a situation of hopelessness, others see you as helpless and begin to try to prey on you. Yes, there were leacherous men at my door. In the first place, they knew I was young and they knew I had received the money from the railroad insurance. I bought this house. They were after me. I suffered from hot flashes for several years. But I shouldn't be telling you all this, I hardly know the two of you. What must you think? Please, please, let's forget this conversation . . . as if it didn't happen, don't you agree?"

"Yes." they replied.

For their part, it would be better if they never talked to the lady in private again.

It seemed to Adolfo and Manuel that, more often than not as they were leaving the house through the corridor, that they could see the lady sitting on the couch covered with doilies, her hand nervously fingering the lace work, and she sobbing gently. It seemed, also, that she purposely had opened the heavy curtains so that they could see her. Finally, out of curiosity one night they stopped and asked her if they could be of any help.

"No," she replied. "At least not at the moment."

They continued on their way satisfied that at least they had not ignored the lady. "It would be terrible," Manuel said to Adolfo, "if later on we discovered that the lady had taken her own life and we didn't care enough about her to help."

"You're right," Adolfo replied. "Now it's out of our hands. If she kills herself, it's her fault."

The practice continued until the two men went to the lady one night and asked again if she needed any help.

"No," she replied, "but it's just that I've been so lonely since my young daughter died."

They were stunned: first the husband, now the daughter. "This woman has suffered more than the Virgin Mary," Adolfo reflected.

"And Mary Magdalen too!" Manuel added.

"It was a tragedy also," she explained. "She was well one day, dead the next. The doctors could do nothing."

"You poor woman," Manuel said, "you have suffered so much in this life. Surely you will go directly to heaven when you die. Your hell has been here on earth."

"The death of a child hurts more than anything in the world. There is nothing as tragic," she informed them.

Manuel felt like crying. After all, he reasoned that possibly, only possibly, he could have a child somewhere in Mexico. Adolfo, not the sentimentalist, wished they had not stopped to talk to Anna. After all, they had tried once and she had said that she was doing alright. It was Manuel that had stopped to talk to Anna, as far as he was concerned, he felt some sorrow for the lady, but this whole conversation made him anxious to go drink beer.

"I agree," Manuel said, rubbing his hands together, "I have even heard of mother's doing themselves in after one of their children die."

He looked at Anna to see if he could detect any inclination toward suicide. Not seeing any, he continued, "but I'm sure those women are off a little in their minds and are very few."

"The thought entered my mind many times," she said. She had taken one of the doilies and had spread it between her thighs and was pressing on it with her hands. "But then I saw the uselessness of the act. What would it accomplish? Sure, my husband had been cut in half. But his death was so sudden, even comical, now that I think about it. Suicide is out of the question, anyway."

Later on as they walked to their favorite beer joint, Adolfo remained quiet for a while, then he asked, "Why would she say that her husband's death was comical?"

"Well," the Professor said, "imagine the things that have to occur and the sequence in which they occurred and the exact timing, the split second timing, in order for her husband to be killed. One second early, he falls between the rail-cars and nothing happens. If he falls one second later, he lands on top of the hitch and barely hurts his head."

"Well," Adolfo said, quickening his steps as he was ready for a beer, "I just don't want to die in a comical way."

"No one does," Manuel replied, "but someone has to."

And as Adolfo had just gotten through making that statement, he almost got hit by an old car, as he tried to cross the street without looking.

"See," Manuel said, taking the opportunity to rub it in. "You almost got killed in a comical way."

"Getting hit by a car is not comical to me," Adolfo said. "Useless, maybe, but not funny. Anyway, these ignorants around here could take lessons in driving from other parts of the world."

Anna's true intentions came to light one afternoon when she caught

Adolfo by himself in his room. She had sent Manuel to run an errand. She had opened the door gently without knocking and she had surprised Adolfo while he was walking around in his shorts. He quickly grabbed the top sheet from the bed and wrapped it around his waist. He still believed that a woman should not see a man without his clothes on. And more recently, he was becoming more and more ashamed of the way he looked undressed. Had she but seen him when he had been the young athlete, he wouldn't have covered himself up as fast.

He arranged the sheet to cover his upper body also. The pendulous growth of his breasts embarrassed him.

"I am a woman of few words," she began.

It was hard for him to believe that, he thought. He was more embarrassed now when he noticed, while looking down, that he had not trimmed his toenails in a long time. He tried to curl his toes downward under his feet, as if he had some affliction of the extremities.

"I was left with a lot of appetites that my husband had just begun to fill. In the tree of life, if I can speak like that, only a few of my apples have been plucked. I remain loaded with fruit and my branches are burdened by their weight. So much so that I feel as if my whole body will break."

Adolfo was trying not to look at the lady. Now he was embarrassed by what she was saying, whatever she meant by all this tree of life business.

"My tragedies have made me very strong and I feel it is a waste of time not to speak my mind. To put it bluntly, Adolfo, you and I, and especially you, are getting old. What are we saving it for?"

He was stunned again! As far as he could remember, Anna had now stunned him three times: the episode concerning her husband's death, her daughter's death and now this. He had never met any woman like her. Even Antonia seemed restrained, even coy, in her advances.

"The earth is going to eat it up anyway," she continued. She was standing at the foot of the bed, leaning forward speaking slowly, making sure Adolfo heard every word. "Do you understand what I'm saying?"

He was devastated, but encouraged. He had always been the one making the advances. He had always been the one in pursuit of women. It was he that took the initiative. He didn't know what to say. His encouragement came at the surprise that he could still attract women.

From this point, it was just a matter of time until she got him into her bedroom. And although he did not perform as she had expected him to, she was satisfied most of the time and it seemed to please her. Her apples were fewer now and her limbs seemed to be relieved somewhat from the pressure of the weight of the fruit.

And although she appeared to be rough spoken, she gently assuaged his feelings of inadequacy at having been seduced. Her demeanor changed. She did not cry anymore. Obviously, she was sad at times when she reminisced. But her sudden crying and moods of depression were gone. She had been right. She needed a man.

Adolfo was not as pleased as she was. From his childhood days, he had been raised ever the gentlemen. And yet in his double-standard morality, he knew at what time he could be the impregnating scoundrel. He had mastered the technique, the turning off and on of the charm. In this relationship, though, there was nothing to turn off and on. This displeased him. He felt like he was playing the woman's part in the affair. Indeed, he was.

For all that he had been, he had never been the gigolo. Every affair, he thought, had been meaningful and special and he remembered most of them fondly. This one he would just as soon forget.

He had also never met anyone like Anna, who demanded to be loved no matter how she behaved. As an example, he told Manuel, Anna had passed wind while in her sleep. "How do you expect me to like someone like that?" he asked. Manuel shook his head. "You mean to tell me that women don't fart?" he asked.

"Not mine," Adolfo said in a short tone. "My women have always been ladies."

"I got over that a long time ago," Manuel said. "My women did a lot of things. They even went to the toilet."

"You're making fun of me and I don't like it," Adolfo said. "You know what I mean, she's so pushy, so masculine in her ways."

"How long is it since we've paid to live here?" Manuel interrupted.

"Two or three months," Adolfo replied.

"Then don't complain. Hurry up and go screw her again; we have no other place to go to."

CHAPTER 7

Maria dreaded the visit, and although her oldest daughter came to visit only every two to three years, she still could not make herself enjoy her daughter's company. She had grown up to be just as contrary as she had been as a child. She could not understand what had possessed her not to discipline the child. It was too late now, she told herself. She must control herself. And it was this precise feeling, what she was going through now, that irritated and exhausted her. Here it was still not the day of her arrival and already Maria was angry. She had awakened in a bad mood over a dream she had had about the Young Maria and it had ruined her day.

She had dreamed that her daughter had come to visit. She had brought her ever-pleasing Eddie along, but in the background she could see many people also. Apparently, in the dream, Young Maria had invited all these people to come along and visit Maria. It would be just like her, Maria thought, as she swept the yard. The sweeping of yards was a common practice in those days. No one had the grass lawns one sees today. The ground was swept of all topsoil and after a while it was as hard as concrete.

But, she came. There was no holding her back. Once she said she was coming, she didn't care about anything else. Maria could have written and told her not to come, but it wouldn't have made any difference. She still would have come. She knew that Young Maria would have her way. And if Maria had indeed informed her that she would be out of town, Young Maria would have ignored the letter, as if it had never been written, for she knew that her mother had to cancel all plans just to satisfy her. What's more, Maria knew it. What was irritating (again we go back to irritation) was that she, Maria, couldn't do anything about it.

To Maria this love-hate-guilt relationship with her daughter drove her mad. Young Maria played on these feelings to impose her will on her mother. After all, Maria would think, she *is* my daughter. If I don't do it for her, who would I do it for?

She arrived late afternoon with a severe headache and her smiling husband, Eddie, and her son, Junior. She ran into the house and barely said hello as she ran past Maria and into the bathroom. Eddie came right after her and shook Maria's hand, embraced her and kissed her. Junior embraced her and was told by his father to give Maria a kiss. He did so but only as a matter of duty. Shortly, Young Maria came out of the restroom and briefly, just briefly, hugged her mother and said, "Mama, you must bathe more often. How long has it been since you've bathed?"

"I bathed this morning, but I've been working all day getting ready for your arrival."

"Then you must be having some kidney problems. Maggie, my friend in Sacramento, had a kidney problem and she started smelling like that. It got to where her husband couldn't get near her."

"It's just that I perspired while working," Maria said, her feelings hurt.

"That's what happens when you live alone," Young Maria continued, not having heard the explanation or, if she had, ignoring it. "You start not taking care of yourself, not caring how you look. Oh, but I've got a headache! A migraine! Everytime I come here I get a migraine. I don't get migraines in Sacramento. It must be this eternal blowing wind and dust. I felt it coming about two hours ago. I just had to vomit." She was sitting in the the small living room bent forward at the waist and holding her head up in her hands. "What a horrible way to feel."

"Well, Baby Doll," Eddie said, "do you want me to go to the store for some aspirins?"

"No," she said, "I already took six."

"Well, did you bring your headache medicine?"

"No, I had not had a migraine in so long that I didn't think of it."

"Junior and I will go to the store," Eddie said, and with that, he grabbed Junior by the shoulder and both went out the door. "What's the name of that stuff you take all the time?" he asked as he reached the first steps.

"It's called bromide," she said and grabbed her head together in her hands. "It hurts even to talk," she said.

"Why don't you go to bed and see if that'll make it go away," Maria asked her. She was feeling sorry for her.

"I think I will," she said. "Where could I sleep that it's not very dusty?"

"You'll have to use Carmen's old bedroom," she said, wishing that Carmen were there with her now. "I've kept it cleaned up all this time."

"How's Carmen, anyway?" she asked.

"Oh, she's doing as good as can be expected. She will be out soon. I received a letter from her just yesterday and she says that she is feeling a lot stronger."

"I could have told her she would have trouble in San Diego," Young Maria said. "Didn't I tell you?"

"Yes, you did. But what are we to do? We can't all do what you want us to do all the time."

"That's the trouble with this family. It has no direction from anyone. If I don't step in who will? Adam? Arnoldo? They won't lift a finger. They will lift a bottle, though. If Carmen had paid attention to me and what I told her, she wouldn't be in this mess."

"I thought you said you were going to sleep."

"I will, but you can't get rid of me this easily. I'll read Carmen's letter when I wake up. Be sure not to let me sleep too much."

"Yes," Maria said. She had always been the baby that never slept, always fidgeting, always having to have something to do, something to say. For once, now that she was older, Maria hoped Young Maria would slow down and enjoy life. But, of course, she couldn't. "She reminds me," Maria wrote to Carmen, after Young Maria had left, "of the little dog we used to have that wanted to eat out of two bowls at the same time. She wants to have a say so in everything."

By sundown Young Maria had slept a few hours and the migraine had gone.

"You'd better drink the powders anyway," Eddie said. "Better be safe than sorry."

Junior had stayed inside the house playing with a new card game that he had brought with him. He barely spoke to anyone and to Maria this was a sign that he was being adversely indoctrinated by Young Maria. God only knows what she had told the boy about the family. Whatever it was, knowing Young Maria, Maria knew it wasn't good. Anyway, he kept to himself and didn't seem to enjoy Maria's company. Right now he was the only grandchild she had. The boy had always been puny and sickly and Young Maria had had a difficult time having him. She was one of the few females at that time that had required hospitalization. The doctors spoke of some blood-related disorder. And since Maria could not remember, would not remember, any member on her side of the family having similar troubles, she blamed Eddie's side of the family. They were so trashy anyway, she had thought.

She met them when Eddie's parents and a sister had come for the birth and had stayed for two weeks, making Young Maria sick with worry. Eddie's family had sat around all day long, drinking beer and raising hell. His father was a full time mortician in northern California and he had a hernia as big as a volley-ball and every time he sat down, the bulge between his legs would cause him great difficulty and pain, and when he tried to stand up, he almost had to be propped up by the wife and daughter. As a result of the beer drinking and the hernia, the man was frequently trying to get up to urinate. Several times he had dribbled urine and had soiled Young Maria's furniture. Young Maria had heard him fart and it had scared her. She thought the man had come undone at the crotch, what with the hernia and all. Eddie's mother was a part-time waitress. She only worked, she bragged, whenever she needed to. She had worked enough during her life already, she said. She had bulging eyes and a snaggle-toothed mouth with very thin lips and she smoked Bull Durham cigarettes that she rolled, one after another, all day long, and smoked in two or three puffs. His sister was an over-weight, over-bearing divorcee who joined in the beer drinking with her father and mother. She was out of a job, she had told Maria, but regularly she was a beautician and thought she could give a woman a permanent better than anyone else. In truth, she ruined Young Maria's hair for several months when she tried a new wave permanent using ammonia from a cleaning jar. Why Young Maria had let her do it, was beyond Maria's imagination. "I thought she was so smart," she had told Carmen. Maria left as soon as the boy was born. Young Maria suffered with her in-laws for a while and eventually they left after all the money and food was gone. She told Eddie that if they ever came back again, she would be leaving. Eddie had laughed.

They were sitting outside in back of the house on the hard ground. Young Maria had just finished taking a bath and she and Eddie joined Maria who had been sitting there cooling herself, as was her habit, after having cooked by the hot stove most of the day.

She had Carmen's letter in her hand and she gave it to Young Maria.

A frail lady appeared from around the house yelling, "Maria! Maria!" She wore a shawl over her head and held the corner of the shawl across her face.

"We're back here," Maria yelled.

It was Umberta, her closest friend.

"Come over," Maria implored her. "Come, come. Young Maria is here visiting. She and Eddie came in this afternoon."

"How are you Umberta?" Young Maria asked. She did not take her eyes off the letter to greet the woman. Eddie greeted her also. He liked Umberta since she was considered to be a very good cook.

"Didn't Junior come with you?" Umberta asked.

"Yes, he's here. He's inside." Maria answered, embarrassed that she had forgotten to mention the child.

"Junior!" Young Maria yelled. "Come out here and say hello to Umberta."

After a while Junior came out, shook Umberta's hand and returned to his toy inside the house.

"He's so tall," Umberta said. "Since the last time I saw him I'll bet he's grown three or four inches.

"He's not going to grow very much more." Eddie said. He had pulled over a heavy slotted wooden lawn chair and was sitting between Maria and her daughter. "He'll be like me. I grew very fast one year, just like he did and then I stopped. It runs in the family."

When he said "family," the picture of Eddie's mother, father and sister instantly appeared in Maria's mind, as if in a bad dream. She asked him how they were, but in a soft voice, hoping that Eddie would take it to mean that she didn't really want to know.

"They're fine," Eddie answered. He was always ready to talk.

("Worse than a woman," Maria had told Umberta.)

"My mother was in the hospital for a while, but she's okay now."

Why couldn't that have happened to Carmen, Maria thought. On second thought, she might not fulfill her promise to God. Her convenant she took seriously and if God didn't, she would not comply with her end of the deal. Her logic was that Eddie's mother never went to church and smoked Bull Durham all day long and she got well quicker than Carmen. God should have taken care of Carmen first, then cured the old lady, Eddie's mother. His priorities were not her priorities. The promise was off.

"And did she get well fast?" Maria asked, trying to find out if God had favored the old woman.

"Oh," Eddie said, "she was in and out in a couple of days. She's as good as new."

That was it, Maria thought. The promise was off. She could play God's game also.

Umberta had taken a kitchen chair that Maria had brought out. Young Maria passed the letter back to Maria. She folded it neatly and placed it in her apron pocket.

"She really has messed up her life," Young Maria said. "She should have never gone to San Diego. That is the worst town for T.B. in all of California. That's where all the riff-raff, the low downs, go to when they can't get work. They carry all kinds of diseases. One of my best friends (Here she goes again, Maria thought to herself. Why must she always have a best friend that knows everything?) was telling me that her aunt got sick in San Diego just walking around the beach. There were so many winos spitting on the side-walks and everywhere. She says they came on home right away. They said they'd never go back. And Carmen insists on going there."

"Well what could the poor girl do?" Maria said. "She felt a need to get away. Adolfo was going. It was a perfect time. It was either then or maybe never.

"That hateful Adolfo encouraged her, didn't he?"

"I suppose so," Maria said.

"I don't see how in the world you can put up with people like Adolfo. There's no necessity to her doing it." She told this to Umberta.

"I don't do it out of necessity, Maria," the old Maria replied with a sternness to her voice. She was getting irritated at the attack on Carmen and now Adolfo.

"You have no business taking in people like Adolfo, who take from you and never give anything back. And I'm talking about money, not just work. Look at all the work you have to do for him. That's without spending a nickel on him. You have got to be crazy to do it."

"Well, maybe I am," Maria said. "But I've done it for you also and I never asked for a dime from you."

"But you took it," Young Maria said angrily, "when I offered it."

"What was I to do? An old lady that needed it."

"You weren't old then."

"I've always been old, don't you understand? And I've always been poor to boot. What harm is there to help someone like Adolfo out? He has nothing . . . the poor man never accumulated anything in his life. While others were working in the fields earning a little here and there and raising a family, he wandered around playing fool's games with a stick and a ball and then the end came for him. What do I do with him? I'm the only living relative that cares for him. Someone had to do it. But you don't understand. You've always been selfish and greedy. I raised you wrong Maria and I'm paying for it."

"You raised me?" Young Maria had stood and was in the middle of the circle of chairs. "Are you complaining about that? What else could you have done, given me away, like a little bastard?"

"I never once thought of giving you away."

"No one would have taken her," Eddie said, trying to be funny.

"Shut up, you damn fool," Young Maria said to him. "I'm talking to my mother? You're not very funny!"

He got up and hurriedly walked inside the house. He slammed the screen door so hard that Maria thought he had broken it.

"I never, never, thought of giving you away," Maria said.

"Never, never?"

"Never. I loved you so very much from the moment you were born. And I suffered for it. There were those who said I should give you away, hide you somewhere, but I never, never thought of that. I loved you so very much, Maria, as I love you now. But you must understand that others have a right to their own lives. I realize that you have helped the family so much, that you sacrificed part of your life for us and I and the rest of the family are eternally grateful. Your brothers may not show it, but they are. Carmen adores you. You have been like a sister-mother to this family. There were days when I didn't know what I would do without you."

"And what would have happened to you if you had given me away?"

"Don't talk like that. I never gave it a thought. I would never have done it."

"And so you blame me for your early troubles. Is that what you're saying?"

"You're not making sense. I never blamed you for anything. It was worth all the humiliation to have you at my side. I loved you so, as I love you now."

Poor Umberta was nervously looking about, trying to act as if she was not interested in the conversation. Her bird-like eyes darted around from one corner of the house to the other, trying to ignore what was going on besides her. If it had been up to her she would have just as soon disappeared.

"I think it's getting late," she said as soon as she could get her comment in. "I have to get up early and help. Tomorrow is the first day for the lettuce crop. They say that this year we will harvest more lettuce than ever and I believe it, just by looking out across the field. Anyway I'd better be going."

"Don't leave yet," Maria said, "I haven't even offered you a cup of coffee."

"Oh no," Umberta said waving her hands in a negative way, "If I drink coffee, I won't be able to sleep."

Maria, of course, knew this. The ritual of offering the coffee and the reply that came with it had become a part of them, a way of saying good-bye, that they had repeated hundreds of times. Why they did this neither one knew nor even thought about.

Umberta's husband had died about seven years ago. It was one of those insignificant deaths that occur every day everywhere. She couldn't remember how long he had been dead, nor could Maria. Everytime his death came up in their frequent talks, they would calculate, subtract the year from today, and then they would agree that it had been longer than they thought. She had not loved the man.

Umberta's husband had stolen her from a dance at a ranch on a Saturday night where she had had to change dresses twice; she had perspired so. She had so kicked at the swept-hard ground that the following day she could hardly move. As thin as she was, she could dance forever, or so it had seemd to her. Yes, she had noticed the young man for several years and she liked him. What did she have to lose when he asked her? There may never be another one to ask me, she had reasoned. Her mother and father were mockingly angry, but that had been all. But, oh, what a miserable man he had been. She had given him four children, everyone one year apart, and all boys. And he had been more trouble than he was worth. She suffered silently, though, and Maria knew of many of her troubles, but both remained quiet about them, ignoring them as if they had never happened. This stoicism on her part was due mostly to her upbringing. A woman should not expect much from life. Wasn't a popular Mexican song of those days entitled *God Made Woman for the Pleasure of Man*? And if this philosophy extended throughout their cultures it was even more so for Umberta's family of farmworkers.

Young Maria's visits always brought back the bitter memories of those days when she was young, sixteen, and Young Maria had been a child. Maria did not mind her coming in the least. But she knew full well the many emotional peaks and valleys that she would go through during the next few days. She loved Young Maria very much. She had raised Maria as an ally. Both together had lived through the hard times: she the young mother of an illegitimate child and Young Maria the bastard-daughter of a fallen woman. The bond had grown strong. No one could ever break it. In an odd twist of logic, this explained why they would always argue. The argument was a show of love, of care. "After all," Young Maria often said, "if I didn't love you, I wouldn't care."

"That is true," Maria said. "I only wish sometimes that you didn't love me so much."

The love she had for Carmen was another kind of love. She had raised Carmen not as a daughter, but as a grandchild. She had been forty when she had Carmen and in those days forty was old for a woman to be having children.

Of her two sons, she preferred Arnold. He was the kindest and most thoughtful of the two. Adam was a scoundrel who was always running out of money. She managed to tolerate him and give him whatever she could. He was a gambler and a heavy drinker and did just about everything in excess. He ate a lot, drank a lot, gambled a lot. You would expect him to be a fat man, but on the contrary, he was thin and hawkish and pock-marked from a small pox infestation as a child. Maria had thought at the time that she had lost him, but he got well and never gained weight. This was one promise to God that she kept. She went from her house, the same one she was in now, to the same church on her knees praying the rosary. "Thank God no one saw me," she said in the morning after sun-up, while she rubbed camphor-laced alcohol on her knees.

Arnold, on the other hand, was the more serious of the two and he was robust. He had grown tall, like Adolfo. He drank to excess, but that was all. He saved his money and spent it wisely. He lived at the opposite side of Mexican Town from Maria in a clean, bright home with a wife, Dora. Dora and Maria did not get along, so Arnold visited his mother by himself. He quit making excuses for her after the first year of marriage. Dora's main objection to Maria was that she, Dora, had been raised believing that Maria was not a proper and clean woman. She promised to marry Arnold, but she told him early that she would not want to have anything to do with his mother. Arnold had never told Maria exactly why Dora didn't like her. He would never hurt her feelings. He preferred to say that Dora and Maria were much the same and they couldn't get along.

Adam's wife, Alba, was a foul-mouthed woman who had been married before. Maria hated her. Just the mere mention of her name would make Maria grit her teeth and she would say, "I'll chew her up, but I won't swallow her. How could Adam have married such a woman? What a mouth she has! She talks worse than a man." Not that Maria didn't curse, it was that the woman expressed herself in a crude way. She had no wit, no charm about her, as Maria had.

Both her sons worked in the fields by day and drank by night, as was the custom in this society.

Maria heard Adam and Arnold come in through the front door. Inside they could hear her sons and Eddie hollering and laughing. They had not seen Eddie for a couple of years and they could tell it from the noise going on inside the house.

Maria felt uncomfortable. The last time Eddie had gone out with them, he had been sick for several days. They had laughed at him except for Young Maria. She had been disgusted with him. She had taken it as a personal insult that her husband had made a drunken fool of himself.

Umberta excused herself again, shook each of the women's hands and walked away silently, stooped, as she had come.

"I'll talk to you later," Maria told her.

"Yes, perhaps after young Maria has left," Umberta replied. She had placed the shawl over her head and had whisked both ends around her small-ish neck.

The argument between Eddie and Young Maria started over whether Eddie should be allowed to go drink beer with Adam and Arnold.

Eddie had pleaded and Adam and Arnold had promised that they would behave and would come back reasonably sober and at a good hour, whatever that meant. Maria had interceded on Eddie's part. "Let him go," she said, "he's a man and should be able to take care of himself." Junior had started to cry over the argument and Young Maria had taken him with her to Carmen's old room. Her headache had started again. Finally she said through the door that she was dying in pain from her head and that Eddie could do as he damned pleased. She and Junior were going to bed after she took her bro-mide. Maria tried to help her, to help ease her pain, but she refused to open the door. As far as Maria was concerned, she could do without all this noise and these arguments.

Eddie, Adam and Arnold left and Maria could see them acting like chil-dren as they ran to the car and drove off in Arnold's car.

At the first beer joint they had encountered, *El Tigre*, the broad-black complected man who had threatened Adolfo. Upon seeing them, he had made several remarks about Adolfo and the three finished their beers and left. They had agreed not to talk to the man and even when he called Adam by name, they refused to be drawn into an argument.

They finally settled on going to a small place run by a friend of Adolfo's and, like Adolfo, a veteran of World War I. He did not tolerate much foolish-ness in his place, so consequently he did not have much business. When they arrived, they found the owner and an old man sitting at a table having a con-versation. They were the only ones there. He greeted them warmly and asked for Adolfo. They informed him that Adolfo had written and had found a fine place to stay and was enjoying good health.

"That's good," the owner replied, wiping the table. "When Maria writes to him, tell her to send him my best wishes. I miss the old son-of-a-gun. The stories he could tell. Whew!" He was shaking his head in disbelief.

"What, Adolfo?" the old companion said. "Why Adolfo could tell more stories and has seen more things than anyone around here. What a great pitcher he was!"

"One of the best," the owner replied. "One of the best."

"But unfortunately he drank too much," the companion said, repeating what had probably been said about Adolfo many times before. "You can't drink like he does and be an athlete. It just can't be done."

"He drinks, that's for sure," Arnold agreed. "Bring us each a beer," he said to the owner, and the owner got the beer from behind the counter and served them.

"The story I liked best was the time Adolfo told me about a game in Mexico in a small town somewhere. They were playing an exhibition." The owner sat down by his companion and wiped his ice-cold hands with a rag he carried draped across his neck. "Adolfo said he hit the ball, a little single blooper over the second baseman's head and as he ran for first he noticed the second-baseman would reach down and try to get the ball, but he acted like he couldn't, so he ran for second and as he approached second base, the center-fielder and the short-stop and the second-baseman were running around the ball, but they couldn't pick it up. So he ran for third! When he got there he was going to slide but his team-mates yelled for him to come on home! He came into home standing up. And he won the game with an inside-the-park home-run. Do you know how he did it?"

Of course everyone did. Adolfo had told the story many times, but someone always enjoyed hearing the ending all over again, so no one admitted to knowing about the story. It would have destroyed the teller.

"They found out later that the ball had rolled into a rattle-snake hole and the snake kept striking at whoever tried to pick up the ball. In the meantime, Adolfo rounds the bases and wins the game — four to three."

"Do you notice that he always scores the winning run?" Adam asked the group, laughing.

They all laughed, but it was true. Adolfo always, in his own stories, managed to win the game, score the winning run, strike out the last batter with the bases full. It wasn't true, but to do otherwise, to tell the truth, would have made the stories not worth telling, or so Adolfo thought.

"I don't want to bring up bad news," the owner said, solemnly, "but I just heard say that the Turtle is dying."

"When did you find out?" Adam asked him. He was mildly shocked. After all, she was not an older woman.

"Just now," he replied, "my friend here just told me." He pointed to the small man sitting across the table from him.

"Yes," the man said, turning over to face Arnold, Adam and Eddie. "She's been sick for several weeks now."

"No wonder I hadn't seen her," Arnold said, "I knew there was something wrong. But then again, I thought that maybe she had left town for a while. Has she got syphilis?"

"No one knows. She didn't want to go to the doctor. She wants to die in peace, she says, or so someone told me she says."

"Well is she at the house?" Adam asked the man. He was the one most interested in her since she was one of the older prostitutes that Adam knew.

"Yes, that's what they tell me."

"Poor woman," the owner said. "Poor woman. I hadn't seen her in a long time. She didn't work around here much."

"No, she was working out of her house," Adam replied. "She only worked her old friends and even then she turned a lot of men down."

"I don't see why anyone would go to her," Arnold said, thinking how awful it must have been. She wasn't called 'the Turtle' for nothing. She did remind one of a turtle. She was appropriately nick-named."

"Yes, but she was a knowledgeable woman, if you know what I mean." Adam winked at Eddie and Eddie started laughing. "She knew more about men and what to do to them than any other woman I ever met."

"You mean you went to her?" Arnold asked, not believing that his brother would stoop so low. "You mean you went to bed with her? As ugly as she was?"

"Is," said the little man.

"As ugly as she is," Arnold repeated, correcting himself. "I don't believe it, Adam."

"Why not?" Eddie said, "he's probably gone to bed with a lot worse."

So after many beers and conversation about the prostitute called "the Turtle," they decided that they would call on the sick lady, late as it was.

She lived like all the prostitutes in town, just east of where the taverns were. Some lived in courts, as they were called then and a few, the older ones who had retired, lived in small frame wooden houses that had never been painted. Typically, the houses had small porches and sat high off the ground to secure better ventilation. They were divided into a living room, a kitchen and a bedroom. There were two doors, one led from the bedroom to the outside and the front door led into the living room. By the side of the house was the ever-present water faucet, as it stuck up three to four feet from the ground. Here at the faucet, the daily ritual was performed: the brushing of the teeth, the wetting of the hair, combing, washing of the feet, neck, hands, torso, in fact, the cleaning of most of the body parts. At night, in the silence, the women would wash their bodies, squatting under the cool water as it dribbled slowly from above. At the back of the property was the one-seater outhouse that smelled of fresh decaying humus.

They could tell in the brightness of the moon that the woman had recently re-roofed the house. The one last act of a true home-owner. She had also arranged some large stones in semicircles around the porch and had painted them white with lime. They could see the glow of a kerosene lamp and some figures walking about inside the house.

Not being able to support themselves very well, they leaned into each other as they walked up the steps. Once on the porch, they steadied themselves and Adam knocked lightly on the door.

"Who is it?" came the voice from inside the house.

"It's Adam and my brother Arnold and our brother-in-law."

"Come in," a coarse looking woman said, opening the door.

Once inside, she asked them, "Did you come to see Virginia?" This was "the Turtle's" real name. No one called her by her nick-name to her face.

"Yes," Adam replied. The other two agreed by nodding their heads.

"You're too late, I'm afraid," the woman said. "She died just a few minutes ago."

The other women in the house were cleaning and dusting and re-arranging the furniture. Some were in the kitchen cleaning the stove and mopping the floors.

"What did she die of?"

"Syphilis, don't you understand? It got to her brain and when it did, she was dead in a week."

"She was a good woman," Adam said. "She was a very good woman." He couldn't think of anything else to say.

"Yes she was," the woman said. "There aren't too many like her nowadays. She helped us all at one time or another." The other women, the ones who heard her words, agreed and they spoke softly about her as they went about their work.

When they walked into the dimly lit, kerosene-smelling room, they could see her body made into a ball and not yet covered. Apparently she had died in pain. They covered her up after cleaning the saliva from her mouth and after straightening her body out. She had lost weight, Adam thought. She had been much bigger than this. How long had it been since he had seen her? He tried to remember as he went from one side of the bed to the other, helping to roll her up in a quilt and sheet, but he could not remember.

The doctor arrived shortly afterwards, as they all stood in the kitchen drinking coffee and telling stories about Virginia, "the Turtle." He was a small man who took care of most of the Mexican-town residents. He was not a very good doctor, simply because he did not have to be. What was the point? He already knew more than he practiced. His continuing education consisted of reading the newspaper every day. Unless it was something serious, he usually wound up the house-call telling the patient something about the feature story on the pages of the *Valley Times*. He was a nice and kind and gentle man and most everyone loved him. Dr. Chichester was his name and since no one could pronounce it, they called him Dr. Chi — the favorite Mexican word for urine. Oh, how the children snickered and laughed when they heard the old people talk about going to Dr. Chi.

He ordered the three drunk men to unroll the body and help him undress her. After a very cursory examination, he pronounced her dead. "What did she die of?" they asked.

"Syphilis," he replied. "I had just seen her a few weeks ago. It was in her brain. I was expecting it."

He sat at the kitchen table and took out an official looking form from his bag. "Name?" he asked.

"Virginia Gonzalez," the woman who had opened the door for them answered.

"Occupation?"

They all laughed even though the dead woman was in the next room.

"What can we put down?" the doctor asked them.

"Housewife," they said.

"Address?"

"Same as the house, I guess."

"Well," the doctor said, writing, "we'll just write down the town's name."

"Age?"

No one knew. They argued and agreed on fifty-nine.

He signed the form and had one of the prostitutes who could write sign as witness and then he left.

"You can get the funeral home to take her now," he said as he crossed the room.

They had difficulty moving the body off the bed when the hearse got there. The driver, a small middle-aged man named Hector, could hardly roll the dead woman over unto a stretcher so they helped him. First they covered the body again, since Dr. Chichester had uncovered it to do his examination. Then they kept rolling the woman until the quilt and sheet was completely around her. It took all four and some of the women's help to get the body through the kitchen, the living room and out of the house. Once inside the hearse, they rolled her over to one side and placed a large board on her free side, so that she would not roll. Eddie, playing his role as part-time embalmer, rode back with the driver. Arnold and Adam followed in Arnold's car. It was three o'clock in the morning and they were still drunk.

The funeral house was behind an old ice-house and the hearse went past it slightly, in order to be able to back up and go between the ice-house and the fence. Arnold and Adam stopped in front of the ice-house and watched as Hector very expertly backed the hearse through the drive-way barely missing by inches the corner of the building. It was apparent that he had done it many times before.

They placed the body on a galvanized steel table and Hector began to work. They uncovered the body and saw her, Virginia, "the Turtle," for the first time under a good light. She had lost a lot of weight, but it was still her. Adam could see what an ugly sight she was. Part of her charm while alive had been her animation, her facial expressions. Now dead, she appeared plastic and very hard — ugly hard. Arnold went over to the sink and vomited. Adam felt like it when he heard Arnold but he held it back with all his might, because he thought it would be disrespectful to vomit. Eddie and Hector started cutting into the inside of her legs and dissected out a vein and an artery. They attached glass canulas to the veins and began the slow process of removing the blood from the body and injecting salt water through the arteries to replace the fluid lost. Adam then vomited and left the room. Arnold had left as soon as he had spit out all the mucus and liquor accumulated in his stomach. Outside, they waited in the car, feeling better in the fresh air and wondering what else the two men were doing to "the Turtle."

When they arrived at Maria's, the living-room lamp was still on. That meant trouble for everyone, especially Eddie. Arnold and Adam decided it would be better if Eddie went in alone. After all, he was the only one that smelled of formalin and could explain what had happened.

"No sense in all of us getting the shit kicked out of us," Adam had reasoned to him. "She's yours anyway, Eddie."

"And your sister," Eddie had reminded them, trying to get them to change their minds.

"No way are we going in," Arnold said, emphatically. "In the first place, we don't have to and you do, and in the second place, I've got to go work today. I'm running awfully late as it is."

"Besides," Adam said, "you wanted to go out just as bad as we did."

"You guys are setting me up," Eddie pleaded. "I'm taking all the blame."

"Well, aren't you the big macho like you always brag about. Where's your macho now?" Adam was taunting him.

"I guess you guys are right," Eddie said. "I'll see you sometime down the road."

"When are you going back?"

"Well," Eddie replied, he had seen an opening for a funny line. "We were *supposed* to stay a week, but now I'll probably be going home tomorrow."

"Hey man," Adam remembered, "you can't do that. We've got a lot of things to do. We haven't gone rabbit hunting yet. We haven't cooked our famous cow-shit stew. Where's all the fun going to be if you leave?"

"Well, I don't know," Eddie said. "I don't know what's going to happen. Contact me tomorrow."

"Tomorrow?" Arnold cried. "You're crazy. This won't blow over for three or four days. You're going to be stuck with the two Marias for a while, I'm afraid."

"Maybe I can keep them from fighting," Eddie said as he opened the door and stumbled out of the car.

"You haven't done it yet," Adam said. "They've been angry at each other all their lives. No one can keep them from arguing."

Eddie looked up at the stars for the first time that night and, as he stretched his neck backward, he saw them race by his eyes at an incredible speed. He had no idea he was that drunk. He immediately pitched forward and fell on the bumper of the car and started vomiting. The other two rushed out and picked him up and dragged him to the first steps and left him there. They took off as fast as they could, never looking back, as if doing so would keep Young Maria from seeing them.

Young Maria was so angry that, when she saw Eddie walk in bleeding from the head, she was speechless. She ran and grabbed him and took him inside the kitchen and raised his head over the sink. She started to scream when the blood-stained water ran off Eddie's head. Maria rushed in, startled by the screams. She saw Eddie bent over the sink with blood dripping from his head. "Eddie, Eddie, what have you done to yourself," she pleaded, "what happened to you? what in God's name happened to you?" She had grabbed him to help Young Maria hold him up.

Junior awoke and came into the kitchen, saw the spectacle of his father bleeding from his head and he ran back to his room crying in terror.

"So help me God," Young Maria said, holding Eddie's head under the faucet, hard, "if you get over this, I'm going to kill you!"

It was not the custom in those days for the general population to attend prostitute's funerals. It just was not done. To do so was, people thought, an admission of familiarity and who knows how deeply that went. So to avoid any criticism, only the prostitutes went to prostitute's funerals.

The priest had refused to allow the body in church. She had not been a good Christian and he had never seen her in church. Not only that, he would not officiate at the funeral. He announced that she would be buried as an agnostic (no one but he knew the meaning of the word) and without his blessings or the blessings of the Holy Mother Church.

Maria, though, persuaded Adam to tell Hector that the least they could do for the poor dead woman was to drive her past the church, maybe slow down a little in front and stop, fake some car trouble and that maybe, just maybe, that would be enough for her to get to purgatory. From purgatory, Maria had thought to herself, it would be a simple matter for her to pray the dead prostitute up to heaven in no time — two or three years of rosaries at the most. And what is two or three years in the eternal life of a woman's soul? Why nothing, just a fleck in the space of time.

And so they did. Hector, dressed in a black suit and white shirt and black tie with torn white gloves, drove the hearse around the town square while people watched and slowly drove to the front of the church and slowly he came to a stop, got out, checked his battery, and up to purgatory "the Turtle" went.

Eddie's wound had been a small cut on the top of his head. The sharp metal bumper had probably nicked a small artery. Adam and Arnold had checked it and had determined it to be of no danger. That being the case, they decided just to leave him there. The wound was not serious enough for them to face Young Maria.

The two Marias had been arguing during Eddie's absence. Maria felt that Eddie was being held against his will by the Young Maria and that if it were up to him, he would leave.

"Eddie?" Young Maria questioned. "Eddie leave? He doesn't have the guts to leave. He relies entirely on me. Who do you think runs the house?"

"I know you run it," Maria said. "And I don't think it's right. Look at what you've done to the man. Look at what you're doing to Junior."

"What have I done?" Young Maria yelled. "Tell me, I'd like to know. Everyone blames me. You blame me. *Eddie* blames me. *Junior* blames me.

Adam. Arnold. Everyone is on me like I was some kind of animal. Well, I'm not. Who was it that kept this family together when things were bad during the Depression? Didn't I knock myself out helping you and everyone else? Didn't I hold down two jobs so that Adam and Arnold could stay in school? Believe me, I'm not an animal. Animals don't do things like that. Have I ever asked Adam and Arnold and Carmen for anything?"

"No," Maria replied. She had her there.

"I could have. I could have asked for the years I put into this family and all this without a gesture of gratitude. No thank-yous. If Eddie allows me to run the family, it's because he wants me to. Don't you understand? He loves it. He loves not having to make decisions. He loves just hanging around without any responsibilities, drinking beer and being a swell guy to everyone he meets. But at home? He never takes Junior anywhere. He stays away from him, but acts like he loves all the neighbor's kids. He's a hypocrite and he knows it, but no one else does, except Junior and me. Well, and I guess you do too. As a matter of fact, a lot of people know he's a hypocrite. I just didn't realize it until after I said it."

"But you must give him something to do."

"Like what?"

"Well," Maria said, and she knew her argument was losing ground, "you could let him have some time off from you."

"I'd be glad to. Don't you realize that it's he that doesn't want to leave. He's more secure with me than without me. He's lost without me. All this argument about going out is a farce. He can go; I don't care. I feel used up already. Here I am forty-two-years old and I feel old. I guess I've lived enough for a forty-two-year-old woman."

"You're young, Maria, you've still got a long way to go. Look at me, at my age, and I'm still going strong. I can work from sun-up to sun-down and I can still do a lot of things that most women my age can't do."

"Like walking on your knees from here to church at three o'clock in the morning," Young Maria said, jabbing at her mother.

"Yes, and what of it. It's my business."

"But hasn't the Priest told you not to do it?"

"What does he know?" Maria asked angrily, as if Young Maria should know better.

"Well, he's the Priest, mother," Young Maria said, "and if he doesn't know, who does?"

"It's just that he doesn't understand our ways, our customs. I'll bet you that in Spain they do things that we think of as crazy."

"Like what?" Young Maria asked challenging her.

"Like something, I don't know, but I bet they do."

"You're always saying things about something that you don't know about. Do you realize this?"

"Like what?" Maria asked. She asked as if Young Maria didn't know what she was talking about.

"Like betting about things they do in Spain being crazy."

"Who's betting?" Maria asked.

"You said that you would bet that the Spaniards did things we would consider crazy."

"My God," Maria replied, "you don't really think that I meant bet, bet? Bet is just a saying. I don't really want to bet."

"But you're always betting without betting," Young Maria said in exasperation, "and it makes a nervous wreck of me."

"That's your problem," Maria replied, seeing a tremendous opening to hurt the young Maria. "You've always been too nervous."

With that, Young Maria let out a small controlled scream and stamped her foot. She turned quickly away from Maria and went to her room. How could she argue over something that Maria said about her? After all, she was her mother and knew her well. But she knew that Maria was wrong. She had not been nervous always. She had been as nervous as anyone else, but to say "always" made her seem unstable and she resented that deeply. Hadn't it been she that had finished paying for the house? Where were Adam and Arnold then? Hadn't she put Carmen through high school? Hadn't she tried unsuccessfully to keep Adam and Arnold in school? Who did Maria turn to when she needed something? It was she. It wasn't anyone else. Had Adolfo ever offered to pay for his keep? Why did she have to bear the insults from everyone else? And yet, she didn't dare bring this out for fear of hurting her mother's feelings. Yet, they could hurt her. No one really appreciated what she had done and she resented that very much.

She was about to announce to Maria that as soon as Eddie came in that night, that they were leaving right then and there and never coming back. As she opened the door to go find Maria, she had run into Eddie and his bloodied head and by the time they had stopped the bleeding and put Eddie to bed, they had both silently forgiven each other.

This was not the end, though. They would start at it again the next day and the next day and each day. Young Maria would pack to leave and then unpack until she left, when she was supposed to, taking Eddie and Junior with her, much like a hen that gathers her flock to her and protects them and needs them to protect.

Maria waved at them from the front yard as they left and she cried. She loved Young Maria so much. She would give the whole world for her and she would have given her life ten times over for her, but God only knew why they never could get along.

"So be it," she said to herself, "in this life I have been given an ox-cart to pull and I guess that's all there is to it. I've got to pull it!"

CHAPTER 8

"Carmen's letter to Maria had been two-fold. In the first place, and happily she wrote, she would be leaving the hospital. The doctors were very pleased with her progress and would estimate that she could leave anytime soon. As soon, Carmen wrote, as they could check her out completely and she tested negative. Carmen wanted to know what she should do, or rather, what Maria thought she ought to do. Maria thought about it as she read the letter in Spanish and the decision was beyond her. She felt she had interfered in Carmen's life enough already and that the decision should be Carmen's.

She wrote back to Carmen and told her that she should do as she pleased. Carmen read the letter and, assured that Maria did not want her back, with much relief she began planning on returning to San Diego, that most dreadful of towns, if Young Maria was to be believed.

The second part of the letter concerned an episode in world affairs that few in Maria's isolated neighborhood had thought much about. This was the beginning of the war in Europe. Carmen had been reading about it and had been exchanging information over the war with her friends. She feared, she wrote to Maria, that the whole world was to be at war in a short time and she was worried. Maria had answered Carmen's letter by writing that the Gringos and the Germans and all those other people could fight all they wanted, but the Mexicans would be left alone. How wrong she was. Anyway, she wrote to Carmen, don't worry about those things. President Roosevelt was a friend of the world and a very good president and he wouldn't get us in a war if he could help it. She admonished Carmen to rest and not to worry about such foolishness, after all, her health came first.

Maria wrote to Young Maria and sent Carmen's letter along in the same envelope. Young Maria was indignant. To think, she wrote to Carmen and Maria, that Carmen had the gall to be worried about such far-away wars. She should be concerned about her own health rather than the health of the world. Young Maria then told them, Carmen and Maria, that Eddie was back to normal and you could hardly see the scar and that now he was embalming at least two people a week. Junior was a tenderfoot scout.

Carmen placed the letter on the top of her bed and sat down on the chair beside it. She had a premonition that the war would be something that would affect the world as no other event had ever done. Usually, she had never thought about world events. She had been isolated in the Valley in southern California, where such things were not even talked about. Her stay in the hospital had brought about a change in her. She felt more a part of the outside world. Her luck with death had opened her mind to other people's lives and pains and she considered herself a better person for it. She ignored Young Maria's and Maria's advice. She would worry about events that occurred across the world. She would care. She was tired of worrying only about herself.

So little by little Carmen had changed. When she was discharged, she was more of a woman than a girl. She knew what she wanted.

She was given the clothes she had been issued at the sanatorium and five dollars and a bus ticket. As she stood at the bus stop looking back at the ominous building, she could hardly imagine she had been there as a patient. Her memory only offered seemingly fictional glimpses of what her life had been there. It was as if she had been there only in a dream. She could not explain it further. She felt giddy.

She loved the people she had known and she knew she would like to study to be a nurse. In fact, the night before she left, she sat down and wrote in proper order the things that were important to her. She wanted to have a good marriage and children, and, secondly, she wrote that someday she would become a nurse. Lastly, she wrote that she wished with all her heart that her mother Maria would live forever.

Maria had prepared herself for her ordeal. Carmen had left the sanitarium and Maria could not rationalize her way out of the promise she had made God that she would walk on her knees from the front porch of her house to the front steps of the church. Umberta had been recruited to help pave the way for her. Umberta had a small broom and she whisked away the small rocks that stood in Maria's way. Even then, when Maria felt an uneven place with her knees, she would reprimand the poor Umberta in a whispering but grating voice. "Don't blaspheme me so much," Umberta said in a whisper. "This may not do you any good then and you may have to do it all over again. These things happen, you know."

"No, mam," Maria said in obvious pain, trying to hold onto Umberta's arm, "if this is not good enough for God, then I'm sorry. Then I'll know I'll surely never be able to satisfy him."

And so they proceeded, Maria exposing her white dimpled knees. With one hand she held the dress up in front of her and with the other, her right, the one she used on Umberta, she held a candle. Umberta held a lantern as she lit the narrow path that she cleared for Maria to use. "Make it wider, Umberta," Maria said of the path. "Remember, I am a big woman with large knees. God must truly love me," she added in her torture. "Who else would do something like this. And to think that Carmen may not even appreciate it."

"I'm sure she does," Umberta said. "Carmen loves you so."

"If she loved me so," Maria huffed, "why doesn't she do this for me? Surely God will accept a substitute."

"I have heard that he doesn't," Umberta replied. She was very serious about her job.

"Oh, what do you know, Umberta? Don't you know that there are a lot of ifs, ands and buts in the Catholic Church. Just ask Father Segura, don't take my word for it. But you're making me talk too much and I'm losing my strength. If I had known you would talk so much, I would have invited someone else."

"Like who?" Umberta asked, innocently.

"There are many who would consider it a privilege. Be careful how you sweep there in front of me. I see you're leaving more and more pebbles in my way. I thought you promised to do well, but I see you're getting worse as I go along in my martyrdom. And many would have come to my aid. You better believe it, Umberta."

"Well, I'm just glad to oblige and I'm glad to be here. I have nothing to do, especially at three o'clock in the morning."

Slowly they covered the distance. As they approached the church, not ten yards away, they saw the flicker of a match and the silhouette of a man as he lit a cigarette. He was sitting on the steps. It was the drunk Father Segura! He had not been able to sleep.

"Who's there?" he asked.

To Maria this was the greatest of dilemmas. If she stood up, she would not have fulfilled her promise. She had to touch the church steps. She had come a long way — four blocks. Would she have to do it over again? Umberta surely would insist that this one had not counted. She continued on her knees as the Priest shied away from them.

When Maria fell forward to touch the steps, the Priest recognized Umberta by the lamp light.

"Umberta!" he yelled. "What in God's name are you doing and who is that midget with you, and why is it holding a candle?"

"She's not a midget, good Father," Umberta replied, "she is Maria on her knees."

"My God, Maria!" the Priest screamed, "are you at it again?"

"Yes, Father," Maria replied, meekly, "but I promise you this is the last time."

The bus-ride was pleasant compared to the ride that had brought her to the sanitarium. The doctors had checked her out several days before and pronounced her well. She had gotten well very fast and they attributed this to her good nature. Indeed, she had been the most liked one at the sanitarium. And the staff told her so. Once she was well and had recovered her strength, she had helped out among the more seriously ill, ignoring her own well being. The doctors had warned her not to over-do the help she was giving, although they appreciated it. They were in desperate need of help. She cleaned pans and changed bedding and generally did what she thought needed to be done. She was born to be a nurse, a patient had said.

She had seen suffering she had never seen before. She thought in her simple way that she had suffered, but after helping the terminally ill, she knew what it meant to die in agony. *La Agonia*, the Mexicans called it. It was the first step before death. From there, there was no turning back.

In this stage of death, she had seen many things which changed her life. She now believed in God more than ever. So many times had she been with a dying person, his face askew and wringing with pain, only to see the beauty as death took its hold and gently, serenely, changed the countenance into a mask of peace. And at the end, when the final breath seemed to come on and on for what seemed a painfully interminable time, these same dying people would speak of seeing their mother or father or some loved one long dead. She would cry wih them as she shared the joy of their death, their end to suffering. "There is my mother with my father sitting beside her and they are waving at me to come home," one dying lady said. An elderly man, who had been dying for some time, shared his experience with her and he spoke of seeing his father take him by the hand and leading him through a void in space and at the end he was re-united with all of his deceased family. He had died in peace.

She had learned also that life was not to be taken for granted. Death was around us always. It amazed her at her age how removed she had been from all of this. She had been amazed even more by the randomness with which death strikes, how each dead person was not perceived by her as being the next to die. After a while, she gave up trying to predict who would be next. Her own death had entered her mind from time to time, but the minute recovery set in, she felt it. It was as if a suffocating veil had been lifted from her lungs and she could breathe normally again. So now she believed in miracles. She believed that Luz de la Garza had helped her achieve this miracle and she would be eternally grateful to her and she was sorry that Luz was not there to share in the joy of her departure. Better still she wished that both of them had been able to leave together.

Of all the people in her bus when they arrived at the sanitarium, she was one of the few that had survived and for this she thanked God.

The illness had not left her deformed. She had not had to undergo the dreaded chest surgery. Later on in her years, she would have a shortness of breath, but that would be all.

She had written several letters before she departed. She wrote to Maria to tell her what her plans were and when she expected to be in San Diego. Just as important was a letter to Fernando de la Garza, Luz' husband. In the letter she had reminded him who she was and that she and Luz had meant a lot to each other. She also took the opportunity to ask if it was possible for her to use his name as a reference for any job application she might make at the Naval Base. Fortunately, he had answered immediately and had insisted that she use his name as a reference. He wrote that, although his position was not very high, he still knew a lot of people who might be able to help her. In her letter she had mentioned nursing as a career and he agreed that she had chosen a field that Carmen was well suited for. The only problem, he had written, was that she needed to begin at the bottom and eventually work her way to a nursing job. He could help her. She wrote back excited at the thought that he might be able to help. She knew full well that she had to begin at the bottom.

She had written to Isabel to tell her of her release and her expected time of arrival, so that when the bus pulled up into the covered barn inside the bus station, Isabel could be seen behind the glassed-in lounge waiting patiently for Carmen. She smiled brightly as she saw Carmen come off the bus and she could hardly contain herself as Carmen waited for the small cardboard suitcase to be given to her by the bus driver.

"Carmen, Carmen," Isabel said, embracing her. "How good it is to hold you once again in my arms. How Maria must long to see you and how happy I feel for her also, now that you are well. I have fixed your old room and you can use it for as long as you want. I want you to stay with me always. I missed you so much."

"And how is everyone?" Carmen asked.

"Ruben is fine. He's in Pearl Harbor and he writes that he'll be there for a while. There are a lot of strange things going on, he says. He's not scared of the Germans. He says the Japanese are the ones to watch.

"And Adolfo?"

"Oh, him," she said and she made a sour face, as if the thought of the man was repugnant to her. "I don't hear from him. I never did, so I really don't expect to hear from him now."

"Poor Adolfo," Carmen said to her, "Maria tells me he's in Los Angeles living with a woman who owns a boarding house."

"I wouldn't doubt anything that Adolfo does," Isabel replied. "He's such a scoundrel, but he'll get to your heart. I know, he got to mine a long time ago and look at what happened. But," she interrupted herself, "we're standing here talking when we ought to be getting home."

With that, she picked up Carmen's suitcase and insisted on carrying it. When they arrived at the car, Carmen saw that Carolina had driven Isabel over. As soon as Carolina saw her, she jumped out of the car and ran to Carmen and embraced her. "Carmen!" she shouted. "I knew very well I could not contain myself when I saw you. I told Isabel that I wouldn't be able to contain myself. It is good to see you well again. You made a very fast recovery." She was still the muscular woman with heavy arms and legs. Her face was rougher now and she needed to shave. Isabel had said that Carolina had been destined to be a man, but God somehow changed his mind. She handled the car like a toy, one hand on the steering wheel, the other arm dangling outside the door. "Well, Carmen," she said, "nothing much has happened since you left. This town will always be the same. The only problems we have had at the theater have been in replacing you. Everyone Mr. Cohn hired has robbed him. Mrs. Cohn left him for a while, but he begged her to come back and she did." She kept the car going at a good rate. Isabel was uncomfortable with her driving. "They say it cost him a lot of money to get her back." She turned left and the wheels made a squeaking sound. "Marcos died about a year ago. Aside from that, nothing has changed."

"Except at the base," Isabel said. "There's a lot of activity at the naval base, and they're hiring, Carmen. They say they have jobs for anyone that wants to work. We're going to take you over there as soon as we can and see if you can turn in an application. Carolina's niece just got hired at the laundry. Didn't she?"

"Yes, she did," Carolina said, trying to pay attention to the conversation and the road at the same time. "And she didn't even finish high school. You finished, school didn't you, Carmen?"

"Yes, I did," Carmen replied. She did not want to work at the laundry. She wanted to work at the hospital.

"That's one good thing about Maria," Isabel said. "She made you go to school."

"She sure did," Carmen replied. "And so did Young Maria, my sister. Both of them made me go to school. But I also wanted to go."

"You were smart," Carolina said. She had lit a cigarette. "I wish I had gone to school. I wouldn't be where I'm at, if I had gone to school. You just don't get anywhere without an education. But try telling that to me when I was young. Shit, I was boy crazy. I thought the whole world revolved around boys. And how wrong I was. Right?" She looked at Isabel and Isabel agreed, nodding her head.

"Yes," Isabel sighed, "if only someone had told me. But it's hard to say. Maybe I wouldn't have listened to anyone, anyway. Who knows? Life's so complicated anyway. Why make it worse by thinking about what could have been?"

"At least with an education I could get a promotion," Carolina said. She took a drag from her cigarette and held the smoke in her lungs for a long time.

"Are your lungs alright?" Carmen asked her.

"Oh sure," she replied, "I've never been sick. Ask Isabel. How long have you known me?"

"Twenty-five, thirty years I guess."

"Have you ever seen me sick?"

"No," Isabel replied, thinking carefully trying to remember whether Carolina had ever been sick. "Yes, I remember several times you stayed home from work sick. You had the flu."

"Yes, but the flu doesn't count. Everyone gets the flu. I'm talking sick. Sick where you're really sick."

"Well, I don't remember," Isabel said.

Carolina threw the cigarette out the window and Carmen watched it go by the rear window. She was afraid it had stuck to the old car, but nothing happened and she relaxed.

"Maria said she wanted to come see me," Carmen said after a brief moment of silence.

"Well, she's welcome at my home anytime," Isabel told her. "In fact, I would love to see her. I haven't seen Maria in such a long time. I probably wouldn't recognize her if I saw her out in the street."

"I don't think she's changed much," Carmen said.

"Well, that's because you were with her all these times, day after day," Carolina said. "You don't see the aging then. But boy, you stay away a while and then come back and you can really see it. Just like my late husband. Remember, Isabel?"

"Yes," Isabel said. She knew the story Carolina was about to tell.

"Remember," Carolina said, "when he went away for a year to work at Yuma and he couldn't get back to San Diego? The poor man looked horrible. Carmen?" she said, making sure Carmen heard this. "Carmen, when he came back walking down the street toward the house, you know where I live don't you?"

"Yes," Carmen replied. "I've been there so many times."

"That's right," Carolina said, slapping her forehead, "I keep forgetting. Anyway, when he came back, he was walking toward the house and I started to get my shotgun out thinking this man was an intruder. What a dissappointment he was to me then, all shriveled up by the Arizona sun."

"Like the Indians," Isabel volunteered, "they're shriveled up with the hot Arizona sun."

"That's true," Carolina agreed about the sun. "That's what did him in, really. That sun in Arizona is so hot that it shrivels you up like the Indians. Carmen?"

"Yes," Carmen answered, politely. She really had missed them both, but after a while, their conversation would begin to frazzle her a bit.

"Carmen, you've never seen an Indian in Arizona real smooth skinned and tall, have you?"

"No, I guess I haven't," she replied. She felt like she didn't want to participate in the conversation. It had, she thought, taken an idiotic turn.

"There are no Indians like that in Arizona because they're all shriveled up by the Arizona sun. And I'll swear to you on my mother's grave, God have her in heaven, that that is what happened to my husband. He came home fried."

"And he wasn't big to begin with," Isabel said, and they both started laughing. Carmen started laughing also. Now if she only had Maria, she would be home.

The activity at the naval base was more than she had imagined. She couldn't figure it out, except that she kept reading where Germany was at war with Poland and that Italy was taking sides with Adolf Hitler. She had always thought of the Italians as a peace-loving nation. That is what she had read. If that were the case, she thought, and Germany was to be the enemy, then most of the activity should be taking place on the east coast and not the west coast. Even so, Ruben, Isabel's son in the navy, had written from Pearl Harbor and had sent his picture in an insert next to a huge ship and his feelings were that, everywhere in the Pacific where they had sailed, there was a feeling of war. He didn't think that was possible, since his commanding officers considered Japan to be so small and the only thing they could do would be to cause a few problems for the United States. Carmen thought that surely there was a conflict in what was being written and what she was seeing at home. In any case, she didn't think very highly of Ruben or his opinions.

Every building she went to in the process of applying for a job had been over-run with people scurrying from place to place. This was not typical of the base. By the dock-side she could see many large ships tied to the pilings with huge lines groaning to hold the vessels to their moorage. Crews worked to load the cargo into their hold.

After all she had gone through, she was informed at the final station that she could not work there because she had had tuberculosis. Carmen questioned the woman about the rule, but she wouldn't budge. When asked to produce the rule in writing, the woman refused to do so. Several of the applicants became irritated with the woman and finally she showed Carmen into a small private office.

"Why do you want to work at the hospital?" she demanded.

"Because I want to," Carmen explained. "Don't you understand that that is where I want to work?"

"The only Mexicans working at the hospital are cleaning pots," she said. "Do you want to do that?"

"Well," Carmen replied, "I didn't intend to start out as a doctor, if that's what you mean."

"Don't get sassy with me, Mexican," the woman said, irritated at being put down, "or you'll never work anywhere."

"Listen," Carmen replied, "it's not up to you to hire me. I'm sure there are other people higher up than you that do the hiring."

"Yes, deary," she said, bitterly, "but you've got to get past me to get hired."

"No I don't," Carmen said. "I'll just take my application directly to the hospital."

"No you won't!" the woman demanded.

Before she could do anything, Carmen grabbed her application from the woman's hands and walked off.

At the hospital she came upon a receptionist walking down the hall and she asked for Mr. Stevens, the name she had been given by Luz' husband. The receptionist, a small fragile lady, took her to the personnel office at the end of the hallway and introduced her to another lady sitting at the desk. This lady took her wrinkled application, studied it and asked her to have a seat. The first receptionist excused herself and left. Carmen sat by herself waiting for the lady to come out of the office she had just gone into. Isabel and Carolina had stayed by the car and had not wanted to accompany her as she walked through the governmental maze of trying to apply for a job. In a short while, the lady appeared with a man and he introduced himself. He was Mr. Stevens. She found him to be a pleasant man, very mild mannered. He talked of Fernando, Luz' husband, as if he had known him for many years. And indeed he had. "Fernando and I started working at the base in the same year," he informed Carmen. He had asked her to step into his office and had sat Carmen across the desk from him. "You understand Carmen," he told her in a very serious voice, "that I'm doing this as a favor. Fernando spoke highly of you. I'm willing to take a chance on you, but you had better not let me down. You understand, also, that you must prove yourself at the bottom of the ladder." Carmen listened intently to the gentleman. She would not disappoint the man, and somehow he felt it when he looked at her. He was the assistant personnel director and he could help her. Carmen's determination impressed him. When he asked her what she had in mind concerning a job, she replied that she wanted to clean pots. She would and could do anything. And about the history of tuberculosis that she had written on the medical records sheet? Mr. Stevens knew all about it. Fernando had told him her story. If she had been released as cured, there was nothing the government could do to prevent her from being employed. However, she was told that she had to submit to another test before they could hire her. It was just a simple precaution and Mr. Stevens felt she would understand. She would be in close contact with a lot of people and he and the hospital needed to be absolutely sure. She agreed and that same day as Isabel and Carolina waited for her, she was radiographed, given a sputum test and a skin test. She went through an ordeal during the following three days. At first, she thought she saw a reaction to the skin test. Then the next day, she was sure she had one. On the third day, her arm was red and swollen at the injection site. She was postive she would fail. Isabel tried to comfort her. There must be an explanation for the reaction, Isabel had assured her. Carmen was despondent. If only she could talk to Maria, but her mother was not there. Carolina spoke to her about a friend of hers that had the same problem and Carmen didn't know whether to believe her or not.

On the day she was to report to the hospital, she almost did not return. But something happened while in her room as she sat nervously thinking of what to do next. Would she have to return to the sanitarium? She couldn't take that. And yet, if she was infective, she couldn't be living with healthy people and contaminating every one of them. As she thought of her alternatives, she reached in her purse and there she found stuck to the inside corner a small medal that Maria had given her many years ago, one which she thought she had lost. Along with the medal she found the money that Adolfo had given her when she first came to live with Isabel. She had never used it. She took it as an omen of something good. When she left for the naval base, she was feeling better. Isabel tried to cheer her up.

The reaction, she was told, was normal for someone having had tuberculosis. Why had she not reacted on the last test before she was released? The doctor explained that at that time her resistance was lower and she had fewer anti-bodies to fight the disease. As a matter of fact, he said, the reaction now meant that she could fight off any new infection that much better. Her chest and sputum tests were negative. Mr. Stevens reassured her that the interpretation of the rule concerning tuberculoids was such that a person not having the active disease could be hired. The doctor was also impressed with her determination to work at the hospital. "You realize," he said, being as gentle as he could, "that most people of your race don't get very high jobs in this field."

"Yes, I know," Carmen replied, "but it's something that I want to do. And who knows, I might just be the first one to do well."

"I hope so," he replied.

Her employment was temporarily interrupted by the interpretation of the rule concerning tuberculoids. It seemed that the lady who had had an encounter with Carmen did not want to process the application. Finally, she gave in and the doctors prevailed and Carmen started her job. She was doubly happy. Maria was coming to visit and she had her job.

She took every opportunity to thank Fernando for his help. She knew that if it had not been for him, she would not have gotten the job. She phoned him immediately after the first interview and he had been happy for her. He became a source of advice and friendship for her during her years at the base.

Maria arrived with Jesus early on a Saturday afternoon. As she got out of the car, Carmen could hear her calling Jesus a drunken fool. "We almost got killed several times because this idiot still hasn't learned to drive. Who ever heard of anyone stopping on the road just because a big truck was coming toward us? Have you ever heard of anything like that?" she asked. She was talking to herself. Carmen ran outside and grabbed her and they both embraced. "Carmen, Carmen, Carmen," she said, crying out loud, "how I have missed you. You are so lovely." She took her face in her hands and she admired her. "You look beautiful. You look so well. Remember that last time I saw you and you looked like a drowning rat!" Carmen nodded in agreement. She was so happy and crying so, that she could not speak. "You even looked all drawn up and fishy-faced, remember? But look at you now."

She turned around to face Jesus and she cursed for the first time in many years. "That shit-head," she said, "here I was coming to see my beautiful Carmen and he almost killed me on the road several times. I believe some Mexicans were just not meant to drive," and both began to laugh. They were still arm in arm as they walked inside the house. Maria turned around before entering and spoke to Jesus who was leaning against the fender. "Don't forget, we leave tomorrow early in the afternoon. I don't want to be with you in that car when night time comes. You're bad enough as it is during the day."

"How come you treat me like a dog, now that I got you here?" Jesus yelled at her. He had taken enough. "You never said a word about my driving during the trip."

"Well," Maria reflected, "do you think I'm crazy or what? I have better sense than that."

"Well," Jesus replied, "maybe I won't come back for you tomorrow, if that's the way you feel. Let's see how you like that. Maybe you want to take the bus. How'd you like that, huh?"

"I think," Maria replied holding onto Carmen, "that that would be a blessing." And to Carmen she said in a whisper, "he always tries to be my equal, but he knows very well that he can't be. He comes from very low families."

"How are you, Carmen?" Jesus asked her, ignoring Maria's last remarks.

"I'm fine, Jesus," Carmen answered.

"Have you heard from Adolfo?"

"No," Carmen replied, "I haven't. Have you?"

"No, but they say he's having a great time in Los Angeles. They say he's shacking up with a boarding-house lady. Pretty good, don't you think?"

"Be quiet!" Maria interrupted him. "Don't be disrespectful to Carmen. Don't you understand that she's a young lady. On top of being a bad driver you are developing a bad mouth.

"Well, maybe I won't come for you, then."

"Don't bother," Maria said, "I have money to take the bus. At least that way I'll know I'll get home in one piece."

"Well then, pay me what you owe me," Jesus replied, "I'll take half of what we agreed on."

"Why should I pay you?" Maria said. "It is you who should be paying me."

"Well, a deals a deal," Jesus agreed, "and I guess I'll be here tomorrow. Tonight I'll go drinking and sleep in the car."

"Be careful, Jesus," Carmen said. "It's not a small town like you're used to."

"I'll take care," he said and with that, he got in the car and took off.

Isabel had been waiting just inside the door. She had not wanted to interfere with Maria's and Carmen's reunion. She felt, and she was right, that she would have been out of place.

Once the two women were inside, Isabel embraced Maria and held her for a long time. They were both crying. Carmen was crying. "My God," Maria said as she released Isabel, "it looks like we're at a funeral. I would hate to see what we would do if someone died. My mother always said that even when I was young I should have hired out to cry at funerals."

"You haven't changed after all these years," Isabel said. "And you're still as beautiful."

"Thank you, Isabel," Maria replied, "but it is you who has always been the beauty. It's been so many years and I'm ashamed to say it, but how often I had thought of writing to you or even coming to see you. But the years pass and every year makes it worse."

"I know, Maria," Isabel said, "the same thing happened to me. Here we are not six or eight hours by car and we had not seen each other."

"I cannot tell you how grateful I am for all that you have done for Carmen. You have been like a second mother to her. She writes to me to tell me how much you love each other."

"Oh don't be so grateful. It is I who has been blessed by having Carmen with me." They were both crying again.

Carmen had stepped back and was admiring the two older women. "Sit down," Isabel said and Maria took the sofa and Carmen sat with her. Isabel sat in the old stuffed chair across from the coffee table.

"Tell me, Maria, how have you been?"

"Oh, I've been doing well. You know I can't afford to get sick. If I do, who'll do all the work? I'm like the good mule; I do everything."

"You have really worked hard."

"Not so hard, Maria," Carmen said. "Remember that you said you weren't working as hard. Adolfo's gone and so am I. So you're bound not to be working as hard."

"Carmen," Maria said, fixing a stern look on her, "no matter who's there I'm always working hard. I'm occupied all day long. Look at my knees," she said, raising her dress and changing her conversation.

"What happened?" Carmen asked her. The knees were purplish black.

"I went on my knees all the way to church," she said, "and," she started to laugh, "and the priest caught me just as I reached the steps. Thank God I was able to get there. Especially since the nosey Umberta was there lighting my way. She wouldn't let me get away with anything. You know how she is, don't you Carmen. She's such a busy-body. And then the priest thought I was a midget because it was so dark and he couldn't see that I was kneeling down!"

Carmen and Isabel were laughing uncontrollably. Later on in her life, after Maria had died, Carmen would tell her children with fondness of this mixture of emotions that Maria was able to bring wherever she went. At first she had you crying and then laughing and so it went, back and forth, until the drain on the emotions was too much. By that time, if they had been at home, it would be after supper and it would be dark and night had fallen and everyone would go peacefully to sleep. It would be a long hard day for Carmen and Isabel; it was only the middle of the afternoon.

Isabel had served coffee in her ceramic tray, as Maria was telling Carmen all about Young Maria and Arnold and Adam. Isabel told Maria about her son Ruben, Adolfo's son. He was in Pearl Harbor and he didn't like it. His last letter said that his outfit was afraid that there might be war with Japan.

"I don't know about Japan," Maria said, "but the Germans are going crazy. Adolfo said that they were crazy when he was in Germany during World War One." Then as an afterthought she asked, "I thought they told us that *that* would be the last war?" No one answered her. "Tell me about the job, Carmen. How are you doing?"

The job was exactly what she wanted to do. It amazed her just how much stamina she had acquired so quickly. It also amazed her how much she enjoyed what she was doing. Never in her life had she taken care of a sick person, except at the sanitarium, and here she was helping out at a hospital. Maria was happy and grateful. "Maybe I could say a rosary for Luz' husband," she said. No one felt it would be necessary. During the conversation she took time to thank God for his blessings on Carmen. She felt, though, that as good as God had been, He didn't deserve another promise to walk on her knees. In fact, she promised never to promise again. Then she rejoined the conversation.

There were things not spoken of during Maria's visit. These episodes in both Maria's and Isabel's lives were better left unsaid. They knew what had happened to each other and they could tell without uttering a word that each knew exactly what the other was thinking. To any observer, the only question that he or she could not answer was which had suffered the most. Both had gotten pregnant under similar circumstances. And at that time, in that culture, where ignorance and cruelty within the family were a way of life, one knew that they had suffered and suffered dearly. The only difference had been the personalities of the two women. Isabel had been gentle and kind and more subdued. She had left town in disgrace and had accepted her ostracism. She felt that she was indeed guilty and should be punished. This is why she never fought back. Maria could not be pushed around. She remained at home and she and her mother braved the criticism and the rumors and the gossip. No one told her what to do. She was not gentle. She was a fighter.

That night while it was still early, Carolina came to meet Maria. She had heard about her from Carmen and Isabel and she wanted to meet her. "I am very pleased to meet you, Maria," she said as she shook hands and sat down with them. Isabel, Carmen and Maria had already had their dinner and were sitting again as before, talking.

"I am pleased to meet you and I would like to thank you for the kindness you have shown Carmen."

"Don't mention it," she replied, waving the compliment away with her hands. "I'm just sorry I didn't know her better when she first got sick. I feel terrible now when I think of poor Carmen and Isabel and the torture that they must have been through."

"It was something," Carmen replied. "Wasn't it Isabel?"

"Oh my God, don't even mention it!" Isabel cried. "You should have seen Carmen at that time. Maria, she was like a ghost. I believe that she would have died if she had not gone to the sanitarium."

"She got sick on me one time," Maria reminisced, "where I also felt that she would die. I'll never forget I nursed her back to health with bean soup and corn tortillas."

"They say bean soup is good for your health," Isabel said.

"It's also good to blow you out," Carolina replied and they all laughed. She had the personality that allowed her to get away with innocent vulgarities, even to the point one day of showing Isabel and Carmen why women did not have to keep their word and she raised her skirt and lowered her panties to show them a huge crotch. "This is why," she almost screamed, "because we have no balls!" Maria enjoyed her.

Eventually the conversation turned to the war in Europe. No one except Carmen knew what was going on. This was Carmen's moment to shine, and as she told them of Hitler's rise to power and the Third Reich and the invasion of Poland under false pretexts, Maria became very proud of her. How much she has learned, she thought, and what a beautiful young woman she has become. She admired her confidence.

"And Ruben says that the Americans fear that Japan may start another war," Isabel said after Carmen was through. "He says that there is a lot going on that we don't know about and that even they don't know about."

"Well," Maria added, "I always say that if President Roosevelt doesn't know we don't know, either. And there's not much he doesn't know."

Ever since the days of the Civilian Conservation Corps, Maria had respected Roosevelt. It would be more accurate to say that she loved him, as did most of the Mexican-American people at that time. The Depression had reduced many of them to still more poverty and Roosevelt, they believed, had raised them from it. Maria's two brothers, Francisco and Jose, now dead, the ones hurt most by the Depression, had joined the CC Camps and had built highway stops and bridges and park buildings throughout New Mexico, Texas, Arizona and Southern California. They had come back stout hard, and with a little money. She and her family were eternally grateful to Roosevelt. The Depression was blamed on Herbert Hoover and all the Republicans in Washington. The genuine belief was that whenever a Republican came into office, there would be an automatic depression. The mere mention of Hoover was enough to cause Maria, Adolfo and anyone of that time to spit on the gound. "Hoover ruined this country," Adolfo said. "And I can tell you that I felt it all the way to Mexico when I was there. If you peope thought you had it bad, you should have been in Mexico. Where you were eating armadillo and jack-rabbit, they were eating rats. Yes, rats! I know you don't believe me, but they were."

"Enough, Adolfo," Maria said in reminiscing out loud. She had stopped the conversation.

"What were you thinking about?" Carmen asked.

"Oh, I was thinking of the Depression. Every time I speak of Roosevelt I think about that. If it wasn't for him, we would have been in awful shape. You were too young to know, Carmen."

"No, I wasn't," she replied. "I was six years old. I remember a lot of things. Like not having much to eat and all of that." "We had it bad," Carolina said. "So bad that my father would go out day after day and not come back till we were asleep. He was that ashamed of being around us."

"He felt guilty," Isabel said. "He felt guilty at not being able to provide for you."

"All in all," Maria reflected, "our generation has seen some strange things occur in our life-time: World War One, the Depression that Hoover caused."

"Don't even mention that name," Carolina said, her face distorted as if she had swallowed the bitterest of pills, "it makes me sick!"

"And," Maria continued, "this war in Europe."

"It'll be a big war," Carmen said.

"I believe Carmen is right," Isabel replied.

In the morning as they were having breakfast, Jesus drove up to the house and stepped out of the car. If they had been close to him, they would have smelled the odor of stale liquor floating out of his lungs. He felt bad. His stomach could not tell him what it wanted. He had thought a little water would do, but he had vomited that out the window as he drove down the boulevard. Maybe some food? The thought created a vague feeling. He didn't know if that would make him vomit. Not wanting to take a chance, he had not eaten. He knew from experience that to vomit water was one thing, to vomit food was entirely different.

He staggered around the front end of the car and came over and leaned on the front fender as was his habit. From there the three women could see him holding on to the car, as if he were afraid he would fall. They watched him light a cigarette, but he quickly threw it away, as if he had tasted poison in it.

"He doesn't seem very stable," Carmen observed.

"That's about the way he acts all the time now. Do you know that he drinks every night until he is drunk. And I'm not talking about getting to feeling good, as Arnold says, I mean he gets drunk to where he gets sick and his head hurts and he vomits and can't eat for most of the day. It's crazy," Maria said.

"Poor man, must be hurting," Isabel lamented, feeling sorry for the teetering little man named after the savior of the Christian world.

"Don't, don't feel sorry for him," Maria admonished them. "The sorrier you feel for him, the worse he gets. You many not know it, but Jesus is a very spoiled man. He doesn't work. Doesn't do much of anything. Did you know he was married?"

"I didn't know," Carmen replied. "When did he get married?"

"Oh, about a year ago," Maria said. "Everyone thought he was living with this woman, but it turns out he is married. Not by the priest, though. The priest says that if you live in sin like they did, you can't get married by the church. The church does not condone such things, he said."

"And what good does that do?" Isabel asked, looking at Carmen.

"I don't know, Isabel," Maria replied, "except that for years that's what the priests have been telling us. Like they know what's good for us."

"It seems to me," Carmen said, "that the church would go ahead and forgive them and marry them and take them in. Maybe that way they can become better Christians. Don't you think that?"

"It makes more sense to me, Carmen," Maria said, "but you know how the Spaniards are. They won't forgive anyone anything."

"So he got married," Carmen said, continuing, "and to that fat lady he was always with?"

"Yes, the same one," Maria said. "But all he does is drive people around town from place to place. People laugh about him because they say that he is our taxi. But don't feel sorry for him, Isabel. The saying goes 'there has never been a drunk who will eat fire.' "

Jesus tried to light another cigarette that he had rolled and it immediately caught fire in a flash and he hurriedly slapped it out of his mouth in a panic.

Maria laughed. "Look at him. He's so shaky he can't even roll a cigarette. That's why the paper caught on fire. He dropped all the tobacco out of it."

The dog had been watching from under the porch and now he got up and stretched once, then twice, first one side, then another and then he bowed his back and yawned. He walked briskly to where Jesus was and lifted his leg on the tire and urinated on it.

"Let me tell you what happened to him the other day," Maria said, ignoring what the dog had done, leaning on the table so that what she was about to say would be held in secret. "They caught him and his wife doing bad things on the cot on the front porch of their little house."

"What's wrong with that?" Carmen asked.

"It was in the middle of the afternoon," Maria said and they all laughed.

"What was he doing?" Isabel asked, not sure what Maria was referring to.

"They were doing *it* in the front porch in the daylight. And it wasn't the first time. This is why they were caught. The neighbors had complained and when the police didn't do anything about it, the neighbors went over where they were doing *it* and surprised them."

"Don't they have any sense at all?" Carmen asked. "Doesn't he have any decency?"

"He's too ignorant," Maria replied. "You know what he told the neighbors?"

Carmen and Isabel shook their heads. They knew they could not even come close.

"He told them that she was his wife, his possession, and he could do with her whatever he pleased."

"Did he keep on doing it?" Isabel asked, not believing what she heard.

"I don't know," Maria replied, "they didn't say."

On December 7, 1941, the Japanese attacked Pearl Harbor and Carmen was working on the third floor, surgery, as an orderly. She had just finished cleaning an abdominal incision and re-bandaging it when she heard two doctors walking hurriedly down the hall, whispering about the attack as if the Japanese could have heard them.

On the radio in a lounge on the third floor, she heard the famous Roosevelt speech on the attack of Pearl Harbor. "My Fellow Americans . . . " he began and from there she could not remember the words she heard. She was stunned. The Japanese had really done it and she couldn't imagine why. Roosevelt and Congress had declared war. Around the naval base word spread quickly about the attack. Rumors had it that the Japanese had sneaked a flotilla near San Francisco Bay and that they were attacking the city. Other rumors went that the Japanese were closer to San Diego. Some said Los Angeles. By the end of the day, all of the California coast was under Japanese attack.

Another rumor had it that the injured would be sent to the San Diego Naval Base for treatment. That one turned out to be true. Inside of a week, a hospital ship arrived and the wounded were unloaded. Their treatment began immediately. They were under first priority.

Again, as in the sanitarium, she worked tirelessly, sometimes eighteen to twenty hours a day. She refused to go home, and when she did, it was to rest a while, eat something Isabel had prepared and then return. There was no stopping her, although the needless suffering she saw would almost make her sick.

"Don't work so hard," Isabel said to her, "most people don't appreciate it anyway."

"I don't believe that," Carmen replied. "I know some people won't, but most of them do."

"Ruben wrote and he says that the Japanese came in flying from every direction. He was in bed reading a book and he heard the planes, but he says that he didn't think anything of it. He thought they were our planes. So did everyone else, he says. Then, when they started hearing the firing, they thought it was a practice of some sort. You know how they do. Anyway, he said a bullet came through the wall and bounced around in the barracks and they all looked at each other like they couldn't believe it. It was like a nightmare, he writes." Isabel took the letter from her apron and, wiping tears from her eyes, she read from it. "It was like we couldn't believe it, Mom," she read. "These guys were all over, running and screaming all this stuff about someone gone crazy. I jumped out of my bunk and ran outside in my shorts to see what was going on and man, all I could see were these grey planes flying in all directions at different altitudes and shells were being fired out of their wings. I could see them and I couldn't believe what the hell was going on.

Mom, then I saw the rising sun painted on the airplanes and I knew it. Remember, I wrote to you and told you there was something going on? Remember I warned all of you to be careful of the Japanese? Well, Mom, when I saw them I said to myself, 'This has got to be a dream,' but when the shells started hitting the ground and I saw the ships listing to port and our planes on fire, I got out of there. By the time I ran inside and put on my uniform, it was over. Mom, it was over before you knew it! Don't believe the papers where they say that we were under fire for hours and hours and that we fought back. Mom, we didn't have time. By the time we knew what hit us, the whole thing was over with. The damn Japs had really put it to us. Two of my buddies were killed. Mom, I'm just glad to be alive. We're doing nothing but holding on and expecting reenforcements. If they attack again, it'll be easier for them. We were left without too much defenses. I just hope they don't try it again soon. Holding my breath, your son, Ruben."

She gave the letter to Carmen and Carmen re-read it sitting down at the kitchen table. She could tell that Isabel was very upset with the letter. Before now, she had not shown very much emotion concerning Ruben, but now Carmen felt that the war had been brought close enough to her son that Isabel was beginning to feel it.

"What are we to do, Carmen?" Isabel asked, still crying.

"We've got to fight back," she answered, "that's all there is to it. Not only the Japanese, but we've got to help fight the Germans too."

Her work at the hospital became her first love. She saw Fernando once in a while and he always managed to invite her over for Sunday dinner, but she always found an excuse for not going. Luz' family was doing well. As the war progressed, slowly, she was able to do more things simply by observing and volunteering. Her co-workers liked her and she liked them. Except for her position at the hospital, she never experienced blatant racial discrimination. Her position was demeaning for her intelligence and education, but she accepted it knowing full well that eventually she would succeed. Many were the people who mentioned her by name as the most industrious orderly in the hospital. She was proud that she had gone from cleaning floors to a hands-on position in the treatment of patients.

One day her break came. She was asked to see the hospital administrator and during their conversation he told her he was recommending her for nurses' training in the U.S. Navy. She would be in the service if her application was accepted and she could go to school. If she graduated, and there was no reason why she shouldn't, he added, then she would be an officer in the Navy — Lieutenenat J.G. Adolfo would have been proud. "Not a dummy and an ignorant, but an officer of the Navy of the United States of America. Not some little shitty country like you see in the maps — this is the United States of America."

Maria did not want her to go through with it. She was afraid something might happen. God might not want her to do it. Had Carmen consulted God?

What had he replied? Had he sent her a sign of some kind? A falling glass? A trip over an object? A mysterious voice heard when no one was there? The unexplained movement of furniture? Dizziness? Indigestion? Loss of apetite? Vomiting? Even a little nausea? Abnormal menstrual periods? Surely God had spoken in his mysterious ways. "Carmen," she wrote in her broken English. She believed Carmen had forgotten Spanish. "I didn't slave for you and kept all those promises to God and went on my knees to church every time you got sick, just to let you go and get killed by the Japanese. Surely your mother's words are important to you. God may just not want you to do it and he just hasn't had time to let you know. Give him time. Or maybe he's talking to you and you're not listening. You know how you are Carmen. There are a lot of times that you don't listen. You're hard-headed like your father. That's what did him in. Finally, she wrote, do what you want, but be careful. Be very very careful. You know how God can be mean if you do things he doesn't want you to do. And since when are they letting Mexican ladies be in the Navy, anyhow? Don't they know that our place is at home? Well then, go. But don't blame me if anything goes wrong. Remember what I told you before. Your best friend is a dollar in your pocket. Don't fall in love and get pregnant and be careful of men especially the Gringos who like to take advantage of young women. Or so I've heard." She tried to touch all bases.

Her break had come when a Department of Defense directive was received and read by Mr. Stevens. It suggested that it would be good for morale if some racial minority representatives could be recruited to be trained for the Officer's Corps.

She applied and was accepted and took her training at the Naval Base. She had to move from Isabel's home, as she was staying in the barracks. She saw Isabel, though, as often as she possibly could.

"And to think, she only weighed five pounds when she was born," Maria said, as she and Isabel and Carolina attended Carmen's graduation. Jesus had waited outside, drunk. She graduated at the top of her class.

Not some shitty little class, as Adolfo would say, but a nurses' class from the Navy of the United States of America!

CHAPTER 9

The war was going on against Japan and Germany. Most of the people in Adolfo's social plane were not aware that Italy had allied itself with Germany. Afterwards, when Adolfo found out that the Italians were fighting on the German side, he had said that he was glad, for he could defeat one hundred Italian soldiers single-handedly. Indeed, the war was a special event for him as it made him feel important. After all, he told one and all, wasn't he like a fighting machine in World War I? He would jump suddenly to his feet at whichever bar he was at and with both hands extended he would shoot through his fingers, shoot down imaginary Germans. "That's how I did it," he would say and all the beer drinkers would laugh. And he would laugh also, that weak laugh one heard when Adolfo wasn't sure whether they were laughing at him or with him. "What's that you say?" he would ask the Professor, and Manuel would whisper to him. "Don't make a fool of yourself, you've told that story many times before. You're repeating yourself."

"I don't care," he would answer, hurt that Manuel would embarrass him like that. "It was an important event in the world. Probably more important than this war. This war, as I understand it, is being fought by strategy and on the black-boards. Hell, World War I was fought in the trenches — man to man, some Germans so big and strong you could feel their muscles bulge as they took the poor Americans apart — hand to hand. What an awful sight that was. I still feel like getting drunk when I recall it in my mind."

"It doesn't take much to get you to feel like getting drunk," someone said, and they laughed again.

It was all done in a gentle way. No one wanted to hurt Adolfo. It was just that he was so bizarre, so comical in his gangly mannerism that he invited comments and asides from his audience. He took it in good humor. At first he would act serious as if he had been offended, but then in the wink of his eye he would start the disarming grin that won him many a lady friend.

The war was his time to shine. He would tell stories to the boarders to the point that, whenever they saw him descend the stairs, everyone cleared out. "Wait a minute, there," he would say, motioning with his hand for someone to come closer. Instead, they ran from him. "Wait, wait a minute," he repeated. "I've just thought of another story to tell you. This one is about a goat that we butchered while waiting for the Germans to attack. Well," he would say, disconsolate at not being heard, "maybe some other time." His love affair with Anna was still on. She demanded many things from him and he still felt uncomfortable in her prescence. For one thing, she thought he drank too much and she hounded him daily about his drinking. She required him to bathe daily and, if he didn't do it, she would smell him right away, lift up his arm-pit and stick her nose in there and she would give him the choice. "Either bathe or I'll bathe you," she would say. Naturally, he bathed himself. Once she even threatened to bathe the Professor, but the Professor objected to the insult. "I'm man enough to do it myself and whenever I want to," he said. Later on he was remorseful for his sassiness. He was afraid Anna would kick him out.

"Do you really believe she would have bathed me?" he asked Adolfo.

"I don't doubt it one bit," Adolfo replied, "this woman is hard-headed. Worse than Antonia."

"By the way," the Professor said. "I saw Antonia the other day."

"Did the hex work?"

"She was driving a new car and wearing good clothes," the Professor replied, "you figure it out."

"Hell," Adolfo said. "She had the curse annulled. You can do that, you know. But it takes a special person. Someone like Anna could probably do it."

He still resented Anna's aggressiveness and her total disregard for the niceties when it came to body functions. Under most cases, when he was around her, he would urinate on the edge of the bowl above the water so he would not make noise. Anna would sound like a person pouring water out of a pitcher when she urinated. This disturbed him greatly. Once he saw a small piece of excrement floating on toilet water after she had gone and he almost puked.

"This woman is crude," he told the Professor. "And yet, from her external appearance, from talking to her, one would never get the impression she would be that way. Isn't life strange?" he asked.

"I've told you before," the Professor said, shaking his head in disbelief. "You are not being practical. Life is practical. Nature does not allow you to be impractical, or a fool," he added.

"Do you think she takes me for a fool?" Adolfo asked, being very serious. "Is she making fun of me?"

"Oh, I wouldn't say that," the Professor replied as if he had all the answers. "No one knows that except her. But like I tell you all the time, take advantage of the situation that life brings to you. You've got it good here. I'm the one who doesn't belong, she could care less. You're a fine one to complain," he said. "I haven't even caused a ripple in her heart."

"You mean you like her?" Adolfo asked him, not believing what he heard.

"After all I've told you about her, you like her?"

"No," the Professor said, "but at least I'd like to have the privilege of turning her down."

"Oh," Adolfo said, "you and your philosophy. If you like her, tell her. I don't care. It would be a burden off my shoulders to get rid of her. She bothers me too much. I can't live in peace. I need peace. I need to leave."

"You're angry," the Professor said. "I'm the one who needs to leave. I even heard that they were drafting Mexicans first to fight this war!"

"That's absurd," Anna replied when Adolfo told her what the Professor had said. "What does that little man know about anything. He walks around with his hands behind his back as if he knows everything. I know all about him and men like him. They know all that is not important — little trifling pieces of information that only bother people during their conversations. My husband was much the same way. What a pest he was. I could imagine, and I'm telling you this for the first time, don't you repeat it. Promise?" She tried to be coy with Adolfo and she cooed and baby-talked to him. He was embarrassed. This he hadn't told the Professor. If he knew, Adolfo would never hear the end of it. "Well," she continued, "I could imagine during my husband's wake, and I was crying my heart out, that the last thing he was doing as he was split in half by the train, was uttering his eternal gibberish about little things that he knew. Who cares? Who cares if the Professor knows all the states and their capitals? And he being a Mexican national. Don't you think he would have something better to do? My husband was the same. He memorized unimportant facts. During our conversation he would say, 'Do you know, my loved one, that Jupiter is the furthest planet from the sun?' I wanted a man to hold me and he talked about planets. I guess, Adolfo, that is why the embers glow so fierce within me. All I have in me is for you. Although I realize I'm sometimes crude."

"Oh, no! Who would ever say such a thing," Adolfo lied. He had been caught off guard, or maybe, he thought, she had heard him complain about her body functions. "She farts like a mule," he had recently told the Professor. The Professor had looked at him not believing the whole thing. "It's hard to imagine," he told Adolfo.

It was obvious from the conversation that Anna had not grown fond of the Professor. He did try to lord it over the tenants. Rachel, the seamstress, took pains to get away from him whenever she saw him. He was too condescending, although she didn't know the word. But she knew the feeling. In his presence she felt like she was standing naked in front of her mother. Sylvia, the bookkeeper, kept clear of both of them. She considered herself better than they. After all, she had said, my forefathers were Spaniards and not Mexicans — a big difference. Domingo, the hardware salesman, was jovial enough, but the Professor and Adolfo intimidated him. They had for several months now tried to get Domingo to go with them to the beer joints, but he always had an excuse. He was an old bachelor, of which in those days there were many who lived solely for their work, the loyal, trusted employee, always early, leaving late, the kind who always was entrusted with the keys. For his effort, he received nothing except a regular pay check. It always surprised Adolfo how someone as good as Domingo, a fruitful servant, was always held in contempt by the bosses. He wasn't the first to be let go, but he wasn't far behind. Domingo tried not to associate with either one of them. He wore glasses, thick as bottles, and he walked like a corsetted woman. "Maybe you ought to take him out, he seems more your type," the Professor told Adolfo.

Isaac, the other boarder, was hardly seen by them. His job was so strenuous and physically demanding that he was gone before anyone could see him and he returned late after everyone had eaten and left. He was making good money on produce.

"Anyway," Anna said, taking a healthy sip of cognac, "the Professor is full of shit." She had taken to drinking, but only in a medicinal way.

After a while, though, Adolfo and the Professor began to notice that her drinking became more and more common and less medicinal. "I believe," Adolfo told the Professor, "that if it is medicinal, she must really be sick."

"If she were, she would have been dead long before now." To Anna, her love life was dwindling with each passing day. She knew Adolfo didn't like her ways. Sure, he liked her when she behaved in public, when she was the proper lady. But in the bedroom, she simply felt that it was hers to do as she pleased. If she needed to pass some gas, why not? she asked. I go to the bathroom just like everyone else. And it wasn't that she did it on purpose to aggravate Adolfo. She did it when the urge was there. If nature called, she answered. Adolfo, she felt, was much too sensitive and not as productive sexually as she had imagined. As a matter of fact, she thought that her first husband was a better lover than Adolfo, not that she would ever say this to him. Adolfo was just not "quenching my thirst," she said, "if you know what I mean." She gave her eyebrows a little jerk for emphasis, just as the Professor would do, as if to ask, "do you really get the hidden point?" She had been talking to the Professor on this rare occasion and the Professor felt somewhat embarrassed. After all, they were talking about Adolfo as if he were dead. "He used to safisfy me," she said using the past tense.

She had captured the Professor in the living room, as the Professor was sitting and reading the newspaper. "And how are you today?" she asked.

"Fine," he replied. "It could be better."

"And Adolfo?"

"He's gone to town to see about his pension. He went to get it changed, so that he gets his money here instead of at Antonia's. Antonia has been keeping his check."

"Why's she doing that?"

"Why, to keep the money. She did the same to me, but I got out of it. The woman's treacherous. She is like a snake."

"Speaking of snakes," Anna said, and this is where the conversation lead to Adolfo's sexual problems. "It is very soft most of the time. When it gets hard it is only for a very very short while. You can imagine, sir, the speed with which I have to act. And I'm not built for speed. I like to take my time. This is why I drink a liqueur. You don't see cognac being taken gulp by gulp, do you? Notice that cognac is sipped and enjoyed. Good sex is like that, very slow and deliberate. It's driving me insane, anyway, so much so that I've taken to drinking. If my poor husband could see me now. But no, he had to be sliced in half by a railroad car. What tragedies have befallen me. And then my daughter." She started to sob gently, her shoulders jerking. Once in a while she expired in a sigh.

It was in fact Adolfo who had gotten them together. "It'll do you good," he told both of them. "You'll like it very much, I'm sure." The preliminaries were standard and routine. "He will be good for you. He should be. I don't believe he has ejaculated in the six or seven months that I've know him." She had sat next to him and was fanning herself vigorously, much more than she needed. He felt a twinge between his legs. Their conversation became more and more suggestive. "Do you like *it*?" she asked. "Do you like to do *it*?" she asked again, "Yes," came the weak reply. He was dumb-founded but erectable. "Can you do it many times?" she asked. "I have before," he answered. She placed her hand on his thigh and was dearly surprised, for on it and running alongside of it like a piece of pipe was her wish, far beyond her wildest dreams. The Professor, small as he was and wiry and impish as he was, was endowed!

"It was like getting screwed by a donkey," she said later. "Not that I've done that," she corrected herself, "but it is as I would imagine a donkey screw to be. God almighty," she said, thinking back on the act. "I never believed it to be possible, but it happened. That goes to show you, Adolfo," she said to him, wagging a finger at him, "that you never know."

"That's for sure," Adolfo said.

"And he says we're going to do it for a longer time next time. Dear God what am I to do? My insides hurt me so much afterwards that I had a hard time urinating."

The Professor had an air of confidence about him now. He was eye to eye with Adolfo and his equal.

"The only reason that man has one testicle hanging lower than the other one is to allow him to cross his legs without hurting himself." The Professor said this and Adolfo started gagging on his beer. He choked and coughed and sounded like he was going to die from lack of air. After he regained his composure, he scolded Manuel. "You should never say anything like that while a man is drinking. Don't you know I could have choked to death?"

"Well, it's true," Manuel replied, "and I have thought about it for a long time. What other reason could there be? I mean, nature is logical. You must remember, nature does not do anything without a reason."

"And Anna's nature," Adolfo asked him, "explain that."

"She's a fine woman. It's just that you are too fastidious."

"Fastidious? What does that mean?"

"It means," the Professor replied, "that you don't enjoy the dirty part of the world as it exists."

"I don't believe that," Adolfo said. He was somewhat hurt by this observation about himself. "I've been in places that would have made you sick to your stomach and I've eaten in places where you couldn't see the food for the flies. I've stayed in places where the rats and the roaches and the scorpions were so numerous and so big I could hear all of them walking around, much as one hears an intruder in the night. In Morelia one night, and I remember it plain as day, we were told to stay at the old Principal Hotel and I remember it as if it happened yesterday. The rooms were very small and they opened to the courtyard in the center. I couldn't sleep. The rats were running in the courtyard, sneaking around from door to door, wandering around to see which door they could push open. Once they did this, and I saw them with these two eyes," he placed the two index fingers in the bags under his eyes to show Manuel where they were. "I've eaten snake!" he yelled. He waited for Manuel to react.

"I have too," Manuel replied.

"And a wren."

"A wren?"

"Yes, a wren."

"What did you eat a wren for?"

"Because I was hungry, stupid."

"What good would eating a wren do for a man that's hungry? How much nourishment could you get?" Manuel shook his head in disbelief.

"In Morelia, again, we killed a wren with a stone because we were hungry. It seems I had more trouble in Morelia than anywhere else. I got a girl pregnant in Morelia also. Her father, God have his soul, the poor man, would still be looking for me, if he hadn't died shortly afterwards."

"Afterwards of what?"

"After finding out his daughter had been desecrated. I've never seen a man react so violently to an occasion as that man. He was so mild and meek." He took a long swallow from his beer and said, "You know, Manuel, if it wasn't for the beer, I don't know what I would do."

"Why eat a wren?" Manuel said, laughing.

"It's not funny," Adolfo said, "we were hungry."

"So you split it with someone?"

"Yes, my friend Luis Garza, the short-stop."

"This is idiotic," the Professor said. He had finished drinking his beer and raised two fingers to the bartender. The bartender obliged and brought two beers.

The tavern was almost empty. On the far right, away from where they were, the bartender had gone to continue washing out a small gasoline engine that he had placed on top of some heavy timbers. He would try to start it with the crank handle and the engine seemed to want to start. They had noticed the engine when they first came in and they had seen that the bartender had connected the water pump to an outside hose. Finally, with one great turn of the crank, the engine started and the room began to fill with exhaust.

"This guy is crazy," Manuel shouted above the roar of the engine.

"He's more than crazy. He's an idiot," Adolfo yelled, "He's going to kill us all."

"Turn the damn thing off," Adolfo yelled at the bartender, and since he couldn't hear, he had to walk over to them.

"What did you say?" he asked.

"Turn the engine off." Adolfo yelled. "You're going to kill us all."

The bartender walked over slowly to the running engine and grounded it and it turned off.

"Can't a man have a beer in peace here without you disturbing the peace?" Adolfo asked the bartender.

"I've got to get the engine running, so I can get it back in the car by tomorrow night," he replied. "I'm sorry for the inconvenience, but I have to do it." And with that he poured some gas into the engine and yanked the crank-handle even harder than before and the engine began to start and sputtered and, with his hand still on the crank-handle, the engine gave a tremendous loud back-firing noise, and the handle reversed itself and they heard the snapping as the bartender's arm broke in several places.

"Let's get out of here," Adolfo said getting up, "this place is full of shit."

"You can say that again," Manuel agreed. "Who wants to get involved with an ass like him.

They had decided to leave Los Angeles. The Professor still had it in his mind that he would be drafted.

"Who wants an old fart like you?" Adolfo had asked him.

"Who knows," he replied, "but in the history of the United States, all its wars have been fought by someone else and I don't want to be that someone else."

"That's not true," Adolfo said, showing signs of impatience with the Professor's remarks. "In Germany we fought for the freedom of all of Europe. Weren't we getting killed over there?"

"Yes, but you are a Mexican."

"I'm an American," Adolfo said.

"No you're not," the Professor replied. "To the American you will always be a Mexican, no matter where you're born. Don't think that, just because you were born and raised here, that you are entitled to the same privileges as the Anglo-Saxon. If you think that you are very naive."

"He's right, you know," a well-dressed gentlemen said to them as they sat drinking their beer.

"You see, Adolfo," the Professor said, pointing his thumb at the gentleman, "even this well-to-do man agrees."

"Forgive me for interrupting," he said, "but I couldn't help but over-hear your conversation. I too agree with this gentleman here and I am Anglo-Saxon."

They had been drinking at this bar, one of many they frequented only for a short time. It seemed that they enjoyed it more than any other. For one thing, it was quieter than the others and the place had an air of class to it. The chairs were in good repair and one could sit on them without fear of tearing the seat of the pants on a nail. The tables had an oil cloth on them and they seemed to be cleaned often. The bartender, and there seemed to be only one, was cordial and would join in the conversation, if he had the time. There was no loud music and no one seemed to be in a fighting mood. Adolfo's and Manuel's concern was that they had not found the place earlier enough. Now that they had decided to leave, it seemed a shame. It was far better than the tavern where the bartender had broken his arm on the crank-handle.

"He got what he deserved," Manuel had said, walking briskly on the way home. "He fogged us out of the place like we were roaches."

"I remember," the old man continued, "during World War I when the war first broke out. Do you mind if I sit with you?"

He had been sitting at the next table facing away from them and it was uncomfortable for him to turn and talk to them.

"No, not at all," Manuel and Adolfo replied. They were anxious to talk to someone as distinguished as this gentleman.

He had dressed well in a three piece suit and white shirt, a blue tie. Adolfo still wore his wool suit and a faded shirt and he was no match for the gentleman. Manuel typically wore his khaki pants and shirt.

"You must forgive me," he said as he pulled up the chair behind him and sat down. He had a cane and they noticed it for the first time. He leaned forward with his hands on the cane. "Bring us another round," the man said to the bartender, music to the ears of Adolfo and Manuel.

"I don't come here as often as I used to," he said. "We used to gather here very often, my comrades and I. We started the first association of Mexican businessmen in Los Angeles," he said. He waited for that to sink in before he spoke again. He took a small swallow from his beer. "I used to be able to drink beer for beer with the Mexicans, but I can't anymore. I'm just too old now."

For once Adolfo and Manuel had met someone who kept their attention. For Adolfo it was mostly that he was impressed with the man's demeanor and his dress. The two things that always impressed him. Besides, he knew the man had money. Manuel was positive the gentleman had money and class.

"And you were telling us about the war," Manuel said, prodding the man to speak.

"Oh, yes," he said, "I was. I suppose I was. It's been many years and the reason I agree with you," he said, looking at Manuel, "is that I saw it in World War I. I knew it. I was on the draft board. I knew what the other members were doing. They didn't realize that I had as my friends most of the Mexican-American community in Los Angeles. I had the happy fortune to be married to a Mexican national for some forty years. Don't tell me I don't know the Mexican people. But you see, they were not organized. They had no leaders. Their efforts were spent in other directions. Instead, they should have united. I tried. We had meetings to show the people the disproportionate number of my friends being conscripted into the Army, and all as foot soldiers to fight hand to hand. What a shame it was for me. What a disgrace for the country to send all these poor young men into battle while the others, more richer and powerful, stayed at home and played. I pleaded with the board for fairness." He stopped and a tear began to form in his eyes. He took a handkerchief and wiped the tear and gently blew his nose. "You can have my beer," he told Manuel, "I can't drink anymore. And you see," he said, looking at Adolfo, "you and your friends were taken to fight a war while a lot of eligible men stayed behind. They laughed and I cried and I cried some more when the bodies were being sent home. What a horrible time it was." He wiped his eyes once more as he held the cane with one hand. "One by one they brought them back, dead."

He took out some cigarettes and he passed them around, but Adolfo and Manuel turned them down. He took one out with his long thin fingers. He lit it and inhaled deeply, savoring the smoke as it saturated his lungs. He got up and without much farewell told the bartender to bring his friends, two more beers. He paid and left a tip and he walked out slowly but elegantly with the help of the cane.

"Who was that man?" Adolfo asked the bartender. He had been impressed. And as Adolfo would say, he had been in select company at various times in his life. It took a lot to impress him.

"The gentleman was a lawyer. He's retired now," the bartender said. "He comes in once in a while. They say he used to hang around with the Mexicans all the time around here. But most of his friends are dead now. I guess he comes just to try to remember the good days. He talks a lot, don't you think?"

"I don't think so," Adolfo said, looking at Manuel to see what Manuel thought of the question. "Do you think he talks a lot?" Adolfo asked him.

"No, not really," the Professor replied. He had started to grin. "But then again, I'm used to you," he said.

"I don't talk that much, do I?" Adolfo asked him, offended.

"Well," the bartender said, "it does us all good to hear what someone has to say. Why hold it back, I always say. I tell my wife, go ahead and let it all spill out. It does you good." He swatted a fly on the counter with a crack of the towel he carried around his neck.

"How come you don't have too much business?" the Professor asked him. It had been a source of curiosity to him. Not that it mattered, for he and

Adolfo found the place to be ideal.

"Well, I really don't know," the bartender replied. He had taken the towel and wrung it out over the sink hidden behind the counter and he placed it around his neck again. "I haven't been working here long, maybe about a year, and it's always like this. People are funny. You just never know."

"Don't get me wrong," Manuel said, "we like it this way. It's just right for us."

"It's alright with me too," the bartender said, grinning. "It makes for a lot easier work for me. I've worked places where I've had to break up three, four fights a day. I've had rifles, shotguns, pistols, baseball bats, all these things under the counter. Here, I don't need anything. This is the way I like it. I'm getting too old for that kind of thing. It's okay when you're young and you can take it, but not anymore."

"Who owns this place, anyway?" Adolfo asked him. That had been another source of curiosity to them, for whoever it was, was not making any money.

"Well, that's an interesting story," the bartender said, scratching his head. "It used to belong to an old man named Diaz, but recently I haven't heard from him. The rumor is out that he's living with a woman at another barrio. So now that's who I see most of the time. She takes care of the business and of this place. Her name is Antonia."

They both said, "Oh," at the same time and got up and left.

"I told you the goddam hex and potion stuff hadn't worked," Manuel complained walking with his little side-ways gait.

"I guess it didn't," Adolfo said, and he stopped and gazed into space. He would not reveal what he was thinking, but there was some discomfort showing in his face.

They had told Anna that they were leaving and she started crying. "What will I do!" she lamented, as she wiped tears from her eyes with her fingers. "I've never been happier in my life. Even when my husband was alive I was never as happy."

"I don't know what to tell you," Adolfo said to her, speaking for both of them. The Professor was standing by him and looking at Anna, somewhat distrubed that she was taking it so hard.

They were standing in the parlor and when she started to cry, Sylvia, the bookkeeper, came into the room to ask what was happening. "They're leaving," Anna sobbed. "Manuel and Adolfo are leaving," she repeated. Manuel felt happy to know that his name was the first one mentioned. Usually it was Adolfo and Manuel. So this is how things rate in this world, he thought, priorities.

"Oh," Sylvia answered and she looked like she could have cared less, as if it were more of a relief than anything else.

"Don't mind her," Anna sobbed, "she's very cold."

"Well, we found out that they may be taking all the Mexicans into the front line to fight the Germans and the Japanese and I'm not staying," Manuel said. He had an air of urgency about him, as if he needed to go to the bathroom.

"But surely you'll stay for a while," Anna demanded. She had stopped crying and was trying to wipe her wet fingers on her dress.

"What Manuel is saying," Adolfo went on to explain, "is that we met a man who said that during World War I they took as many Mexicans as they could before taking the Gringos and he's afraid."

"But Manuel," Anna implored, "you're not a young man anymore. What would they do with you in the Army? They are after the young ones, the ones who can fight."

She had dyed her hair. They hadn't noticed before, but now that she had stepped into the light by the parlor window, they could tell. They noticed it at the same time and they both looked at each other, wondering what was wrong. Her hair was now jet black, ceramic in appearance and gathered at the top. Before, it had been slightly gray and combed back into a bun. She was trying to improve herself. She was still trying to dry her small stubby fingers.

"Why hadn't you said anything before about leaving? Why is it a complete surprise to me?" She felt slighted now. "Didn't you think I should know about these things? I do care, you know." And with that, she started to cry again and she walked out of the room, sobbing as she went. "Ungrateful," she whispered as she walked out.

The trip was planned. They would leave Los Angeles by bus and go to San Diego. When Manuel had mentioned going all the way to Tijuana, Adolfo had changed Manuel's mind. Adolfo had it in the back of his mind to stop in San Diego. The reason, of course, was to see Isabel one more time. However, he didn't want Manuel to know just then. Later, once they arrived, he could tell him, or make up a lie or anything. He would come up with something. If he confessed now, it would make him appear too much like a beggar and he didn't want Manuel thinking about him as such. He was running out of chances with her, he felt, and he needed every opportunity to see her. Maybe he could change her mind this time. And besides, he already had another excuse. Maria had written and told him about Carmen and he wanted to see her. Maria had told him also about Arnold. Arnold had been drafted and was in basic training at Ft. Benning, Georgia. He would be an infantryman when he was through there and a Private First Class, the same rank Adolfo had when he was discharged. "They never did promote me," Adolfo would say, "because they knew if they did, I would run the whole show and end the war in week. These people, the Generals and Colonels, they want the wars to continue. They love war. They're not fighting. They're playing inside a sand-box and moving little troops around on their maps. I was out there fighting. You ask anyone who fought the war if they couldn't have ended it faster. Sure they could, but nobody up high wants a war to end. There's too much glory and patriotism and fun during a war. And money? Do you think that the people making money off the war want it to end? Not on your life. That, my friend, is why I and people like me never get promoted."

Adam had been delared 4-F, Maria wrote. She was not told why, nor could she imagine. He looked perfectly healthy to her.

They had one more chore to do before they left. They had gone to the Federal Building, the same one as before, and had been told that Adolfo needed a release, Antonia's signature, before he could receive his pension in San Diego.

The Professor couldn't understand why Adolfo was going to all the trouble to have the check mailed there. "I have some friends there," Adolfo explained, "and I'm going to stay with them a while. Anyway, I need to have the money taken away from that woman.

"I don't understand," Manuel said, knowing full well that Adolfo was holding something back. "Why not send it to Maria?"

Adolfo explained his predicament to a young lady and, when he started to tell her the whole story, she stopped him.

"I'm sorry, sir," she said, courteously, but with finality and holding up her hands, "but I'm not interested in that. I have records here that show you signed over to this lady the power of attorney and the right for her to countersign your check. Is that right?"

"Yes," he replied meekly, he hated to be treated as an ignorant man. That's for someone else, field hands, migrants, but not for him. There was nothing he could do about it, though.

"Well then you need to sign here," she said and she pointed to a new form and she gave him a pen. He wrote slowly and left-handed. His teeth were in place and he looked good. He had shaved. Anna had given him and Manuel all of her late husband's clothes and shoes and underwear, everything except what he wore when he was cut in half by the rail-cars. "Those are clothes that have a lot of memories for me," she had told them, as she threw the clothes from the closet unto the bed.

"Now all you need," the young lady informed him, "is a release-form signed by her on this line," and she x-ed a line at the bottom of the card. "Return this to me or mail it to this address. And be sure and write the address where you want the check mailed to."

They thanked the lady and walked out.

The dead man's clothes had been a mish-mash of sorts. The man apparently had had no taste in clothes except that Anna had kept him from getting out of hand. On Adolfo and Manuel they looked good, passable, yet very good for what they had been used to. His shoes fit Manuel, but not Adolfo. "It's amazing," Anna had mentioned, as she watched them try on their new clothes, "how small Adolfo's feet are for his size, and how big Manuel's are for his size. You know what they say about the size of feet, don't you?" She looked at them and grinned that healthy grin of hers. He couldn't stand her.

"You would have thought," Anna said later to Domingo, the hardware salesman, "that after giving them all of my deceased husband's clothes, they would have at least stayed a little longer when I asked them to."

"They were very ungrateful," Domingo replied, and he knew that she had had an affair with both of them. "And doubly so," he added, "when you consider what else you gave them!"

Anna blushed and held her hand to her mouth.

Antonia was adamant. She refused to let them in her house. Across the way, the three mean sisters were getting restless. They were standing at their screen door listening to Adolfo plead his case. "She took you for all your money, didn't she? She took both of you, didn't she?" Adolfo and Manuel could hear them jeering in the background, "You got screwed in more ways than one," one of them said and they all whooped and hollered.

Adolfo and Manuel were beginning to feel uncomfortable. Anything would set them off. They pleaded. Surely she could let them in, so that they could explain Adolfo's problem.

Finally from inside the house, like the voice of a savior, came a man's voice. "Let them in!" he demanded and she meekly let the two men inside. What they saw was a huge man weighing probably three hundred pounds and sitting on a wooden chair, half of his thighs sticking out on each side. If he was sitting on his ass, they couldn't tell it. It seemed to them that the legs started as large stumps with no feet and went to the torso. His fly was longer than any fly they had ever seen. His upper body was huge, sideways. His head, although fat, looked small for his body and looked as if it could be screwed off and screwed back on. He had trouble breathing and he had to choose his words carefully. They shook his hand; it felt like a soft roast. He did not get up.

"Excuse my not getting up," he said, slowly. He took a deep breath. "But you see the condition I'm in." He took another breath and gulped. "What can Antonia do for you?"

They were both wondering how Antonia had gotten involved with this man. They had never seen him before. Bobbie and Eloise were there. Bobbie gave them his back and did not turn around to greet them. In a short while he left. Eloise, when she saw Adolfo, stuck out her tongue at him and she timed it perfectly, so that only he and not Antonia or the fat man saw her. She walked out soon afterwards.

Adolfo explained what he wanted. "Simply put," he said with some nervousness, "I need Antonia to sign this form. It won't cost her anything. I need to have my checks sent somewhere else. I think it's only fair."

The Professor was watching in the background, as Adolfo was by the table talking to the fat man.

"Well," the fat man said, shifting his weight around on the chair, "I'm Antonia's husband. We were recently married. I don't know what you were doing here or how your check came to be delivered here." He took a breath and placed his hand to his throat. He pointed at it and motioned with his hand for everyone to wait. "I do believe that Antonia will sign your form." He raised his hand again and they waited for him to take a couple of breaths. "Go ahead, Antonia," he said and motioned for her to sign.

She signed without saying a word. And as she did, another man, a frail thin man, came walking into the kitchen. He walked with the aid of two canes. "Has anyone seen my shirt?" he asked absent-mindedly, and when no one replied, he went back to where he came from. "I need to go to the tavern to check on things. Does anybody know if we're still open? Business has been terrible," he said as he turned around.

"You've been doing alright for yourself," Manuel said to Antonia. "I saw you in a new car the other day."

"Oh yes," Antonia replied. "I've been doing fine. The good Lord has been kind to me and my beloved husband and children."

The husband motioned for them to leave and Adolfo picked up his card, put it in his shirt pocket and they excused themselves.

"Look at the two queers," they heard the sisters say, laughing. "You two got screwed in more ways than one."

"Serves them right," another said.

"Those are the two biggest shit-heads I've ever seen living there!"

They walked between the two houses hearing the taunts, but they knew better than to antagonize snarling dogs. Manuel reached into his pocket and discretely threw a small tobacco bag full of burned possum hair under the house. Adolfo had not known he would do this. "What's that for?" he whispered. "I'll tell you later," Manuel replied.

When they reached the side-walk and they had a good headstart, Manuel turned back to the sisters and he could plainly see them sticking their heads out of the partially opened door and he screamed at the top of his voice, "Assholes!" And they both ran for their lives.

"So then, Antonia got married," Adolfo said.

"Apparently so," Manuel said, looking confused. "Unless that's a lie. You never know."

Adolfo was rubbing his chin and trying to figure it out. "He said that they had just married . I don't believe it. Where has this man been all this time? You sure couldn't hide him."

"That's for sure," Manuel said and he scratched his head as he thought out the situation.

"Here are the details," Adolfo said, trying to get the puzzle solved. "Antonia marries this fat man. He completely dominates her. No man could do that to Antonia without holding something over her. Could it be that this is the Uncle Joe that they always talk about. He was never dead, right?"

"Right," Manuel replied, "but where was he?"

"I don't know."

"I know," Anna said when they told her. "I've known him for many years.

Not intimately, you understand, just have seen him. God knows, I would never touch that man for all the money in the world. Can you imagine how dirty he is. Can you just imagine him trying to make love to that hateful woman. But," she said, letting them see the disgusted expression on her face, "can you imagine how he cleans himself after he goes to the bathroom?"

"Please, Anna," Adolfo interrupted her. "Please don't talk like that. Answer the question."

"Oh, him?" she asked. "He's not Uncle Joe. Uncle Joe doesn't exist. Everybody that lived there is Uncle Joe. You two were Uncle Joe and you didn't know it."

"That's not true," Manuel said.

"It sure is," Anna remarked, "and you mean to tell me that as smart as the two of you are you never caught on?"

"Well," Adolfo said, "I'm not the smart one, Manuel is the smart one."

"And the children," Manuel asked her still not convinced.

"I don't know. I don't know the woman at all . All I know is what I hear from the boarders, but I would guess they are from her first husband," Anna answered him. "But you never know, she probably got pregnant from some Uncle Joe living in the house at that time. You knew she was promiscuous, didn't you? Not like me." Anna corrected them before they could even think about the similarity. "She is a whore. I've been very discreet and, besides, you two are the only ones. And I didn't take advantage of you, did I? As a matter of fact, I gave you things, service, food, clothing, shelter, you name it. I gave it. Even money. There is a world of difference between a lady and a whore."

"The difference, I have found to be, is money," Manuel said, looking at her in a serious way. "The poor are whores and the ladies have money."

"That's not exactly true," Anna replied. She had stood by the window again and was showing off her ugly hair, a patent-leather-looking mat that covered her head. "Why did she do it?" Adolfo asked him later when they were in their room and about ready to leave. "The whore charges because to her it is a way of making a living. There is no love, no tenderness." Anna felt that she had made her point and she strolled to the chair and sat down. "I'll miss both of you," she said, staring into space. "What will I do?" she wondered, fretting with her hands.

"You could go with us," Manuel said without thinking. And he knew the moment he said it that he had made a mistake. They spent the rest of the afternoon giving her excuses why she wouldn't like it. But they should have known better. She didn't want to leave. It was just that they were afraid that she might change her mind. The seed had been planted in her and they had to make sure it didn't take hold.

"All right!" she exclaimed in desperation. "I'm not going! I've heard a thousand excuses as to why I wouldn't like it. Relax. I don't want to go. In the first place, this house is too valuable for me just to leave it in someone else's hands. And in the second place, I need to be close to my beloved deceased husband. You may not realize it from the way I talk about him, but he was the center of my universe, the guiding light for my spirit. I grew up under him." She realized that she had made a remark that could be misconstrued and she put her hand to her mouth. "How silly of me to put it in such a way," she said. "Anyway," she continued, rearranging her skirt so that it went symmetrically around her on both sides, "I can't go."

"Don't get us wrong," Manuel said, still trying to cover up their desperate attempts to keep her from going, "we wouldn't mind."

"Yes, you would," Anna replied. "And I don't blame you. I would just be in the way. I'll stay. I mean, I'd much rather stay. To you I guess I was just another piece of meat."

"It's not that we think of you like that," Manuel explained, looking to Adolfo for help. "It's just that we have to go. And now that Adolfo is all squared away with Antonia and I'm ready to leave, well, we thought it would be a good time."

"He's right," Adolfo chimed in, leaning forward over his knees. "And if it hadn't been for that fat man, we maybe couldn't leave. Anyway, thank him for me if you ever see him," Adolfo told her. "He sure told her what to do. He kept her in her place."

Later, after Adolfo and Manuel had left, she was to find out that the fat man had owned a circus and had sold out and had met Antonia at the bus station in Phoenix, Arizona, and was now the drug dealer for the barrio. He was to completely dominate Antonia and her children, something no other man had been able to do. Even the mean sisters were afraid of him. How Anna wished she could have written to them to tell them the news.

They arrived in San Diego late in the afternoon. They had met a gentleman on the bus who lived in San Diego and he vaguely remembered Adolfo from his playing days. Not that he particularly cared about baseball or sports, it seemed to him that he remembered something about somebody named Adolfo. Surely, the Professor had informed him, someone of Adolfo's fame was not easily forgotten. The man, a skinny gentleman, with grayish eyes and a thin long nose, didn't seem to grasp the significance of being a professional baseball player. He wrote the whole thing off as preliminary conversation. He wanted to talk about today, he told them, not about yesteryears. The war was prominent in his mind. He talked about the war until even Adolfo couldn't take it anymore. He went into one war and came out in another. He had wars confused and, if he didn't, he tried to compare what was done at the Treaty of Hidalgo with the Treaty at Munich. He sounded knowledgeable, but the majority of his information was wrong. He almost seemed to have his facts straight. Adolfo didn't care because he didn't know the difference. For all he knew, this man was speaking the truth. Manuel knew a little more and detected some discrepancies in the stories, but again, he wasn't all that sure either. The best part about it was that he had someone waiting to pick him up at the bus station. Adolfo's and Manuel's problem was to get him to take them to where Isabel lived.

He was oblivious of their hints. "Maybe we can all go and get a beer after we get there," Adolfo said, readjusting the man's tie. "Or maybe we can have a game of dominos," Manuel said.

"I don't play dominos," the man replied, "and I don't drink." He stood up and lowered his trousers slightly. They had crept up and were bothering his crotch. He pulled at them from the in-seams and sat down again. The bus driver looked back at him, as if he were about to say something.

They had a flat and Adolfo remembered, as they helped the bus driver fix the nail hole in the tube, that when he was on a bus from Torreon to Aguas Calientes, they had had ten flats in one day. "We arrived on the rim," he said, laughing. "We dug a white line down that asphalt road as pretty as any line you ever saw. Those were the days when players were men and they played for the love of the game. Today," he said as they rolled the tire to the bus, "boys want to start in the big leagues right away. They have no sense, no baseball sense anyway."

"Maybe you can show our friend here something about baseball," Manuel added, hoping to bring the man into the conversation and shut up Adolfo.

"Yes," Adolfo said, picking up the hint, "maybe after we get to San Diego, I can show you something about baseball."

"No," the man replied, "I'm not that interested."

"Well," Manuel asked him in desperation, "just what are you interested in?" He looked at the man across the aisle and then he looked at Adolfo, sitting next to him.

"I'm interested in wars, revolution, things like that."

"That's funny," Adolfo, replied in glee, "I love that stuff myself. Don't you, Professor?"

"Professor?" the man asked, surprised that a professor would be riding the bus and dressed in large plaids. "Are you really a Professor?"

"Yes," Manuel answered, trying to look studious.

"The Professor here is a student of war and revolutions, having lived through the revolutionary war in Mexico, right Professor?" He winked at Manuel when the man looked the other way. He was enjoying this. He felt he was about to dupe someone.

"Yes," Manuel lied, shaking his head, acting as if he was recalling the bitter memories, "I lived through hell."

The bus was beginning to make a loud transmission noise and was having difficulty even on the small hills. The rest of the passengers, tired of hearing this conversation, were beginning to become exasperated. The bus driver, already slightly piqued at the old man's frequent standing and grabbing of his crotch, had begun to curse openly every time he had to shift. Although the temperature was mild, it being May, everyone was becoming irritated.

When Adolfo continued the conversation, he said, "I'll never forget the time Pancho Villa came to see me pitch." One man, rather large, got up and teetered as he held on to the seat and said, "If you don't shut up your goddam mouth, I'm going to shut it up for you. Can't you see we're having trouble with the bus? And that goes for you too," he said, pointing his large finger at Manuel and at the man.

They were silent for the rest of the trip and then everyone else could talk, a more subdued pleasant type of conversation that bus passengers love to create and which Adolfo and Manuel had deprived them of. Manuel whispered to Adolfo, as they arrived in San Diego. They could see Coronado Bay. "I screwed a woman under a tarp in Coronado Bay one night," he said. Adolfo looked at him suspiciously.

When they arrived — the bus barely made it into the station — some people shook the large man's hand. The bus driver threw their suitcases, the cardboard ones, away from the other ones. "I knew these had to be yours," he said, angrily.

"You ought to show more respect," Adolfo told him, as he pulled his suitcase. "This one belonged to a man cut in half by a railroad car."

"I don't care if it belonged to Jesus Christ," the driver said, jumping back into the bus and closing the door.

They spotted the old man inside the station, as he talked to a younger man. "His son, probably," Adolfo surmised.

"I hope he takes more hints than his father," Manuel suggested.

"He appears smarter than his dad."

"How can you tell?" Manuel asked him, as they approached the two men.

"He's not helping carry his father's suitcase."

"You and your jokes. Be serious."

As they approached the old man, he turned around as if the younger one had told him that Adolfo and Manuel were coming. "Oh," he said smiling and he introduced his son to them.

"Which way are you going?" the son asked them and Adolfo told him, told him in detail. "I'm sorry then," the son replied, getting his father's suitcase, "but we're going the opposite direction." And they walked away laughing at some private joke.

"I told you he was a shit-head," a disgusted Adolfo told the Professor.

"I thought you said he was very smart."

"When?"

"Just a few moments ago."

"I said he was smart?"

"Yes, you did. Just a moment ago you said you could tell he was smart, because he wasn't carrying his father's suitcase."

"And then what did he do?"

"What?"

"The son."

"What do you mean?"

"Didn't he pick up his father's suitcase after all?"

"Yes."

"Then he's a shit-head, like I said."

They hitched a ride to Isabel's house in back of a pick-up truck. They had been walking for about a mile, carrying their suitcases, when they thumbed the driver of the truck and he stopped for them. They could not fit inside the cab. The man was carrying his wife and three children up front with him. "There is no way to look dignified while riding in back of a truck," the Professor said, holding his hair down with one hand and leaning into the wind. Adolfo looked ahead bleary eyed into the wind created by the force of the truck. "This reminds me very much of a situation," he said, still looking into the wind, "that occurred to me in Mexico and the day the good Father Carranza from Mexico City helped us out. We were broke. The manager had left the team while we slept and had taken our money. This reminds me very much of that time. We rode in back of an ox-cart then."

Manuel could not tell whether the tears in Adolfo's eyes were from the wind or from the story. Manuel looked at Adolfo and felt sorry for him. You could say the same for Manuel, but he had never attained the heights that Adolfo had and here he was, Adolfo, fifty-seven years old, wearing ill-fitting dead man's clothes and riding in back of a truck. He had never felt sorry for him except now. He had admired the man for being so strong willed, for not letting anyone tell him what to do or how to do it. He had, in the Professor's eyes, gone beyond what the normal lower middle-class Mexican-American man was supposed to do — stoop labor - and he felt, no, he knew, that Adolfo had fought insurmountable odds to achieve what he had and no one appreciated it. In the end though, he felt that Adolfo had payed dearly for being a renegade. Would he have done the same thing if the opportunity and the talent had been there? It was hard to answer. One doesn't know until one has been there, it's been said. The irony was that Adolfo didn't have to be doing all of this. Wasn't living with Maria good enough? Why go to all this trouble? Manuel could uderstand his part in the scheme of things, but he couldn't understand Adolfo and that is why, as he stared at the old man, he felt sorry for him. What a waste of life, he thought.

Adolfo had not continued his story, which was unusual. He had other things on his mind. The story he had begun would be too long anyway and he didn't remember if he had told it to the Professor or to Maria. Anyway, he had to think about what he would say to Isabel.

As they got off the truck, the man waved to them and gunned the engine and left. They straightened out as best they could and Adolfo took his teeth out of the coat pocket amd placed them quickly into his mouth. "How do I look?" he asked Manuel. Manuel looked at him head to toe and stepped back. "You look alright," he answered as he lied. Age was starting to show on Adolfo, as if he had aged overnight.

Adolfo reached into his pocket and pulled out his money. He counted twenty-four dollars. "How much did you say you had?" he asked Manuel. Manuel counted his. "I've got exactly sixty dollars." he told Adolfo.

"That ought to put us in Tijuana for a while, don't you think?"

"I thought you were going to stay here?" Manuel said, confused.

"Oh, I'm thinking if things don't work out for me."

"Well, then it would hold us for a while and I can always get more money," Manuel told him. "I have people there."

"I wish Anna had given me more than twenty-four dollars. And if it wasn't for Antonia, I'd be well off right now."

"Well, that's all water under the bridge," Manuel advised him. "Forget about that. Remember the saying: 'That is why spiders never pee.' "

They could hear the dog growling under the porch and the house was lit only in one room, the front room to the right of the porch. The light seemed to flicker and they could see Isabel through the window as she crossed the room. She held something in her hands and her walk was different, a little older. Adolfo stopped when he saw her through the window and his heart ached. He had never felt like this before. All the women and all the hearts he had broken came to this. His heart was breaking now. He loved her, as he had never loved anyone before in his entire life. And now, at this moment, as he saw the poor wretched woman, he finally realized it. The Professor had been right all along. What a waste of life! What a shame to throw everything away. Right then the thought crossed his mind that he should have never left her. He would be a different man today. A father or a grandfather with a home, a family.

Seeing her again brought painful memories to him. He could see her in a flash running naked that night, as the men came upon them while they were making love by a deserted road in the country. Her father's image jumped at him and startled him, as he ascended the porch steps and her father was chasing him away.

The Professor decided to stay behind. Adolfo had finally confessed to him about his past the night before they left Anna. He had told the Professor about Isabel and, personally, he didn't think Adolfo had a right to intrude in Isabel's life. But that was none of his business. Who knows, maybe Isabel would take him in. He had seen stranger things. He was satisfied to sit on the porch steps and listen. "Come in if you think you can help me," Adolfo whispered into his ear. He could hear the clickety sound of the false teeth as Adolfo spoke.

Isabel came to the door when she heard the knock. "Who is it?" she asked, surprised. "Is that you Carolina?"

"No," came the reply in a husky voice. "It's me, Adolfo."

"Adolfo?" she asked, confused.

"Yes, It's me."

"Adolfo? Adolfo? Adolfo, Carmen's uncle?"

"Yes," he said from behind the dimness of the porch.

She turned on the light and the Professor got up and moved to the street where she could not see him. One surprise was enough, he thought. The light shone on Adolfo's thick hair, tousled by the windy ride on the truck.

"My God, it's you!" Isabel exclaimed, finally believing what she was see-ing. "Come in, come in," she said. "It's been a long time. What brings you here?"

"I'm in town for a while," he said, stepping into the familiar room where he and Carmen had sat about two years ago.

"Well, isn't that nice," she told him. She was genuinely pleased to see him. She had so much news.

She offered him coffee. "No, thank you," he answered, and he realized that maybe he should have accepted. Perhaps it would have signaled to her that he could change his ways, be domesticated, drink coffee, that sort of thing. "Well, maybe I ought to, so that I won't fall asleep early," he said.

She got up and brought coffee in her tray and set it down on the table between them. He took the cup and placed it on his lap and drank from it as he spoke. "How is Carmen?"

"Carmen is fine," she said. "She's here at the Naval Base. She is a nurse already."

"I heard," Adolfo said, "Maria wrote to me."

"She's working real hard and having a good time. She has no time for anything else. You know she graduated at the top of her class and Maria, Carolina and I went to the graduation. You should have seen Maria. She was so proud. We cried all the time. People kept looking at us. We laughed later, because we missed most of the graduation."

"How long was she in school?"

"For six months. She was a very good student. She's living at the Base now. It's more convenient for her. She comes once in a while. When she wasn't so busy, she used to come every weekend. But you know how it is with these young people nowadays. They have to have their fun first and then they take care of their obligations to their family. Carmen is no different. She's a normal, healthy young female and she needs the companionship of a man her age. She's going out with a lot of men, now that she's working at the hospital. She's having a lot of fun and working very hard. Carmen, I told her, be sure and remember the advise Maria gave you: 'Tell me who your friends are, and I'll tell you who you are!' "

"Yes, Maria has a saying for everything that goes on in this world, from spiders to money. And you?" he asked, trying to change the conversation, now that he had Carmen out of the way.

"Well," she replied, stretching out the hem on the apron, like she always did, "I'm doing fine. Ruben is in the Pacific and he writes often, about once a month. You know yourself, you've been in it before, you know how difficult it is to sit down and write when you're young. It's just normal, I guess. He's doing alright. He got promoted and he's going to stay in even after the war, whenever that happens. The Japanese are very smart he says. They are hard to find and hard to kill. But he says the talk is that it is beginning to look better for us. Carmen told me that Arnold was drafted. Adam couldn't go. He was 4-F, whatever that means. Carmen says that Maria wrote and she is back to her promises to God. She says if Arnold and Carmen return safely, she will crawl on her knees in daylight all the way to church."

"In the daylight?" Adolfo asked her to be sure she knew what she had said. He knew Maria was exaggerating.

"Yes, in the daylight," Isabel replied.

"But you, Isabel, I'm asking about you. How are you doing?"

"Alright, I suppose, with the suspense of having my son in the war, living day to day not knowing what will happen. It is depressing. I try to entertain myself during the day, doing all kinds of things. I'm sewing a quilt right now. Carmen says her blankets are not warm. But I don't know when she's coming for it. But," she said after a deep sigh, "I don't know about myself, Adolfo. You know me. I never thought about myself that much, ever. I try to stay busy and help other people. Carolina is sick and I've been helping her. She's the lady that lives three houses down the street. She's been very good to Carmen and she's been a friend of mine for a long time. She's got hepatitis, the doctor says. Her eyes are yellow and her skin is yellow. The doctor says she'll get over it, but it will take several more weeks. I have to cook for her, because she can't and I have to cook everything without fat. She vomits if she smells fat being cooked. So you see, I've been busy and I guess I'm happy. What is happy, anyway? I also have my plants and my sewing. I do everything. I don't do it all well, you know me, Adolfo, but I try." She continued to straighten the hem with her fingers. "And you? Tell me about you."

"I've been living in Los Angeles," he said crossing his leg. This time he was wearing shoes, not old canvas sneakers. His socks matched his trousers. He felt comfortable, prosperous. At least, he had improved. "I've been staying with friends; you know how it is. When you have as many friends as I do, it's impossible to say 'no' to them. That's always been my downfall. You know that. Anyway, I stayed with them for over a year now. Let's see," he told her, and he stroked his chin, "I've been there about a year. That's right. We spent one winter there only, if you can call it that. It was a mild winter, didn't you think?"

"It was. I heard the radio anouncer say that San Diego was colder than Los Angeles this past year."

"Amazing, sometimes the weather is like that. It's unpredictable. How can anyone claim to know what will happen?"

"You're right. Yesterday they were saying it was going to rain today and it didn't. You can see for yourself. It's been hot for being spring. It usually doesn't get hotter than this."

"That's true," Adolfo replied. "And in Los Angeles it can get hot. I was living then with friends, as I was saying, and I had a good time. As a matter of fact, time flew. A year was up and gone before I knew it."

"Maria wrote to Carmen and said you were living with a widow."

"Oh, yes," he said, "that was at first." Then he realized Anna had been a widow also. "Well, I lived with two widows. One, the first one, turned out to be not only a widow, but a shyster, but Maria doesn't know all about her. I haven't had a chance to write to her."

"So what brings you to San Diego?" she asked him.

The question was so straight forward that it stunned him. He had expected to ease into his pitch as the conversation edged along, maybe dropping a hint here and there.

"I have two reasons," he replied, fidgeting with his tie. He stumbled trying to think of the second reason. The first one was that he was here to visit Carmen. The second was, well, something that he had to think of right away. "I came to visit Carmen," he said, finally.

"And the other reason?" she asked him, she had taken a crochet needle out of her apron and was continuing making a doily. "Don't tell me you're still trying to get back with me?" she laughed.

"Oh no!" he exclaimed, rather loudly. He startled Isabel and himself. "I have another reason. I know that you won't take me. It's too late, I guess."

"Well, Adolfo," she said. She stopped her crocheting. "There are days when I would take you back and there are days when I could kill you. I imagine that after all these years, I still love you a little. But don't get encouraged," she added when Adolfo seemed to get interested. "It's not a good healthy love. It's more of a hatred that I feel for you that borders on love. Do you understand?"

"No, I suppose not. But then again, I was never very smart. Let's face it, you don't have to be very smart to play baseball."

"I never considered you dumb, Adolfo," she told him. She was being tender to him, just as he figured she would react when he degraded himself. "I considered you very smart and very talented. That's why I had a crush on you. That's why I lost my footing with you."

"But that's another story," Adolfo said, thinking with pain about the years he had thrown away. "We'll never recover those days. They're gone forever."

"Unfortunately," she replied.

"Maybe I could stay for a while," he said, "maybe just to see how well you would like it."

"No," she said to him. She sighed deeply, "I already know how I would feel. You hurt the wrong woman, Adolfo. You hurt the one that could never forgive you."

He looked down at his feet and couldn't find the courage to look at her.

"You think that all your playfulness, all your silliness, is a man's way of living a good life?" She asked him the question and looked at him waiting for an answer. "Do you?"

"No," he replied, faintly. He was still looking down and he remembered that, as a child, his mother had stood him in front of her and she had scolded him for dropping and breaking a vase of flowers and she had shook him and shook him until he cried. He felt exactly the same way at that moment.

"Do you still drink all the time?"

"Yes."

"Do you still think you are a ladies' man?"

"Yes."

"Do you still stay out till all hours of the night, drinking, arguing, acting like a little boy?"

"Yes," he had to admit.

"And you ask me if it would be alright to try for a reconciliation?"

"Yes, I'm afraid so," he said. He was completely devoid of courage. He was a child.

She took the apron and began wiping tears from her eyes. "Why must you do this to me?" she asked him. "Why must you interfere in my life? I'm as happy as I will ever be right now. I feel sorry for you, that's all." She wiped some more tears, as she cried and the doily was getting wet, so she stuck it in her apron and the needle with it. "I'll tell you what you can do, though," she said. "You can sleep in the washshed tonight. But that's all."

"It's kind of you, Isabel," he said, "but I have a friend with me and we must be going. I didn't intend to stay this long. Anyway it was Carmen that I was looking for. Just to say 'Hello.'She must look beautiful in her uniform."

"That she does," Isabel replied. She had stopped crying and now had the sniffles. "Well, I'm sorry you missed her," Isabel told him, "and I'm sure she would have loved seeing you. But what of your friend? Where are you to meet him?"

"He's outside waiting," Adolfo informed her, looking apologetically towards the door.

"I didn't know," Isabel said, "I could have offered him a cup of coffee."

"Oh, he doesn't drink coffee. Actually, he's not much of a social person. He's very bashful," Adolfo told her, hoping Manuel couldn't hear him.

She convinced them to sleep in the washshed that night and she happily arranged two cots for them, spreading out quilts for them, as the night was crisp. She left the kerosene lantern with them, just in case they needed to get up in the middle of the night. She had forgiven him for the time being. She had cried out her anger.

"She's a wonderful woman," Manuel said. He was covered to his chin with the brand new quilt. "How could you have left her?"

"At the time," Adolfo replied, reflecting slowly, painfully, "it was a matter of my career. Later, when my career didn't come out as planned, it was too late. I guess those are the things that make life so hard and so miserable."

"You shoot for the stars and you land on a pile of shit," Manuel said. "Is that what you're saying?"

"Yes," he replied.

The weatherman was right. It began to rain, at first a drop and then more, until the deluge came and they could hear the noise as the rain pounded the tin roof.

"This reminds me of a time in Texas," Adolfo said, his full body stretched on the cot, his feet sticking out from under the quilt, his long toe-nails yellowish with age, "when we were caught in a hail storm outside of Brownsville. We were in an old bus . . . "

He heard the Professor snore and he felt embarrassed and hurt. "I've been insulted by better men than him," he said, and he rolled over and went to sleep. That night for the first time in a long time he cried.

Carolina had been at Isabel's from early morning on drinking coffee and eating toast left over from Isabel's breakfast. She was feeling better. Her color was returning to normal. She felt like eating. She had heard Isabel's story about the night before. She had grimaced every time Isabel mentioned Adolfo's name. "How can you put up with that sonafabitch," she said, picking up her dress and crossing her leg. "It's hot already and here it is only spring."

Isabel laughed at her. "Which part do you want me to answer?"

"Adolfo," she snapped. "That no good sonafabitch. And I'll bet you he's still in the washshed, asleep. Right?"

"I guess so," Isabel replied. She had not been to take a look at them this morning. "They're still here. If they haven't sneaked out."

She was preparing breakfast for the two men, very carefully rolling out flour tortillas and cooking them on the griddle. "You eat lousy bread and for them you make tortillas. You'll never learn, Isabel."

"Oh, I learned a long time ago. Be pleasant. That's what I learned. If you're angry, you don't live very long and you really don't get your revenge. Not that I ever needed revenge for Adolfo. That's been many years ago. If I had stayed bitter, I would have had a terrible life."

"Oh, you think you had it wonderful?" Carolina asked her. "You think you had it like a queen, or what?"

"No, but I could have had it worse. I could have turned out worse. I can easily see that. I did well, considering. My life was very bad in those middle years, but I survived. If I survived that, I can survive anything. And I'm not only telling you this, I told Maria the same thing. I told her, Maria, you and I went through hell to get to where we're at and no person and no thing is going to disturb us now."

"And what about me?" Carolina asked. She had taken the last piece of toast and had wiped the egg off the plate with it. "You know, Isabel," she was licking her fingers, "you cook the best eggs of anyone I've ever known. Better than my mother used to, bless her soul, and may God have her in heaven with him."

"Amen," Isabel answered automatically without thinking. She had come to sit at the table with Carolina, a cup of coffee in her hand. She had all the breakfast ready, except for the eggs. She would fry them as soon as she saw the men walk out of the wash-shed. That way, she had thought, by the time they sit down, the eggs will be done. "I see that you're feeling much better. You look better," she told Carolina. "And I see that your appetite is coming back."

"I'm feeling better, thank you. You know me, if I can eat I will. God knows, I needed this illness to make me lose some weight." She looked at herself and she didn't like what she saw. "Well, what about me," she started up again. She had gotten side-tracked. "My husband was no glass of milk. You remember that, don't you, Isabel?" Isabel nodded in agreement. "Why, he could be like a snake and then be so loving. Remember when he used to take me to the park? Remember, we used to take you with us sometimes? He could be so sweet, as long as he was drinking in moderation. If he had his drink here and there, he was fine. What a happy man he could be. You remember, don't you? But what am I telling you all this for, you knew him well. But what a bastard he could be once he went over that limit. My God, woman, don't you remember how terrible he could be?"

"He was terrible," Isabel agreed, drinking her coffee.

"Terrible?" she shouted at the question. "Terrible? What do you mean terrible? He was worse than that. Horrible. That was it. He was like a horrible animal!" Then she stopped and thought for a while and she asked. "Why are Mexican men like that? What in the world makes them be like that?"

"It may be all the hot food they eat," Isabel said and she started laughing at her own words.

The men were coming out of the washshed. Adolfo was adjusting his belt and shielding his eyes from the sun as he walked. Manuel looked refreshed. He seemed happier, now that he was closer to Mexico. He had told Adolfo that the air seemed fresher the closer he got. He had shaved using an old wash bowl and some hand soap Isabel had left with them. Adolfo had not shaved. He was not in the mood to shave.

As soon as the two men entered the house through the back door, Carolina stood and allowed herself to be introduced and she excused herself and left quickly.

"He must have been a good-looking man when he was young," she would tell Isabel after Adolfo and Manuel had left. "I can see very well why you could loose your footing with him. You know what I mean, open your legs, that sort of thing."

Isabel blushed and continued working on her quilt. "He was not like the others," she answered her. She began to reminisce. "When you asked why all Mexicans treated their wives badly, I thought about him. Not all of them do, of course. And Adolfo was one that was a perfect gentleman. He knew that tenderness meant a lot to a woman. He was very tender. The trouble was," she reflected as she thought about it, before pushing the needle through the quilt, "that he was also the perfect scoundrel. And it seems a lot of women love that in a man. It somehow makes their juices flow. I know it did mine."

"And how!" Carolina cried out, shaking her hand as if she had touched something hot.

Isabel had asked Carolina if she could drive Adolfo, Manuel and her to go visit Carmen. Carolina had agreed with pleasure. After all, she was feeling much better with Isabel's excellent care. She only wondered if her car could make it there and back. It wouldn't make much difference, Isabel had told her, Adolfo and Manuel were to be dropped off at the Bus Depot and if the car didn't make it, she and Carolina could just walk back. Unless, Isabel thought, Carolina thought the car would be stolen. Carolina had informed Isabel that no one in his right mind would steal the car.

When the four of them arrived at the naval base, Carolina parked the car to one side of the gate. Traffic seemed to be going both in and out at an incredible pace. The four SP's directing traffic were busily keeping everyone moving. When an officer's car went by, they would snap to attenion and salute. Isabel got out of the car. She was riding up front with Carolina. She walked to the gate and the three left in the car could see her talking to one of the sailors. They could see her reach into her purse and show the sailor some identification. The sailor nodded his head as he read the card. Then they saw Isabel turn toward them and point toward the car as she continued talking to the sailor. He shook his head in a negative way and they saw her walk back to the car.

"They say I'm the only one that can go in," she informed them as she opened the door and got in. "I'm the only one with a worker's identification. I suspected something like this would happen. They are very strict now with the war going on. In th old days anyone could go in that wanted to."

"Did you tell them that the great Adolfo was here?" he asked her, making fun of himself.

"That's probably why they wouldn't let us in," Carolina replied and the Professor laughed.

"Tell them Manuel Garcia, the Ambassador from Mexico, is here in the car," the Professor said, in a mock tone. "Tell them he is one of the few survivors of the battle of Moctezuma."

"Yes," Adolfo joined in, "and tell them he has been fighting the battle of the bottle and he has not surrendered, even though he isn't winning."

"You two are crazy," Carolina said, looking at them sitting in the back seat.

"This is serious," Isabel told them. "It means we won't be able to see Carmen, and if you don't see her, Adolfo, God only knows when you'll be able to see her again."

"Maybe we can walk up to the fence and see if we can see her," Adolfo said.

"Are you crazy?" Manuel said to him. "There are thousands of people walking around inside the base. You think Carmen can spot you standing at the fence?"

"He's right!" Isabel agreed. "We can't see her from here, that's for sure. But the least we can do is show you where she works."

So they all got out of the car and, peering across the base through the fence, Isabel showed Adolfo where Carmen worked.

"It's hard to imagine," he said, shielding the sun from his eyes, "that little Carmen works in such a large building. I'll bet," he said, "that as smart as she is, she knows every room and hall in that building."

"I bet she does," Isabel added.

"You don't know her, Manuel," Adolfo said to him in all seriousness, "but she is very smart. The smartest one in the whole family and with that I tell you everything. I'll never forget," he said, continuing into something else, "when she was a little girl and she would run to the store for me. I always gave her a penny before-hand so she could buy something. When she came back she would give me my package and then she would go to the shady part of the house and she would eat her candy, sitting in the dirt. Can you imagine that? Carmen sitting in the dirt?" He paused a while and let go of the fence and he turned around. "Look where she is now, working in a tall building." He adjusted his suit and straightened his tie.

During the ride back to the bus depot he was quiet for a long time. Manuel seemed to be having a good time flirting with Carolina. Isabel was piqued. She had wanted to see Carmen and she had so looked forward to it, not only for herself, but for Adolfo. It depressed her too that Carmen had not been by to visit her in a long time. It had been over two months since she had graduated. That was, she thought, the last time she had seen her. Isabel had thought of going to the naval base to see Carmen several times. And after Adolfo and Manuel had left, she and Carolina tried and, although she had worked there many years, she was not allowed to go into the area where Carmen worked. The government was very sensitive, she had been told, of the wounded and dying. Only the immediate family and the hospital staff were allowed where Carmen worked and lived.

"Tell Carmen I tried to see her," Adolfo said as he opened the door and grabbed his suitcase. Manuel was out and headed for the depot. He was anxious to get home. He turned around, though, when he thought about it and came back and apologized for not saying his proper good-byes. He had to thank them profusely for their hospitality. "It's just that I'm excited at going back home," he explained.

Adolfo had not thought of what to say. This was probably his last farewell to the only woman he had ever loved. She looked up at him with tenderness and he saw that in her eyes and he almost cried. Instead he cleared his throat.

The thought of her naked beside him came to him as they both had been together one night. It was hard to believe that that was all it took to ruin her life. It was a night he had never forgotten. She was the purest, the finest, and the most innocent of all his women, he thought. He had covered her up as she shivered in pain while she slept. And then he saw her running in the brush once more, the men seeing her naked as she ran to hide from everyone.

"Goodbye, Adolfo," she said. She was about to cry, "and may God bless you."

He just didn't know what to say. For the first of a few times in his life he was speechless.

They arrived in Tijuana by late afternoon. The sun had been almost unbearable. Adolfo blamed the weather on the fighting in the Pacific. "It's boiling up the water with all those bombs and torpedos." Manuel just shook his head. The sun had heated up the day and inside the bus the stench of the sweating peope and dirty feet had almost nauseated Adolfo and Manuel. One woman sitting in front of them had a box full of white goat cheeses and she kept them from falling out of the box by pressing a piece of wax paper over them. They had an acrid, rancid smell and Adolfo and Manuel, who were used to eating just about everything, had to hold their noses when the wind blew in their faces. She looked back periodically at Manuel and she would grin a toothless grin. He ignored her, trying to look the other way. Once she stared at him for a long time and he had to face her and she grinned again and he gave a half-hearted smile just to be well-mannered. "That's the way you look when you don't use your teeth," he whispered to Adolfo. Adolfo was not in a mood to be made fun of. "And that's the type of woman you attract," he whispered back to Manuel. He was clearly irritated. But later after the hassle of the custom inspection on the Mexican side, he began to come out of his mood and started to laugh silently to himself.

"What's so funny," Manuel asked him, almost laughing himself at what Adolfo was thinking.

"I remember a time in San Antonio, Texas," he said, half closing one eye and tilting his head, trying to remember the date. "Anyway, I don't remember the date," he said finally, after a while. "Anyway, that's not important to the story. What is important is what happened in the story, the story itself. I'm always trying to get dates right and it seems that they are usually not important to the story. I don't know why I do it. When I do remember, it gives me much pride and elation, like I have accomplished something. My mind relaxes. If I knew the date, I always thought I could tell the story well. I forgot the date. I'm doing this more often, if you notice."

"I've noticed, Adolfo," Manuel said to him.

Adolfo couldn't tell if Manuel was being sarcastic or simply agreeing. He looked at him for a time, studiously or maybe dumbfounded, for he had that look. The look became a blank stare.

"What's the matter?" Manuel asked him.

"I forgot what I was saying," he replied and they both started to laugh.

The toothless woman looked back and laughed with them. Then she pointed at the circular pieces of goat cheese and motioned to ask them if they wanted some.

They both declined gracefully by looking the other way.

When they got off the bus, they allowed the woman to get off ahead of them. They noticed the smell had not left. As they crossed her aisle, they saw that the poor woman was clean. Somebody had vomited on the floor by the side of the bus and that was what they had been smelling all this time.

"She looked ugly anyway." Manuel reasoned to Adolfo, "no matter how good she may have smelled."

"And to think I turned down goat cheese," Adolfo said in remorse, "one of my favorite foods."

They were carrying their cardboard suitcases and walking down the narrow sidewalk full of people. "It's a long walk," Manuel told him, "but we've got plenty of time. My sister and her husband will be waiting for us with open arms.

CHAPTER 10

Maria had been terrified of the war. She remembered the first one, the one where Adolfo served. This one, though, seemed to be worse. A lot of young men were being drafted. Several of her friend's boys were now in the service. A star hung by many windows in those days. She had two, one for Carmen and one for Arnoldo.

Arnoldo had been asked by official letter to report to the courthouse and from there, with all the others going that day, they had been taken in a caravan of buses to the induction center in San Diego. That same night they were bussed home and, after the results of their physical exam had been made known, they were each cailed into a separate branch of the service. Arnold was drafted into the Army. He would be an infantryman. He took the bus to Ft. Benning, Georgia, and from there would be shipped to the Pacific.

He had been furloughed after basic training and he had come home on a bus all dressed in uniform and looking young and handsome. Maria had met him along with his wife, Dora. Dora spoke only very shortly to her while they waited for the bus. She did mention that Arnold had written to say he had lost a lot of weight. Maria had been amiable to her and told her she hoped Arnold would look fine. She didn't want him too thin. Dora walked away from her as Maria finished her remarks and went to sit with her relatives who had brought her over. Maria was there with Adam and his wife, Alba, the one Maria hated. She had cursed at just about everything that had happened to them that day. Adam had bought a used car and had had a flat tire. This had been enough for Alba to break out in a torrent of curses that Maria could hardly believe was possible. Along with Umberta, who had also been invited, she took refuge on the opposite side of the car as she heard Alba's curses against the tire and Adam. Maria felt anger as she listened to the tirade directed at her son. But she kept quiet. She looked at Umberta and Umberta knew Maria well enough to know that if looks could kill, Alba would have fallen dead where she stood. Adam was more tolerant. He said nothing, but seemed exhausted just changing the tire. A man passing by had readjusted his hat and partially covered his face with it as he passed the cursing woman. Adam had looked at him as the passerby hid and did nothing but shrug.

"To think that Adam would marry someone like that," Maria had told Umberta. "This is the only time in my life that I would consider someone's death as a deed worthy of a promise."

"Don't say that!" Umberta had excitedly screamed at Maria, as if Maria were going through with it. "God will punish you and kill you first. It always happens."

"Well," Maria insisted, "it may be worth the risk. Poor Adam," she added as she thought of her son having to live with the woman.

"He could always leave her," Umberta reminded her. "There are no ropes tied to him that I see."

"Well, he probably loves her," Maria said, depressed with the thought of having Alba as a daughter-in-law for good. "You know how dumb men are. The ones that are falling over their faces for them, they could care less about."

"That's life," Umberta said. She had it figured out.

Arnold stepped from the bus and was hardly recognizable. He had indeed lost a lot of weight. He hugged Dora for a long time, then he came over and hugged Maria, and then Adam and Alba and Umberta. The conversation was awkward. Where were they to go next? Maria offered her house, but that suggestion was received with silence and then a change in conversation. Maria had prepared food, she told them, but that also was by-passed. After some discussion among Dora's friends and after the bus had left, they decided to go eat at Arnold's and Dora's. Arnold invited Maria and Adam and Alba and Umberta and they all went. The idea, Maria had said on the way over, was to keep things runnning smoothly while Arnold was there. After all, it was his furlough and he should enjoy himself and not have to mediate a fight between the two families. "I don't know why Dora has all that pride," Alba said in the car, "they have nothing. No money, nothing to be proud about."

Maria felt awkward and soon a٫ter eating, when the men began to drink in earnest, she asked Adam if he would please take her and Umberta home. She could see Arnold by herself the next day. No one had been disrespectful to her, but she knew she didn't belong.

"As Adolfo would say," Maria remarked to them in the car, "these people have no class."

"You know they think that they're better than you, Maria," Umberta said. She was not trying to goad her on; she was merely repeating what a lot of people had been saying.

"I know," Maria said to her, looking straight ahead with her arms folded sternly over her bust, "and it really burns me. They don't know that my people were much better than theirs. In other words, our bastards are better than their bastards. They've got things to hide also. Don't believe they don't." She fixed her dress and rearranged her hat. "Anyway, Umberta," she said, "we've got a lot to eat. I hate for it to spoil."

When they arrived Maria decided that the food would be too much for them and she had Adam take it and give it to the prostitutes where Adolfo had worked. "They'll appreciate it more than Dora and her family," she said, bitterly.

The priest had more or less reached an understanding with his fate. He had changed considerably, and although he still was angry and chastized the parishioners, he was a little more tolerant. He had come to the conclusion that he could not change these people. God only knew why they lived as they did. He couldn't explain it. And after so many years of trying to change them with no results, he had given up. At least they stood up to fight for their country, he had thought, trying to give them some compliment. He had also come to the conclusion that all these people were not necessarily bad. As his uncle Father Carranza had told him when he first arrived in the United States, "Don't misjudge these people. They have no education, no background. All they have is today and they try to make the most of it." The words were still fresh in his memory. Father Carranza had been right. No other class of people he had ever met lived for the present as these people did. Ask them about tomorrow and they couldn't understand. What about tomorrow? Well, that would have to take care of itself. The women, he had found, were the mainstay of the family. And although at first appearances it seemed as if the familes were male dominated, they weren't. The reason for this maternal dominance, he had found out, was that the male did not want the responsibilities of the home. He wanted to be free to go and come as he pleased. Let the woman take care of everything else, those things that he considered insignificant. It was an Indian-warrior type of philosophy. Once he was inside the house, though, he exaggerated his importance in front of the children by threatening the wife. The wife's mentality, he had found out, was that life was a burdensome journey that must be endured. And, if life was so, then married life was infinitely harder. Being married was a master-slave relationship. And the more masterful the man the more slave-like the woman. "You must suffer in order to deserve," was the saying in those days. The wife took the abuses. What else could she do? Ignorant and poor, they had no recourse. Even their own families turned them away if they complained. Why shouldn't they? Their mother's and their mother's mother had to endure much more. He secretly admired the women for accepting such a devastating fate. "What else could they do?" he asked himself. It was not an easy choice. They were ignorant and couldn't work and, if they did work, they couldn't support themselves and their children. So it was an economic problem, he had surmised. "One day," he said to himself, "when the Mexican woman becomes educated, there will be no Mexican marriages." He was wrong, of course.

In the six-months period before World War II, he had lost both his father and mother. His mother died first. The home-coming had been painful. His country was at war also. The Spanish Civil War was ending and the Fascists had won for all purposes. Franco had entered Madrid. All over there was chaos. The rail system of which they had been so proud was destroyed. No trains were on time. Few buses moved at night for fear of attacks, either from the Republicans or the Fascists. More disturbing to him than anything else, though, was that Franco was aligning himself with Hitler. He could predict the consequences of that alliance. If Germany won, then Spain would remain fascist. If Germany lost, Spain would be ostracized for many years. It's industrial development would remain behind most of Europe. Either way, Spain would lose.

His father died shortly after he returned to the United States. This time, when he returned for his father's funeral, he understood that, in spite of the pressures from within, that Spain would try to remain neutral. His friends were very depressed that Spain had even aligned itself with Hitler.

Although many very educated citizens had left, there was some evidence that order was being reinstated in Spanish life and he felt somewhat better upon his departure.

He had left Spain through the port of Bilbao. He had traveled by train from his home in the province of Galicia through the small towns that he had known well in his younger days. Lugo, where he had studied; Porferrada, a town where the main kiosk was painted as yellow as a canary. The train had stopped here briefly to take on passengers, mostly Spaniards fleeing the country. Then the train had proceeded to Astorga, a town on top of a small mountain that he remembered well. His father had brought him to Astorga to see about his education. He had met a fine woman here. He remembered her well as a robust lady who had made advances to him. She had scared him when she showed him her long pubic hairs. He had refused her, such had been the intensity with which he pursued his early religion. His mother had been born near Astorga. Leon, was the next stop. There was a one-hour lay over. It was by far the largest city near his birth-place. When the train arrived at Leon they were told by the militia guarding the train that there would be at least an additional two-hour delay. It fit in perfectly with his plans. He had intended all along to see Father Carranza's family, to pay his respects and to bring them a picture of Father Carranza's grave in Mexico City. The priest there, a friend of Father Carranza, had sent him the picture. He felt that they would want to see the place where the old priest had been buried.

He took a bus to the neighborhood as soon as he cleared the military inspection at the train depot. He went to the small street-level house and found that Father Carranza's parents were still alive, well into their nineties. They were blind and deaf and could hardly walk. He spoke to a younger woman there, a niece, and gave her the photograph of the grave. He was disappointed that the parents could not understand who he was and what he had come for. He had expected more of the priest's family to be there, but the niece informed him that they had all fled.

Bilbao was one of the main ports of Spain. The train arrived late at night and the activity in this fairly large city was intense. He did not have to be reminded that there was a war going on. Although Spain was remaining neutral, it seemed to him that there was an emotional display favoring the fascists at that time. There were signs throughout, and some not so subtle, of anti-Jewish sentiment.

His ship was delayed several days, but the passengers were allowed to stay aboard and he was able to catch up on his reading and drinking. The word out was that the German Navy was interfering with shipping lanes.

When normalcy was restored to the Bay of Biscayne and the Atlantic, the ship was allowed to sail.

Once home, he had begun to drink in public. Nothing much mattered anymore. He was accepted for what he was, an alcoholic priest. He knew that, even if the Bishop had known, he still would not have been reprimanded. Who else would go to that parish?

"He says the reason he drinks so much," Maria had told Umberta, "is that he has to live with us."

"That's a good enough reason," Umberta agreed. "Most of these people are heartless. It must really be hard for someone as intelligent as him living among us."

It was December of 1942. The war was a year old. Fighting was intense in both fronts. Eddie had been drafted and was in England. He was a tail-gunner on a B-29. The word from him was that they were starting to win the war. The Russians were beating the Germans and the English and Americans were winning in Africa. The French, he wrote, were still in deep trouble. He had flown twenty-seven missions in two months. He hoped there would be some rest. He told young Maria to pray for him. It was tough going. He always remembered Maria and Arnold and Adam. He had hoped to be with Arnold in the the Pacific, but it had not worked out. "Anyway," he wrote one time, "Arnold and I would have been drunk all during this goddamn war and when it was over, we wouldn't have known about it."

Again the small car came up the road, this time in the dry windy coldness of a late December afternoon. Maria strained her eyes from the porch where she was standing. She was sweeping. She was wearing a heavy black-wool sweater and a muffler around her neck and over the top of her head. She stared at the car as it came closer and closer. She recognized the car and her heart seemed to stop. She hoped with all her heart that the car would turn or stop, do anything but continue relentlessly toward her house. It was the small black car. No, it was not Jesus. This small black car was driven by the telegrapher's messenger. His telegrams spoke mostly of wounded soldiers and dead soldiers. She had not heard from Arnold in a long time and she supposed Dora had not either.

The car stopped slowly as the wind howled around it and the dark-complected man stepped out and walked slowly toward her. He had a telegram in his hands. At that moment she didn't know what to think. Was it Carmen? Was she dead? Wounded? My God, not Carmen! Or Arnold! Which one was it? It had to be Carmen! If it were Arnold, Dora would be the one to know first. "My God!" she screamed, "it's Carmen! Is it?"

The man stood silently. He had been through this several times before. "No," he said quickly, "it's Arnold, but I thought you should be the first to know. The telegram is not for you. We haven't received yours yet. This one is for Dora," he said. He apologetically showed her the telegram. He hated being the bearer of this type of news. "Arnold was my friend," he said crying, wiping tears from his eyes, "how do you think I feel? We had great times together. I'll miss him always and I'm sorry."

The fact that Arnold had been killed stunned her for a short while. But when she realized what had happened, she began screaming and beating the porch floor with the broom. Then in her anger she turned on the man and began chasing him to the car. Her screams could be heard around the neighborhood. Finally, exhausted, she fell to the ground on her knees and began to sob. She rocked and she shook and she bundled herself up in a human ball and cried and cried.

Umberta had heard the screams, but knowing Maria, she had imagined that she was singing or getting after someone, as this was her nature. When the noise continued, she walked out of the house and saw a black form on the ground shaking and crying and pounding the ground. She ran when she saw her and almost at once she saw the little black car, the dreaded car, slowly drive away from the house. The man ducked behind the wheel as he passed her.

Poor Umberta had run to Maria as Maria cried in pain and agony. She reached Maria as the crying and screaming got louder. "No! No!," Maria yelled and Umberta imagined that Maria was talking to her and immediately she asked her, "What happened, Maria?"

Maria continued to cry and couldn't answer.

"What happened?" Umberta screamed. "Tell me, please," she begged as she fell to her knees to put her arms around Maria.

"It's . . . It's Arnold," she screamed. "Oh God! How can you be so cruel! What have I ever done to you to deserve this pain? Tell me it's not true. Tell me that I'm in a dream!"

"Arnold!" Umberta screamed now. "Arnold? What happened?"

"He's dead. He's dead. He's dead," she kept on repeating as the words kept dying off.

"In the name of the Holy Father," Umberta said in disbelief, "I don't believe it. How cruel you have been, dear God, to this poor woman who never has betrayed you. Where are you now, God?" she asked him.

"Why have you abandoned me, Lord," Maria said in her grief. "What horrible thing have I done to you that you have brought me so much misery in my life. Never have I been at peace in this world," and she pounded the hard ground with her fist.

Both women were on their knees looking at the heavens and the neighbors started peering from their homes and began to slowly walk toward Maria's house. First one, then another, the women came and as they heard the tragic news, they in turn began their wailing and supplications to God.

"We regret to inform you," the telegram read, "that your son, PFC Arnoldo Saenz, was reported killed in action on November 10, 1942, in the Pacific Theater. The Department of Defense extends to you our deepest felt sorrow. His country will always be eternally grateful for his supreme sacrifice."

The Company Commander wrote:

"Dear Mrs. Saenz

I wish to personally extend A Company's condolences upon Arnold's death. We shall miss him a lot. He brought great joy and comraderie to his outfit. He was a soldier's soldier.

He was killed trying to save the lives of the men in the squad that he led.

For his gallantry in action I am recommending that he be awarded, posthumously, the silver star.

Sincerely yours,"

and it was signed by a Captain Richard Miller.

Dr. Chichester read the telegram for Maria and he read the letter and explained what the silver star was and what posthumously meant. She shook her head in disbelief. It would be some time before she would accept his death. Even Dora had accepted it and was leading a normal life. Maria never forgave God.

Her thoughts turned to the age-old question of whether God is good or not. If he is, why punish Maria and Arnold's family by killing him? Did God, in fact, Maria asked Umberta, control your life? If so, how could he allow something like this to happen? Why not have Arnold be somewhere else thus avoid the bullet that killed him? Why was he not one second early or late and thus avoid his death? If God was everywhere, as she had been taught, and, if he knew everything, then why allow this to happen? Thinking back, she couldn't remember doing anything wrong that would have given God the excuse to punish her. It was confusing.

She kept thinking that Arnold was alive. She had to remind herself. She had not gone through the funeral, the final ritual for the living upon the death of a loved one. And since he had been gone from her sight, she imagined him alive. At times she asked herself if she was in a dream. But she came back always and steadied herself against something (she was having dizzy spells) and she tried to face the truth. Arnold was dead. How could God be so cruel?

Umberta was at her side most of the day to comfort her. Umberta would go home for a short while, do her chores, and then keep her company. Umberta's own son had been drafted and he also was in the Pacific. "God help us," Maria had said to the women after church, "if Umberta's son meets with some accident. She'll die." The women had agreed.

Although Maria never said anything to Umberta, she wondered about Umberta's son. Why had he not been killed? It would have been just as easy to kill him as to kill Arnold. She apologized to Umberta by being extra nice to her. "I've never known anyone more considerate," Umberta confided to her neighbors, "Maria should be thinking about herself, but she's always thinking about ways to please me."

If God is as powerful as she had been led to believe, then he was cruel. And if Arnold's life had been predestined to end this way, then the whole thing, his life, had been a charade.

The conflict in her mind was partly due to her preoccupation with Carmen's fate. Her deep-rooted Spanish Catholicism would not let her condemn God, not while Carmen was in danger. If she spoke out in her anguish, she was afraid that God would punish her by taking Carmen's life.

She herself started her own charade. Although not eager to go, she went to church where she prayed mass, her novenas, and the stations of the cross. But her heart was not in it. She was going through the motions, hoping that God would not discover what she was doing.

He had taken Arnold from her, but, she thought, he had better not mess around with Carmen. That would be too much.

During the day, as she washed her dishes, she would look out the window through the gently moving curtains and she could see Arnold playing in the vacant fields behind her house. She would cry. He loved candy, she thought, one day. She never could understand why. She would give him a penny and he would run to the little corner store and get his candy and he would run back and, like Carmen, would go to a shady place and sit on the ground and eat it. He was frail as a boy, she remembered, but later after high school, he had put on weight. He had been bigger than Adam. "Now Adam is the soundrel," she would tell everyone. "I never know what he'll do next. And he was alway that way since he was a child. He'd steal from me. Not much, but he'd steal from me. Arnold would ask for things. Adam would steal them."

The period between learning of his death and the funeral was a time which later on she could not recall very well. She had fainted several times and, as interminable as it had seemed, it became a blur of speeding time when she tried to recollect her thoughts.

She knew that the first thought after she had somewhat regained her composure was that there had been a horrible mistake and that soon the small black car would appear, stop in front of the house, and the young man would announce to the great joy of everyone present that Arnold was alive and that he would be coming home shortly.

She thought so much on this that at times it seemed to her that it had already occurred and that she should be getting things ready for Arnold's homecoming.

Maria's preoccupation with events that had not taken place began to trouble Umberta. More than once she had asked Maria a question, only to be answered with an unrelated response concerning Arnold and how he was preparing to come home. "He's coming soon," she said to Umberta. "He's coming as soon as he straightens out this mess. I knew it," she said to herself, although Umberta was there. "I knew Arnold would pull a trick like this. He faked his own tragedy just for fun. He was always playing dead as a child. He was always the cowboy that got shot. He picked it up from the pictures he saw. But I'm sure they will be very angry with him. The Army doesn't tolerate those pranks. Poor Arnold, God only knows when they'll let him come home."

It took two months for the body to arrive. During this time, oddly enough, Maria and Dora were closer than they had been. Through Umberta's interventions the two women began visiting each other. Umberta felt strongly that Maria needed to get out and talk to someone before she completely lost her mind. "You're young," Maria had told Dora in one of her more lucid moments, "and you must start life anew. Thank God you have no children. Look at how much worse it would have been for you. A young widow with children has a hard time getting remarried. Think about yourself now for a while."

"He was a good husband," Dora told her, "and I don't know if I'll ever marry again. It's so painful when you lose someone like this."

"You've been very brave," Umberta said to Dora, blinking quickly with her narrow-set little eyes. "Some wives go to pieces over a tragedy like this. But you have been very brave. You could almost say that you are acting normal." And she looked toward Maria, who was back again deeply into her thoughts. "You must help her, Dora," Umberta said, whispering.

"I will," Dora replied. She was crying softly.

The day the body arrived by train, there was a discussion at the depot as to where the body should go. Jesus was sent over to ask Dora and then Maria and then he was to return to inform Hector, the man with the hearse.

When Jesus returned, Hector and the men had loaded the coffin in the hearse and Hector was leaning against the hearse smoking a cigarette and bragging about knowing Arnold and telling all those present that he and Arnold and Adam and Eddie had embalmed an old whore. They had been passing a bottle of liquor around. Jesus strode to them rapidly and said that Dora had agreed to have the body taken to Maria's house. "She says," Jesus informed them in his smallish voice, "that Arnold belongs to his mother now.

Isn't that a generous way to be?"

"She's a good woman," someone volunteered. "She'll make someone a good wife some day."

"You know what they say about widows," Jesus told the group, winking at them. "They've got the fire inside them."

"What a horrible thing to say," one of the men told him, "and Arnold's body right here besides us."

"Well," Jesus replied, apologizing, "I was just repeating an old proverb, that's all."

"You ought to be ashamed of yourself," the same man scolded him. "Have you no shame?" he added, spitting out some of the bitterness of the liquor from his mouth.

And Jesus meekly changed the conversation and passed the bottle of barreteaga around.

"We'll drink to Arnold," Jesus said, raising the bottle and taking a long swallow. "A good friend and drinking partner who died for his country."

They passed the bottle around one more time.

After the funeral, the families separated. Those that had come from Maria's side gathered at Maria's. It was not that there was any resentment. In fact, Maria felt good that Dora had suggested that the body be taken to Maria's house. Maria had already thought about it, but had not mentioned it to Dora and when Dora suggested it, Maria knew that Dora was a good woman after all. Maria thought a child always belongs to the parents no matter what. Dora can always marry again, she said. Dora can lead a new life. Maria was stuck wih Arnold's death. He would be no more. So it was more a matter of convenience that the families separated. The only bond that had held them together was buried. Maria was to see a lot of Dora during the next months, but gradually, as time went on, she saw less and less of her. There were no children to hold them together.

Adolfo had come the day before the funeral. Jesus had met him at the bus station, eagerly awaiting the return of his drinking friend. He had taken a bottle of cheap whiskey and had given it to Adolfo. "Keep it," he said, "when Adolfo tried to return it after a swallow. "I have another one under the seat. I'm starting to sell the stuff as a business. Sort of on the side."

"How's business," Adolfo asked him, not expecting any truthful reply. He knew Jesus too well for that.

"Very good," Jesus replied. He still had that habit of barely looking over the steering wheel.

"It ought to be, if you're giving this stuff away." Adolfo said. He was making an ugly facial gesture as if he had swallowed something vile. "Where do you get this stuff anyway. It's horrible. And I have drunk some of the most horrible whiskey in my life."

"It's from Mexico," Jesus said, extending his hand to Adolfo. Adolfo passed him the bottle and he took a long hard swallow and he made a face.

"You can't beat it," he coughed, "for the price." And his small voice trailed off into a gasp.

"This is poison," Adolfo informed him, seriously. "Do you really sell this stuff?"

"Well," Jesus confessed, "I only started today."

"Do me a favor, will you? Don't give me any more of this stuff." Adolfo spat out the window.

Jesus took the bottle and examined it as he drove slowly. "Maybe the other ones are better than this one."

"I wouldn't be too sure," Adolfo said, taking the bottle from Jesus and throwing it out the window.

"Poor Arnold," Jesus said, waiting to see how Adolfo would reply.

"Yes, poor Arnold. But that's life. If it's your time, it's your time. And God forgive us if we try to change it. I had a feeling Arnold was going to get it. He wasn't very smart, you know. Now, when I was in combat, I knew exactly where to be. I wasn't going to be no hero. Not for this country. What in the hell has this country done for me? Or you? Or any Mexican? Hell, let the Gringo die for this country. It's his. It's not mine."

Jesus looked at him and nodded in agreement. He hadn't thought about it that way. He had preferred to believe that Arnold was a hero.

"What the hell good is it going to do for Maria and Dora to have Arnold's silver cross?"

"You know about that?"

"Yes, Maria wrote to me."

"By the way," Jesus told him, "Maria has been receiving your pension."

"Yes," Adolfo replied, "she's been sending me the money."

"Where are you now?" Jesus asked. He knew where Adolfo was. He just wanted Adolfo to say it.

"I'm in Mexico. Tijuana," Adolfo replied. He didn't seem to want to talk to Jesus and Jesus sensed this. His feelings were hurt.

"Are you angry or what?" Jesus asked him. He came directly to the point.

"Yes, I'm angry," Adolfo said. This time he extended his hand to Jesus and Jesus reached under the seat and gave him the other bottle. "I'm angry because Arnold got killed. That's all. I'm angry, also, come to think about it, because Maria was hurt so much by this. It's hard to believe, but I'll be okay after a few drinks. I always am."

He took a long swallow from the new bottle and he made a face indicating to Jesus that this was as bad as the first one. "Let's just throw the goddam thing away. Don't you agree?"

"Wait!" Jesus shouted. "Let me see," and he took a drink and swallowed it and made a grimacing expression and *he* threw the bottle out.

"For all we know," Adolfo said, working his tongue in and out of his mouth, trying to clean it, "those goddamn Mexicans sold you bottled shit."

"It does taste kind of bad," Jesus agreed.

"I'll tell you something, Jesus, you're not going to sell much of that stuff. And if you do, you'd better leave town. I know some Mexicans that would kill you for less than that."

"I think you're right," Jesus agreed.

Carmen had arrived the day before the funeral also. Maria had been so happy to see her that she cried alternately from grief and joy. The other women around Maria, Umberta and her other church-going friends, were gathered around her in wooden chairs next to the living room where Arnold's body rested and when Maria began to cry, they all joined in. And as if on cue, when Maria stopped, they stopped. Maria would talk a little, reminisce about Arnold, and then she would began her wailing again. To Carmen, the wake was an experience she had almost forgotten. It brought back painful memories of her childhood and the many funerals and the wailing. Now as a grown woman she couldn't understand it. It was partly the hypocrisy involved and partly the shallowness of the emotions that bothered her. As an example, most of the women there except Umberta had not known Arnold that well. She knew that as soon as they left, they would go home to criticize Maria for something or other. It was not their nature to be generous in someone else's grief. Primarily, these women were there because, if the same thing happened to them, they also needed the support of women friends. It was strictly the Mexican way of doing things and it bothered Carmen.

"You should get some sleep," Carmen told Maria in a firm voice. The other women attending to Maria sensed that Carmen was trying to get rid of them, to break up the wailing.

"She's right," Umberta said, wiping her nose and sniffling. "Carmen is right, Maria. You need rest. Tomorrow will be another day."

"Tomorrow will be a long day for you, Maria," a friend said, patting her on the hand. "You had better do as Carmen says. After all, she's a nurse and knows about these things."

They got up as if they were one and Carmen showed them to the door. Once outside, Carmen heard one of them ask, "Did you see how rude Carmen was?"

"Yes," another replied, "and they didn't even offer us a swallow of coffee."

And like magpies, they wallowed in their long black dresses toward the darkness and disappeared into their homes.

Outside, the group of men were standing in a circle drinking. This time Adolfo had secured a bottle of good barreteaga and the other men, Adam and the rest of them, had brought beer and other hard liquor. They spent the night of the wake drinking and telling jokes and once in a while someone would say, "Poor Arnold," and Adam would cry and they would be silent, looking down at their feet, and when Adam quit crying, someone would say something funny and they would laugh and Adam would laugh wih them. As they drank more and more, they talked less and less and finally at the break of days they were standing and swaying and no one remembered anything. Soon the group dispersed and Adolfo went in and Adam went with him.

Young Maria was having a fit. She could not tolerate the men drinking at the wake. She would go out and fume to herself and then she would storm back inside. She thought that her presence would be enough to make them stop drinking. But they didn't. In fact, they ignored her and one of Arnold's friends mentioned that his sister (Young Maria) was sure worried about something, the way she was coming out and going in. "Don't pay attention to her," Adam told him. "She never wants anyone to have a good time."

"Where's her husband?" he asked.

"Eddie is fighting in Europe." Adam told him.

Carmen had a difficult time sleeping in her old room. She started to cough and her throat seemed inflamed. Maria had gotten up in the night to check on her, but Carmen wouldn't let her rub her chest with liniment. It wouldn't do any good, she told Maria. Maria tried to insist, but Carmen absolutely refused. "You're the nurse," Maria told her, finally giving up, "you ought to know."

"It's nothing that liniment will cure," Carmen said to her. "It's the dust in this house. Everything is so dusty." She stroked her fingers over the night stand and showed Maria the dust.

"I can't help it, Carmen," Maria replied. "I live next to the fields where they are plowing day in and day out. I can't keep the house clean. And besides," she added in her defense, "I've been very heart-broken by Arnold's death. It seems that at times I have lost the sense of time. It hasn't been a good time for me, you understand. I just haven't been keeping up with house-work."

"Maybe I could find someone to help out. I could pay for it. It's no good living in a house like this. It's filthy!"

"Has it changed that much?" Maria asked her. "Is it really that much dirtier than when you lived here?"

"She's not used to this anymore," Young Maria said to Maria. Young Maria was standing by the table with a cup of coffee in her hand. There was a trace of sarcasm to that remark.

"I've never been used to dust," Carmen replied to young Maria. She was defiant. She had broken loose from Young Maria's influence and Young Maria knew it. Now Carmen felt superior to her, and truthfully, she was. She had sought more and had accomplished more.

Young Maria had aligned herself with Maria in hopes of deflating Carmen's ego. But it hadn't worked. Maria knew exactly what Young Maria was up to and Maria consequently doted more on Carmen than ever before. To Young Maria it was an insult and throughout the funeral she acted hurt. She was beginning to hate Carmen and if Carmen hadn't left right away, the afternoon after the funeral, there surely would have been an argument between them. Young Maria was ready for one. Carmen didn't pay that much attention to her. But it seemed to Young Maria that whenever she said something, Carmen would correct her. After all the years that she had dominated the family and had helped them out financially, Young Maria's power was beginning to erode. No one needed her anymore.

"How ungrateful Carmen has turned out to be," Young Maria had told Maria after Carmen had left.

"Why do you say so?" Maria had asked her. She wanted Young Maria to be specific. She knew how vindictive Young Maria could be. She knew, though, how to handle Young Maria and she said, "It's funny that you should say so, because she spoke so highly of you and what a good mother you had been to the whole family in times of need. She really appreciates you."

"She said all that?" Young Maria asked, surprised. She had thought Carmen had spoken badly about her behind her back. "Well, it's just that I thought she was ungrateful by the way she acted. It wasn't anything in particular, you know what I mean."

"Well, I can say that Carmen has changed," Maria said. "I can see where she's used to other things now, other customs. She's living a different life and I admire her for it. But I know what you mean. She's different now." She thought a while and then she said, "She's not the little girl that left here with Adolfo. I can assure you of that."

"Do you think she's changed that much?" Young Maria asked, still trying to get Maria on her side, "or do you think she's putting on airs?"

She had wanted Maria to agree with her. Then she could begin her attack on Carmen. Maria didn't answer for a while. She knew exactly the reply Young Maria wanted. She would not agree with Young Maria. She would never allow Carmen to be victimized by anyone.

"I think she's changed," Maria replied to her and she got up as if to leave for bed. Her walk had slowed down. Arnold's death had taken a lot from her. "As a matter of fact, I think she's changed so much that we won't see very much of her from now on. What a pity," she sighed. She could not cry anymore. "How cruel life can be. I always told my children to stay close by, not to leave home. Carmen just never understood. She always wanted to leave home."

A knock came from the front door. Dr. Chichester had come to see how Maria was doing. Young Maria showed him in and she was impressed that the doctor had come over. Doctors had always impressed her.

"How are you, Maria?" Dr. Chichester asked as he walked into the kitchen. "Are you feeling alright?"

Maria understood him fairly well if he spoke slowly. "Fine," Maria said, although she felt weak.

"Let's see about your heart," the doctor said as he opened up his black bag. He pulled out a stethoscope and listened intently to Maria's chest. "You're fit as a fiddle," he remarked and put his stethoscope back into the bag.

Maria looked at him, confused.

"The doctor says you are doing fine," Young Maria told her in Spanish.

"Tell the doctor," Maria said to Young Maria, "that my heart has always been good and it has always been in the right place. It's just heavy with grief at the moment. Tell him that some day if he has any children and if he loses one of them, he'll know what pain and grief are."

Young Maria translated the words to Dr. Chichester and he nodded his head. He was wearing his black string tie, his trade-mark. He was a tireless worker.

"Tell your mother," he said to Young Maria, "that I admire her very much. She's a good woman."

Maria beamed when she heard the translation. "Yes," she said in one of the few words she knew in English.

"Well, I must be leaving now. Tell your mother how sad I feel for her in her hour of grief. Arnold was a good boy." And with this he walked out as Young Maria accompanied him to the door.

"Thank you so much," she said to him.

"No problem," he replied. "I'll keep an eye on her. It seems to me that she has recovered her mental alertness. We were worried for a while. I think she's going to be alright. She's a very strong woman."

When Young Maria returned, Maria was already in her room preparing to go to bed. Umberta was asleep in Adolfo's old room. She had decided to stay the night in case Maria needed her. Young Maria was sleeping in Carmen's room. Adolfo had left that afternoon.

"I still say that Carmen is ungrateful," Young Maria said to her as Maria got into bed slowly.

She looked at Young Maria for a while and said, "You know very well that you and I have been through a lot. So don't think I don't love you. I love you just as much as I love Carmen. It doesn't look good for you to try to run Carmen down."

"I wasn't doing that!" she screamed at her mother. "You never understand me!" she screamed again and she stamped her foot and left the room. She banged the door shut and woke up Eddie Junior.

"What's going on?" he asked rubbing his eyes.

"Oh, shut up and go to sleep," his mother said.

Adolfo had not had much of a chance to talk to Maria in private. And when he did, it was mostly about Arnold. She asked him how he enjoyed Tijuana and he had replied that he didn't. It was a little too dirty for him. He was living with a couple that had a corner grocery store. He was helping them out a little, not much. Yes, he was receiving the pension checks that Maria forwarded to him and he appreciated it. Adolfo explained to her that he had changed the address on his pension from Isabel to Maria when he realized he was not staying in San Diego. All in all, he said, he was doing fine. Not as well as it could be, and yet not as bad as he could be. His friend, Manuel Garcia, the Professor that he often mentioned in his letters, had left and had gone into the interior of Mexico. They laughed that Manuel was afraid that he would get drafted into the war.

"Well," Maria said to Adolfo, wiping tears from her eyes, "you know you can always count on me, if you need me. I'm getting older and I don't know how much longer I can hold out, but you can count on me."

"You're the only cousin I really ever had. And I guess, come to think of it, that you're the only friend I ever had." He was wiping tears from his eyes also as they both stood side-by-side in the small hallway.

"Oh, you can't say that," Maria scolded him. "You've had many, many friends. That's been your life, taking friends out, entertaining friends, living with friends."

"But it didn't do any good. Look at me now," he said, showing himself to Maria, "just look at me. Old and without anyone. It didn't do me any good."

"You didn't expect it to do any good, did you?" she asked him. "I know you well enough that I know you didn't expect any good to come out of it, not in the long term. You did it just to have fun. You never thought about any consequences and now you're paying for it."

"You're right, Maria," he said, admitting to her that his life had been a failure. There was no sense denying it any longer. He had known it for years and she had too. "The only true friend, and I mean true, is you. All the other ones were just along for the ride."

"Well, whatever happens to you, you know you can count on me," she said and she felt another one of her dizzy spells overtake her.

"You'd better get some rest," Adolfo said to her. And he led her to her room.

Adolfo had spoken to Carmen and he sensed the difference in her. For one thing, she had become a grown woman. Gone were the girlish ways that he had loved about her. She was a serious young lady now. They spoke of her career, the war, her boyfriends. He told her of the time when he and Isabel and Carolina and Manuel had gone to see her and couldn't get into the base. "They're very strict now because of the war," Carmen explained. "Even Isabel, who worked there forever, isn't allowed in some parts of the base, not the part I had been working in."

"I've never been to the Phillipines," Adolfo had said to Carmen.

"They are beautiful islands, but right now I don't think anyone would like to visit them. The war is horrible right now."

"It's always horrible," Adolfo corrected her.

"No, not really," she responded. "At the beginning it was exciting. Now it's horrible."

He also sensed a change in her attitude toward him. He noticed that she did not embrace him or Maria, or Adam or Young Maria. It could have been shyness. She was always shy, he had thought. And when Jesus' wife, the small, fat, dark-skinned lady with snaggled teeth, had insisted on cooking after the funeral, Carmen had refused to eat. It was as if she found everything around her repugnant. Then again, he thought, it could have been the war. Her nerves maybe were getting a little frayed.

It wasn't the war. Carmen had changed. Her exposure to another way of life had opened her eyes. She had gone from a culture steeped in ignorance into another world. It was unbelievable to her that she had grown up with so many misconceptions.

CHAPTER 11

After walking for what seemed several miles, carrying the heavy suitcases full of a dead man's clothes, they had finally arrived at Manuel's sister's house. It was an unpainted building sitting on the corner. It was more than a house. As Manuel walked in through the open door, Adolfo realized that they were inside a grocery store, a small neighborhood type store that carried a small amount of staples: beans, flour, bread, spices, herbs, candles, cans, a small table full of used clothes, school supplies. The store consisted of one fairly large elongated room and at the end was a counter. There was a small space between the counter and the back wall. On this wall there was a door, with a curtain that led into the back part of the building. This was the living area for the family. Just looking around, Adolfo could see that there was not much variety in stock. There were only a few cans of each item. A huge burlap sack of pinto beans was open, resting on the floor and leaning against the counter. A large scoop was buried deeply into the beans and only the handle could be seen. They could hear someone talking in the next room.

"That sounds like my sister," Manuel said to him. He seemed excited.

She came through the door wiping her hands on an a large white cotton apron. "Could I help you?" she asked without noticing who they were. Then, suddenly, as she lifted her eyes she caught sight of Manuel and she ran to him and hugged him. "Manuel, Manuel," she kept repeating. "It's so good to see you." She looked at Adolfo as she hugged Manuel and she smiled. "This must be Adolfo, the one you wrote to me about," she said as she extended her hand to Adolfo.

"I'm pleased to meet you," she said, graciously.

She appeared very genuine and sincere.

"The pleasure is all mine," Adolfo replied. He liked her. He liked her the first time he saw her. Too bad she was married, he thought.

"Well, well," she continued, as if she intended not to let the conversation die off. "Let's go to the back. I wasn't expecting you today. What did your letter say, Manuel?" She turned to Manuel.

They were walking to the back of the house, Adolfo at the rear.

"I didn't know exactly when we would be here. I just didn't say when. We've been taking our time about getting here, haven't we Adolfo?"

Adolfo was still looking at Manuel's sister. She was beautiful. There were no other words to describe her. She wasn't short like Manuel. She was even taller, he observed, by at least two inches. Her complexion was smooth and clear. She looked full of life, ruddy and ready. Her large dark eyes seemed to dance to the sounds of her words. He could tell she was easily exciteable, but in a vibrant, controlled sort of way. "Oh yes," he replied to the question. He had not paid much attention to what Manuel was saying. He guessed her age to be about forty. He was wrong; she hid her age well. She was fifty.

"Come, come," she said to Adolfo and she motioned to him with her hand, inviting him in. "Come in. Make yourself at home."

She didn't realize that Adolfo had purposely stayed behind to observe her. He wanted to see her body.

"Where's Pete?" Manuel asked her.

She had sat the two men down and was pouring coffee. "I was just making this coffee," she said, hurriedly placing two cups and saucers in front of them.

"And you?" Manuel asked her.

"I'll be having some too. I just need to get another cup." She was looking through the cupboard.

They heard someone holler from the store side. She went quickly through the curtain and disappeared.

"Your sister is very beautiful," Adolfo said, "much more beautiful than I ever thought."

"She takes after my mother."

He was stirring the coffee slowly, trying to get it cool enough to drink. "My mother was even more beautiful," Manuel said to him. "She was a little darker than Yolanda. A little more darker and a little shorter. I don't know where Yolanda inherited her height, but she seemed to grow. As a child she was small and frail, but then I remember she began to grow tall in secondary school." He took a swallow and his eyes gleamed, "Ah!" he groaned, "this is coffee! Good coffee, how I missed it."

They could hear Yolanda talking to whomever it was buying some groceries to take home. She could be heard adding figures out loud and then making change. Soon she was back and sitting with them. Adolfo had never seen a more vibrant woman in his life. He drooled at the thought of her. "Her eyes twinkle," he said to Manuel afterwards, all excited. "Yes," he responded, "they always have."

A door opened slowly behind Adolfo and Pete came in the room. He had been asleep. He yawned with an open mouth and stretched out his arms. His name was Pedro, but he preferred to be called Pete. No one knew why, except that he went across the border very often and he sometimes tried to affect California ways. Mostly, people ignored him. He was what was called "heavy blooded" in the Mexican culture, a person who is hard to like, an ass-hole. He worked at odd jobs, never wanting to get tied down from nine to five, five-six days a week. That wasn't for him. In that respect, he was like Adolfo, but there the similarity ended. Pete was crude, low-life. He was, as Adolfo would say, "low-down, an ignorant." How he ever married Yolanda he could not figure out, except that he had seen this type of marriage before: a beauti-ful, delicate woman with some breeding married to someone very inferior to her. Why it happened, as he said, he didn't know. The two had nothing in common. He mainly did what he pleased. He had a little thirty-six Ford and he used the car to ferry people back and forth across the border. When he wasn't working, he could be found playing pool or drinking beer. In other words, he had the perfect arrangement and it irritated Adolfo very much, especially since Adolfo was not in his shoes. This was exactly the situation Adolfo was looking for. And here was Pete, a man lower in social standing than he, who had what Adolfo found impossible to achieve. What gall of the man, he thought to himself, to even think that he deserves a woman as perfect as Yolanda. He was already in love and he hadn't been there one hour. He could easily take her from her husband. It wouldn't be hard. All he had to do was use his charm, his wit. And what about Isabel? His sub-conscious reminded him. Well, he said to himself, she had it coming to her for the way she treated him. He knew that there was a reason for all this madness that had followed him these three years. No one, none of the women he ever knew, could take Yolanda's place. The truth was, that although he professed undy-ing love for someone, he was never capable of committing himself to a lasting relationship. He felt that tomorrow or the tomorrow after that would bring him something better. He had waited all his life.

He instantly hated Pete.

"This is Pete," Yolanda said to Adolfo and he turned and shook hands with Pete. Pete was small, to make matters worse, and thin. He smelled of last night's whiskey.

"How do you do?" Adolfo asked him and shook his small hand.

"Fine," Pete replied and yawned again. "I'm still sleepy," he said as he sat down.

Yolanda sprang like a puppet and hurriedly poured some coffee for him and then opened the oven door and took out a slice of cake. "I'm sorry I don't have enough cake for everyone," she apologized as she set the cake for Pete.

Pete didn't offer to share.

"That's alright," Manuel said, looking at the cake, "we ate just a while ago," and he looked at Adolfo to make sure Adolfo had caught on.

"Yes," said Adolfo. "We just ate and we're full."

"What a pity," Yolanda said in her gentle voice, "I was going to prepare some ribs for you, and also some rice and beans with flour tortillas."

"That means," Pete figured out as he ate his cake, "that I don't have to go out and buy all those ribs."

They had messed up again. "Why did you say we had already eaten?" Adolfo asked Manuel later at night when they were alone.

"I didn't want to embarrass my sister," he replied.

"And to think," Adolfo said to him, disappointed and hungry, his stomach growling, "that we turned down the poor woman's cheese."

Maria was a bitter woman since Arnold's death. She had received two blows that had made her change. First, Arnold's death had taken a lot out of her. She was normal, mentally, but she was more subdued, as if she had to sort out a lot of things in her mind and she didn't want to be bothered by anyone. Umberta understood. However, she felt it was better for Maria to talk to someone and she tried to get Maria out of her shell, and she would sit with Maria in the backyard and she would talk to her. Sometimes Maria answered; sometimes she didn't. At first, before Arnold's body arrived, Umberta had been very worried about Maria's health. Now she knew Maria would be alright. She sensed the boiling anger under the surface as Maria sat and thought.

The second blow was the loss of Carmen. She had protected Carmen from Young Maria all the time Young Maria had been there for the funeral, making excuses for her, but the only thanks that Carmen had given her was in a letter that Carmen wrote to Maria from the Phillipines. In it Carmen explained how alien she had felt staying at Maria's and associating with Maria's friends and even with Young Maria. Adam, she detested, she wrote, and if possible, she would appreciate it if Maria would keep him away the next time she visited.

Maria couldn't believe that she was reading a letter from Carmen. In four years Carmen had changed and Maria didn't think it was for the better. Carmen also wrote to say that she was seriously thinking of becoming engaged to a naval officer. His last name was Johnson, and Maria almost died. She did not want Carmen marrying a Gringo like Young Maria had done. She wrote to Carmen in Spanish and told her so. She wrote that she didn't mind being insulted about her friends or her house or Adam or Young Maria. That was Carmen's right. But when she said she was marrying a Gringo, she was going too far!

She quit going to church. For Maria this was as big a decision as she had made in her life. Indeed, to her way of thinking, it was probably as important a decision as the one to keep Young Maria. She had given up on God. God was vindictive, hateful, mean, and he didn't keep his promises. "Let him take Carmen if he wants to!" she yelled at Umberta with all the anger she could muster. "Fuck him!"

"No, no, Maria," Umberta begged her, nervously looking at the heavens to be sure no one was hearing. "If God hears you, he will surely punish you and maybe even take Carmen away."

"Let him!" she screamed. She had her jaw set for a fight with God. "If he wants to do whatever he wants, who is going to stop him, you?"

"No," Umberta responded, wringing her hands. She wanted no part of this conversation. Lately, when Maria spoke, it had been with a vengeance against the Lord.

"What about Father Angel?"

"No," Umberta replied meekly. She didn't know.

"Of course you don't know," Maria told her. "No one does. All religion has done for me is to complicate my life. Why didn't God help me?" she asked, and she started crying, her face in her hands.

"I don't know," Umberta replied. "I'm only a poor woman who is not educated. I don't have the answers to your questions."

Still, at night, as she lay in her small bed, she would pray the rosary to the Virgin Mary. It was her way of complaining to the Lord's Mother about how poorly her son was running the world.

Dr. Chichester had come to see her about once or twice a month and he seemed to enjoy her company, although they had a little trouble communicating. Dr. Chichester knew more Spanish than Maria knew English. So they conversed about her health in Spanish and she was able to understand the main point of his questions.

Once, Dr. Chichester came earlier than expected and she wondered why he was there. She and Umberta had let him in and he went and sat at the table, placing his black bag on top. The two women looked at him in anticipation. Umberta understood less English than Maria.

He tried to find the words to explain to Maria about what was happening. He had been putting things off for a while, a long while in fact, and now the time had come. He hated to be the bearer of bad news, especially to Maria, who already had received a severe blow with Arnold's death.

"Am I sick?" Maria asked him, confused about his unexpected visit.

"No, Maria," he replied and he shook his head. He hated to tell her. "It's Adam," he finally said.

"Adam?" Maria asked him and she looked at Umberta.

"Yes, Adam," he reassured her. "How long has it been since you've seen Adam?"

"Oh, I haven't seen him in a long time, since the funeral. But he's a scoundrel. He only shows up when he needs money and he hasn't needed money in a long time."

"He's been sick a long time, but Adam did something he shouldn't have done," Dr Chichester said. He shook his head again. "He's been sick with syphillis for a long, long time and he never told anyone and he never sought help from me. It's crazy to think about it. This is nineteen forty-three. We can treat syphillis."

Maria didn't know what to say. She was not that familiar with the disease. She didn't know what to ask. Was Adam dying? How long did he have to live?

Was he treatable? She didn't understand, except she saw that Dr. Chichester was being very serious.

"We have to see about his wife also. I hope he hasn't infected her, but as long as he's been sick, I'm sure she's got it." And he gathered his bag, drank the last of his coffee and left.

Could it be that she was to suffer another blow so soon after Arnold's death? Was God not a forgiving God?

She sat down and Umberta sat down with her. They were stunned. What had he meant? "Surely God will spare me this tragedy," Maria said to Umberta. "Don't you think so?"

"I would think so, yes," Umberta replied. "God is very good, Maria," she said trying to reconcile Maria to God. "Look at it this way," she said, "as the saying goes, 'there is some good in all bad situations.' "

"How could the illness of my only surviving son be coming from something good?" Maria asked her. She couldn't believe it.

"Well," Umberta said to her as she got up to leave, "you'll see. God's work is always a mystery."

Maria didn't bother to reply. She only shook her head.

Manuel had divided Anna's husband's clothes according to size and he had packed his suitcase. Adolfo was still asleep in the small bed next to him. They had said their farewells that night when they both went out and drank heavily. It had been a sad time. They had both tried to have fun, but they wound up crying, then laughing, going over their times together. It had been a bitter-sweet experience. One bartender had run them off, claiming they were ruining his business. He couldn't remember very well, but he thought that Adolfo had met a prostitute and had stayed with her. He had lost him on the way home. But apparently not, for there he was asleep in the bed. He tried not to disturb him. He didn't feel like he had a hangover, probably because he was still a little drunk. If he moved his head too fast, the whole room would spin around. He dressed quietly and without moving his head very much. He shook Adolfo's hand as Adolfo lay in the bed asleep.

"Good-bye, good friend. It was good knowing you," he said, softly.

He hated to be going, but he needed to keep moving farther south, back to where he was born. He and Adolfo had gone by the bus station and had checked the schedule. He had not bought a ticket then, a sign that had encouraged Adolfo.

"You're not sure of leaving?" Adolfo had asked him.

"Oh yes, I'm sure," he replied, "It's just that I don't want to carry the ticket around all day. I might lose it."

He stepped out of the room into the small dining area and he quietly said farewell to his sister. She already had coffee made. She insisted that he have breakfast, but he refused. He would miss the bus. He had a half-cup of coffee and they embraced and she sobbed quietly. "When will I see you again?" she asked as she wiped the tears from her beautiful dark eyes.

"I've stayed too long as it is," he said to her.

"Only four months," she replied. "That's not a long time."

"It is a long time," he told her, "but you are such a good person that you don't complain. Someone else would have kicked us out, as bad as Adolfo and I are."

"You weren't any trouble at all. I'll miss your help with the store."

"Adolfo can help you," he said. "He's pretty good at that work."

"I hope he can," she said, wiping away one more tear.

"Treat him well, will you?" Manuel asked of her. "He's been through a lot."

"I can tell," she replied, "and I'll treat him well. For your sake."

He turned slowly getting out of her grasp and he picked up his heavy suitcase — he had kept the one with the metal rivets — and walked through the curtained doorway, through the grocery store and out into the street. She followed closely behind and she stopped at the outer door and watched him slowly walk down the street, bent side-ways balancing the heavy load that he carried and he turned the corner, waving, and he was suddenly out of her sight.

Adolfo awoke in the early part of the afternoon. His head felt like it was being squeezed in a vise, but strangely enough, it hurt less when he pressed against his temples with both thumbs. He got up slowly and placed his teeth in his mouth. He stood and scratched and made sticky dehydrated noises with his mouth. He went through the door into the common hallway, went into the toilet and took a shower. The water felt good, except that it hurt when it fell on his head. By the time he was dressed, Yolanda was fixing lunch for him. She was a good cook. Better than Isabel.

"Come in, come in," she said to him, gesturing with a large spoon for him to sit down. "How do you feel?" she asked. She knew exactly how he felt.

"I feel poorly," he replied still trying to get his tongue moist.

He sat down.

He had not been able to get her to like him. She was nice enough to him, but he knew that she was oblivious of him, as if he really didn't matter. He resented it, but there was nothing he could do except try as hard as he could. He tried to be charming around her all the time. He took special pains to dress as well as he could with what clothes he had brought with him. He bathed daily, shaved daily, and she never, never, saw him without his teeth. *El hambre lo tumba, y la vanidad lo levanta.* He had remembered what the Professor had told him while passing the meat market one day. "See the chicken's ass over there?" and he had pointed at a dead chicken hung on a nail. "Well," the Professor had gone on, "that's the way your mouth looks when you don't have your teeth in." He would never allow her to see his mouth like that.

Almost everything he did, he did for her benefit. He was consumed by her,
her beauty and her charming ways. He came to feel, genuinely, that Yolanda
was a thoroughbred and Isabel was a plow horse. That's the comparison that
came to his mind.

But still, in spite of everything, she ignored him.

He resented Pete very much. He hated Pete. That would be a better way of
expressing it. "What does she see in him?" he had asked Manuel, her
brother. Maybe he had some insight into her mind. After all, they were raised
together. But Manuel didn't know.

"I don't know," he had told Adolfo. "He's not really her type."

"That's it!" Adolfo said, excitedly. He had known it from the beginning.
"They don't go together. If you put them in a room, no one could tell they
were married. They don't make a couple. They don't seem made for each
other."

"That's life, though," the Professor replied, "if you could figure life out,
then it would be kind of dull, don't you think?"

Adolfo agreed up to a point. But this marriage just didn't fit the mold.
"He's ugly," Adolfo kept on, insulting Pete.

"Well," Manuel responded, "he's not handsome. There is a difference.
He's not ugly, ugly, though."

"Well," Adolfo said, "he's ugly to me. Compared to Yolanda, he's ugly
and he's short and skinny looking, like you could knock him down with a
straw. And he doesn't work! Can you imagine that?" He couldn't believe it,
how a man like Pete could be so lucky. "She works all day in the house and in
the store. And all for him. What's the deal?" he asked.

"My sister has always been in love," Manuel answered. "I guess it's
love."

"Manuel's gone?" he asked, sitting down gently — everything hurt.

"Yes, he left early this morning," she answered. "He's half-way home by
now. He didn't want to wake you up. He was very quiet. I almost didn't even
get to say farewell to him myself. I was glad I was up early cooking breakfast
for Pete. Pete didn't see him go either. Pete had eaten and was gone before
Manuel ever got up. Manuel said for me to tell you farewell again. He said
that he will miss you and your friendship."

She placed lunch in front of him.

"He's a good person. Very sincere," he remarked. "He'll always be welcomed anywhere he goes. He was, I guess, the best male friend I ever had,"
he said to her and he started laughing and then he remembered the headache.
"Ask him one day when you see him again about his experience with witchcraft."

"Witchcraft?" she asked, puzzled.

"Yes, witchcraft. He'll know what you're talking about. He ate lunch
slowly, making sure it wasn't going to nauseate him. When he was through,
he gave her part of the money that Maria had sent him. She took it and placed

it inside a drawer by the open sink. "I hope this is enough," Adolfo said. He was trying to speak as softly as he could to keep his head from exploding.

"Yes, yes," she responded and she dried her hands on her apron and asked him if he wanted more coffee.

"Where did Pete go?" Adolfo asked, trying to hide his disdain for the man.

"Oh, he got up early and went to the market place to pick up a fare," she replied. "He's going into the United States today. He'll have a busy day. He's constantly working at something or another. Pete is one of a kind," she added.

"Yes, you can say that again," he answered her, full of envy.

He left by easing his way through the conversation. He was sick of talking about Pete. Her Pete this and her Pete that nauseated him as much as the hangover. As he walked to the outside, she asked him to be careful. "Some woman might pick you up," she said, laughing at him. He could have killed her, if he didn't love her so much.

She didn't know how close to the truth she had been. Adolfo, disgusted with her, had set out to find the prostitute that he had met the night before, the one Manuel had vaguely remembered. She had let Adolfo have a good time with her. It had cost him three dollars, but three dollars was a lot in those days, especially when you consider that his pension amounted to almost thirty dollars a month.

He found her at her house washing her panties. It was a good omen, he thought.

Maria had returned from visiting Adam. He was very sick, but he still got around, walked a little. He had developed some lesions in the nervous system. He walked with a limp, as if trying to pat his feet on the ground. Maria remembered having seen some men walk like this around town during her life. She had not realized at the time that this was an indication of an advanced case of syphillis. He was pale and had grown thinner, as if he were wasting away. His wife, Alba, had been treated and was doing well. She never knew she had anything, she told Maria. Dr. Chichester had treated Adam also, but he felt that it was too late. A lot of the damage had been done. He would have to wait and see. He would not give a prognosis, but if pressed for one, he would have had to say that things did not look good. At the most, he gave him one year.

Adam had been hiding his illness for a long time, four to five years, as well as he could recollect. Now, it had gotten to the point that when he urinated, he would be in intense pain. He would have to hold on to something stout as he urinated, such was the pain. Many were the times that he refused a bottle of beer, knowing full well that if he drank it, he would have to urinate. No one had ever seen Adam turn down a beer. Many were the times, though, that he rattled the water pipes that came down the ceiling to the urinal, as he grabbed them and shook violently as he urinated.

Dr. Chichester did not have to go far to find out who had infected Adam. "The Turtle" had been the carrier. Now she was dead. God only knew how many men she had infected. At least in dying she had stopped the continual re-infection.

Maria heard a knock and a small voice calling to her. "Maria," the little boy screamed.

"Yes, what is it?" she asked him. She recognized him. He was a little boy who lived down the street who often ran errands for Maria.

"Maria!" he yelled.

She could hardly control her laughter at seeing such a loud voice come from such a small boy. "Alright, alright," she said to him. "Don't be so loud. Don't get so excited. What do you want?"

"They want you at the grocery store. There's a phone call for you," he said. He was being very serious.

"What is it?" Maria asked him. She sensed in the child an urgency that she had never seen before in him.

"There's a woman crying on the telephone. She needs to talk to you right now. Hurry up," he said. Then he started to stutter. "Hu . . . hu . . . . hurry up," he finally said.

She wrapped her black shawl around her and she followed the little boy as fast as she could. What had gone wrong? My God, she thought, he's taken Carmen! I'll never forgive anyone for that — not the Virgin Mary, Jesus, God, and all his saints. Her heart beat faster as she thought about it. She was half a mile away from the store and she tried to go as fast as possible. "Hurry, hu, hu . . . hurry," the child would implore her. "They ca . . . ca . . . can't keep the telephone open fo . . . fo . . . for you all the time."

He was looking back for her and pleading with her to quicken her pace.

"I'm going as fast as I can," Maria said. "I can't go any faster."

She felt her heart skip a beat. Was she dying? She couldn't. She wouldn't let herself do it. If she were going to die, she said, gritting her teeth, it would be in bed, not running to the grocery store to answer the telephone. It was Carmen. She was positive. She felt in her bones. Something had happened to Carmen. Maybe it wasn't serious. Maybe whoever was crying on the telephone was crying for joy. Carmen had gotten married. That was it! Did they have telephones in the Phillipines? Why not just write? Why make her go through all this running? Carmen was going to do what she pleased, anyway. Why bother her?

When she arrived at the grocery store behind the little boy, she grabbed the telephone and answered it. "Who's there?" she asked, holding her breath.

"It's me, mother," she said crying.

It was Young Maria! She recognized the voice immediately. Then there was silence and all she thought she could hear was someone sobbing, but she couldn't tell. It was long distance and the telephones were not very good. "What's happened?" she demanded.

"It's Eddie," Young Maria answered. "He's dead," and she started crying again.

And from there on she couldn't understand a word Young Maria said. Later, she was told that Eddie had been shot down over Germany. All the crew died when the plane exploded in the air.

There would be no funeral, nothing was ever found of him.

The possum-eyed middle-aged man with a pencil mustache read aloud as Adolfo sat back and enjoyed his prose. His name, Benito Orozco, had been recommended to him at a tavern. Orozco was a notary who in those days wrote letters for clients, prepared quasi-legal documents and served in a general way as the learned class among the illiterate. He also considered himself a poet, sometimes reading his works among the strollers at the city park or wherever a docile crowd could be found.

Adolfo was there to see if Orozco could possibly write something for him that would impress Yolanda. He was desperate. Although he had not moved from Yolanda's, he was living with the prostitute.

The prostitute had put it to him bluntly, marry me or don't come around anymore. She was kicking him out soon. She was not about to put up with him, not unless she was married. "For problems like yours," she informed him, "I can find twenty men in one day. I'm looking for a good man, a good relationship. I know problems are a part of it, but I need to be recognized as a person. I'm tired of being fucked and forgotten. I feel like I'm a piece of meat with a hole in it and I don't like it anymore. I want to be a human being. I want to join the human race. Do you blame me for that?"

If Adolfo couldn't, who could? That's what *he* was looking for also. So he recognized her problem. It was mutual. The thing was that he didn't love her. He never liked crudeness and, like Anna, she was crude, even more so. When he found her laundering her panties, he had seen stains that were unspeakable. Still, like Anna, he had developed a fondness for her. He didn't know what to do. He decided to try out what he thought was his main option, try to gain favor with Yolanda.

He had come up with the notion that he could charm her with words. So he found Orozco and Orozco had obliged by writing a series of poems for him. He couldn't guarantee anything, he said, flicking his mustache, but if he were a woman, he would fall for it. He had been successful with many clients before. His reputation as a writer was secure in the neighborhood. Adolfo agreed.

"Tell me," Orozco pleaded, solemnly reading from the page, "tell me what you want; tell me what you need so that I can place it at your feet. Tell me what you feel; tell me what you feel, so that I can change it from a dream into reality," he sighed.

"It doesn't rhyme," Adolfo said, perturbed.

"That doesn't matter," Orozco said, scolding him. "It's not supposed to. Anyway, no one speaks in rhymes in this day and age. This is blank verse, free verse. Don't you feel the freedom in the words as they are spoken? This is not Shakespeare, this is Orozco!"

"But still, I would like something that rhymes," Adolfo said, adamant.

"Alright," Orozco replied. He took off his glasses and wiped them with his handkerchief. "Come by tomorrow and I'll have something that rhymes.

The following day, Adolfo came early by Orozco's office, a small front room at his home. They haggled over fees. Adolfo did not want to pay for the poems that did not rhyme. Orozco claimed that those took more time to write, they required more imagination, more creativity, and therefore he should be intitled to some compensation. Finally they agreed on five dollars.

"Shit," Orozco informed him. "You want a Browning and you only have money for an Orozco."

Yolanda was behind the counter at the grocery store when he arrived. He had practiced what Orozco had told him, but he felt it wouldn't work. He had the sheet of paper, though, and he tried to read it beforehand on his way over, but it was no good. One poem said that he loved her as a dog loves the moon — he couldn't take that. He was afraid she would laugh. There was one that said something about the love between a man and a woman, where it begins and how it ends, using an old Aztec Indian theme about lovers who tear their hearts out when separated by a volcanic eruption. It was better, but he couldn't read all of the long Indian words in bad handwriting. Orozco had thrown in another poem, this one he almost guaranteed fail-safe, about the love between a butterfly and a moth and the impossibility of it all. Adolfo couldn't understand this one.

"How are you," Yolanda said. "It's been a while."

"I've been fine," he answered.

"I hope you didn't leave angry? Are you coming back?" she said to him.

She looked beautiful this morning. He couldn't figure out what she did to herself, but her color, her eyes, her disposition, was beautiful. He just had never seen a more completely beautiful woman in his life. If only she had some flaw.

"Tell me," he said to her, surprising her, "tell me what you want, what you need, so that I may bring it to your feet."

"What?" she asked, a perplexed smile on her face. She had not expected this.

"Nothing," he replied, embarrassed.

That one had not worked, and none would, not with Yolanda.

He decided to try his best method, the direct approach, and he began to tell her how much he loved her. She was stunned. She never figured he would even take a second look at her. She felt herself ugly. He couldn't believe it. He told her how beautiful she was. He was getting carried away. Finally, he proposed to her, if she could get rid of Pete. She didn't want to, of course. She was still very much in love with him. But didn't she see his flaws? "Yes," she answered, "but look at all of mine." In comparison, she told him, she was getting the bargain. Adolfo couldn't believe it. The more he criticized Pete, the more she defended him.

Nothing worked. The prose, the poems, could just as easily have been left out. She thought they were nice but silly. He was left defenseless, stripped of all his plans for conquest. Yolanda didn't like him, much less love him. She hated to say it, but she thought him comical, a pathetically funny man with no substance, a scoundrel with nothing to offer anyone.

The truth stunned him and he left, trying desperately to ignore what she had said.

"How did it go?" Orozco asked him.

"Fine," he said, flatly, with a vengeance. "So good that I thought about giving you a tip, but I don't want to spoil you."

There was just enough sarcasm to his remark that Orozco couldn't figure out if he were serious or not.

Adolfo pulled out the poems that Orozco had written for him and threw them on the desk.

"Did you read them to her?" Orozco asked him, putting his feet up on the small desk and unfolding the pieces of paper.

"Yes, as best I could," Adolfo replied, angrily. "It didn't go off well at all."

"You just didn't read it right," Orozco said, trying to placate him. "I knew you couldn't read it."

"I tried," Adolfo responded. He was feeling very depressed and angry at this time.

"Well, read this one for me," Orozco demanded, handing him one of the poems. He was insistent.

Adolfo opened the poem and read it in an angry and halting voice:

"We are dissimilarly similar,
you and I.
We are like the moth and the butterfly.

We are dissimilarly similar,
but from the same cloth.
You are the butterfly; I am the moth.

We are dissimilarly similar,

we both can fly.
But I am a moth; you are a butterfly.

We are dissimilarly similar,
the butterfly and the moth.
You are the beauty,
I am the sloth.
Yet great love can come from dissimilars,
great love if we try.
I am the lowly gray moth,
You are the beautiful butterfly."

Orozco looked at him with a cocked eye. He couldn't believe how poorly Adolfo had read his poem. "No wonder," he exclaimed, "you were turned down in your conquest. You did a horrible job of reading. And after all the time and effort, the sheer mental effort of writing the poem. I'm very disappointed."

"You're disappointed?" Adolfo cried. "How do you think I feel. And I paid for the poem."

"It was worth every cent you paid for it. Goddamn it, 'The Butterfly and the Moth' has won many a lady's hand in Tijuana."

"It sure didn't win this one!" Adolfo said angrily.

"Her trouble," Orozco told him, referring to Yolanda, "is that she is ignorant and does not appreciate good poetry."

"She laughed at it," Adolfo told him, "she just sat there and giggled the whole time."

"She's very juvenile," Orozco said, dismissing her criticism of the poem.

"Juvenile?" Adolfo responded, stroking his chin, "she's forty-some years old!"

"Age is no difference," he implied. "I've seen mature women at an early age and immature women at an older age."

He got up and extended his hand, palm up.

"I've already paid you," Adolfo said to him, "you son of a bitch."

"Well, then, I need to leave. This notary work is a never-ending job," he said. He dismissed Adolfo by hurriedly accompanying him to the door. "I'm sorry the lady was not as receptive as she should have been," he said.

Maria had boarded up the house and had been gone for almost two months. She had gone to stay with Young Maria. She felt that young Maria needed her for some time to help her adjust. Young Maria had not asked for the help, but that's the way she was. And Maria knew it. She knew that Young Maria would try to go through the crisis by herself. This was her way of showing the family how strong she was. Anyone else would have asked for Maria's help. Well, maybe Carmen wouldn't now, but there was a time, as Young

Maria kept on saying, that Carmen couldn't tie her shoe-laces without Maria's help.

"I still say she's ungrateful," Young Maria said to Maria.

"Leave her alone," Maria implored. She was sick and tired of hearing the constant talk about Carmen. "Concern yourself with your life," Maria advised her, and it was good advice. Maria feared that Young Maria's poking at Carmen was destroying Young Maria. "You have no quarrel with her," Maria added. "It's me that has a quarrel with her. Look after yourself and Junior. What kind of life are you going to lead now that Eddie's dead? That's what you ought to be worried about."

"Oh, I'm worried alright," Young Maria replied. "I really don't know what to do. For the first time in God knows when, I don't know what to do."

"Well, you have your house," Maria said, "and you can begin with that."

"I'll have Eddie's insurance," Young Maria said. "That will help me also. And I'll have a pension for me and Junior that will keep us from being poor."

"Remember," Maria said to her and she was dead serious, "not to fall for some man and then find out all he wants is your money."

Young Maria laughed gently. She had not laughed in a long time. "Don't be silly," she replied. "No one would look at me now. And besides I have Junior. No one would treat Junior like Eddie did. I would die if I married and the man didn't like Junior. I would leave him."

"I understand," Maria said. "That's why I'm warning you, although you think I'm being foolish. Be careful, that's all I've got to say."

By the end of the two months, they had begun to get on each other's nerves and argue. Maria had some peculiarities about her, innocent habits, that made Young Maria irritable. It wasn't any one thing in particular. It was the accumulation of several old habits multiplied by time that wore on her nerves. She had complained about Maria's idiosyncrasies, but Maria never changed, as if she were deliberately trying to get the best of Young Maria. Of course she wasn't. It was just that the situation in which Young Maria found herself, the tension and grief, exaggerated anything that Maria did.

One morning Young Maria had enough and they went through one of their long arguments and Maria's feelings were hurt. She packed and left the same day. In a way she was happy, she thought, as she rode back on the bus, for she knew that Young Maria was her old self again. And that mattered more to her than anything else.

When she arrived it took her several days to open the house. She stayed with Umberta while she worked. The little boy who stuttered helped her clean the house. She showed him how to do chores and he caught on very quickly. "Someday you'll go to school," she told him as she sat with him drinking coffee, "and you will do good. Don't work like these other men. Don't be like your father and mother, working all day with a hoe and getting paid almost nothing. I feel that you can be somebody. Get all the schooling you can. Look at me," she said to him. He looked at her intently. "I never amounted to anything. I'm in the night-time of my life, as the saying goes. I have really nothing to look forward to. I have only a few years left in me. What a horrible life I have lived. I have even lost all my faith in God."

"You . . . you . . . did?" the little boy asked, surprised. He never knew anyone that had said something like that before. "And . . . and . . . Go . . . Go . . . God didn't ki . . . ki . . . ki . . . kill you?" Suddenly he became embarrassed with his speech.

She ignored it. She knew how painful it was for him.

"No," she said, laughing. "He didn't do anything to me. He already had, come to think of it. But he didn't take Carmen."

"But . . . but . . . he . . . he . . . ca . . . ca . . . can," the little boy said.

"Let him," Maria said, "I've already lost her to someone else."

A gentle knock came from the door. It was Dora. She came in and embraced Maria. Maria started to cry. Dora was crying. The little boy walked outside to keep the women from seeing him cry. Dora opened an official looking package. Dora had already opened it beforehand, since it was addressed to her. Inside were two jewelry boxes. Maria opened one and it was a medal in the shape of a heart suspended from a purple ribbon. "That one is the Purple Heart," Dora said. "That one is for being wounded."

"I've seen this one before," Maria said. "There are a lot of these in the neighborhood."

She opened the second box and in it was a silver star medal with its red white and blue ribbon. "That one is for valor," Dora said to her. "I don't think you've ever seen this one before. You have to be a hero before you get one of these."

"Can you imagine, Arnold a hero." She grinned as she looked at the medal. "And he was always so scared of everything when he was a child. He used to hide under my skirt when he knew he was in trouble. I never had to spank him. All I had to do was talk to him and he would start to cry."

They both cried and afterwards, after much fondling of the medals, Maria closed the boxes and returned them to Dora.

"No," Dora told her, "they belong to you. Arnold always belonged to you. I just had him for a little while. I only think it's fair."

Maria couldn't talk, she was under such great emotion. She tried pushing the medals onto her, but Dora kept refusing. Finally, when she was satisfied that Dora was being genuinely honest, she took the medals and clasped them to her breast and they both cried for a long time, as if the wound had been reopened for the last time.

They talked briefly of Young Maria and Junior and how they were doing. Maria did not mention the argument that had led her to come home. Why should she? She was not about to talk poorly about her children. Even in their conversation about Carmen she did not mention any animosity between Carmen and Young Maria. Dora asked about Adam and Maria told her that Adam was doing very badly and was in much pain. Dr. Chichester didn't see much hope for him. Besides that, Alba blamed Adam for her not getting pregnant. "She may be ruined for life," Dora told her, expecting Maria to feel sad.

Instead Maria thought that it was one of the best things that had ever happened to the human race.

It had been a year since Dr. Chichester had spoken to Maria about Adam and Adam was still alive. He had suffered much as Dr. Chichester had told them he would. They could expect the worse. His mind was gone and he could not walk. But, he was alive. Maria had moved him to the house because Alba was not taking care of him. Alba had used the illness as an excuse to start going out on Adam. It was all over town. Maria knew it, Umberta, everyone. Maria figured she didn't love him anymore and that he would be better off at her house. Alba agreed immediately. As a matter of fact, Maria felt as if Alba had put the idea in her mind in the first place. She always suspected that she used witchcraft. How else could she have married Adam. "What a cheap woman," Maria told Umberta. Umberta, with her little eyes dancing and making the coversation more serious than it really was, looked at Maria and said, "You never know how things will turn out. Who would have thought that Alba, the ugly one, would wind up having so many lovers. And even getting married too. Her marriage was a surprise, don't you think, Maria?"

"It sure was," Maria responded. They were sitting in the back-yard in the coolness of the late afternoon shade. "I don't see how Adam ever married her. She was always so ugly."

"Wasn't she always very dark?" Umberta said. She was always concerned about complexions.

"She used to be darker. Her lips were purple when she was a child. I remember her coming over to play in the dump. She alway liked Adam. I could tell. God have mercy on us when a woman like her gets it in her mind that she likes someone. She followed Adam until he fell for her and her witchcraft. What a pity. He could have married someone better."

"That's true," Umberta agreed. "He could have done better. By the way, how is Adam?"

"Oh," Maria replied, shaking her head. "He's not doing well. Some days it seems like he can recognize me, other times it doesn't seem like it. Take today, for instance, he said some words and he started crying, like he remembered something."

"Poor you, Maria," Umberta sighed. "You have suffered so much in this life."

"And it's not over yet," Maria said, thinking to herself. What else could go wrong?

The next morning the little boy was there early. She had told him to be there at eight and at eight on the dot he knocked on the back door. "It's mmm . . . mm . . . me!" he screamed. Maria had grown to love the child. He was what she never had — a bright, punctual, dependable boy. Arnold had come close. But Adam? She didn't even want to think about that.

"You need to go to the post office," Maria told him without letting him in.

"I know," he answered. "I already we . . . we . . . went."

"Did I get anything?" she asked. She was both surprised and impressed with the boy. It was unusual for her to see someone his age that would do things without being told.

He tried several times to say "Yes," but he couldn't and he finally nodded his little head.

"Well, come in and show it to me," Maria said to him, rubbing his head as he walked in. He had that particular gait common to some children that grow up before their time, already a manly walk.

She poured him a cup of coffee, just one, as Maria had told him, because coffee stunted growth and she wanted him to grow up to be a big man.

"Like Adolfo?" the little boy asked.

"Yes, like Adolfo. Except that you're a hundred times smarter than he is."

The letter was from Carmen and Maria opened it with trembling hands. Thank God it was in Spanish. She was getting married, she wrote. She wanted Maria to know and she hoped that Maria would be happy for her.

Maria didn't know how to feel — happy or not happy. It was odd, but she had never envisioned Carmen getting married this way. The other children had been predictable. Carmen had not. She had always thought that Carmen would get married by Father Angel in the old church. She had seen her marry a good man, educated, of her same race. (No, never one who worked in the fields.) She had not anticipated this. In a way, she was happy for Carmen. Carmen had finally gotten what she wanted. On the other hand, she felt sorry for her. She knew that, except for very special occasions, she would not see Carmen again. If that is what she wanted, she said to herself, then let her be. She's old enough and smart enough to make her own decisions.

The little boy sat quietly looking at her as she read the letter and as she sorted out her thoughts in her mind. He waited patiently, drinking in sips of his coffee like a little man.

"Carmen is getting married," Maria told him, finally.

"Who to?" he asked.

"I don't know," Maria replied. "Can you imagine the state of the world today. My daughter is getting married and I don't know who to?"

Adolfo looked down at the Justice of the Peace. He was a short fat man, very dark, and with puffy lips, much like Pancho Garcia, the farter, "The Skunk". In fact he reminded Adolfo a lot of Pancho. He started wondering during the ceremony what Pancho would be doing right now. Whatever it was, it wouldn't be what Adolfo was doing.

He was getting married!

The Justice raised his voice to an emotional timbre and Adolfo came back to reality. The problem was that in between the high timbre part, the Justice's voice became such a low and droning sound that it mesmerized him. It rocked him in his shoes.

Adolfo had given up on Yolanda after the episode with the "Dissimilarly Similar" poem. The whole event had embarrassed him to the point that he couldn't stand to look at the woman. He still loved her, but the embarrassment was too much. He felt that he had played his hand, shown his cards, and she had turned him down. What else could he do? Maybe, he had thought, he had made his move too early. She just wasn't prepared. It just wasn't like him to be turned down. But come to think of it, he remembered, Isabel had treated him in much the same way. He knew life had its quirks, and one of them is that God never gives you everything you ask for, just enough to keep you asking. If He did (he was referring to God), then surely He would give Adolfo a woman with Anna's money and Yolanda's looks and personality. Why couldn't He? Why *didn't* He? He could do anything. It was just a matter, probably, of saying one word and the deed would be done. Still, it was not to be. God didn't agree with him. He had better things to do than tailoring concubines for Adolfo's pleasure.

So here he was now standing in front of the Justice of the Peace marrying a whore, the only woman, he felt, left in his life.

He had moved in with her for good after he left Yolanda's house. It was an act of desperation. Yolanda had not wanted him to leave. She and Pete needed the money. She just wanted Adolfo to forget what had happened. It wasn't the first time someone had proposed to her, she had told him, when he went to pick up the rest of his clothes. She was used to it. She had nothing against Adolfo. "Take your time about leaving," she said. But it was no use. He was tired of being rejected but he didn't tell Yolanda that. It was enough that he knew it. Why spread it all over town? Manuel had written to him, a flowery type of letter using a lot of unfamiliar words, pleading with him to stay with Yolanda and Pete. But, he was disconsolate.

Purificacion was her name, a most inappropriate name, he had thought, but what the hell. He had known prostitutes who were very caring. This one was not. He couldn't figure out if she loved him or not. (Love? He was still looking for it.) She was a woman of few words and, when angry, her stare could melt him. He didn't know whether she was mean or not. She never had to prove it. One stare was all it took and everyone did what she wanted done. He remembered a sergeant like her in his outfit in Germany. "That sonofa-bitch could talk with his eyes," Adolfo remembered.

He couldn't figure out also whether the marriage had been his idea or hers. At first he thought that he had initiated the courtship. Later on he wasn't so sure. Regardless, the excuse she used for marriage was that no one had ever lived with her wihout marrying her. She had her scruples. She also was one of the few prostitutes that didn't need a pimp.

The year is 1944. The war is ending, the loss of lives that it caused in the United States from 1941 to 1944 was finally drawing to a close. Germany had fallen. Only Japan was still fighting, but it was just a matter of time. Roosevelt, the great white father to the Mexican-Americans, had died. No one knew who Truman was. Maria couldn't even pronounce his name.

Adam died in 1944 before the war ended. His death was a welcome relief for Maria. She had taken care of him for over a year and it was affecting her health. She had grown much older in that short period of time. She had come to rely on the little errand-boy more as the days went by. He had learned to write and he would sit by Maria's bed and write letters for her. Then he would read them back in his little stuttering voice, a voice that she had learned to love. He would add to the letter as he saw fit and she would agree that it was much better his way. He would write stories for her and would read them to her, much to her delight.

Maria was sweeping the kitchen when she heard the hard knock on the door. "Who is it?" she asked, slowly walking to the door.

"It's me," came the large voice.

She couldn't quite understand. "Who?" she asked again.

"It's me, Adolfo," came the reply.

"Adolfo?" she asked, finding it hard to believe.

"Yes, Adolfo!" he shouted.

"Adolfo? Is that you?" she asked, shielding her eyes from the sun coming through the door.

"Yes, it's me."

"What on earth are you doing here?"

She opened the door and embraced him. After all these years he finally placed his long arms around her. "Maria, Maria," he repeated, savoring the emotion he felt for her at that moment. "I knew about Adam, but I couldn't make the funeral. I was broke. How much you have suffered."

"You're right," she said softly, "I knew there was a good reason why you couldn't make the funeral. I knew you were probably having trouble." Then standing back and looking at him from head to toe, she said, approvingly, "You haven't changed much. You've got better clothes."

"You haven't either," he replied. "You're still the same Maria. A little older, but the same Maria."

"Do you want some coffee?" she asked, leading him into the kitchen.

"Just a swallow," he responded. "I don't drink much coffee anymore. I feel better when I don't."

"My, my," Maria said, mocking him, "now you're watching your health. Since when?"

"Oh, I'm getting old. Just taking care of myself better, I suppose."

"You quit drinking?" she asked. She couldn't believe it.

"Oh, no," he replied, feeling guilty. He knew he should have done that instead of cutting down on coffee.

"I knew you hadn't," she said. She knew he never would. "I received the letter saying that you got married. How is it going?"

"Not well," he said. "I'm not married any more. I left her. Mexican marriages don't take with me."

"What's the matter?" she asked him, "the woman was after your money?"

"Yes, I think you're right."

"Didn't I tell you long ago about that?"

"Yes, you did, but I guess I never listen."

"Poor you, Adolfo," she murmured quietly, shaking her head. "So it's come to this. You're back, I hope."

"Yes, I'm back," he said and quickly he got up and went to the porch. Jesus had left Adolfo's suitcase on the porch and was now gone, a cloud of dust following his little car.

Adolfo came back in and stood at the door, his large body covering most of it, his suitcase dangling from his arm.

"Adolfo," Maria laughed out loud, "you are a pile of shit!"

"Yes, I know," he replied, grinning, "but I don't know what to do about it."

"Well," Maria started to tell him, but he raised his hand to stop her.

"Please, please, don't tell me how bad I am," he said, quietly, "We've been hurt too much already."